PRAISE FOR REBECCA HANOVER

"A fast-paced thriller about identity a

"Episodic and fast moving with plent_____ big turn
that will delight mystery readers."

—*Booklist*

"An engaging ride . . . the novel calls attention to larger questions of
identity, selfhood, and what it means to be human."

—*Kirkus Reviews*

"Fascinating. I was captivated."
—Francine Pascal, bestselling author of the Sweet Valley High and
Fearless series

"As immersive and fast paced as it is shrewd, compelling, and
heartbreaking."

—Ray Kurzweil, inventor, futurist,
and *New York Times* bestselling author

"A page-turner that more than delivers on its premise."
—Allison Raskin, *New York Times* bestselling
author of *I Hate Everyone But You*

THE
LAST
APPLICANT

ALSO BY REBECCA HANOVER
FOR YOUNG ADULT READERS

The Similars

The Pretenders

THE
LAST
APPLICANT

A NOVEL

REBECCA
HANOVER

LAKE UNION
PUBLISHING

Published by Lake Union Publishing, Seattle

www.apub.com

Amazon, the Amazon logo, and Lake Union Publishing are trademarks of Amazon.com, Inc., or its affiliates.

ISBN-13: 9781662513626 (hardcover)
ISBN-13: 9781662509285 (paperback)
ISBN-13: 9781662509292 (digital)

Cover design by Eileen Carey
Cover image: © Paul Moore / ArcAngel; © Kinzie Riehm / Getty;
© Spiroview Inc / Shutterstock; © Tupungato / Shutterstock;
© hydebrink / Shutterstock

Printed in the United States of America
First edition

To Ethan,
for the last two decades

And to Benee,
for being nothing like Audrey and Sarah . . . but loving
them anyway

PART ONE
AUDREY SINGER

Chapter 1

I'll act like I don't remember you.

I'll listen politely, with an eager and open face, while you ramble on, shifting your weight nervously in your chic No.6 clogs that do nothing to counterbalance four decades' worth of insecurities. You won't be aware you're even doing it, but I'll notice you clutching the strap of your Celine Micro Belt Bag close to your chest, like a bulletproof vest. It's your trick, your tic. You all have one.

But that's coming in a minute. You still haven't spoken to me. Not yet. You're waiting impatiently for your order, your eyes scanning the barista behind the counter between furtive glances at your phone. When your name is called, I notice you've ordered a black coffee with a dash of almond milk. Nothing too decadent; you're counting calories. It's admission season, after all.

You're picking up your order and thanking the preoccupied barista an unnecessary number of times, in case I'm watching and taking notes. You're right to wonder, because I am.

Thirty seconds later, you'll pretend to spot me for the first time.

"Ms. Singer?" you'll exclaim. "Audrey Singer? I can't believe it!" you stammer, and I lift my lips in a knowing smile.

"New York City. Truly a small town," I answer, my voice sounding kind, and approachable, and you won't know that the inflection is rehearsed. How could you know that I've been here, done that, more times than I'd ever admit to you.

"I dropped off Owen's application not five minutes ago!" you go on, suspecting you sound desperate but praying pitifully that you don't. "What are the odds I'd run into you here? But of course—Easton's right around the corner!" You act like you've just figured that out, when, in reality, you've been observing me for the past five minutes, possibly longer, debating exactly what to say. Obviously you know Easton's around the corner. Obviously, you know everything there is to know about Easton.

That's how it always plays out. Time after time after time. You see me across Fifth Avenue, or at Citarella, and you freeze, conflicted about whether to seize on this moment of pure kismet. Unsure whether you're the luckiest woman alive, to have run into me, or the unluckiest. Because making the wrong impression will be so much worse than no impression at all. Perhaps you should leave. You consider quitting while you're ahead. But then . . . the other applicants won't have this same, entirely fated opportunity. You simply can't ignore this chance, handed to you like a gift from the private school gods, and walk away from it. That would be ludicrous, and you know it. Worse than ludicrous: in your circles, bordering on criminal. So you steel yourself, doing a silent breathing exercise before approaching me and remembering your therapist's words of wisdom, the ones that cost you $450 a session, out of pocket. You have value. You are deserving. You matter.

Your heart pounds like a jackhammer in your chest, and you begin to sweat off the makeup so meticulously applied this morning in your en suite bathroom. You have value. You are deserving. You must talk to me, right now, unscripted. You must leave an impression so indelible that your child's future will be undeniably sealed.

I can almost see your brain cells spinning as you try to come up with some witty one-liner. A conversation starter that will put you on the map—my map. A topic or anecdote so inspiring, and endearing,

I'll have no choice but to return to my desk at Easton and mark your child's file folder with a scarlet *A*.

For *Accepted*.

When you do finally approach, after four and a half minutes of working up the nerve, I pretend I'm meeting you for the first time, that I've never seen your face or your exquisitely highlighted hair and deep-set blue eyes framed by dull, average features, and I act like I don't recognize you.

I remember everyone who fills out an Easton application. Every single parent who slips through the Easton doors for a tour. Every individual eager to grace the Easton lobby.

It's my job to remember you. It's my job to know *you*, not just what you choose to reveal in the essay questions.

It's what you don't write about that I remember the most.

———

"Stella is truly an original. I'll never forget the day she came home from preschool with a full blueprint of a house she wanted to build with LEGOs. Little architect in the making! We do have several engineers in our immediate families, as well as an inventor. You could say building is in Stella's blood!"

I'm curled in front of the fire with a glass of pinot, flipping through the stack of file folders I brought home. A hundred and seventy-five applications, and it's not even September 30 yet. But New York parents vying for spots in the elite K–12 schools don't wait for deadlines. They act, immediately. Expeditiously. Some desperately.

I should know.

I have a system for evaluating applications. It's complex and involves a Google spreadsheet with twenty tabs—but anyone who thinks admissions is a simple game of yes or no has no understanding of how delicate, and intricate, a process it really is.

"The vultures descend," Luke says, topping off my glass of wine.

I feel myself relaxing. Calvin is down for the night; Hazel's in her room avoiding us, as teenagers do; and I even had time to jump on our refurbished Peloton after work. A short twenty-minute ride, but still. I feel the stresses of the day draining off me as the pinot warms me from inside out.

I kiss Luke, breathing in his familiar scent. This is a man I would do anything for.

And he, me.

"So these are Cal's future classmates," Luke muses, thumbing through Stella's application.

Our son will be entering the kindergarten class next year along with these families—that is, the ones I ultimately choose to join Easton, which is arguably one of Manhattan's best, most lauded independent schools. Acceptance means a child's path is paved through high school. It's synonymous with a top-notch education, but more than that, it means stability until college—with any luck, the Ivy League. It's a lot of pressure to place on a bunch of five-year-olds. That doesn't stop these parents from playing the game.

I, too, am a player this year, but I won't have to sing the song, do the dance. My son will attend Easton next fall—it's a given—and I have the power to decide who will make up his class. Who Cal will be friends with. Who Luke and I will socialize with. I wouldn't dream of exploiting that power. I have a duty to choose the best families for the school, regardless of my personal preferences.

"Hands off. You're messing with my system." I swat the file folder out of his hand. "But yes, these are our future friends. A select few of them, anyway. Not that one. Her parents think she's the next Monet."

"'Felix is already showing quite the propensity for chess,'" Luke reads from the essay section of a file he's just picked up. "God, Audrey. Don't you ever get tired of reading these?"

"Like you get tired of developing film?" My eyes are twinkling, the drink dulling my edges. We've had this disagreement before. I'm not annoyed that he finds some aspects of my work mundane. I could never spend all that time in a darkroom the way he does. I'd panic, crack a window, and ruin every last photo.

Luke swishes his wine. "That's different. These are all the god-damned same. It's like no one has anything remotely interesting to say."

"But I'm not reading what they're saying. It's what's between the lines that's pure gold. Look at this one. The parents keep reiterating how many friends have told them about Easton. Easton this, Easton that. But they can't actually name anyone. Not a single Easton family."

"So they're full of shit."

"Overflowing," I confirm.

"Pick some regular folks, then, will you?" Luke smiles, and I melt. "I don't want to spend the next twelve years hanging around a bunch of complete asshats."

"Noted," I lie. It's a minor fib. An omission of the truth, which is that I know I can't deliver. There aren't any regular folks in the applicant pool. The tuition is excessively steep, and most families, unlike Luke and me, don't receive a hefty staff discount. Those who do qualify for scholarships are a small percentage of the school's population, albeit an important one. My own unique situation, as Easton staff, isn't something I'm particularly proud of; if I'm being honest, I spend a fair amount of time making sure no one is ever reminded of that, or of the fact that Hazel initially started at Easton on a scholarship before I even worked there. My reputation depends upon it.

Don't misunderstand. Luke's one of the most successful people I know. He's an award-winning photographer whose work has appeared in all the greats—*National Geographic*. The *New Yorker*. A spread in *Vogue*. But art doesn't pay. Luke's esteemed, but we don't come close to owning a private jet, or even traveling on one. The trick is to impress upon people, in your every interaction, that you do important things.

That you matter. Then they might look past your run-down condo building, your absence from the philanthropic circuit. Social media can be deceiving. I use it to my advantage.

Still, I wouldn't trade him, or us, for the world. Not for all the club memberships and gala invitations. Luke is my rock, and I his. I lean over and squeeze his thigh—an invitation, of sorts. It's been a while.

He doesn't take the bait. He's busy thinking. I wish I knew about what.

"Dinner's almost ready," he announces. He springs up, padding out of our living room past the less-than-luxurious drapes that were here when we moved in. With my fingers, I absentmindedly cover a small stain on our couch, musing about how easy it is to make unpleasantness disappear. We aren't wealthy, but we are happy. Still, Luke and I haven't always been this way. I haven't always been this way—settled. Content. Secure.

I down my glass of pinot and try not to think about the woman I used to be. As desperate as many of these applicants.

No longer. I have a man I love and who loves me. I have a five-year-old son who thinks I built the world with my bare hands. I have a daughter who—what can I say about Hazel except that she's thirteen? I don't blame myself for her testiness, or the fact that she turned on me six months ago and decided I'm completely embarrassing and out of touch. She gets her stubbornness from her father, and God knows my ex-husband Samuel's flawed personality isn't my fault. In spite of Hazel's mood swings, Luke and I and the kids—we're good.

Which brings me to my job. I fucking love my job.

It hasn't always been this way. I haven't always been this way. There were the scrappy years, the downward-spiral years, when I came this close to throwing it all away. When it felt like I deserved all my bad luck. When it felt like I'd never belong—not here.

You could say it's a little ironic. That an outsider, someone who fought and scraped her way into this world, kicking and scratching and clawing, now wields so much power over Manhattan's elite families. Power to make their dreams come true or fuck them to little bits.

Sure, there's a certain symmetry in it for me. I like being the decider, for once in my life. But it's not why I do it.

The truth is, I love the cyclical nature of admissions. The way one season melts into a second, and a third, and time marches on determinedly, a new crop of eager applicants submitting themselves to me every September. It's comforting.

I'm stacking all the folders neatly on the coffee table, returning them to their rightful order before I follow Luke into the kitchen for some rigatoni and more wine, when I casually check my inbox. There's a new email message, from a sender I don't recognize, and the subject line catches my eye.

Subject: Help! One last applicant?!!
To: AudreySinger@Eastonadmissions.com
From: sarahbex50@gmail.com

For some unknown reason, I open it. It's surprising, even to me, because I get emails from applicants every day, and I delete nearly all of them. Applicants are encouraged to contact me through the Easton portal, not directly. Of course, they still do email me, but I don't guarantee responses. I can't; my colleagues and I would be fielding messages all day long.

Still, I start reading. Against my better judgment, perhaps.

Dear Ms. Singer,

I can't believe I'm doing this. I've been sitting here for twenty minutes debating whether or not to write. Between glasses of merlot. Three glasses, tbh.

I glance down at the glass in my own hand and commiserate. It's indisputably wine o'clock.

I almost didn't write you. I thought about shutting my laptop, running into the closet, and locking the door. But if I did that, I'd be reinforcing what I've long suspected everyone thinks about me: that I'm a failure.

Let me explain. I've worked on my son's Easton application for the better part of two months (truthfully, four, but I promised myself I wouldn't admit that to you, of all people). I won't go into how long I debated whether it was ready and all the self-doubt and indecision I tortured myself with, but you can imagine my horror when I logged onto the Easton site, my essays at the ready, and realized that, even though it's not the deadline yet, so many others had beaten me to the punch and already applied. I had no idea you cut off the applicant pool after a certain threshold and that the Easton portal would be closed to new applicants!

Which brings me to here. The tears streaming down my pathetic face and right into my fourth glass of merlot, as I stare at the Hot Wheels cars scattered across our living room floor, a visceral reminder of how I've let down my son. (Joking about the Hot Wheels, of course. All Eli's toys are constructed of either wood or sticks, no plastic anywhere on the premises.) I'm quite certain I've completely derailed his future. Easton has always been in my plans for him—even as a pipe dream!—and now, realizing I can't even apply on his behalf . . .

I'm not going to lie, Ms. Singer. It's absolutely devastating.

I'm just so . . . ashamed? Guilty? Certain I have no shred of self-worth left?

It was my job to plan for Eli's future. My only job.

If there's any chance you might consider taking one last applicant for next year's kindergarten class . . . I'd be eternally grateful if you considered Eli.

Yours,
A truly disconsolate Manhattan mom

She's right. The system cuts off applications after 250. I hadn't realized we'd hit that number today, but a quick check on the portal on my laptop confirms it. There's a logic to this. My team and I simply can't adequately evaluate more than that many families, and the board decided five years ago that it was more democratic, and less political, to simply take the first 250 applications on a first come, first served basis and deny the rest. Even certain donor and legacy families aren't guaranteed admission—not anymore. Families must stand out. They must do more than shine; they must sparkle.

I've seen many a legacy family march through my office door over the years, convinced they had that "it" factor—and a checkbook hefty enough—to ensure all they had to do was grace me with their presence. Not so. There are families we simply don't invite in past the tour. If that seems unfair, or cruel, it's not meant to be personal. It's simply a capacity issue.

Each December, we meet personally with 150 applicants. It's draining, putting on that same affected smile for each couple that walks into my office, so certain their lives are on the precipice of mattering.

The truth? If they don't matter already, Easton won't change that. Not that I'd ever tell them as much. That's the whole trick of it, the sleight of hand. It's my job to reaffirm the whispered conversations they've heard for years, over craft cocktails at Little Sister, in the pre-school courtyard at drop-off, at the Met fundraiser, and over filets at Le Coucou. Those conversations all boil down to one thing. Acceptance to Easton is akin to membership to an elite club, for life.

I sip, then reread the email twice, three times. I have to admit—I'm intrigued.

This "sarahbex" woman, there's something so . . . raw about her. So real. It's strangely refreshing. Most exchanges with potential families are so dull, so tedious, so generic and cookie cutter; no one risks saying anything that could rock the boat in any way or jeopardize their child's chance of admission. Weaknesses must be spun into positives. Potential red flags must be massaged or covered up.

I see right through those families. Everything they think they're hiding is right under the surface, like a skeleton costume on Halloween, and it takes a mere flick of my office light to reveal it all.

But this woman, she requires no illumination. Without any encour-agement at all, she's laid herself bare. Shown me every ounce of her insecurity in one self-deprecating email.

And something else. It makes me feel. Like I know her, or could have been her, once. Or maybe even was. Because I understand how she must see herself, right now. As utterly worthless. She could have edited that email before sending it to me. No one put a gun to her head, forcing her to spill all those details, her innermost fears. But she did.

I click on the reply button and begin typing.

"Babe!" Luke calls out from the kitchen. "Pasta's almost ready!" My body leans toward his voice, the one I fell in love with nearly eight years ago, when I first heard it at the Press Lounge, where Easton was hold-ing a fundraising event. Luke was photographing it for the semiannual school newsletter, glossy and thick as an old-school *Vanity Fair* maga-zine. Filtered through the clinking of glasses, the useless conversations between Manhattan anglers, those trying to impress and those trying to drown in their Dewar's, was Luke's baritone. It was deep and halting in a way that sent shivers down my spine. I knew instantly when he shook my hand, gripping it with his own overlarge mitt, that I could fall for him, hard.

I was the lowly assistant admissions officer back then, but I felt especially on my game that night. My outfit was on point and bolstered me from the outside in: Isabel Marant shift, the Jimmy Choo booties I snagged in near-perfect condition off Poshmark, and a fresh blowout I'd barely squeezed in between work and rushing home to get then five-year-old Hazel settled with a sitter. But when Luke's eyes met mine through the viewfinder of his camera, all that confidence deteriorated. I instantly felt my lack of class, my lack of polish, and a secret shame that my underwear was ratty and torn, my nails ragged.

I recognized Luke's face from *New York Magazine*. He'd won some fancy photography award and had been featured in a spread of self-portraits he'd shot on black-and-white film. He was sexy as hell—that wasn't debatable—so the fact that he was giving me the time of day surprised me, delighted me, and scared me shitless. This was a man I could lose myself for. I'd been down that road with my ex. Had regretted every minute of it, except that it had given me Hazel.

When we finally spoke, he told me he felt like a sellout for taking this gig for hire in the first place.

"I'm an artist, you know. Not that anyone here gives a damn about art." He lowered the camera from his face and shrugged, revealing a half smile that made my knees pathetically wobbly.

"Don't they?" I asked, not sure if my words were forming properly.

"Oh, they care about Art." He swept a hand around the room, presumably encompassing every single parent, board member, and trustee in his statement. They were a "they." But I wondered if I was exempt from his sweeping commentary. If we could be a "we . . ." "They are patron saints, they are contributors, they bankroll the museums and the galleries, and they bid on the Banksys and the Kusamas. But real art? The kind that you struggle and pine and starve for? They wouldn't know it if it hit them in the face."

I took in a breath, feeling shaky in this man's presence and trying to get a grip. You'll never see him again, I reminded myself. This conversation's a one-off. Disposable, like the plates we're eating off. It doesn't matter.

Our life now, our family, our little unit, is proof that somehow, Luke and I did end up mattering. We became a "we."

He's calling me again to dinner, and I want to go, I do, but first— this email. My mind is fixed on this applicant and the unsent reply bubbling up on my fingertips.

Luke can wait.

"There in a second," I call out, gulping down the rest of my wine before continuing to type.

> Dear Truly Disconsolate,
>
> This is feeling very *You've Got Mail*. I'd suggest we meet in person at an adorable dessert shop, but I'm happily married.
>
> Unfortunately, you are correct, the Easton portal tracks applications, and we have reached the max for this year. I encourage you to seek other options for Eli; there are a host of wonderful schools in New York City.

I pause. Here is the part where I will lie.

> And though Easton is, quite frankly, one of the best, it is not the sole choice for a bright boy who has spent his life in the company of educational wooden toys.

But—

I stop myself. What am I doing?

"It's getting cold, babe!" Luke's voice rings out. He can keep waiting, but I don't want him to have to. My hands hover over the keyboard.

But I like you.

I hesitate. I don't know this woman and certainly have no obligation to help her out.

But in some way, I understand her.

Sure, she could be anyone. There's no way of knowing if she's a complete wack job holed up with a dozen cats or a serious applicant. Still, offering her a chance to apply isn't the same thing as admitting her son. There's little harm, or downside, in writing her back.

I type.

And I appreciate your honesty. So please attach your application to this email. And I will see what I can do.

I hit send and shut my laptop before I can think too long or too hard about what I've just done, then scurry into the kitchen, taking my empty wineglass with me.

Chapter 2

The email, and my impulsive response to it, is still nagging me as I pad down the hall to Hazel's room and push open the unlocked door. I find her spread-eagled on the bed, her eyes closed, her AirPods firmly in place.

"Hazel," I say calmly. When I get no response, I repeat myself. Her name, her dear name—Hazel Holloway. Alliterative. An ideal combination of letters. A name I spent hours marinating in my mind, convinced it was winning on every level. It was perfect, until her father threw me out like last year's garbage, and I began to resent the alliteration, because the *h*'s in her name reminded me of a time when I relished being Audrey Holloway. I couldn't have expunged the name from my life more quickly than I did; our divorce was barely fresh before I reverted to my maiden name, Wilson. As soon as I married Luke, I adopted his last name—Singer. It's the last name change I'll ever make.

"Hazel," I repeat, taking in my daughter's features. A fifty-fifty blend of her dad and me. His eyes, my nose. My doggedness, his wit. Her brown hair falls naturally in the kind of waves people spend hours trying to re-create artificially at Drybar. I'm biased; every parent is. But she's so stunning it hurts.

I lean down and pluck one earbud from her ear. Then the other.

"Mom!" she shouts, bolting upright on the bed. "What the hell?"

"Dinner's ready," I tell her. "Pasta night."

But she's already popped them back in.

"I don't eat carbs anymore," she mutters. "But thanks for remembering." She snaps her eyes shut.

I don't react. I calmly turn and walk from the room. If I stay, I'll yell at her. I don't want to be that mom, that person. So I keep our interactions as brief as possible when her mood's like this. And when she eventually comes up for air and sidles up next to me on the couch and puts her head on my shoulder, and I have my daughter back for one minute or—blissfully—a full hour, I savor every second. That's when the floodgates open. She'll talk about school, her friends, what she's reading, what she's watching. Those are the moments I live for. They make the ones when she sees me as an uncool, out-of-touch monster more bearable.

In the kitchen, I pull out our flatware from the drawer and refresh my pinot. Luke's pouring his favorite whisky—Japanese Hibiki, a bitter swallow. He always offers me some, and I always decline. I like my drinks to go down easy. I watch him as he fishes, barefooted, around the freezer for the square ice cubes we save for cocktails, and I'm filled with a kind of contentment that both buoys and unsettles me—and I don't know why. I'm happier than I've ever been, and yet—I seem wired to never appreciate it, not fully. Maybe it's because, like everyone, I worry it could all go away. That it could all be taken from me, in an instant.

I slide up to Luke and wrap my arms around him from behind, feeling his strong torso in my grasp and breathing in his scent.

"Hazel?" he asks, spooning the rigatoni from the colander into pasta bowls.

"She can nuke hers later. I'm not in the mood for a fight." He nods. He never contradicts my parenting when it comes to Hazel. Perks of stepdad life.

"Let's eat," I tell him. "Then Netflix? Then bed?" I breathe into his neck, but he doesn't lean into me. I tense.

"Audrey, honey, you are my soulmate, but if you get any closer to the masterpiece while I'm still working . . ."

I laugh, throwing my hands up. "Say no more. I'll wait to be served."

My phone beeps—the telltale text ding—and I reach for it instinctively on the counter, sneaking a peek as I settle in at the table. My screen is cracked, has been for a month. It's on my to-do list to get it fixed, but I'm avoiding the chore, at least in part. I don't mind the crack. I have a history of ruining new things, of tarnishing them. Better my things are already tarnished to begin with.

I feel a momentary pang of guilt about having my phone out at the table, but it's fleeting. Luke and I tried to enforce a "no devices" rule at meals months ago, but since Hazel's refusing to grace us with her presence, it feels moot. Sure, we could talk to each other. But like most married couples, we are, for the most part, all talked out. That's normal, Audrey. Normal, normal, normal. Which is exactly what you've always wanted.

And yet the thought of it disturbs me.

The text is from my best friend, Chippie—not her given name. Her birth certificate reads Caroline Chippenfield Crane. But when your family's richer than the Gettys, you can be "Chippie" from birth and no one bats an eye. The story goes that her eighteen-months-older brother couldn't say the *r* or the *l* in Caroline, so a great-aunt suggested an alternative. It stuck. Chip tried to shake the nickname at Columbia, but by then, reinventing herself seemed impossible. I never understood why she even wanted to. I would have given anything to be as casually monikered, as only the über-wealthy are. I'll admit I didn't help matters by flat-out refusing to jump on the Caroline bandwagon. I was her best friend, and I knew she wasn't serious enough for her given name.

can you believe that twat second grade mom is accusing me of trying to upstage everyone else at the auction with my skincare products?? I can't help it if they're valuable!

I begin my reply.

How much $

A new text pops up almost instantly.

I'm GENEROUSLY gifting 40k in creams and serums! Hello it's for the CHILDREN and it's coming out of Quince's profits. Sorry if she feels overshadowed but WTF? Can't anyone do anything NICE anymore

I fire off another text.

scale it back? take out the liquid surgery serum?

An instant response.

fuck no that's the showstopper!

. . .

fine! I'll curate. But I'm not apologizing for being in a position to help. i could just donate the $5m capital campaign goal and save everyone a whole lot of time & energy but then I'd be castigated for ruining everyone's fun!

I quickly write back.

please don't do that or talk about doing that or even THINK about doing that. Just . . . ignore this woman. Please.

She responds.

I HATE WHEN YOU'RE RIGHT.

I set down my phone with a sigh. I know where this second-grade mom's coming from. It's hard to stand in Chippie's light. You always get overshadowed, or worse, burned. Chippie's not a person; she's a force. With her three hundred thousand Instagram followers, her face that defies aging, the wardrobe that looks like it came straight off a runway—not to mention Chippie's success as the CEO of her bespoke SoHo skincare shop, Quince—she can be hard to swallow.

I spent years trying to reconcile my love of Chippie with the ever-present resentment I felt that she had the world at her fingertips, and I didn't. As much as I've "made it," I'll never have her wealth, her ease, her certainty that she belongs. That resentment has diminished over time; it's rare that I truly pine for her life anymore, charmed as it is. Probably because I know, deep down, that Chippie's never truly been happy.

Luke has brought the pasta over, along with the fancy pepper grinder that was on back order for five months from France but was worth the wait in Luke's estimation, because it was "the one."

"It's good, babe," I say after spooning the artfully plated pasta in too fast, remembering that I haven't eaten since 11:00 a.m., which would explain my sudden-onset hunger. "Really good."

"Too much basil," he observes, but I know he's being hard on himself. He's an artist. Self-criticism is his drug of choice.

"Mommy?" says a voice behind me. "I'm too hot! I am never, ever, ever going to fall asleep!"

Calvin. My five-year-old, standing on our creaky wood floor in his dump truck pajamas and bare feet, a Pull-Up peeking out from his PJ pants, his hair tousled from sleep.

I check the clock, not surprised it's 8:37 p.m. It's an unfortunate pattern that's arisen these last few weeks. We put him down at 7:00 on the dot; he's awake again not two hours later. And that's when it starts.

The long, drawn-out process of him refusing to go back to bed. A special kind of parental torture.

Still, every night when I kiss his cheek and read him "just one more" Pete the Cat story, refill his water cup, tuck him in, and gingerly close the door to his room, I tell myself the lie that he'll stay down. It's the lie every mother of young children tells herself, because as much as we love our kids, the most blissful time of all is when they're fast asleep, and we can gaze upon them lovingly before heading into the kitchen for some desperately needed "me" time. Preferably with wine. And sex.

So as I'm staring at my little one, clutching his favorite giraffe stuffie, that's what I'm thinking. That Luke and I actually haven't had sex in weeks.

And Calvin is why.

I keep falling asleep next to my son, in his twin bed with the Spider-Man sheets, during his second bedtime of the night.

I know I'm weak. I should have the willpower to get up from his bed and walk away after two minutes. But fuck willpower. My days of Calvin needing me are numbered. Hazel's newly minted sour teenage mood has highlighted that fact for me in fluorescent ink.

"I'll get him down," I say to Luke, ignoring my husband's exasperated look. I shovel in two more bites, then half carry, half propel Calvin's willfully limp body down the hallway to his room and get him resettled in bed.

It's 9:55 p.m. when I wake with a start next to him, check that he's breathing, slide out through the crack made by his bed rail and footboard, and tiptoe out of the room, paranoid I'll wake him before I reach the hallway. I close his door, cursing that squeak we can't get rid of, and let out that familiar sigh: he's out. Thank God.

The kitchen's empty. Two marinara-smeared plates rest in the sink: Luke's and Hazel's. I had a feeling the carb comment was bullshit. I unwrap the foil from my own and begin to shovel the remaining pasta into my mouth by the forkful, not even bothering to sit. I lean over the island instead.

Then I pick up my phone. Being away from it for more than an hour has already made me anxious to see what I've missed.

I catch myself, acknowledging how absurd that is. My life is here, between these walls. Not in the cloud.

Ten texts await me from Chippie, each progressively more furious at the accusing second-grade mother, who apparently escalated matters by looping in the head of the PTA. Chippie claims she's being targeted and that another family offered up a weekend at their private island. But no one's even mentioned them! That island is worth way more than my stupid creams. This isn't about the creams. It's PERSONAL. The last one reads, Fine you're probably having sex, just call me tomorrow goddammit, with an inappropriate emoji and a heart. God knows where she gets the various penis emojis. They aren't standard on my phone.

Her text rattles me. I'm not having sex, because I keep falling asleep next to Cal. But I do come back to our bed eventually. It should be happening then.

I notice a fresh email in my inbox that wasn't there a moment ago. It's a reply, from her. Truly Disconsolate Mom. I open it.

Dear Ms. Singer,

Thank you. A million times, thank you. Please find Eli's application attached. And, can I ask one more favor? I realize that must seem positively farcical given you've just granted me the biggest one of all. But . . . . . .

Can you delete my initial email and wipe it from your inbox—and your memory? Because I am truly, deeply embarrassed by how juvenile and frankly, insane I must have sounded! Let's face it—New York City school admissions can drive a person over the edge. I know I'm not the first to say that. Perhaps I'm the first to admit that, to you, in an email that will likely color your entire perception of me, and my son (but hopefully not my son), till the end of time!

Is it possible I've now written you two highly questionable emails? (Rhetorical question; please don't answer). I'm going to hit send, regardless. I don't trust myself to self-edit without making this whole situation far worse.

In all seriousness: thank you again.

Yours,
Disconsolate

"Work email?" Luke's standing behind me. I turn, dropping the phone, like I've been doing something illicit.

You were reading an email. From a mom. Nothing strange or even remotely illicit about that.

"No. Well, sort of," I admit, gulping down my last bites. "An applicant," I tell him. "She's either delightfully nutty or a woman who's going to be found dead in her apartment surrounded by cats. Jury's still out."

I'm still processing the email in my mind. I can't decide if her words were charming, desperate, pathetic, or all of the above. I'm usually an excellent judge of character; it's what makes me so good at my job. I can suss you out. I can take what you tell me and reduce it to the exact thing you don't want me to know. I can read you, no matter how hard you try not to be an open book.

This woman is an open book. Or, at least, she presents as one. But that's what's so odd about it. I can't place her. And I don't like not knowing what her game is, or if she's even playing one.

I'm dying to read her application essays. Wondering what they'll reveal, if they'll be as raw and uncensored as her emails or as boring as everyone else's. There's every possibility that her extreme authenticity is strategic, an act in itself.

But Luke's still awake. As much as Disconsolate intrigues me, her application materials can wait. I have more pressing concerns.

I know what's going on with him. He's forgotten, if only momentarily, how good we are together. One amazing night, and this little dry spell will be just that. A blip. A pesky scab that will heal into a faint pink line and be entirely forgotten.

Nothing more.

I'm going to have sex with my husband tonight.

Chapter 3

We didn't have sex.

This isn't typical for us, I think as Hazel and I down our coffees and round the last block of East Eighty-Fifth Street, crossing to the Easton gates. I allowed her to start drinking half-caff last year. She swears all her friends do and that Easton demands so much attention and acuity, I'd be putting her at an unfair disadvantage if I denied her her morning latte. I suspect she's playing me, heading to Starbucks after dismissal with her friends, but it's not an argument worth having with her.

Hazel hates that I still accompany her to school and keeps her earbuds firmly in place the entire ten blocks from the subway to the Easton gates, in a show of protest. Normally, I'd be ready with an argument as to why, at thirteen, it's perfectly reasonable for her to still walk with her mother to school. But today, my thoughts are occupied by Luke and his continued lack of interest in me last night after we finished an episode of *Schitt's Creek*.

"I'm tired," he said sleepily, then pulled out his Kindle and turned away from me. "Love you."

Luke keeps finding any and every excuse to avoid me, and it has been starting to feel extremely personal.

I hope it's not what I think it is.

"Mom!" Hazel's nudging me in the side. "We're here. You almost kept walking." She rolls her eyes at me, then turns and waves to her friends as we approach the Easton gates.

Without a single glance back, she leaves me standing there as her giggly, long-haired girlfriends surround her, whispering and shooting what they think are furtive glances at a pack of nearby boys. As Hazel's face disappears from my view, and all I can see is the back of her head, her colt-like body hidden beneath layers of baggy clothes all the kids her age insist are trendy . . . I wish I could physically hold on to her as long as possible. Instead, I let her go. It's what every mother faces, starting at birth. The long, painful journey to severing the ties that so solidly bind us when the baby's born. It's why I cling to Cal so tightly. Because I know what's coming. While other moms my age are in the throes of raising several under-fives at once, too busy to notice the time rushing furiously by, I have the privilege, and burden, of watching Hazel slip from me right as Cal needs me the most. The juxtaposition sometimes takes my breath away.

I head in the side entrance to the school, avoiding the clusterfuck that is the front double doors. My office is a few steps down a wood-paneled hallway. This building is a relic, a nineteenth-century beauty deemed historic by the city, cracked and worn in places but still awe inspiring, and I pull out my key, unlock my office door, and head straight for my desk. It's immaculate, and I follow my procedure on entering my work space. Bag goes on the small leather love seat, softened by years of nervous couples submitting to my interviews, desperate to be seen. Keys to my condo belong in the heart-shaped Kelly Wearstler dish on the corner of my desk, a birthday gift from Chippie. I slip the Easton application files from my bag before placing them in a neat stack in front of me. Then I pull out my keyboard and log into my email.

I'm sitting down and typing before I even notice them there, on the desk, out of the corner of my eye.

A vase of flowers. Hydrangeas. Tastefully arranged, delicate white-and-green buds that are perfectly fresh and came here straight from the florist, probably mere hours earlier. What's curious is how they got here.

I rack my brain to remember what transpired moments ago. I unlocked my office door, which means it wasn't open. Someone from maintenance must have intercepted the flower delivery, used the master key to unlock my office, deposited the vase here on my desk, and then relocked the door. This must have happened early this morning, while I was still stepping out of the shower, putting my makeup on. Or while Hazel and I walked to school.

Even though that all makes logical sense, something about the whole thing bugs me. I stare at the flowers, momentarily flummoxed, trying to work out why. Usually we have to pick up packages and deliveries from the main office. And that's especially true for me; I can't tell you the number of random gifts I've received from applicant families over the years. It's against school policy for me to accept them, which means the goods get corralled in a no-man's-land by the Easton secretary, Joyce, who shows them to me, for kicks, before she returns them to the sender. It's always the same rotation of generic items: coffee-table books, chocolates, expensive tea. Once, a cashmere throw so gossamer soft that letting it go felt momentarily painful. But I had to. If I accepted those gifts, they could influence the admissions process. Everyone knows that. Everyone except the families who send them.

The white-and-green hydrangeas are mystifying. They must not be from an applicant family, I conclude. I stand up, leaning over my desk to search under the thin petals for a card. They could be from Luke. My heart speeds up as I consider why he might have sent them. He feels bad about our dry spell. He wants to make it up to me with a date night: dinner and a walk down Commerce Street—a twisty, tucked-away corner of the West Village that feels like it hails from another era. We like to stroll there, dreaming about retiring one day to a brownstone. If we could ever afford one.

But there's no card, so they can't be from Luke. I know him; he'd want credit for sending these. I sit back in my rolling desk chair, adjusting my legs one over the other, my brow furrowed. I instantly stop myself and relax my forehead. The fewer Botox appointments I have to make with my dermatologist across town, the better.

"That fucking second-grade mom!"

I hear a familiar voice from my doorway and look up. It's Chippie, standing in the threshold. She has this way of always posing, frozen in midair like some preening bird. She'd completely deny it if you brought it up, but the fact is, she's photo ready anytime she leaves the house. Even her athleisure wear is couture.

Today, she's dressed the part of a perfect Easton mom. Her hair is freshly highlighted and blown out in soft, effortless waves. Her eyebrows are artfully shaped, her outfit notable, as it always is: a black Chanel sweater sporting hot-pink interlocking *C*'s, paired with flared APO jeans, frayed just so; Fendi boots with a patent-leather detail on the spike heel that makes them seem unattainable; and a serpentlike chain of swirled lock-and-key necklaces, all dangling at different lengths over her perky chest. I recognize the gold chains as custom made from Chippie's local jeweler, each one costing a small fortune and sporting the highest-rated diamonds.

I feel plain in comparison. Drab. I know my own ankle-length white jeans and cashmere cardigan are nothing to scoff at, even if my sweater does have a tiny hole in the sleeve that I absentmindedly cover with my hand. Still, I always feel this way in Chippie's presence. I have since we were teenagers.

Chippie sweeps into the room, not bothering to ask if I'm busy. She flings her bag on my couch.

"God, she's a twat. I am this close to cornering her and, and . . ."

"And what?" I prompt, suppressing a smile. I'm certain Chippie can't even think of a good threat, because she'd never do anything remotely threatening. She's the most cynical person I know, but it's all talk. She's far more likely to kill someone with kindness than say anything bitchy to their face.

Instead of answering me, Chippie pouts, flouncing onto my sofa and slipping off her sunnies. My eyes wander to the hydrangeas again.

"Wait, did you send these?"

Chippie's picking at the shiny gunmetal-gray polish on her fingernails. "Obviously not. I don't do flowers."

"Of course you don't."

"I mean I do flowers! Naturally." Chippie laughs, that delightful tinkle that's as familiar to me as Cal's cherubic giggle. "But I don't buy them. I haven't purchased flowers since the early aughts. Of course, that doesn't stop them from appearing in my home every morning, freshly arranged. I have Ana for that."

Ana is one of the nannies who raised Chippie when she and her brothers were children, and now she's helping raise Chippie's daughters. I adore Ana; she's the most genuine person you'll ever meet. A necessary presence in Chippie's life. Not that Chippie isn't authentic. She truly is who she appears to be. But Ana is . . . something else entirely. Warm. Not a sarcastic bone in her body.

"I believe what you mean is that you have an entire staff for that? But sure, how is Ana?" I tease, trying not to think of how much the line item for "flowers" must be on Chippie's yearly bank statement. And how much she must pay the nameless staff member who fills the vases. But I don't have time to dwell on the outrageousness of Chippie's lifestyle; it's not something I'll ever reconcile. I'm still trying to work out in my head where these flowers came from and coming up short.

"Audrey." Chippie snaps her fingers at me. "Focus. I have a major personal crisis happening here?"

"Right," I answer her, toggling my computer mouse to waken my monitor. "Auction Mom. Ruining your life."

"She actually went to Hurst over this!"

Headmaster Hurst is the head of the school and my boss.

"How do you know?" I ask, feigning outrage, even though Chippie's problems are always of the first-world kind. The ultimate first-world kind. I know we all breathe rarified air north of Central Park, but Chippie's life is especially oxygenated.

"I heard. Because I hear everything. And I don't like your resting bitch face," she accuses, pointing a manicured finger at me. "This is serious! My whole reputation could be trashed! I could be canceled. That mom is telling everyone that I'm vying for attention. That I'm pulling some kind of stunt."

"Chip, forget it. No one's going to believe that. Or care. Besides, you think anyone on the planet, or more specifically the Upper West Side, would cancel you?" They wouldn't dare risk the social suicide, and she knows it.

She flops back onto the love seat, sighing. "Stop being right all the time. It's exhausting."

I laugh. I'm about to remind her that she's never once given a flip what anyone thinks about her, and she shouldn't start now. But I don't get the chance to say anything at all. An alert pops up on my computer monitor: the first Easton school tour is today, in exactly one hour. Much as I'd love to spend the next sixty minutes commiserating with Chippie over Auction Mom, I have no time to waste.

"Chippie, I love you to death, but I have work to do, and anyway, you're late for spin." I click on the list of tour attendees for today and begin pulling their files from the pile on my desk. There will be nineteen prospective parents in attendance, split into two groups. I don't have to physically lead them around the school—we have the parent volunteers for that—but I'll greet them at the start of their tour and answer questions once it's over. I'll be making mental notes of the questions they ask and how interested they seem in Easton. Naturally, they're being judged. Every second they're at Easton is a chance for me to evaluate them. But what they don't realize is that there's very little they can do to sway the process one way or the other.

My gut hasn't failed me yet.

"The fact that you know my exact schedule should scare me because it's borderline stalkerish? But don't you dare stop, because I need you." Chippie gathers up her Goyard bag and feels between the cushions for her sunglasses. "You're more reliable than my assistant. I should pay you her salary so she can go be an influencer, which is, let's face it, what she really wants."

"I'll send you an invoice," I joke. I don't look up from my computer but hear the door slam.

As I'm stacking up the files, noting the names of today's applicant families—the Porters, the Stones, the Wus—and of course, Disconsolate Mom. "Sarahbex50," whom I now know to be Sarah Rebecca Price. I'd printed out her essays late last night after Luke practically brushed me off in bed, and I'd found Sarah's answers to be the perfectly ordinary, mundane ramblings of a typical Manhattan mother. That was all. There was certainly nothing scandalous to be mined from their depths, and her entire tone—the self-deprecating voice that was laced through her emails to me—was gone. I decided her emails were one-offs, the products of too much wine and a lot of self-loathing. I couldn't believe I'd been so intrigued yesterday. Intrigued enough to make an exception for her. It was not in my nature.

I focus on the next fifty-four minutes until my tour starts. I could sell the school in my sleep, and let's face it, Easton doesn't need selling. But I still must study these candidates. Know exactly who I'm dealing with. I dive headfirst into the files, learning everything I can about the Porters, the Stones, the Wus, a single mom called Anabel Stern, Julia Hawthorne and Jennifer Mehta (moms to Asher), and the Jarrod-Smiths. Of course, there's Disconsolate Mom—Sarah and her husband, Adam—and a few others.

It's ironic, I know. It's hardly about the children at all. I'll get to them. Later. There will be the playdate and the evaluation of their kindergarten readiness. And, of course, I'm not simply selecting a handful of disparate kids. I'm creating a class. But right now, at this early stage in the game, it's about the parents. It always is.

By the time my computer dings, alerting me that the tour starts in five minutes, I'm ready. I know what makes these folks tick. I also know how truly unremarkable they all are.

I leave my office, taking my handbag with me, and lock the door behind me. I duck into the dusty bathroom—it's all vintage details and refinished hardwood floors that are original to the building—and reapply lipstick and mascara. I stare at my face, thinner than it used to be but still respectably "young looking," thanks to a steady stream of La Mer and the occasional aforementioned Botox, not to mention free swag from Quince: the expensive skin creams that Chippie slips in my bag, unsolicited. I pluck a stray gray hair from my temple, reminding myself to confirm my salon appointment for next week. Another maintenance chore I don't have time for. As I stare at the fine lines between my eyebrows, I can't help it. I wonder if Luke isn't attracted to me anymore. Not like he used to be.

Because you're getting old. And constant—too constant.

That's what happens in marriages. Husbands get complacent. So do wives.

I'm busy scrutinizing my face when a voice cuts through the string of unpleasant thoughts racing through my mind.

"You look like you could use a Xanax. I've got one in here somewhere."

I turn to look at the person standing across the bathroom as she digs through her oversize purse.

"What?" I ask, taken aback. I'd thought I was alone.

"A Xanax," she repeats, still searching through her bag. "To get through this hideous tour. I mean, I want to be an Easton mom more than I've ever wanted anything in my life. But that makes it all the more pressure filled, doesn't it? I'm so nervous. What if I fuck up? Say the wrong thing? Ruin my son's chances at ever going here? Have you considered that this next hour and a half of your life might actually determine the rest of it? Where your child goes to kindergarten, and after that, college? Then graduate school? Who he meets at those institutions and what job opportunities he gets and even who he marries—"

This woman's about my height. Coppery waves fall to her shoulders. I can't tell if her hair's been highlighted or not. I bet she instructs her stylist to give her that effortlessly "untouched" look.

She's thin but not too thin. A size two or a four. She wears a crisp, tailored outfit of black capri pants and a plain white button-down shirt, leopard-print flats on her feet, no doubt to add a flair of interest to an otherwise forgettable ensemble, and she clutches a bag that's far too big for her. I wonder what she could possibly have stashed in it. It's huge and has the effect of swallowing up the left side of her body.

I know instantly who she is, of course. Sarah Price. Disconsolate Mom. Minutes ago, I looked at her photo in her application materials. I find myself suppressing the urge to laugh. Her essays might have been staid and boring, but everything she's just said, it fits right in with those initial emails she sent me. So she is as erratic and honest as she first appeared. Or she wants to be perceived that way.

She's looking at me now, really looking. An expression of embarrassment creeps over her face. It must be because I haven't answered her, and she's waiting for a response.

"I'd love a Xanax," I tell her, my voice even, controlled. "But that might interfere with me running this tour."

Chapter 4

"No," is all she says in response. Then she shakes her head. There's a look of recognition, and pure anguish, on her face. "No, no no. You can't be Audrey Singer. Can you?"

Her eyes well with tears that she should brush away but doesn't.

I offer a small smile. "I've tried to become someone, anyone else, for much of my life, but sadly, none of my efforts have been successful." I shrug and return to my reflection, brushing powder over my T-zone areas, swiping my makeup containers from the counter and back into my purse in one efficient motion, and giving my face a once-over before hustling toward the door . . . and this woman. This applicant, whom I probably never should have given the chance to even be here.

"But—" Sarah sputters. "But no. This can't be happening. " I push open the door, indicating that she should exit the bathroom, and she has no choice but to slip out ahead of me. I follow her into the brightly lit hallway, where a few students are wandering on their way to classes, seemingly oblivious to us.

"Thanks," she mutters, looking increasingly flustered and upset. "I just—"

"It's already forgotten," I say. "Look, you're a lot more memorable than anyone else who's going to be on this tour, if that helps."

"It doesn't," she whispers. "Everything I just said. I can't imagine what you must think of me. And after—" I assume she means the emails.

I continue down the hallway, my pace brisk over the vintage runner. My tour begins—no, began—two minutes ago, I confirm on my watch.

I don't think anything about you, at least, nothing new, because I already thought you were a nutter.

"You've written me off," Sarah says in a hushed tone as she hurries to keep up with me. She's intense, this woman, and at the same time, flimsy. Small and delicate like I could nudge her, and she'd break. "I know you have. You're not saying that, of course, because you don't want to crush every last shred of hope I have left, but there's no way I have a chance now. If only I could have a do-over." I'm finding myself increasingly unnerved by her. Her wide eyes, the way she flits next to me like some kind of nervous bird. "You know," she says conspiratorially, a tremor in her voice, "I'd love a do-over of my entire life, if I'm being honest. Everything except for my son. He's my shining achievement in an otherwise mundane and, frankly, mediocre existence . . . a lifetime of mistakes, errors in judgment, and not living up to my potential. Please, Ms. Singer. Please don't make my kid pay for the mistakes of his mother."

We've reached the main lobby, where today's applicant families have gathered. They stand in little clumps under the antique chandelier. It casts ambient light over the room, illuminating every nook and cranny. It's a stunning foyer—a relic of another time, another place, with books lining the entire height of the ten-foot walls and crimson crushed-velvet sofas inviting students to sit and read in front of the gas logs in the fireplace. Not that I've ever seen a student actually do that. Keeping up with Easton's rigorous curriculum and the inevitable APs necessary for college prep is a full-time job. There is no time for pleasure reading at Easton, according to my daughter.

"I'm mortified," Sarah whispers. I wish she wouldn't stand so close to me. Our elbows are this close to touching. Even without looking in her direction, I can feel her presence beside me. I inch away, hoping she won't guess that I'm actively trying to put distance between us.

I scan my eyes over the parents clustered in small bunches, all nervously talking, picking lint from their clothes, trying to pretend this isn't, in their minds, one of the most important moments of their adult lives. "Consider it forgotten. You and I will never speak of it again. Agreed?" I look at her directly now—straight in her eyes—so she knows I'm serious. And so she knows the conversation is over. I have no time for this, or inclination—I have a job to do.

Sarah nods unconvincingly as she shifts away from me, resetting her path toward a trio of parents to my right. They instantly absorb her into their group. It's not that these folks are so generous to a newcomer; it's that they don't want to appear otherwise. Being polite to fellow applicants is all part of the game.

I take advantage of this time before we've formally begun the tour to check off the applicants in my head. We require them to include a family photograph, so naturally, because I've scanned their pictures, I can match up who the Porters are. The Stones and the Wus. Of course, I already know Sarah.

"Welcome to Easton." I address the group in the practiced tone I reserve for prospective families. In the seven years I've been doing this job, I've perfected it, down to the last inflection. I'm confident but not overly cocky. Approachable, but not enough to confuse them into thinking I'm their friend. If I've learned anything over the years, it's that applicants will take any—and I truly mean any—opening. Any opportunity to get "in" with me, to forge a connection that they believe is ours and ours alone. I simply cannot encourage that.

My eyes land on Sarah Price. She's shifting her weight from one foot to the other in her leopard flats, standing a few feet from me, next to the Wus. I force myself to look away. I broke my own rule by writing her back; I'm not too proud to admit that to myself. Too late now, though. What's done is done.

I spot my colleague Babs across the room consulting with Morgan—the Gen Z admissions assistant who is my barometer for everything hip and current, as well as my bullshit meter. They both work for me and will make sure our parent volunteers are ready to begin the tour process. Babs nods at me from over by the fireplace. Thank God for Babs. In her pleated skirt and button-down blouse, her silver shoulder-length sheath of hair neatly combed à la Helen Mirren, Babs is perpetually sunny and the perfect second-in-command, even if she has worked at this school for longer than I've been alive. If she resents me, she never lets on.

"Welcome to Easton," I repeat, scanning my eyes over the applicant parents, their eyes widening as I speak. This happens like clockwork; all I have to do is breathe the Easton name, and it's as though I'm about to reveal the secrets of heaven. I get the sense that some of them could be driven to orgasm right about now, simply by standing in this hallowed lobby.

They would all seem so pathetic if I hadn't once been in their shoes.

As I glance over the parents, I take lazy stock of their attire. Most wear expensive clothing procured from Neiman's or the kind of unassuming Manhattan boutiques in SoHo where a scarf sets you back two grand. But it's all so subtle—no one wants to stand out in any way that might be construed as a red flag. So while the women wear solid-colored, wide-legged pants and a few don flowery dresses—all accessorized with the most current shoes, bags, and understated fine jewelry—the men mostly wear suits, save a few in business casual jackets. One dad has on colorful Nike Dunks. I mentally give him points for not taking himself so seriously.

I continue my introductory spiel—I could recite it in my sleep—about excellence, inclusion, and diversity, how we "know each child well" and cater to individual learning styles with our progressive educational philosophy. The parents watch me, rapt, nodding along. These tenets aren't a joke—Easton is every bit as magical as these parents believe. If it weren't, I wouldn't have given an arm and a leg for Hazel to go here. I wouldn't take my job as seriously as I do.

One mother catches my eye, and I'm certain from my pretour cram session that it's Olivia Jarrod-Smith. She's been sending me weekly emails for the past month "checking in," asking for confirmation that I received all the supplemental files she submitted along with her son's application: extra preschool teacher recommendations, a glowing letter from his Suzuki piano teacher. Her heavily made-up face is a smidge too eager; her hair is a little too coiffed. I'd feel sorry for her, but there's no pity allotment in my day. I have too much to do.

"Any questions?" I ask once I've finished my rehearsed speech. I brace myself for the onslaught of tedious inquiries and comments. Most applicants ask what they think I'll want to hear. Or worse, they show off their encyclopedic knowledge of the school under the guise of inquiring about APs and the reading curriculum.

Olivia Jarrod-Smith's hand shoots up immediately. "Yes?" I prompt her.

"I know everyone's thinking the same thing, so I'm going to go out on a limb here and ask the big burning question," Olivia begins, her eyes glistening brightly. "Take one for the team, if you will."

"Well, don't keep me waiting." I laugh, hoping my casual tone sets everyone at ease. "This sounds like it's going to be good."

Olivia chuckles, a high-pitched, awkward sound. "How many spots will there be, actually, in next year's kindergarten class? I know there are two classes of twenty-four each, but that doesn't account for siblings of current students and multiples, because those families take two—or three!—spots apiece, no judgment . . . could you please put us out of our misery so we can calculate our specific and terrible odds?" A tall man next to her, her husband, shifts uncomfortably in his loafers. Meanwhile, beads of sweat are forming on Olivia's upper lip, but she's not perspiring out of nerves. She looks practically rapturous. Like she's so close to greatness it's almost too much for her to bear.

"I can't give you concrete numbers at this time," I answer her, organizing my features into their most sympathetic pattern before scanning the group. She's right; the others would kill for this information too. Only she had the guts to broach the topic. "We're still solidifying our sibling applications. If I had to guess, we'll have space for thirty nonsiblings."

I hear an audible gasp from a mother in a flowery dress. Thirty isn't many. Not when you consider how many families apply.

Another hand shoots up, tentative. A woman in a neat pencil skirt and heels. Stacey Wu.

"Can you talk more about Easton's social-emotional philosophy?" she asks, like she's reading from a script. She's put together, on point, and devoid of emotion. If she thinks this question will score with me because it sounds thoughtful, like she's done her homework, she can think again. It's not that it's a bad question. It simply doesn't matter that she asked it. Hundreds have asked it before her, and hundreds will again. I answer her succinctly, then address a question about varsity sports in the upper grades before wrapping up my comments and directing the couples to the parent volunteers. Two of them spring up and begin ushering the applicants to various corners of the school. God bless those perky parents who sign up to operate these tours. Former CEOs and prematurely retired parents who need an outlet for all their higher education and energy. The school wouldn't function without them.

As they split into groups, I notice Sarah, who's stayed silent so far, sliding into step after the Wus. She's still alone. I had assumed her husband would be joining her, but from the looks of things, he's a no-show. That would be a strike against them, if they didn't have a host of strikes against them already.

"Audrey," says a voice behind me, on the shoulder. I spin to find Babs standing behind me, looking worried. "Luke's here. In your office. Didn't you get his text?"

"Oh, thanks, Babs," I say breathlessly, my wheels turning. I don't let on that I'm surprised, that I had no idea he'd be stopping by.

Why is Luke here?

He could be here to say he's sorry. To tell me he misses me. To explain why he's been so distant as of late. He might not even wait to apologize—he'll pull me toward him, and we'll fall back onto the love seat in my office, making sure the door is locked . . .

Or he could be here for some other reason. One that you don't see coming.

My pulse starts to race, and I want to go find my husband, but Babs is still talking. She's chattering on about work and making a plan to discuss parent interviews, and did I see that article in the *Atlantic* titled "The Emotional Cost of Private School Admissions"? My cardigan is stifling me, rendering me so hot I have to pull it off. I do my best to respond to Babs, but it's another five minutes before I can excuse myself and hurry down the hallway back to my office.

I slow my steps, channeling calm. There is no reason at all to think . . . not that. Luke loves me. I, him.

I stop short when I reach my locked office door.

He is standing in front of it. I feel my heartbeat begin to accelerate again at the sight of him. His lean physique, his tall frame accentuated by slim jeans and a pullover. I love this man so much it hurts.

What I don't expect is who he's talking to. A woman whose back is turned to me. But right away, I recognize who she is from behind. The slim cropped black pants, the oversize bag on her arm, the leopard-print flats—Sarah Price.

She's standing in front of my office door. Talking to my husband. I can only wonder why.

"Luke?" I approach them warily, my eyes traveling from Luke's familiar visage over to Sarah's as she turns to face me. Her tour group has already left; she's missing the main event. Odd, but then again, this woman is the very definition of the word.

"Babe!" Luke says, with a little more enthusiasm than I'm used to from him, as he squeezes my arm. I feel my blood rush to my toes and am reminded that this is the first physical contact we've had in weeks short of my own lame advances.

"What's going on? Is it Cal?"

"Cal's fine," Luke reassures me. "Not a peep from preschool." I can tell there's more he wants to say, but he won't, or can't, because there's the issue of Sarah Price. She's still standing to my left, pretending inelegantly not to listen to our conversation. I still can't compute why she's here.

I don't care, honestly. Whatever awkward thing she's come here to do, or say, I'm over my interactions with her. More to the point, I don't have time for her; I need to know why Luke showed up midday at Easton. I can't ask him in front of Sarah Price.

Which means I'm going to have to get rid of her.

I spin to face Sarah, plastering on my most diplomatic Admissions Director Face.

"I'm sorry—was there something you needed?"

"Sort of." Sarah looks from Luke, to me, to the floor, her eyes darting manically in a way that increases my sense of unease. Maybe she's on something. It would certainly explain her behavior. She wouldn't be the first Manhattan mom with a drug problem. Prescription pills . . . half the parents at Easton take something . . .

"I came to apologize," she chokes out. "For my erratic behavior in the bathroom. For my rambling emails," she adds quickly. "Those were mine, duh. I'm sure you've already figured that out. I'm—she. I mean, her. And I'm sorry. For all of it."

I'm about to cut her off, send her on her way, but Luke jumps in before I can. "Sarah . . . it's Sarah, right?"

She nods. "Yes. Sarah Price."

"Admissions stress people the fuck out," he says warmly, with the kind of irreverent tone he pulls off so well. "You know how many parents email Audrey weekly with all kinds of strange requests? Loads." He shrugs. I don't bother shooting him a look. We both know he's full of it. But he's being kind, generous—that's how, that's who, Luke is. It's why I fell for him in the first place. He makes you feel like you're the only one in the room who matters. Sarah likely cornered him in the five minutes before I arrived, and he felt sorry for her. And now he's trying to smooth things over so she doesn't feel so completely foolish. I'd love him for it—I do love him for it. Except in this case, I wish he'd blow her off.

"Honestly," Luke goes on. "And I say this with all due respect to my lovely wife . . ."

I grimace. Where's he going with this?

"This whole process is bananas. The stress, the pressure . . . it's a wonder half the moms don't crack before they even make it to their interviews."

I refrain from rolling my eyes. Now he's going a bit far. Is this song and dance necessary?

It seems like it's egging Sarah on.

"Thank you," she whispers, looking on the verge of tears. I study her, that smooth, attractive face and those beachy auburn—no reddish, in the right light—waves. She's not conventionally beautiful, but she has one of those faces you feel like you've known forever. "Look," she breathes out. "I know everyone says this. I know it's clichéd and stupid and so incredibly pedestrian, but my son Eli is . . . the sweetest boy. He's—" she sputters, seemingly searching for the exact right words. "The thing about Eli is, he's so observant. You think he's this adorable little elf who loves rainbows and sparkles and baking and *PAW Patrol*, but then he'll bust out with the most apt comment about something you had no idea he even understood. About the earth. And tectonic plates,"

Sarah adds. "And all you want to do is hug and cuddle him because he still lets you? He's not one of those five-year-old boys who's disgusted by his mama. He would attach himself to me all day like a barnacle if I would let him. He would climb back in my womb if he could. And I know I've blown it about six times already, but please, Audrey. We're a good family. And Eli, he's a good kid. When you meet him—" She stops, suddenly looking down at her leopard flats like they're a lifeline. "I'm being presumptuous. If you meet him, if you invite us . . . you won't ever want to let him go." She looks nervously from me to Luke; then, seeming to sense she's overstayed her welcome: "I should probably catch up with my tour."

"Third floor," I tell her. "In the library. No one will even notice you were gone."

Sarah nods, gives an awkward wave to Luke, and brushes past us down the hall, but not before glancing back once more at me. I smile—a closed-mouth, tight-lipped smile, nothing more. She acknowledges it with a nod, then goes. I watch Luke watching her walk away. It's strange—all I wanted was for her to leave so I could find out what Luke wants, what's brought him here. But there's an odd feeling now of emptiness in this hallway, now that she's gone. I shrug it off.

"Spill," I say to Luke, my attention completely on him.

"It's Hazel." He sighs, dropping the carefree attitude he'd projected with Sarah. "Hurst called me. Apparently, she wants to meet with us. There's a problem."

I feel my heartbeat in my chest. Hazel . . . in trouble . . . what the hell? "What kind of problem?"

Hazel doesn't get called into Hurst's office. Hazel's my nearly straight-A student. Sure, she's had attitude lately. But that's teenagers. At least, I think that's teenagers.

"I don't know, Audrey, that's all the info I got. Hazel's there already, in her office." He doesn't have to say more; I'm already heading toward the second floor. As Luke follows me, the thought crosses my mind that my husband had the perfect excuse to get Sarah out of here far sooner. All he had to say was that we were late for an appointment with the head of school. But for some reason, he didn't. It's possible he didn't want to air our business in front of her. But whatever the reason, he let Sarah linger. Not for long; it couldn't have been more than five minutes, max. But still.

Chapter 5

Hazel is quiet when I meet her at dismissal, sulking in the front courtyard. I don't push her.

School is out for the day, and our meeting with Hurst feels like it was ages ago. I've hardly thought of much else. It's tense meeting with your child's head of school when that head of school is also your boss. But Hurst handled it deftly—like the professional she is—and I get the sense that Hazel received no preferential treatment. Nor did Hurst punish her excessively simply to make a statement. Hazel may be a "faculty and staff" student, but she hardly drank on campus or was busted with drugs. This was a fight with a classmate. A tiff.

Hazel got away with a reprimand, and so did the other student— Sadie Young, a girl Hazel's never particularly been friends with. Of course, I knew who Sadie was before we ever stepped foot into Hurst's office. I know every family at Easton, at least by face and name. It wasn't me who admitted Sadie—I didn't start working in the admissions office until halfway through Hazel's kindergarten year—but Hazel's classmates and their parents have been a pseudo family of sorts since she started here at age five, in kinder. It's true, after all: the community that all those applicant families are clamoring to be a part of is real. We come together when there is tragedy and loss. We complain, as all privileged parents do, that the lunch program could be more organic and the capital campaign should raise more funds. We fall asleep at night knowing we're the luckiest parents on the planet. We are part of Easton. We've made it—if nothing else, at least we have that.

"I'm not going to ask. Not now," I say to Hazel as the wind nips at our shoulders. I don't know if I got the full story in Hurst's office. I suspect I didn't, that there's more to it than "She said something nasty, so I threw my water in her face. Jesus, it was water."

I'll find a way to get it out of her later. She needs the space to work this out first. I know she'll tell me when the time is right.

But do you know that? Or do you simply hope that's the case?

"Can I go with my friends?" Hazel presses me. This is the second time she's asked. I see her waving to the same group of girls she joined this morning; they're exiting the school in a clump. I think these are nice girls, friends who have been by Hazel's side since they all played Barbies together and got their first bras. But who knows, really? They could secretly be doing drugs or having sex. Probably some of them are. I feel dread sinking like a stone in my gut. What if what happened with that Sadie girl is part of something much larger? A pattern?

"Mom! I asked you if I can go with my friends! I'll come home by five. Promise," Hazel practically growls at me. "The fight was nothing. I told you. That girl is a complete bitch—"

"Language," I tell her halfheartedly. I don't actually give a fuck if she swears, but it's one of those parental "shoulds." I feel like I should call her out on it.

Hazel knows this, which is why she rolls her eyes. "Sorry, a complete witch. She said something mean about a friend. I was defending her. That's all. Please can I go?"

"You can go," I tell her. "But tonight I want the full story. The unabridged version."

"Okay, okay," Hazel mutters, before grabbing her backpack—it's slumped onto the pavement—and rushing to catch up with her friends.

I sigh, watching her leave me again. This push-pull, this loosening of the threads that bind us. It's startlingly painful. I'm beginning to understand why parents say the teenage years are the hardest of them all.

I head back into the school. I've been so preoccupied today; I want to get in a few more hours of work, and Luke said he'd pick up Cal from preschool, which he does every so often, especially in the fall, when admission season is ramping up. On my way, I text Samuel, my ex. I feel that familiar tightening in my chest when I pull up his name on my phone. Even after all these years, the thought of him, sight of him, even the idea of him causes something akin to rage to rise in my torso. He hurt me. I don't know if that feeling will ever go away.

Hazel in a fight. Not a big thing. She's fine. Will fill you in when I know more. No need to call.

It's my duty to inform him of what's happened, even though I'd prefer not to interact with that man any more than I absolutely have to.

I don't wait for the three little dots to cross my phone screen. I turn the ringer off and put my phone away. He probably won't write back, anyway.

———

It's seven o'clock when I finally leave Easton for the day. I've had my head down in my applicant files and responding to administrative emails. So wrapped up in work I haven't noticed that it started drizzling and the sky is nearly black. Thank God Luke texted to say he could feed the kids. I needed this catch-up; my entire afternoon got co-opted by worry over Hazel.

I curse myself for forgetting to bring back my umbrella and head into the street with the collar of my trench coat pulled up. Hopefully it won't start raining sheets before I can get home.

I consider jumping in a taxi or Lyft, but it's rush hour, and a car ride will take a lot longer than the subway. My entire commute is a quick twenty-two minutes, if timed perfectly. It's one of the things I love most about living in Manhattan. It's such an efficient city. Like me. So I begin my walk to the Eighty-Sixth Street station, moving at a brisk pace, up one block and across the avenues. I want to get home to Cal, and Luke, and most importantly, to Hazel. I need to know how serious that fight was and if she needs consequences for what she did, or whether it was a one-off. A misunderstanding.

I'm still rattled by Luke. I'm not ready to confront him. It feels so silly and paranoid to be worried about us, when nothing's happened . . . yet.

The raindrops grow fatter and begin pelting my face. I consider ducking into a bodega and buying a cheap umbrella, but that would end up costing me time, and I want to get home, where I can curl up in front of my fireplace with a glass of wine. It's my favorite part of the weekday. Waiting for Luke to finish whatever culinary creation he's been plotting. Knowing my family is all home, and warm, and safe.

I cross Second Avenue and am stepping onto the opposite sidewalk when I sense someone behind me.

It may be dark, but it's only 7:00 p.m. And this is the Upper East Side. Of course there's someone walking in step with me. There always is. No such thing as an empty New York City street.

I quicken my pace. Not because I'm uncomfortable but because this damn rain is going to end up soaking me to the bone, and it's growing colder by the minute. Time to pull my puffer jacket out of my closet and wear it to work tomorrow.

My phone dings—I turned my ringer back on—but I don't slide it from my pocket. If it's Samuel, finally responding to my text about Hazel, I can see what he has to say later. I doubt he'll be particularly helpful. He rarely is.

I'm nearing the Eighty-Sixth Street subway station at Lexington. I'll take the 6 train one stop, to Seventy-Seventh, and walk four blocks to my condo. The person behind me quickens their step. So I walk faster, unable to ignore my heart rate elevating in my chest. It's stupid, because I'm sure they're just another commuter, like me. Still, I'm feeling a bit anxious and consider pulling out my phone. I could have it in my hand, at the ready, just in case.

Audrey, I admonish myself. Stop listening to all those true crime podcasts Chippie recommends. You're heading to a major subway terminal. This person probably is too.

I scan my surroundings anyway, in search of other people who could give me that sense of security I crave. In New York, a street dotted with people is a comfort. It means that if you screamed, someone would hear you. A stranger, yes. But another human nonetheless.

I walk faster still. I'm nearly soaked through now and beginning to shiver. I allow myself a quick glance back to see if the person is still behind me. The figure, in a black coat and boots, keeps a six-foot distance but seems to be following at my pace.

I turn my head back around swiftly so I can keep walking, picking up the pace further. Because of the rain, I tell myself. Nothing more. I see the outline of the stairway to the subway station up ahead. In mere moments, I'll be able to run down the stairs and into the shelter of the dry station.

I'm shaking now from the cold as I practically jog to the entrance. I'm here now, my foot skimming the first step. I look back one last time to see if the figure has followed. They're gone.

I'm in front of the fire in my coziest loungewear, shaking off my rain-soaked walk to the subway. I was letting unsettling thoughts take over.

No one was following me; it's New York. People are always on the street. People are always close to you. It's built into the DNA of the city.

"Mommy?" A small voice reminds me where I am: at home, in my favorite spot, my legs curled underneath me, my phone resting on my knee.

I'm about to open my Instagram app for a quick social media pick-me-up, but Cal is pulling on my arm. He needs help with fixing his truck. He shouldn't still be up, but Luke never got him to bed, and tonight I'm feeling too wiped to care. I set the phone down, help him fiddle with the wheel until it clicks back in. He scampers off as my phone dings. It's a note from Robert, our building's doorman.

Evening, Audrey. You have a package. Would you like to come down and pick it up?

I quickly type a response.

Thanks, Rob! Amazon? Shopbop?

If it's nothing important, I'll head down later. I'm super comfortable right now and don't feel like moving.

Rob writes back immediately.

No. There's no label. A woman dropped it off for you earlier. 4pm.

Weird. I'm not expecting anything, but then again, I can hardly keep up with all the details of daily life.

I'm curious, though, so I text Robert back.

Be right there.

I shove my feet in the first pair of shoes I can find and holler at Luke that I'll be back in five minutes. "Watch Cal!" I look like a slob, but the beauty of my condo building is that not a soul who lives here is part of the Easton circle. A blessing and a curse.

"Mommy?" I hear Cal ask, clearly puzzled as to why I'm rushing off.

"Package. I'll be right back, sweetie," I reassure him before heading to the front door. I'm down in the shoebox of a lobby in two minutes flat and standing in front of Rob's desk when he hands over the box.

It's medium size and plain cardboard, like an Amazon box, but there's no writing anywhere on it, no branding.

I accept it, gingerly, thanking him and turning it over in my hands while making small talk. Asking about his kids, his wife, his chronic back pain.

I don't want to open it here, so I take the elevator up to the fifth floor, back to my condo, and slip in the front door. Cal's left his kid scissors on the bench in the front hall, so I grab them absentmindedly and slice the packing tape on the box.

I lift the flaps and find white tissue paper on the top, covering the box's contents. Whatever waits there, nestled in the flimsy paper like an omen or a sweet treat, I don't know, but I'm mostly curious, slightly bemused. Maybe Luke sent me something.

My mind flashes to the hydrangeas from this morning, realizing I never figured out who the sender was. I'd forgotten about them with all the Hazel stress. I make a mental note to text Joyce, the school secretary, about them.

Reaching in and slipping the tissue paper aside, I'm hit with a wave of nerves. Unmarked box, delivered by unknown woman . . . strange, but not exactly the stuff of one of Chippie's crime thrillers. I shake off the thought and dig in.

What I find inside gives me pause.

Buried deep in the tissue paper is a wooden nesting doll. The face is painted in broad strokes, her eyelashes dramatic and over the top, with red dots for cheeks and roses painted on her torso. I grab the doll, yanking her two halves apart to reveal a smaller doll inside. As I do, I feel an immediate sense of something I can't place, not at first.

It takes me a few moments, as I pull apart the second doll to reveal the third, to recognize and name what the feeling is: dread.

I open the dolls until I reach the final, tiny one. Then I walk over to the bench and set them all down there in a line, wanting to release them, feeling like my hands are contaminated.

They're harmless dolls, I remind myself.

Except they're creepy. Jarring. If they're from an applicant, which I'm guessing they are, they're a bizarre gift to send me. A coffee-table book, or the latest artisanal small batch of honey, I'd understand. A generic choice like that would give off the right vibe, something akin to a housewarming gift. It would be slightly aggressive but not unnerving. These matryoshka nesting dolls, on the other hand, feel weirdly specific, even personal somehow. An unwelcome invasion of my privacy.

I completely remove the tissue paper, checking for a note. Something that would indicate who these are from. I find one, jammed into the stiff cardboard fold of the bottom of the box. It's a blank card, on fancier paper than your standard index card. But there's no engraving on it; it's unembellished stock. Written in black ink, in scrawling letters, is a message.

> Dear Audrey,
> I can't thank you enough for your kindness today. I know I've acted like a crazy person, but I hope you can put that aside and still consider Eli for Easton's kindergarten class. Even if I don't deserve it, he does.

The nesting dolls are a little thank you. A reminder, if you will, that I have more layers to me than just this (unpresentable!) one.

Yours,

Disconsolate Mom

I let the note drop out of my hands and waft to the ground.

Sarah's ramping up her game. She dropped the dolls off herself. She was here at my building. My home.

That's when it hits me: this woman knows where I live.

Chapter 6

I haven't felt this thrown in a long time.

Be rational, I tell myself. There's probably a good explanation.

But nothing can explain how Sarah found me. Our address isn't publicly listed online. Luke's a stickler for privacy and made sure of that when we purchased this condo. It's listed as being owned by a trust—a very small one, mind you, the one his grandma set up for him in his twenties that allowed him to live the artist's lifestyle in the first place, though it's slowly dwindled as we've dipped into it over the years to pay our mortgage and preschool bills. You can't see anything more than that online.

I can't figure out how Sarah got my home address. There must be a loophole she took advantage of.

Then I remember my office. She was standing there, outside it, when the tours first began this morning, after I greeted and addressed the group. I suppose she could have slipped out of my talk, headed straight to my office, and gone inside. I had locked it before heading to the bathroom where I first ran into her. At least, I'm pretty sure I had.

But if I hadn't . . . if I'd forgotten or been too distracted . . . Sarah could have walked right in and grabbed a piece of mail from my drawer. Even a loose catalog, strewn on my side table, would have borne my address. I don't bring personal mail from home into work, at least not often, but it's possible.

Or she could have logged onto my computer.

That thought is chilling. Even Luke doesn't have my passwords.

Then I remind myself that the screen locks every five minutes, triggered by inactivity. There's no possible scenario in which Sarah was in my office within five minutes of me stepping away from my desk. We were chatting in the bathroom for longer than that before the tour, when she offered me that Xanax. And when I saw her there after, my screen definitely would have been locked.

"Audrey? You okay?"

Luke has scooped up one of the Russian dolls from the bench; he's studying it. "Where'd this come from?"

"An applicant," I tell him, my eyes glued to the doll. I'm hoping he won't ask if it was sent here, to our house, or why. I don't want to have to explain something I don't even understand myself that's stressing me out. Besides, it's not a big deal. We live in a doorman building. It doesn't even matter that a stranger knows my address.

"We should talk to Hazel tonight, shouldn't we?" he asks me in a low tone, so Cal, who's trailed Luke and is pulling on his leg, won't hear.

"Already planning to." I sigh, leaving the unmarked cardboard box on the bench and walking away from the dolls. "You're off the hook." It makes the most practical sense; if we both swarm Hazel, outnumbering her, she'll be on guard. Way less likely to talk.

"Daddy!" Cal pulls hard on Luke's arm. "You said you would come look at what I built!"

Luke bends down and grabs Cal, swinging him into the air and causing our little boy to dissolve into giggles. "You bet I did! But first, I need your help, buddy. The vegetables are burning! We must rescue them! Grab reinforcements!"

Cal shrieks with laughter, and they run off together to the kitchen.

I'm relieved for the respite and happy to see them bonding over Luke's cooking. He takes it very seriously, has already started teaching Cal how to perfectly sauté an onion, cook an egg. Thank goodness I don't have to. Left to my own devices, I'd eat peanut butter and jelly in between saltine crackers standing over the kitchen sink. I hate cooking. Good thing I have Luke.

And you do have Luke, I remind myself.

Cal's run back to me for a hug. "Wait, Mommy. I want to show you the ramp I made for my monster truck! It's epic!" I scoop him up under his armpits and rest him on my hip, kissing his neck and promising him I will come see it, in a minute. As he snuggles into my chest, I try to remember that everything's okay, that I'm okay. Luke and I, we're okay too.

I hear a ding on my phone and startle before my eyes shift toward it: it's a notification for a comment on one of my Instagram posts. I halfheartedly check it. The comment is on my latest photo from my morning commute, a snap I took of the New York City skyline. This is my public-facing "Easton Admissions Director" account, and it's one small way I show my enthusiasm for the school and keep up appearances. I want the world to never question that I'm current, up to speed, on point—and that I belong. My photos are curated and elusive. I don't post pictures of Cal or Hazel on here, and my shots are generic, like this one.

I often get comments from applicants, though, which I make a point of never responding to.

This case is no different.

The commenter is someone with the handle "Olivia J-S." Her note reads: Today was EVERYTHING. I am so in love with Easton. But I guess you know that already. Thank you for all you do. Five pink hearts follow her comment.

I click on the commenter's profile and see it's Olivia Jarrod-Smith. She's been an eager beaver ever since she first turned in her bible of an application. But flattery is not the way to win a spot at Easton. Still, something about her enthusiasm is endearing. I like Olivia. She may come off as desperate, but we probably could have been friends in another lifetime.

Another comment pops up before I can slip my phone back into my sweater pocket. It's in response to Olivia's initial comment.

I so agree. Audrey, you're amazing. So good at your job. Hope you love the little gift I left you. XOX.

The handle of the commenter reads "sarahbex." I click on her picture.

Sarah Price.

I feel a sinking in the pit of my stomach. Disconsolate, leaving me a note. Referencing the Russian dolls.

I notice a little red conversation bubble icon appearing in the top-right corner, indicating that I have seventy new notifications.

That's more than usual. A lot more. It's not like I'm Chippie, with her massive social media following and hundreds of DMs per day. My curiosity piqued, I click over to the heart at the top of the screen and am directed to my "likes" page.

Within seconds, I see that all seventy of the new likes—seventy-two now, all posted in the last few minutes—are from the same account. Hers.

Sarah has liked every single one of my posts, going back several years, and she's commented on a bunch of them. Feeling my mouth going dry and a fluttering in my chest, I read some of the comments. Things like LOVE and this is everything and even a sorry not sorry but I'm an Audrey fangirl.

I thumb back to her profile. I'd noticed her photo before, but nothing else, and now I see what it says in her bio, under "sarahbex."

Mom of Eli. Wife of Adam. Manhattan native. Prospective Easton mom/fanatic. I HEART EASTON.

She hardly has any posts—three, only. The oldest is clearly of Eli—cute kid. The second is of the Brooklyn Bridge. A third, the most recent, is a selfie. She looks slightly harried, though the photo is flattering. But that's not what stands out to me. What's notable is that she's wearing the exact outfit she had on earlier . . . and she's standing in front of the Easton steps.

Without thinking, I scroll to the date each picture was posted and confirm what I had already begun to suspect: all three photos were posted today.

It's clear what Sarah's done. She set up this account specifically so she could comment and like and be a voyeur of other people's Instas. Many of the accounts of our peers, of fellow Manhattan parents, will be set to private. But not all. The question is whether she created her account to be able to comment on a bunch of people's accounts, like Olivia Jarrod-Smith's, and some of the other applicant families'.

Or just mine.

I set the phone down, feeling shaken, and even more unsettled than before. I tell myself that Sarah could be locating every parent she met on the tour and connecting with them. Not a terribly crazy thing to do, though not the most subtle. But if I'm honest with myself, I don't suspect that's what she's doing. She seemed to be watching, waiting for Olivia to comment on my post, so that she could comment back. Sitting there with my post up on her phone to see if someone gave her an opportunity, an in.

Which makes me wonder if this isn't about sussing out the kindergarten competition at all. If it is, somehow, about connecting personally with me.

Sarah's clearly obsessed with Easton, obsessed with getting her child in. She calls herself a fanatic in her own profile. It's unclear to me whether she thinks anyone would ever look at it. She has no followers; the zero stood out like a sore thumb . . .

I pick the phone back up. Her profile's still on my app. I study it more carefully this time, my eyes devouring the page. At the top, to the right of her photo, are her stats.

3 posts

0 followers

1 following

I don't even have to confirm it. I know it in my bones. The one person she's following is me.

Chapter 7

I was agitated for the rest of the evening. After shutting off my phone and trying to force myself to think about anything but Sarah's disturbing Insta profile—throwing myself into Cal's truck ramp, dinner with Luke, and an awkward interaction with Hazel in which she guilted me into leaving her alone, citing too much homework for a long, involved talk—I walked back into Cal's room to put him to bed and found him engaging in imaginative play . . . with the Russian dolls.

Overreacting, I snatched them from his hands, taking them from the room and shutting them in a dresser drawer. Cal didn't understand why he couldn't keep playing with them, and it had taken quite a bit of creativity on my part to distract him. Then I dreamed of the dolls all night, restlessly waking in fits and starts, imagining them larger than life. I knew it was all silly—at least, I hoped it was. So, Sarah was over-eager. Borderline compulsive about Easton. She wasn't dangerous.

———

I'm in my office now, diligently reviewing applicant files, responding to emails, and momentarily entertaining texts from Chippie. I haven't filled her in on Sarah's Instagram feed or the dolls; she'd want a play-by-play. I'm behind on work as it is, and I'm annoyed with Sarah Price for co-opting my time like this. It's time I'd rather be spending with my family. Specifically Luke.

I'm five minutes late when I burst through the door of Ella's Nail Salon. Babs and Morgan are already here; it's our standing biweekly team-bonding event. Morgan came up with the idea, originally. In spite of our vastly different grooming styles—Babs faithfully gets the same neutral manicure she's had for thirty years, while Morgan is a fan of whatever the latest trend is—gingham, zigzags, tiny glued-on pearls— we all still need to refresh our nails every two weeks; why not do it together? Morgan proposed. When she'd first suggested it, I'd loved the efficiency of the idea and had put it on our calendars as a reoccurring event every other Wednesday at 1:00 p.m. We never miss it.

Today, Morgan is already instructing Stacey, the nail tech who at this point has heard far too much about Easton admissions, to give her a double french manicure—in bright orange, which will clash beautifully and effortlessly with her plaid pants but complement her oversize nerd glasses and chunky bangs—while Babs is soaking her toes in the tub at the base of her massage chair and pretending to relax. I know she isn't, not really. She's struggled with this plan since we first started coming here. I think she finds it challenging to let down her guard at work, to "chill out" on Easton time. I don't know if it's generational—Babs is sixty-two—or simply the way she's wired. Her beige pants are pushed up inelegantly so that they don't get soaked, and her prim cardigan is draped shapelessly over her shoulders. Chill isn't in her DNA.

I slip into a tan faux-leather massage chair between the two of them, say hello to Stacey, and request my signature color: gunmetal gray. It's neutral but still edgy, it goes with everything, and since I don't have time to plan outfits around my nail color, it fits the bill.

"You're late," Morgan deadpans to me as she inspects the work Stacey's doing. Morgan has an eagle eye. It's one of myriad reasons she's a critical part of our admissions team. "The cuticles," she reminds Stacey. "They're a fucking disaster." Stacey nods, not offended—once you get to know Morgan, you realize she has two modes: blunt, and more blunt. Plus, she tips Stacey generously, in spite of being the youngest on our team. It's all part of her master plan to one day rule the universe. I have no doubt she will. In the meantime, I need her. We can't run the Easton ship without her on board.

"Where are we on tours?" I ask, jumping right to business. I can tell Babs is pleased. She sits up straighter, relieved we aren't playing some team-building game outside of her comfort zone.

"Five down, eight to go," Babs reports. "We've made good progress on whittling down the pool. Justine identified our overlap—"

Justine is the admissions director of Dalton. We are in constant contact with her and the other teams, comparing applicants, homing in on who is more serious about which schools.

"Fine," I tell her. "Update the sheet with anyone you're cutting . . ."

"I prefer 'phasing out,' but yes, will do," Babs says brightly.

"What Babs is strategically omitting is that Justine is trying to steal my candidates," Morgan says flatly. "I have seven top choices, and she's practically declared all-out war. I swear to God that woman was born to piss me off."

I smile to myself. Every year, Morgan sets her sights on a few kickass families she wants to admit—either they're incredibly interesting, outrageously successful, changing the world in some way at a fundamental level, or so wealthy they could bankroll a new gymnasium. And yes, those few unicorns apply to every school, and yes, they usually get in all of them, though we try to make deals with Justine and a handful of other directors. A trade here, a trade there. I don't get nearly as invested as Morgan does; I don't let myself. She feels some responsibility to the school to "win" the most compelling applicants. It's like her own personal game, one-upping the other admissions teams. It may sound silly, but it makes her invaluable to me, to us.

"I'll talk to her," I say, "but you know I have no pull." I've never been able to tell if Justine likes me, but I sense she doesn't. I'm a hurdle to her getting the best candidates herself. We aren't friends. We are only tangentially colleagues.

Ella, the owner of the salon, appears smoothly at my elbow, sloughing off my chipped gray polish and thrusting my hands into a bowl of soapy water. "How's your daughter?" I ask her, aware of how we must sound to her—if she's even listening. Does she think we're shallow? Is our chatter annoying or simply par for the course in New York City?

"Teenagers." Ella shakes her head. "I want to kill her every day. Otherwise, she's great!" Ella's daughter is exactly Hazel's age. I frown.

"Teen girls are the worst," I commiserate.

I'm about to tell her that Hazel got into a girl fight, but I stop myself. Babs and Morgan do not need to hear about this. Our community is incestuous; Chippie's right, in a way, to care so much what people think. You can't hide at Easton.

I steer the conversation back to work. "Getting down to business. Scholarships. Babs, any updates?" She shakes her head no. "Morgan, reach out to interview families. Let's begin the scheduling now to avoid last year's clusterfuck." Ella indicates that I should sink my feet into the warm water.

It calms me. I can almost forget about Sarah and her unnerving behavior. I consider it for half a second. Telling Babs and Morgan everything that's happened. I could confide in them about the emails, the Russian dolls, and Sarah's Instagram comments, gauging their reaction. If I brought the whole thing up casually, like it was something to laugh about, they'd likely insist on seeing her Instagram account. I can imagine them huddled behind me, poring over every like . . . Babs would be generous and diplomatic, calling Sarah "dynamic." Morgan would not mince words. I can already hear the derision in her voice, how she'd chide Sarah for making such a gauche social media faux pas . . . then we'd cut her from the applicant pool. And that would be that.

It would be a relief, really. To hear them say that she's weird but suggest that nothing she's done is particularly out of line. To hear them dismiss her as annoying but hardly threatening.

But they might not react that way. Sarah's behavior might actually worry them. Freak them out the same way it freaked me out, setting off little alarm bells, causing them to escalate the whole thing. They might take all this info to Hurst, confirming my darkest suspicions: that Sarah's actually a problem I must deal with.

If they started digging, and asking questions, they'd inevitably realize how this whole thing started. They'd find out I was the one who responded to her emails, bending the rules to get her a spot. They'd put it together that Sarah never would have even been at the tour if I hadn't made an exception for her.

They'd realize what I already know. It's my own fault I'm even involved in this mess. My fault for feeling like I understood this woman and leading her on. Letting her manipulate me. Still, I had no idea she'd do all this.

No, I can't tell them.

". . . and her husband didn't even show up," I hear Morgan saying to Babs under her breath.

I snap to attention. "Who? Whose husband didn't show up to what?"

"That woman on the tour. The redhead?" Morgan isn't looking at me; her eyes are glued to her nails as Stacey polishes them. "Guy couldn't be bothered to fucking show."

The redhead. My stomach drops.

She's talking about Sarah.

It's like they read my mind, somehow. But no, it's a coincidence. She left a strange impression on them too.

"It happens," Babs says calmly.

"Sure, but not to people who are serious about Easton," Morgan retorts. "Miss the tour without a good excuse? Big fat oh no way."

All I can think is that I don't want to talk about Sarah Price. I must change the subject.

"Luke!" I shout. They both look up, surprised by my outburst.

"What about him?" Morgan narrows her eyes at me.

"He was at the school because of Hazel," I explain, addressing Babs. "She's fine, it was a school thing. Thanks for, um. Helping."

A lame excuse, but at least I've steered the conversation from Disconsolate.

Before they can maneuver it back, I jump into boss mode. I bring up work topics: financial aid, Hurst's latest addendums to the school calendar, and the updates I'm making to our system. When the conversation inevitably deteriorates into petty Easton gossip—the Zellermans' very public divorce, who is or isn't attending some pointless gala—I wiggle my feet in the aromatic water and try to calm myself.

Bullet dodged. Sarah doesn't come up again.

An hour later, our nails are glossy, and we're gossiped out. The time has been meditative. Letting Babs's and Morgan's voices wash over me and my mind zone out has allowed me to think clearly for a second, and I've made a decision. I'll set my Instagram account to private. I don't know why I hadn't thought of it before. I'll block Sarah, which will send a strong and clear message. We aren't friends. We can't be and never will be.

Morgan's gingerly gathering her things; the bright-orange mani looks straight off an influencer's feed. Babs is slipping on flip-flops while her pedicure dries. Her freshly done nails look characteristically neat and prim.

"Did you run our cards yet?" Babs calls over to Stacey, who's at the front desk. "Please add our usual gratuity . . ."

"Not necessary," Ella says, walking over with a smile. "No charge today."

"What do you mean, no charge?" Morgan looks suspicious. "We aren't letting you comp us."

"Not a comp. The previous customer covered all your treatments." Stacey smiles. "Pay it forward, I guess!"

Something about this doesn't sit right with me. The previous customer paying for three manicures and a pedicure . . . no way a stranger did that. No one in New York would be that generous to someone they don't know. They might pick up a Starbucks latte, theoretically, for the person behind them in line. But even that would be pushing it.

"Was her name Chippie?" I venture. She's the one person I can think of who knows about our standing date at Ella's. But then again, Chippie wouldn't ever come here. She has her own standing nail appointment with the most expensive and chicest nail salon in SoHo.

"No." Ella frowns slightly. "I would have remembered that name." She hurries to the desk and confers with Stacey. "She was insistent she pay," Ella continues to explain. "She said she's a very good friend of yours, Audrey, and it would be her pleasure to treat all of you. 'She deserves it' were her exact words."

I look from Babs to Morgan. They shrug blankly. "Weird," Morgan says. Babs frowns.

"Well, don't keep us guessing. Who was she?" Babs asks.

"Reddish hair. Nice lady. Name was . . ." Ella beams up at us after checking the computer screen. "That's right, Price. Sarah Price."

I have never felt a greater need for fresh air in my life. I mumble a quick thanks to Stacey and Ella and am out on the sidewalk in moments, the world dipping and tilting around me as I dial Chippie. It rings once; best friends are like that. They pick up when you need them.

"Bitch, what's wrong. You never call." Her voice is silky smooth and comforting. Especially right now, when I feel physically off balance. Unsure whether I'm overreacting or whether I am right to feel extremely unsettled.

"Chippie." I hesitate. "I think I'm being stalked."

Chapter 8

Chippie's legs are tucked under her on my office couch. I've locked the door and am pacing the threadbare rug as she studies Sarah's Instagram profile on my phone. I watch her scroll through it, trying to read her facial expression but getting nothing. Chippie rarely emotes; fine lines are a no-no for a skincare guru. As the seconds pass into minutes, I can hardly bear the anticipation. Finally, she lets out a breath and flings the phone onto the cushion next to her.

"Well?" I stand directly across from her, aware of every beat of my heart.

"You want me to call my PI?"

"Your PI? God, no. Chippie. That's completely unnecessary!"

"But is it?" Chippie presses. "This is the part in the crime podcast where the woman wakes up the next day stabbed in the eye with the heel of her Jimmy Choo."

"How cliché. And rewind for a second," I tell her, feeling the need to shove the genie back in the bottle. We've gone from obsessed mom to gore and death . . . I should never have told Chippie about any of this. I need to take things down a notch. "We don't know that this woman is dangerous. She could very easily be your basic, desperate weirdo. And you listen to too many of those goddamned shows."

"And you're my best friend on the planet, and I don't want to find you dead tomorrow strangled with fishing wire. Or shoved down your own trash chute." She slips out her phone and starts typing away. "I'm assuming you haven't done an extensive Google stalk? And don't tell me it's not appropriate. Google stalking is one hundred percent socially acceptable. It isn't the same thing as actual stalking at all."

"Of course I've googled her," I tell Chippie. "I found nothing. The Instagram account was new, remember? Otherwise, she's a ghost."

"Shush. Let the professional work." Chippie's slender fingers tap away at her phone's keypad. I walk over to my desk and open the top drawer.

Early this morning, after I woke up and Luke still lay asleep, tangled in our covers, I wrenched open the dresser in my closet, the one where I'd shoved the Russian dolls the night before, and slammed them into a tote bag. Then I brought them here, to my office. I didn't want them in my house. I felt safer with them here.

I locate the dolls now and deposit them unceremoniously into Chippie's lap.

"Explain to me," I say, holding back the emotion from my voice, "what kind of person delivers a gift like this to a person they barely know? And finds out where they get their manicures and follows them there, saying she's their really good friend. Please don't say a psychopath unless you actually mean it."

Chippie picks the dolls up, one by one, opening them and depositing them one inside the other, so when she's finished, they're back together as a single whole. She takes the remaining largest doll and sets it on my desk, then wipes her hands on her rag & bone jeans like she's getting rid of leftover residue or a lingering stink.

"Someone sad. Someone really fucking sad sends dolls to a person they barely know." Chippie picks at her fingernail, and I want to scream at her, Don't mess up a perfectly good manicure, but I hold it in. "I think this mom is sad. I think she has a very ill-conceived idea about how to ingratiate herself to you. But I also think she's harmless."

"Okay, but what about all that stuff about being choked by my own shoelaces that you were spouting with quite a lot of conviction?"

"Surely you know about my overactive imagination by now, Audrey." Chippie runs her hands through her hair, examining the ends. They, too, are perfect and anything but split, but that doesn't stop her from checking. "I think this woman's totally lost the plot, but she'll give up, eventually. And once she does, you'll never have to hear from her again. Or I'm completely wrong and you'll be dead tomorrow!"

I'm shooting Chippie a withering look when my phone beeps with a text. Before I can grab it from the sofa, Chippie's reached it herself. She adopted this aggravating habit years ago and has been doing it ever since we've had smartphones. I've even caught her fiddling with my sharing settings on Find My Friends; she doesn't think there's anything about my life that's not her business.

"Chippie, give me my phone."

Now she's avoiding looking at me. My stomach starts to churn. "Chippie?"

She's staring down at the phone screen, looking like she very much does not want me to see it.

A feeling of dread starts to creep up and down my spine.

"Chippie? What the actual fuck?"

Finally, she looks up at me, meeting my eyes. And for the first time today, she seems . . . flustered. Genuinely worried. Uh-oh.

After a bloated second, she hands the phone over. I take it from her and read the words written there in a green text bubble.

Hope the mani-pedis were amazing! My treat! XOX

The message is from an unknown 646 area code number. A New York City number.

My stomach churns.

A text. I'm guessing from her.

I look back up at Chippie, not bothering to mask the fear that I'm sure is evident on my face. I can barely whisper the words. "She has my fucking cell phone number."

Before now, I'd thought I was overreacting. I was sure that I was. And Chippie agreed! Crime-obsessed Chippie. But now . . .

Don't go there, I tell myself. Don't go to that place . . .

"Chippie, what the fuck."

"Okay," she says, still not losing her cool in spite of the fact that I've completely lost mine, and all signs point to that being 100 percent reasonable. "We need to look up restraining orders. And how you file for one. I'll text the family lawyer . . ."

But I'm not ready. I can't deal. This is too unreal. Too scary. Too . . . outrageous.

"How did she even get it? How did she get my address and my cell? What doesn't this woman know about me, Chippie? My bra size? My Starbucks order?"

"I can call my guy. Not a PI," she clarifies. "I know you're weird about them since the divorce, and I don't blame you. This is a tech guy. He can scour the web. No one's actually invisible online, not if you know where to look. Then at least we could find out something about this woman."

"I know where she lives," I say, vocalizing some internal thought that's bubbled up from my consciousness. "Every applicant's information is in their submission materials on the server," I explain, gesturing toward my computer. "Of course, I'd never use that information against anyone. That would be a gross misuse of my position of power, and I'd be fired in two seconds if I ever did anything with it—"

"You can stop talking like a brochure because this is different," Chippie insists. She stands up into an effortless triangle pose. Even in her jeans and gold-and-black cashmere sweater, she's limber as fuck. "She's the one harassing you, not the other way around."

"I can't," I tell her. As much as I'm tempted to do it, I'd be crossing a line and putting my job at risk. That's not something I could ever jeopardize. My life here at Easton is everything to me.

Still, I feel my resolve wavering.

There's a knock at the door. I force myself to slip on my Admissions Director Mask and open it to find Babs standing there, smiling nervously once she notices Chippie in the room. She gives her a little wave. Chippie nods back.

"Am I early?"

Leave it to Babs to think she's intruding on an appointment we already set. I check my watch; she's exactly on time.

"No, now's perfect. Chip?" I hope Chippie takes the hint. She must know I don't want to discuss this further, not in front of Babs.

Chippie sweeps her sunnies on and goes, promising to text me later. We both know this isn't finished. But the thought that it isn't over—it's enough to chill me to the bone.

———

It's 4:00 p.m., Babs has gone, and I'm seated at my desk. The white-and-green hydrangeas stare back at me, taking on a new, ominous tone. Did Sarah send them too?

They've drooped since I studied them yesterday. Suddenly much more motivated to learn who actually sent them, I feel all over the vase and even inside the blooms for a card, a note, anything that would explain where, and who, they came from.

Nothing.

Dammit. There are too many mysterious pieces of this puzzle. Too many question marks. It doesn't seem like Sarah even sent them; she always leaves a note.

Ugh! That makes me think of those serial killers who leave a signature every time they kill.

I stare at my computer screen. I know it would be wrong to access Sarah's address. It would most definitely be wrong, or at the very least, ethically dubious.

But it's all I have.

I toggle my mouse and access the server, where it's waiting for me: the Price family digital file.

Bingo. With a noticeably thumping heart, I scroll to the information page and note her address.

452 West Seventy-Ninth Street.

Right across the park. I could be there in ten minutes.

I know it's crazy, but I can't help it. I need to know where Sarah Price lives. I need to learn about her home, about her family, about her. And I can't quiet the voice in my head that's urging me to go there, now, and see what her house looks like.

And possibly catch a glimpse of her too.

No, no, no. I absolutely do not want to see her. She's the stalker, not me. I simply want to learn some facts, some details about this strange person, and put together the puzzle pieces of this odd narrative so that I can write her off as a nuisance at worst, a kook at best.

I can't go. The idea is insane. I close the tab on my computer and force myself into my work, letting it consume me. Putting Disconsolate out of my head. I have to.

———

I can't even come close to sleep. Everyone in the house is out cold—Luke, Cal, even Hazel . . . I checked, slipped her phone out of her hands while she dozed and tucked her covers over her. I'm awake, unable to stop thinking about it all. Sarah. Her intrusions. Her gifts. Her text.

There's a string of texts from Chippie, all checking to see if I'm okay and asking if I want her to send a security detail to look after my family. I laugh off that suggestion, assuring her I'm fine. We're fine.

At 11:00 p.m., the urge is too strong. I'm climbing into the back seat of the Lyft before I can talk myself out of it. As we head off into the night, to the Seventy-Ninth Street Transverse, where we'll cut through the park and shoot out the other side, I compose a quick text to Chippie.

Still no word from you know who bet she's given up. Lunch tomorrow? Xo

I can't tell her the truth. If anything, she'd be proud of me. That thought makes my stomach turn. I don't want to be doing this. I didn't ask to be put in this position.

We jolt to a stop at the side of Seventy-Ninth Street.

"Miss? We're here."

I look up, surprised, to find that we've stopped in front of an unassuming brownstone. I squint for the street numbers, spy the 452 in scripted wrought-iron on the gate.

Sarah and Adam Price's house.

I'm instantly nauseated. I thank my driver and wrench open the car door, eager to get to the street and the cover of darkness.

But as soon as I step into the chill, and the Lyft tires squeal away, I feel even more exposed. What if she stepped out of her house right now to take out the trash or go for a walk to the nearest bodega? What if she has a dog and it needs to be walked? The likelihood is that she's home, in bed. Any sensible person, any sensible mother over the age of thirty, is in bed right now, or at least in the kitchen nabbing a late-night snack before heading to bed. Still, I imagine her walking out and catching me like this, red handed. I dart to the pathetically small and scraggly tree near me and lean against it, hoping that in the cover of dark, my body will blend in with the tree's form.

I stare up at the deceptively modest brownstone. It looks like every other one on the block, like every other one on any number of Upper East and West Side Manhattan streets. Grand and Italianate, yet unpresuming in its own way. There's nothing flashy about a brown-stone, but there doesn't need to be. Everyone knows they are prime New York City real estate, that they start, at the very least, at a cool five million. Most of these would sell for ten million or more.

And yet they don't look opulent. They are simply stout and solid, well designed, with small details you have to know to look for and wide, sturdy steps, elaborate enough, but still simplistic compared to other architectural styles. Like the aloof faces of the society women who inhabit them, they seem to shut you out while simultaneously hinting that what lies inside is covetable . . . if you could earn an invitation in.

I can't help but feel jealous as I stare at her home. Luke, Hazel, Cal, and I don't live in a brownstone, or anything close to it. And though our condo is nice enough, it doesn't have the history, the space, the status of a home like this one. It never will. I'm reminded that I never will.

I'm surprised, somehow, that this is where she lives. I don't know why; I had no reason to think she'd live somewhere more shoddy. Somewhere more like, let's face it, my home. I stare up at her house and study it, searching it for clues, for some small sliver of information that could tell me more about its owners. The windows are dark. The house is a blank mask with few identifying features. It's five stories, like the others on the block, with a curved bay window and pedimented front windows. There's nothing in front that's out of place—no Amazon packages or stray kid's bike, not that I'd expect there to be anything personal on the front steps; in NYC, leaving an item out, unsecured, is the equivalent of giving it away, since it'll be snatched up in two seconds flat. I remember the time I was moving apartments in my twenties, when I set a bookcase down and turned my back, only to have it gone a minute later. The first of the month is humorlessly dubbed "free fur-niture" day in NYC, when people too lazy to deal with their stuff set it out on curbs to be adopted by overeager twentysomethings. In my case, someone got way too eager. The bookcase had been one of three pieces of furniture I owned. Then, I was down to two.

I shake off the unpleasant memory. The Prices probably have a sizable backyard or patio for trikes and toys, which is why there's nothing for me to see here.

I'm going to go. This was a terrible, misguided idea; I can't believe I let myself fall into Sarah's trap. What she wants is for me to connect with her. She'd likely be delighted if she caught me here, at her house.

The thought makes me sick.

I'm turning to go when a light goes on in one of the windows. I'm assuming from the hour that it's probably a bedroom, unless it's an office and someone's up late working, like Luke sometimes is. The window, now lit, is on the second floor, and I can make out the top portion of a framed gallery wall of photos and prints that scream "little boy"—a red truck drawing, a black-and-white, artful print of the solar system.

Her son Eli's room. It must be.

I shrink back into the tree, feeling hot, clammy. I tear my eyes from the window. I shouldn't be here. Someone's up with Eli in that room, either Sarah or her husband, and I'm literally standing here like a freak, watching, waiting . . . stalking. Chippie's words echo in my head. She's the one harassing you.

But right now, that's not how it feels.

The light blinks back off, and I flee.

Down the block, as fast as I can, shivering and sweating all at once. I cross the street and head south one block, to Seventy-Eighth Street. I don't want to be anywhere in the vicinity of the Prices' house, not now, not anymore. Satisfied that I'm completely out of their orbit, I pull out my phone with shaking hands and hail a Lyft. I have to get home and put this behind me.

I'll pretend I never came here. And no one will know except my Lyft drivers. I won't tell Luke; of course I won't tell Luke. And naturally, the last person I'd tell is Chippie. She'd want every lurid detail. I feel my cheeks flush with shame. I can't admit to her what I've done. Sure, she'd approve—she was encouraging it! But I'm not that person. If anyone at Easton ever were to find out . . . Babs or Morgan or Hurst . . . Chippie wouldn't understand. She jokes about her reputation being ruined, but the truth is that her standing at Easton is ironclad. She can do no wrong. I don't share that privilege.

It takes me far longer to get home than it should. My first Lyft never shows. As I stand in the cold, dark night, watching the little car icon on the map circle two streets down, then head backward in some kind of rideshare Bermuda Triangle, I finally give up and call an Uber. That car arrives ten minutes late, and as I wait, I'm certain this is all my fault, a punishment for what I've done. I can barely breathe again until my driver drops me in front of my building, home at last.

I nod to Rob at the front desk, and he gives a small wave, clearly understanding without my saying it that I'm not in the mood for chit-chat. He won't breathe a word to anyone about my comings and goings. It's Rob's job to keep the residents' secrets.

The condo is dark when I slip in. I set my purse on the kitchen counter, kick my shoes off en route to the island, and turn the lights on low on the dimmer. My heart pounding, I head straight to the wine fridge and unscrew the open cap to a bottle of merlot.

I feel like a criminal. I know that's an overstatement; all that I've done is take a drive by someone's house to look at it . . . but I remind myself that it wasn't exactly someone. It was an applicant's home. I've never done this, never thought I would; I've never used an applicant's mailing address to satisfy my own curiosity or entered their physical space without being invited.

Of course, that's exactly what she did. Texting me, and leaving a gift at my home . . . Liking all my Insta posts and paying for those mani-pedis . . . What I've done isn't any different, I tell myself as I pour wine in my glass. If anything, her acts were actual intrusions. What I did was nothing; she never even saw me.

But you're in a position of power, I remind myself. And she isn't.

I know it's true. I crossed a line today, and thank God no one knows about it. It was wrong, however you slice it, and Sarah Price could probably sue the school if she knew about it. I'd lose my job, probably be blacklisted from ever working in Manhattan again. Luke would divorce me and get custody of Cal . . .

Stop it, Audrey. No one will ever find out what you did.

I let the thought comfort me. It's true, after all; I'm allowed to access the applicant server. I'm allowed to take car rides and stand on sidewalks. Sarah never saw me. People do worse every day, corporations and politicians . . . I'm too hard on myself.

I down the merlot too quickly, letting the warm fruitiness embrace my esophagus and calm me almost instantly. I'll grab a snack and slip quietly into bed. Luke'll have no idea I ever left.

In the half light, I pad over to our fridge. I'm contemplating whether I want leftovers of Luke's pasta or my old go-to, cheese and crackers and chocolate. I open the refrigerator doors, instantly bathing the kitchen in a bright, soft light. And that's when I see it, or rather her.

She's standing about five feet from me, half-hidden in shadow in the still-dark living room, her hair wild and unkempt, her face strangely angular and drawn in various planes like a face in a comic book.

I freeze right where I am, my heart stopping for what feels like a full minute in my chest as she meets my eyes.

It's undeniably her. Standing there, watching me. Waiting for me. Stalking me.

In my house.

PART TWO
SARAH PRICE

Chapter 9

I walk in the double doors of Easton on a September evening at 6:00 p.m. and fall in love.

It's one of those perfect fall nights. Naturally, I was early for the information session, planted myself at a nearby coffee shop for at least an hour beforehand to sit and wait. I didn't want to risk not being able to secure a taxi or hitting traffic. God knows that would be my sort of luck. This is too critical; too important. It's Easton, after all. There can be no mistakes, no errors. As it is, Adam isn't with me. A last-minute work meeting came up with investors, and I went into damage-control mode that morning, my wheels spinning as I considered our limited options. Should I email the admissions department right away, letting them know he'd be unable to attend? Ask them to reschedule us? No, that would be a definite red flag, and they might take our family, and Eli, out of contention.

Eli. My single A-plus accomplishment. The one thing in my life I'm purely proud of. Failing him is simply not an option. I must simply pray the universe will grant me this small favor. That the admissions committee will not strike us down because I've come to the first event alone.

Rounding the corner of Eighty-Fifth Street and taking in the sight of Easton's grand front steps, I have to stop to catch my breath. At risk of sounding dramatic, everything about the school feels magical, like it's been doused in starlight and fairy dust. From the historic building, cracked and crumbling in places, but appropriately austere and sublime, to the antique carpets that your high heels sink into upon contact . . . a hushed feeling pervades the lobby, giving the impression that the books on the shelves are laced with the secrets of the world, and that the conversations that have happened here are sacred. Surely it's irrational. Surely it's illogical . . . but walking into the lobby, I feel somehow that I belong. It is what I want for Eli. This place. This school.

I slip into the small crowd of eager applicants and am greeted by a prim older woman named Barbara—or so reads her name tag—who instructs me, warmly, to fill out my own name tag, then mingle with the other families before the official program begins.

They stand in tight clusters around tables bearing tea, scones, and elegantly displayed individual Perrier bottles—all untouched. Not a soul wants to be the first to break bread, to be so uncouth as to actually eat the food or fumble with a water cap. What if they spilled? God forbid!

I have the fleeting thought that perhaps these same water bottles have been dusted off and trotted out for decades. Those scones might be years old, hard as rocks.

My name tag firmly in place on the breast pocket of my crisp, slim button-down, I choose a clump of parents to approach. They all sport plastered-on smiles, and I am no different. I can feel myself grinning as widely as any of them, afraid my cheeks might permanently freeze in this artificial position.

"Welcome to our club," a man in a spiffy blazer addresses me in a British accent. "It's for stressed-out parents of five-year-olds who are wondering how to pass their devil children off as the greatest thing since sliced bread."

We all laugh, some of us genuinely amused, others reacting in the only socially acceptable way, given the circumstances. Deep down, we're all grateful for his well-timed icebreaker.

"I don't know what you mean," another mom, bolder than me, pipes up. "My child has already read *Hunger Games*, and he's recently mastered division. Long." She's a petite woman with hair parted on the side and sharp blue eyes. Her name tag reads Jules. Something about her intrigues, no, entices me.

I stare at her. The other parents stare, too, for what feels like an excruciatingly long time but is likely a mere thirty seconds. *Hunger Games*? She can't be serious . . . can she?

"Kidding! Jesus, I'm so completely kidding!" Jules looks from one anxious face to the next, beginning to laugh. "I'm sorry! That was a seriously lame attempt to follow up his very witty joke with my own . . ." She trails off. "I promise you, my kid is not reading *Hunger Games*. If I even try to teach him anything, he acts like he's being tortured."

The rest of us smile, relieved. All of us but one mom in the group, a tall supermodel of a woman whose name tag reads Ulla and whose face appears unlined, like she's never been touched by the emotional ups and downs of being human. She bears no emotion, no hint of a smile. "Have you tried simply explaining to your child how important reading is? I have some resources I'd be happy to send you," she says. We all stare at her.

It's a welcome reprieve from this woman and her resources when the admissions directors—Barbara, from the front door, and another woman, a boldly dressed millennial who introduces herself as Morgan and seems like the kind of person I would have noticed in a college class and admired from afar, assuming we could never be friends— announces that we should take our seats.

We scramble, en masse, for the folding chairs. I sit down gingerly next to Jules, who has made a good impression on me and whose warmth seems to radiate from her smart blazer. We chat casually about our children as we wait for the program to start. Jules is a woman I can imagine being friends with, and Eli with her son, Jack. I've noticed how free from my usual anxiety I am. I suppose it is surprising, but then again, I love talking about Eli. It calms me. And that is the whole point, isn't it? The reason any of us are here, subjecting ourselves to this dance, this overly orchestrated and high-stakes game? Because of our kids.

———

It is nearly 8:00 p.m. when the presentation concludes, and I feel surer than ever that Easton is where Eli belongs. Where all three of us belong. I feel special sitting here among these parents, among these other hopefuls who know as well as I do that this place is sacred. Over the course of the last hour, as Barbara showed us PowerPoint slides about Easton's curriculum, outlined extracurriculars and Easton's core tenets, explained how the robust scholarship program works, and, finally, gave the overview everyone really wanted: the admissions timeline, I felt a stillness inside myself. A hunger, yes. But also, a kind of peace, like coming home. I suspect the others felt it too.

The program is over now, and while the others return to mingling, I sneak off to the bathroom, hoping I won't miss anything critical during the two minutes I'm gone. But I drank too much coffee. I must slip out to pee. I'm rounding the corner of the empty hallway leading back to the foyer when I run into him.

He's tall, and very attractive, with that universal type of good looks that could have cast him as a lead or a villain in a blockbuster movie, were he an actor. I wonder at first if he is an actor; he looks familiar. Maybe he has one of those familiar faces. Besides his looks, the second thing I notice about him, right away, is the elaborate camera hanging from a strap around his neck. This is no point-and-shoot; it's vintage, and robust, and expensive. It gives off an air of professionalism and heft, and it grants him a vibe of importance, if that's even a thing.

I'm not looking where I'm going, which is something I'm often guilty of. He seems to not be looking where he's going, either, which is how we end up doing that awkward and strange dance where we try to sidestep past but end up standing inches across from each other, gridlocked.

"Sorry!" I squeak. "I wasn't looking . . . ," I stammer. "Information night. It's like auditioning to be a character in your own life . . . in a film you wouldn't even enjoy if you were forced to watch it."

He doesn't react at first, which makes me wonder what he thinks of me, and that comment, which I'm already regretting. The silence is maddening, so I do what I sometimes do best—I keep running my mouth.

"Are you . . . taking pictures?" I glance at his camera.

"Ah! No. Was finishing up in the darkroom before I popped over here. I love film. I'm old school. Which is another way of saying . . . I'm old." He smiles, one of those real smiles that reaches the eyes, crinkling his crow's-feet even more.

I don't know how to respond to that, except to say, "Oh." He still hasn't explained who he is, and why he's here. Unless . . . "Are you applying too? Are you a dad?"

"Guilty as charged." He shrugs attractively. Why do attractive people always make me sweat? "Though I have to be honest with you, I have a rather significant leg up in this whole process. I've kidnapped the admissions director and demanded immediate acceptance for my child."

I think I hear myself laugh—it's a pretty good punch line, after all—but I'm not really sure. Something about this man is getting under my skin.

"I'm joking, of course," he goes on. "But not about the leg up. Said admissions director is actually my wife."

I feel my heart skip a beat in a way that I know is not a sign of some underlying cardiac problem because I've asked my doctor about it happening sometimes, seemingly at random, and have been repeatedly told it's normal. Did he say that his wife is the admissions director? Of Easton? He can't mean Babs or Morgan . . .

"Audrey Singer," he supplies. "She's not here tonight; she saves her strength for the marathon that is the rest of this goddamned process. Our son, Calvin, is five."

Holy shit. This man . . . this man is actually married to Audrey Singer. Head of admissions Audrey Singer. The head honcho. The decider. When I signed up online for this information session, it was her name and signature on the email I received, reminding me of the date and time. Babs and Morgan work for her.

I have to say something, I have to answer; I can't stand here not responding or I'll seem even less competent than I already do. Speaking on autopilot at this point, robotically, I manage to utter: "My son is Eli. I'm Sarah. Sarah Price."

"Luke Singer," he says, holding out his hand. I hesitate a moment, frozen in my own anxiety. Then I work up the nerve to take it. We shake, and I feel the heat of his palm traveling up my skin. When our hands detach, I let mine fall loosely to my side.

"Nice to meet you, Luke Singer." I cannot help but contemplate how statistically fortunate I have been. I could have run into any parent from the tour. I ran into him.

Perhaps he'll remember and tell his wife about this. A stupid thought; I am certain this moment will be forever etched indelibly on my mind, and likely not on his at all.

We exchange a few more niceties before moving off in different directions. Me, back to the lobby. Luke, to pick up something from his wife's office. I am sad to part from him. Our conversation barely lasted a few minutes, but it looms in my mind as the highlight of the evening. A chance encounter that now feels like kismet.

Back in the lobby, the scene looks hardly changed, but I feel fundamentally altered.

I go through the motions of the next ten minutes. Morgan encourages us to sign up for an applicant tea, each hosted at a current Easton family's home. There are several dates, and I choose the first-possible one, noting the day and time. Of course I will be there. Hopefully so will Adam.

I'm saying polite goodbyes to the other parents I've met. Jules and I even exchange email addresses, promising to commiserate over this whole stressful application process. I nab an Easton brochure from a table beside the front door, then step out into the windy New York night.

"Can't get out of there fast enough, huh?" a smooth male voice says. I spin to find Luke standing by the side of the building, smoking.

"Um, well, it's over." I shrug. I am moderately shocked by the cigarette in his hand. Who smokes outside Easton of all places?

He sees my eyes land on the ciggy, but he doesn't make a move to snuff it out. "Don't tell my wife," he says with a wink. "It's been a day. You want one? You could probably use it, after all that."

He means the information session. The anglers and strivers and competition of it all. Little does he know that I actually enjoyed myself this evening. I felt like I finally found my place. Eli's place.

"I'll take a drag." I'm surprised by my own voice, the confidence in it. I've never smoked. Not once. But he's right: tonight has been intense. What can it hurt? I don't want my own cigarette. That feels too bold, like too big of a commitment. But trying Luke's feels . . . achievable.

I step toward him, feeling myself cross some unspoken invisible barrier as I do, and reach out for the cigarette. His fingers graze mine as I take it from his hand. It's the second time we've touched, I note.

The cigarette feels foreign in my hand, like a new, odd appendage. I make a mental note of the fact that this is very much not me. But something about this night, about him, about the high that I get from Easton . . . somehow, I don't even care that this cigarette has been in a stranger's mouth. I take a drag.

The smoke hurts going down; I cough. I was too afraid to try smoking even in college, when my roommates offered to show me how.

This really is a first. "Virgin," I say to him, laughing it off as I pass the cigarette back.

The word slips out so easily, and I register that I'm flirting a bit. What am I doing?

"I wouldn't refuse some tips," I go on, shocked by my own boldness. "You know, about this whole kindergarten admissions thing. Nothing you aren't supposed to tell me. No insider stuff!" I clarify. "This whole process, as you said, it's so opaque . . . I bet you've picked up on all kinds of dos and don'ts over the years. Occupational hazard via marriage, right?"

I dig a pen out of my bag and scribble my phone number on the front of my Easton brochure, then hold it out to him.

He takes it, glances down at my number, and stuffs the brochure in his back pocket. He doesn't say anything, and I wonder if I've offended him. Instantly, I regret what I've done. Have I crossed a line?

Certain I've fucked up, and that any sense of dignity I might have has left the building, I don't wait for Luke to answer.

I turn around and flee the scene of my crime.

Chapter 10

I feel nauseated for most of the cab ride home.

What possessed me to pull out that brochure and scribble my number on it? Why did I think this man's polite chitchat, his small talk, was anything other than what it so clearly was? He wasn't interested in talking to me. We'd simply been thrown together, and he was cordial. That was all.

I hope that Luke will forget about it. Please don't tell your wife. If he does . . . my son's chances at Easton could be shot. How could I have been so reckless?

The taxi continues through the park, but I hardly notice my surroundings. I run a simulation of sorts, in my head, of what Luke might do, trying to calculate how likely he is to report our odd exchange to Audrey. Perhaps it's wishful thinking, but I decide, in the end, that he probably won't breathe a word of it to her. Why would he? After all, the interaction sounds sketchy when I describe it to myself, and I was there, and could confirm that it wasn't sketchy in the slightest. My chat with Luke—two chats, if we're counting—was casual, offhand, and, frankly, G rated.

You gave him your phone number . . .

Yes! But! It was a friendly gesture, nothing more. Two parents commiserating. End of story. I'm married, and he knew that! I did mention Adam . . . didn't I? Still, if Luke were to even try to explain to Audrey what had happened, she'd be suspicious. She'd wonder if he had some-how solicited my number. In his body language, or by innuendo.

No. He won't tell her about it. I am sure of that now.

I rest my head back on the cool leather seat of the cab as we exit the park and close my eyes, trying to calm my racing heart and recapture the ebullient feeling of earlier this evening. Easton is everything; securing Eli a spot is not simply something I might do, or should do, but something I must do.

I feel an intense urge to see Adam. Opening my eyes and scanning the streets as we wind our way toward my house—a nondescript brownstone that we renovated and moved into when Eli was two—I feel it like a compulsion. I have to make my husband understand how important this is. Before tonight, I had vague intentions of applying to get Eli into Easton, but the idea was unformed, lacking strategy. Amorphous, like a dreamscape. Now, it is an imperative. The application is due in a month. I've already toyed with the essays, drafting them after Eli's bedtime, a glass of wine by my side. I've enjoyed scribbling down my thoughts, but now I must uplevel. Get serious. I'll have Adam take a pass too. He should lend his eye and ear to the answers I've tried to make sing. Our pithy essays will need to shine. So many other families have everything we have, and more. We will need to stand out.

We will declare Easton our first-choice school. I've read about this technique on the Reddit forums: announcing to the school in not-so-subtle terms that you will absolutely accept admission if it's offered to you . . . and that you are applying to no other schools, because the rest are inferior. This is the route we must take. These schools appreciate flattery. They are not immune to begging or shows of loyalty and gratitude. I have every intention of giving them all of the above. Because I understand, on some primal level, that Adam and I are not special. Eli is a different story—from his cherubic smile to the way he mispronounces *artichoke*, he is the kind of child who brings joy to everyone he meets. He deserves a spot at Easton, and I am not about to let my own mediocrity hold him back.

The cab pulls up in front of my house, and I hand the driver a twenty, not waiting for change. Then I hurry up the front steps and enter our darkened foyer. The door to Adam's office is closed, and I know from a brief text he sent me that he returned from his work commitment and is on another call. When I check the time on the clock on the wall, it reads 9:00 p.m. Way past Eli's bedtime.

First, I pour a glass of wine. Second, I open my laptop and stand at our oversize kitchen island, googling Jules. I know her last name because we traded email addresses; it is spelled out right there in my phone: "jules.warner@gmail.com." I find her instantly. Her Twitter and Instagram profiles are public, and she has a website. She is a writer, apparently, and many of her articles are linked. Ones on motherhood, political pieces, and the biggie: a link to her nonfiction book, forthcoming by Knopf in the following calendar year, about how "leaning in" is an unrealistic insult to working moms.

There is no denying it: Jules is impressive. She will stand out to the admissions officers as being legitimately interesting and smart and cool in a way that I am not and have never been. I don't work, not anymore; I left my publishing job when Eli was one, deciding that staying home with him made more sense and was ultimately more fulfilling. The world doesn't exactly view it that way. I have seen it in the reactions of old friends who seem disappointed I am no longer an editor at Random House. Though I can never really tell: Are they disappointed for me? Or did they simply like introducing me as their "editor friend"?

Being a stay-at-home-mom is unpaid, unglamorous work. So many of the other mothers hoping to get their kids into Easton will also be SAHMs—the majority of them, even—but they will never present themselves that way. Unlike me, these women are sure to have some "special sauce." Either they come from moneyed legacy families; or they're influencers, whatever that means; or they run charities or helm fundraising efforts—or all three. These women regularly attend galas and lunch at private clubs I don't even know about. Adam and I are wealthy enough, modestly so compared to rich New Yorkers—but that doesn't mean we are in any way unique. We aren't rich enough to even be noticed. In Manhattan, we are the definition of average.

Then there's Jules. As I click on her family photos—she and her wife, Amelia, and their smiling son Jack—I feel a pang of something I hate to even name. Envy. Jules and her family are better candidates than us. Jules is a great mom, and she has a book deal. On top of that, she's charismatic—I was drawn to her, wasn't I?—and she would likely ace the parent interview.

It's not that I regret my choices. I chose to stay home with Eli so that I could be there for his every milestone, his preschool graduation, his playdates. So that I could take him to soccer and trips to the carousel in the park. I did that. That mattered! And yet, it was unlikely that the mundane ramblings of a privileged Manhattan mom were going to mean much to Easton. They would probably see my choices as mediocre. Small.

I stayed home because Eli needed me, more than other children need their parents. Because he had more doctor's appointments than the average child. It was another reason I didn't want to entrust his care to a nanny. No one would ever love Eli the way I did; I belonged by his side. I was his mom. It was an easy decision to make, and Adam supported it wholeheartedly.

But it doesn't make for very good application material—does it? It is all I have.

"You're home." I spin at the sound of Adam's voice. He stands there bathed in half light, still in his work clothes, his hair rumpled. "How was it?"

Where to begin? So much has happened since I left the house. I feel like I've lived more in the last three hours than I have in weeks.

"There's an applicant tea," I tell him. "We have to go." I'm putting the cart before the horse. There is so much else to tell him, to explain. "Next week. Oh, Adam—it was, I can't even say it, I don't know how to say it . . . unicorn-level magical."

He smiles a little at me, a tired smile that doesn't reach his eyes and signals to me how hard he's been working. "I'm going to finish up these emails, and you can tell me all about it before bed."

"'Kay," I answer. I turn back to my laptop and hear him pad out of the room. I need to gather my thoughts. Collect the evidence, make a solid case. It will be my job to make sure Adam understands what's at stake. His usual chill attitude will not be sufficient this time. We must be strategic. Focused. We need to think like winners.

Jules is a winner; that much is clear. She deserves to be one, based on everything she's accomplished. I hate feeling jealous of someone I've just met and who is perfectly nice! But Jules's child getting in means one fewer space for Eli. Jules and I can't be friends. Not until, or unless, both our children are accepted to Easton.

My phone buzzes with a text. I pick it up off the counter. It's from an unknown 917 number.

Here's an Easton tip . . . act like you don't give a fuck. Play hard to get

Chapter 11

I shut the door to Eli's room, then pad out into the hallway. What parent doesn't sneak into their child's room to peek at them while they sleep? They say that love can be so painful that heartbreak can nearly kill you. I never felt such pangs when I met Adam. Sure, I loved him, thoroughly and securely. He was safe, and solid; he was the cozy socks I'd been searching for my entire adult life.

But I never felt that fever when we first started dating, those intense jolts of love people write about in romance novels that cause you to lose sleep, drop ten pounds, and channel all your energy into pining after this new person in your life. That was all reserved for Eli. Likely because it took us forever to meet him—six years is a long time to wait to meet your first and only child.

It is 10:00 p.m. I received the text a mere half hour ago.

When it landed on my phone, it had no signature, but it was clear it was from Luke. I asked him for tips on the admissions process. He was following up with one.

After reading it, I immediately set my phone facedown on the kitchen island and slipped up to Eli's room. There, I hid in the dark on the lounger where I'd nursed Eli for so many long months. I can't deny what I was doing: avoiding what waited for me downstairs.

Reading the text caused me so much anxiety it was almost visceral. I could barely look at it. I did look at it, of course. I memorized it, every word. But seeing it glaring up at me from my screen: it was too much. My head felt fuzzy. I felt . . . woozy. Drunk, almost.

Standing now in the dim light of the kitchen, I stare down at the phone and take in a breath, flip my screen faceup, hit the side button to turn it on. I hold it up across from my nose, letting the Face ID activate, then press the little green "text" icon.

There they are. Luke's words. Still blue. Still awaiting a response, from me.

Why am I so nervous? Why do I feel shameful, like I've done something wrong? When I force myself to think rationally, I recognize that my predominant feeling is relief. Luke texted me; he chose to do that. He doesn't hate me. He didn't write me off, isn't offended, and definitely didn't throw the brochure with my cell number in the recycling. Not before typing my number into his phone, anyway.

This is a good thing, I remind myself. My actions didn't sabotage Eli's chances. Luke's text isn't the response of a person who went to "report" me to his wife. It is witty, and generous, from a fellow parent who understands how stressful this process is and wants to help. It shows his sense of humor too; I laughed when I read the text and nearly cried too. People can be kind if you give them the opportunity. Luke is kind. All is not lost.

The text glares at me, demanding a response, but I still don't know what to say back.

For starters, there's the content of the text, Luke's pithy advice to "play hard to get" with Easton, which I have no intention of following. Surely he realizes that those words are synonymous with giving up. If I were someone famous, or supremely desirable, then his advice might hold water. But I am mediocre, and that means I have to try harder than everyone else. Of course, Luke doesn't know that. We've had one interaction, and I certainly can't expect him to know, based on that, what a screwup I am. Anyway, he's biased. He has the luxury of not even having to apply. I'm sure there's some faculty and staff application he's expected to fill out, but it will be a mere formality.

No, Luke's advice is not sound. It is not applicable, not to me.

After rinsing my wineglass in the sink and turning off the kitchen lights, I take my phone back with me to bed and climb under the covers, suddenly feeling fatigued. Doomscrolling headlines, I refrain from doing what my brain really wants me to—googling Easton to look for something, anything, that might give me a leg up with Eli's application.

At 11:00 p.m., I awake with a start, my phone still in my hand, Adam asleep beside me. I feel suddenly, distinctly aware of the fact that if I don't respond to Luke soon, I will miss the socially acceptable window to text him back. Luke went out on a limb to give me the time of day. The polite thing to do would be to dignify his message with some kind of emoji or witty one-liner, or, at the very least, a common courtesy like.

I contemplate what to say for far longer than is necessary, finally settling for a **Thanks! Duly noted**, a smiley emoji next to it, and a brick house that is the closest approximation to the Easton building I can find. It will have to do. Then I hit send before letting my phone drop down beside me onto the covers and eventually drifting into a fitful night's sleep.

———

It is one of those stunning September mornings when the weather in New York City is ideal. Sunny with clear skies, the temperature tiptoeing around the low seventies. The heat of the summer has blown off, and the first hints of foliage are bursting out in Pantone hues. Adam's on a bike ride with his college friends, which he does twice a year, and I always make a point of encouraging it. We can't become one of those married couples who lose touch with our friends because we're too busy being parents. We faced an excruciating road getting pregnant, and as we struggled for five years to conceive, completing round after round of failed IVF cycles that resulted in multiple miscarriages, I began retreating into myself. It took time; it's not like it happened overnight. But by year four, with no baby in sight, I began declining invitations to celebrate our friends' kids' birthdays. I stopped wanting to brunch with our parent friends. It's not that they were unsympathetic. Far from it. They were everything you'd expect them to be: caring to a fault, thoughtful not to inundate us with cute stories about their kids. Considerate enough to never complain about the sleepless nights or toddler tantrums. In group settings, my best friends were masters of steering conversations away from babies; that's how fiercely protective of me they were. Still, it was hard. They were moms, and I wasn't, and that divide became increasingly difficult to bridge. I detected pity in their voices, much as they tried to remain upbeat, to hide their shame at what I was experiencing. I shrank from their happiness, their joy, because it amplified my own emptiness.

Once Eli arrived, things were different. I was nervous about being the center of attention—no baby showers for me; I was too super-stitious. By the time I had one infant, my friends had full broods to handle. They were thrilled for me but too busy to live in my worry. Too "been there, done that" to answer my fearful middle-of-the-night texts (How do I know if he's breathing? Can babies choke on breastmilk??) with anything other than a Don't worry! He'll be fine. Once again, I felt like I was going it alone.

I didn't want that for Adam. And so, on this September morning, I urged him to go on the bike ride, reminding him that we didn't have to spend all weekend together as a family. It is Adam's preference; his time with Eli is so limited during the week that he cherishes our family breakfasts, our walks through the city, our visits to the farmers' market. But I don't mind taking Eli on special outings, just the two of us; I live for these opportunities.

This day is no different. Eli and I are out for an exploration day—I called it a "noticing-things walk"—and he's clinging to my hand as we stroll at toddler speed down Central Park West. I push the UPPAbaby VISTA with my right hand while he holds tightly to my left. I'm afraid I've made him slightly terrified of oncoming traffic and have drilled pedestrian safety so relentlessly into his toddler mind that he absolutely refuses to walk down a city sidewalk on his own. Part of me feels guilty, worried I'll pass my neuroses onto him. He's already genetically predisposed, at least from my side of the family tree, so it would be in his best interest for me to curb my constant anxiety in his presence. In spite of that knowledge, another part of me is pleased. Eli is careful, thoughtful, and hesitant enough not to throw himself into dangerous situations. Even at such a young age, he has stellar impulse control. He won't be one of those teenagers to make terrible, drunken choices, knock on wood.

The stroller is in case Eli gets tired, but for now it is a decent place to stash my purse, a snack bag, wipes, and any other items we pick up while we're out. But more than being a convenient catchall, the stroller is something I take deep pride in. Even being able to order it online, after I was finally twenty weeks pregnant and had passed all the scary ultrasounds with flying colors, was a victory for me. I knew the UPPAbaby was a stupid status symbol, that its offensive price tag was nothing but marketing, but the meaning I derived from it could have come from a five-dollar umbrella stroller. It meant I was a mother. I was a part of that club, a member for life.

"Mommy, can we go see the penguins today? Puh-lease?" It is Eli's fifth time asking me in the last ten minutes. He's angling to go to the Central Park Zoo, but it's twenty blocks south, on the other side of the park, and when I check my phone, I see it's already 11:00 a.m. By the time we ride the crosstown bus and subway down, find a bathroom, pay our admission, and enter the zoo, it will be lunchtime. Eli takes his time eating these days, and we'll be pushing at the edges of his nap if we try to squeeze all that in. Then he'll be cranky when Adam gets home . . .

I kneel down to his level and brush his bangs from his eyes.

"Next weekend, okay, bubs? I know you want to go. I know you want to see the animals. Let's look for animals in the park!"

He stares at me with those brown eyes I never take for granted. "Okay . . . ," he consents. "Fine! But I want to read Curious George when we get home!"

He stamps his little foot like this is some crazy demand I will never accept. I smile but try not to let him see. "All right, I suppose we can do that. But just one Curious George. Okay, fine. Twelve Curious Georges!"

Eli laughs, appreciating the joke, and tugs me over to a park bench.

"I'm hungry, Mommy. I want a snack."

"And how do we ask for that snack?"

"Please!" he yelps. "Give me the please!"

It is an inside joke between us. He has been saying a lot of "give me this, give me that," and when I sat him down for a lesson on manners, he decided that "Give me the please!" was an acceptable compromise between "Gimme!" and "Please!" I have to admit it's clever.

As I fish around in the snack bag for the grapes I diligently cut up into quarters and packed in a Tupperware, Eli climbs up on the bench and begins a balancing act where he tries not to let his feet touch anywhere between the slats.

"Mommy," he says, seemingly out of nowhere. This is the way of small children. Always about to ask you the most profound question of their lives . . . or tell you they have to go poop.

"Yes, cutie?" I respond, half listening as I people watch, reveling in the beauty of the day, the shoppers toting crisp, overlarge bags of bounty, and the elegant stone buildings that frame Central Park West.

"Why can't I have a sister or brother?"

I feel an instant wave of something—anxiety. Anguish. Shame. My pleasant surroundings fade, and all I can see are the cracks in the sidewalk and the scuffs on my shoes.

I let out a breath, steeling myself. "You know why, sweetie. Because you are enough. Because you, me, and Daddy are the perfect family."

"But . . ." He stops his gymnastics game and climbs over onto my lap, grabbing the grape cup that I stabilize as he cradles it in his chubby hands. "But at school, we did family day. And everyone else had a big brother or sister. Or a baby. We could get a baby! The stork could bring us one. Right, Mommy?" He says this with quizzical eyes, in part because, I can tell, he doesn't buy into the stork bit.

"Families all look different, honey. Some families have two people. Some have seven, or ten, or more! Just because ours is three people, that doesn't make it any less perfect."

Eli chews a grape quarter, considering my words. "But if we had a baby . . . it would make you so happy."

It feels like someone has scooped my insides and turned them outward, exposing my organs for the whole world to see. Eli has never said anything like this before. It is so strangely wise for a child his age. Too wise. Too true. It makes me ache inside, knowing that he's picked up on this sadness within me. This failure to give him the moon—sibling included. The grape container nearly topples out of my shaking hands.

"Mommy and Daddy decided after you were born that we were going to be a family of three. And that you were so special. And so sweet. And so smart . . . that way, we could save all our love for you."

The words break me into a thousand kaleidoscoped pieces. It is true, every word of it. We did decide. Childbirth was dangerous for me. I suffered from placenta accreta, which meant the placenta attached too deeply to my uterine wall. Within moments of giving birth, I lost two-thirds of my blood and had to have multiple transfusions. Having another child, Adam and I decided, was too risky. We would be content as we are. And we are content.

"I have an idea," I say, standing up and tossing the grapes into the seat of the stroller. "Let's get ice cream."

"Really?" Eli's face lights up like the Empire State Building. "Right now? Before lunch?"

I hesitate. It isn't great parenting, is it? Distracting my child from his lack of siblings with treats? Or is it I who needs the comfort, to avoid reliving my traumatic labor?

"Yes," I answer. "Before lunch. And I don't even mind if you get a double scoop." He lunges himself into my arms, and I feel his hot breath on my neck as I cling to him for dear life.

Chapter 12

The first thing I notice about Genevieve Williams is that she's extremely pregnant.

I stand alone in the doorway of her home. Alone, because Adam at the last minute bowed out of the Easton tea. Though I know this work dinner that came up is a legitimate conflict, I suspect he didn't try as hard as he could have to get out of it. It's not that he doesn't care; he simply doesn't understand the stakes. But I won't think about that now. I will represent us, and I will do such a bang-up job that no one will notice he isn't here. Besides, it's a social gathering. They won't be taking attendance.

The Williamses' brownstone is the kind of home people envy. Built in a more elaborate Italianate style than our own, and much larger, it's truly impressive, sweeping and ornate. I am five minutes early for the applicant tea, but it looks like I'm not even the first to arrive. The marble-floored foyer is ricocheting with polite chatter, and there is a flurry of movement as someone hangs up coats and a waiter crosses the room balancing a tray of Hokkaido scallops with lemon balm and uni, or something equally gourmet. Of course, I have zero appetite, so they hold no appeal for me. I haven't eaten all day.

Genevieve is as luminous and gracious as you'd imagine an Easton mom in her element to be. Dressed to the nines, she's all sleek lines in a vaguely flapper-inspired dress that accentuates her baby bump, neon-pink heels, showstopper chandelier earrings, and on-point hair and makeup.

The pregnant stomach is a surprise; I didn't know, but then, why would I? I've never met this woman until now. As she greets me and ushers me into her foyer, I'm accosted by a larger-than-life family portrait of her, her husband, and their four sons. Smiling, combed, and smartly dressed, they are arranged in a perfect stepladder and look to be about twelve, ten, eight, and six. I have to assume every one of them attends Easton.

Noticing me notice the painting, Genevieve leans toward me, her tone conspiratorial. "It's a girl this time." I pass my coat to a woman dressed in a snappy uniform, who is reaching out to take it. "I try not to advertise that, although I guess I just did! Every time someone squeals with delight for my good fortune, my boys get self-conscious. 'What's wrong with being a boy,' they want to know? I tell them nothing, but I know they don't believe me. They're so young, and they already have a freakishly accurate bullshit detector!"

I look around, seeking confirmation that Genevieve has directed this comment at me. There is no one else in our immediate vicinity.

"Any baby is a blessing?" I blurt out, and she laughs.

"Exactly," she trills, rubbing her bulging belly. I notice she speaks in a slightly affected manner, almost like she was British in another lifetime and can't help herself. "Such a blessing we did IVF this time around and chose the one healthy female embryo we got. But who wouldn't, you know?"

Who wouldn't, I echo in my mind, averting my eyes from her bump. Pregnancy is still a painful topic for me. A sore spot of sorts. Mine was so hopeful, so happy, so long in the making, following round after round of IVF. And then . . . my labor, when I nearly died and left Adam alone with an infant, came as such a blow. I still don't like witnessing others' pregnancy bliss. How has this woman managed to have four, going on five, successful pregnancies, while I've barely scraped out one?

I banish these unpleasant thoughts as quickly as they come. I can't get off track, not here, not now. This event matters—a whole lot more than the information session. Ostensibly, this tea is about mingling and asking questions, but I know the truth: we are being judged. All of us. And I am ready, my armor polished. My game face on.

"Should I go in?" I ask cheerily.

"Oh, where are my manners?" There's that British lilt again. Likely faux. "Pregnancy brain, clearly. Please, go ahead! The party's just started."

I move into the heart of the foyer, past a few couples who seem deep in conversation with each other, and make my way into the spacious sitting room, which looks like a page ripped out of *Architectural Digest*, all plush rugs and drooping curtains and more places to sit than people. More prospective parents hover here, some exuding confidence, others covering their nerves with false bravado. Still others drift in concentric circles around Babs, who stands in the center of the room by the low velvet coffee table, holding court.

In this world, Babs is a celebrity. I don't blame a single parent for wanting to linger in her orbit. I feel that pull too. Babs doesn't just represent Easton. She is Easton, or a key to it, anyway. I don't see Morgan here, or any sign of Audrey Singer. I wonder when I will finally meet her. But it makes sense she isn't here. They probably split up for these; there are too many events for each of them to attend them all. For half a second, I wonder if Luke will make an appearance. But why would he? He doesn't have to trot around at these things, putting his best face forward. His child is, for all intents and purposes, already in.

Rather than feeling nervous, I note a contentment begin to settle in my bones in the presence of all these other parents, in spite of my urgency to make this count. To impress. To prove that Eli deserves a spot. To prove that I can secure it for him.

I won't lie; I feel strangely empty without Adam by my side. It pains me that he bailed, but it's also my fault, at least in part. I should have convinced him to be here.

"Oh, thank God!" a voice calls out. I see Jules Warner approaching me, smiling warmly in my direction. At her side is her wife, Amelia. I recognize her from the photos I glimpsed of their family online. I feel color rising to my cheeks at the memory of it, of how I pseudo internet stalked them. I'm not particularly proud of that, but then again, doesn't everyone look each other up online? Isn't that par for the course these days? Luckily for me, I never went down the social media rabbit hole and therefore have few ties to the ether. There is very little information about me, or Eli, or Adam out there for anyone to find.

After introducing me to Amelia, Jules thrusts a champagne flute at me that she's snagged from a passing waiter. I'm momentarily surprised; isn't this supposed to be a tea? I suppose they use that term loosely. I take a tentative sip, aware I've eaten next to nothing today and not wanting to compromise my mental faculties for even a moment. I have to be on! But it would be impolite not to imbibe, for the sociability of it.

"I'm so happy there's someone else normal here," Jules is saying. "That woman," she continues under her breath, indicating a statuesque blonde a few paces behind us, by the fireplace, "is a goddamned influencer . . . who talks about nothing but herself. I considered spilling my drink on her to shut her up . . ."

"But I wisely grabbed it out of her hand and forcibly removed her from the situation!" Amelia chimes in, shaking her head. She is a petite woman with a sleek black bob and chic glasses. "I literally don't know what to do with my wife sometimes."

"Her daughters pose. On Instagram. In caftans." Jules almost spits out her wine. "Every. Single. Photo. Another caftan. I had no idea caftans came in so many colors and patterns. But let me assure you, according to her feed, they do. She showed me, by the way. That's how I know all this."

"I think they call them 'nap dresses,'" Amelia says, correcting her. "And the photos are a bit much. Something a little . . . faux aristocratic about them." She shrugs. "They seem to be perpetually going to a garden party. I don't know how they manage to find so many gardens in New York . . ."

"Everyone!" trills a voice, and we halt our chatter at the sound of the clinking of a glass. "If I could have your attention for a moment." It is Babs, addressing the crowd. It takes less than ten seconds for the entire room to go silent. I look around me. There are about forty parents in attendance, so roughly twenty couples, give or take. There are a few who, like me, don't have a partner with them, though I'd hazard a guess I'm the only one whose other half didn't come. This brings up an unpleasant feeling in my gut, but I squash it. Now is not the time to think about Adam. It will derail me, and I must not let that happen. I focus back on Babs, who is beaming at everyone, seeming moderately comfortable in the spotlight. I wonder how long she's been doing this job for. It's probably old hat to her by now.

"Welcome to the Easton admissions tea," Babs goes on. "This is your opportunity to chat with other applicant parents and, most importantly, to ask your burning questions of me and the other Easton families in attendance. You've all met the Williamses, of course: Genevieve and her husband, Lance." Genevieve and a tall man in a suit wave at us; my stomach roils in an uncomfortable way when I look at them, and I set the champagne flute down. Best not to drink. "We are grateful to them and their sons, Fisher, Hunter, Sailor, and Bishop, for opening their home to us. With four children at Easton, they truly are experts, so please. Ask away! Also in attendance is Madeline Chu, our PTA president," Babs continues, as an elegant woman who appears lawyerlike in a conservative suit waves from behind the massive settee. "Her daughters, Avery and Zoe, are third-grade twins. And Stephen Goldstein, who would love to chat with you about inclusivity and all the different family structures at Easton. He's a single dad to daughter Regan and son August and heads up the LGBTQIA affinity group." A slightly balding, chipper-looking dad waves from the other side of the room. "Please, one last request. This food will go to waste if you don't consume it. If I don't see you eating and drinking, I'll be quite disappointed!" This elicits some chuckles from the crowd. A few parents hungrily stuff hors d'oeuvres into their mouths, eager to please. "So now, go forth and enjoy yourselves!"

Babs has barely stopped speaking before she is accosted by a couple who look like they have a serious agenda. The wife is wildly gesturing while the husband nods aggressively. Everyone else resumes their chatting, and Jules snags a couple of mini avo brioche toasts from a nearby tray, picking up right where she left off. "Do you think we should try to talk to them?" she sputters between bites. As a flake of toast flies out of her mouth, I squeeze the strap of my purse; Jules is starting to get on my nerves. She really should wait till she's done talking to chew. I assumed she'd be a shoo-in, perfect Easton fodder from what I discovered about her online, and from her relaxed vibe at the info session, but now I'm beginning to wonder . . . and worry. She seems too relaxed. What if I'm hanging out with the wrong people? What if there are more suitable candidates, true winners I should be associating with, like the influencer with the caftans? Jules is still droning on. "I guess we should figure out some brilliant question to ask Madeline and what's-his-face . . . I mean, what really is the point of this tea, anyway? Who's going to even remember we were here? And is anyone asking any substantive questions, or is it all a game?"

"Game." Amelia sighs, sipping her champagne. "We've been over this, honey. You're not going to derive any deep meaning from this event, much as it pains me to tell you that."

I feel a twinge of something. A strong urge to detach myself from Jules and Amelia. It's not that I don't like them. It's more that I feel I am wasting precious time. It's easy for them to joke; Jules and Amelia have a kind of natural confidence I lack. But I want to be around people who care, who feel how imperative this all is. I feel a pressing need to do something, anything, strategic that can get me noticed. Standing here listening to these two prattle on is not going to help Eli's case. I can see how I look to everyone here: like a mere fixture, blending into the luxurious furniture, hardly even here. A sickening thought occurs to me: if I don't make this tea count, it will all be for naught. An entirely useless exercise, a waste of two hours, and more pressing, a waste of a chance to secure Eli a spot. There will be no do-over. It's not as if I can sign up for a second tea. That would be a nonstarter. But what to do to optimize this moment. Who to approach? What to say?

"Stupid bladder," I bark to Jules, who has switched topics to her upcoming book launch, "ever since I had a kid, it's pee every hour on the hour, or . . ." I shrug, hoping my excuse sounds plausible.

"If you see any, get us more of those avo toast thingies when you come back, okay?" Jules calls out. I nod, weaving my way toward the hall. I'm not really looking for the bathroom, of course; I'm strategizing. Reading the room.

"Sarah Price?" says a voice behind me, and I whirl, startled. The woman staring at me quizzically is the last person I ever expected to see here. Thin, nondescript, but pretty enough, Lauren is a former Harvard Business School grad turned philanthropist mom. We were close, once. I feel instantly sick. I start to say her name, but it sticks in my throat.

"Wow," she says. "It's been . . . ?" She trails off. She knows how long it's been. Of course she knows.

"A long time," I say, fixing my eyes on her face. It elicits no feeling in me. Almost as if she's a stranger. I guess she is, now. "How's Beatrice?" I find my voice, switching the topic to something safe. Her daughter, whom she is obviously trying to get into Easton. It's why she's here at this tea, of course. That thought is unwelcome but true. I didn't expect it. Or her. Not here. Not today.

I notice Lauren clutching the strap of her designer bag. Her knuckles are white. "Beatrice is as stubborn as always, headstrong and a total girl boss. But otherwise, fine," she adds quickly.

"They were such cute friends, weren't they?" I respond loudly; if anyone is listening, I want to appear friendly. Who knows how we're being judged? Social skills are important for Easton families. I don't want to appear inept. "Remember that rock game they played? Pretending like the rocks were treasure?"

"Sure," she answers, staring at me, seeming put out. "I mean, of course I remember the rock game. Look, Sarah, I wish we hadn't lost touch . . ."

"Please, it's old news." I wave her off, feeling my mouth forming the words for me and praying I sound normal. "Forgotten. In the past.

Look, I'm sorry to do this, because I really would love to catch up properly, but I was on my way to talk to Babs. She looks available now, so . . . I don't want to miss my chance."

"Oh," Lauren answers, still staring at me strangely. "Of course. Go."

I disentangle myself from her, inching to the side of the room. I grab a champagne flute from a side table—is it half-drunk? I don't even care—and swallow it down in one gulp. Seeing Lauren here is . . . extremely unexpected. But of course; why wouldn't she be applying to Easton for her daughter? Lauren is "perfect," too, with her nannies and her causes and her fishmonger and organic snacks. Things didn't end well between us. And her presence, here, it threw me. Hard. I feel my chest tightening, the all-too-familiar anxiety settling in. This was not the plan. This was so far from my plan for today that it is laughable. Lauren is the one person who could show up here and make this tea untenable. And here I am, trying my hardest to be on my game. It is almost like she came here knowing she held the power to ruin this day for me. Almost like she did it on purpose. I know, rationally, that she didn't. We haven't spoken in a year. Still, I can't help but feel like she came here to spoil things for me.

I spin around, scanning my eyes back to the spot where I stood talking to Lauren. She's alone. Where is her husband, Mark? Did he even come today? I feel a wave of dread wash over me. Lauren is alone now, but soon she'll mingle. What might she say about me to any of the prospective parents here?

I must act. Seeing Lauren has thrown me into a tailspin, and I need to recover my course, to redirect my brain to what is important. Oh, how I wish Adam were here with me . . .

I whirl around and notice Stephen Goldstein, the Easton dad whom Babs introduced earlier, standing solo by the fireplace, scrolling on his phone. Perfect. I won't even have to fight my way into a conversation with him. He's alone.

But first, liquid courage. A passing tray of champagne flutes catches my eye, and I grab one and down it. So much for keeping a clear head.

Maybe the key to the Easton tea is to be wasted or at least buzzed. Maybe every parent here is lubricated, and that's how they manage the whole affair without losing their minds. Maybe that's how Lauren talked to me about her precious "girl boss" with a straight face. I'm a lightweight and barely ever drink more than a glass, but I will pace myself. All I need is a boost. I approach Stephen.

"You look bored," I offer, feigning confidence as I stand a mere foot away from him. "Let me guess. They bribe you into coming to these things?"

I'm surprised by the looseness of my words. Eyes on the prize, Sarah. Being nice and forgettable has not worked. It is time to try another tactic.

Stephen laughs, genuinely amused by me, it seems. "Blackmail is more like it. The things they have on all of us . . . you know this place is nothing more than a common cult, right?" I must look shocked, because he chuckles, running his hand through what's left of his salt-and-pepper hair. "Kidding, of course."

I smile to give the impression that I'm in the know. "Of course." Thank God for that extra champagne; without it I fear I wouldn't be up for this task. Conversation on this level isn't my strong suit. Encouraged by how well I'm managing, I grab the next glass that floats by me on a passing waiter's tray.

"What I'm supposed to be saying," he admits, "is that Easton is a magical place for magical people, and if your child attends, they'll live a magical fucking life forever."

"That's true, isn't it?" I swish the bubbly around in my glass, staring at his face. It's a nice face. I like him. "From what I can tell, I'm standing here, and you're standing there, and your life has begun, and mine's . . . in purgatory."

Stephen laughs. "Well, yes, I suppose in a sense that's true. Easton is as amazing as advertised. Of course, it's all an illusion of sorts, isn't it? What truly makes a school so good that people would kill to get a spot in it?"

"Easy for you to say," a voice chimes in, and I turn to see Caftan Lady standing to my right. "You're already in. You might have killed for a spot," she muses. "How are we to know? I'm Ingrid, by the way." She holds out a hand; I numbly shake it. Then Stephen follows suit. Of course her name has to be Ingrid. See? Already interesting out of the gate. Plus, tall. Why are tall people always so intimidating?

"I'm Stephen," he answers genially, now solely focused on Ingrid. "I know you, for what it's worth." Stephen's mood seems to lift a little, which I note with a pang. It's not that he's been bummed out talking to me, exactly, but I can tell that Ingrid has piqued his interest. "Ingrid on Time, right? I freaking love your feed."

"Thanks," she answers modestly. "Can you believe when I started it ten years ago it was this little nothing thing, and now . . . ?" She sighs. "It's a lot of work, but when it's your passion . . . you have to feed the muse, if you know what I mean. The inspiration finds me! I just channel it!"

I smile for their benefit, not that either one is even looking at me. Then I steal a glance at Ingrid's long, floaty dress, the fabric cut flatteringly to emphasize how thin she is, her toned arms and tiny waist. The whole effect of it is ethereal and stunning, giving her the air of some fantastical being. "Ingrid on Time" must be her Instagram handle. I feel something bubbling in me that I know is envy. Ingrid is another winner. I'm drowning in a sea of winners . . .

And this one is currently upstaging me. I came over here to talk to Stephen alone. Now Ingrid is homing in on my progress. It is not okay. With every passing second, I am blending into the furniture again.

But what can get me noticed? What do I even have to offer? I have never been a popular girl; even in grade school I didn't understand how to navigate the tight social circles of the pretty girls around me. I stuck out—the skinny redhead—like a knobby carrot. Is this middle school all over again—or worse yet, high school? Am I going to lose out because I don't understand the politics, am not well versed enough in social cues, and don't even have an Instagram account? I haven't started one because I'd be useless at posting. How people manage to seem interesting on social media, and not "bad" interesting . . . it's the exact problem I'm having right now.

"Ingrid?" says a voice behind me, and I snap my eyes over to see the woman Babs introduced as Madeline—the head of the PTA—walking toward us. "I can't believe it!" Madeline squeals.

Ingrid stares at Madeline for a half a beat before her eyes widen, and she opens her arms to pull her into a tight hug. When they separate, Ingrid is smiling. "Fuck you, Madeline Chu. You haven't responded to any of my DMs!"

"Some of us have jobs . . ." Madeline sounds perturbed but looks genuinely happy.

"PTA president is a job?" Ingrid responds.

"At Easton it is," Madeline answers, all business.

"Fair point." Ingrid laughs, turning to Stephen. "I suppose I have no leg to stand on, not as a prospective parent. God, how long has it been? Reunion five years ago? Princeton '06," Ingrid clarifies to Stephen to loop him in. "Maddie and I were in the same freshman dorm."

"And, coincidentally, so were our husbands," Maddie quips. "It's so good to see you. Tell me about life. Of course I know everything about your gorgeous girls from Instagram, but I want the unvarnished scoop."

"We've been renovating the Hamptons house for ages." Ingrid sighs. "It's a drag, but I make it sound fun on Insta because I have to, and naturally I don't want to come off as a spoiled rich bitch!" They both laugh. "But the truth is, it's been a nightmare. Production delays are killing me. You'd think the stone from Italy had to be chipped out with a teaspoon, with how long it's taking . . ."

Stephen nods, jumping in to commiserate about contractors and the absurdity of living with half a kitchen while your butler's pantry is being remodeled.

I tune them out. It's as though I've muted them, and I'm merely watching these three interact, studying their hand gestures, their faces, and feeling absolutely sick. This is the definition of a clique. I have no place here. I don't run in the circles of these people and never have. I don't understand their ways, can't make this kind of small talk. There is no real reason I can't jump in and give my two cents about house renovations. I could add a pithy comment here, a sarcastic remark there. I own a house, after all, and it's nice, even by New York standards. But what to say about it? It is a home, a place to live. I have no opinion about Carrara marble, nor can I make one up. I'm not wired that way.

I feel an extreme pressure building inside me that is only partly caused by champagne bubbles. I down a third glass while Ingrid rambles on about custom stair railings. The room begins to dance.

"Excuse me," I say to the three of them. "Excuse. Me." This time I say it loudly enough for them to actually look up, pause their conversation, and remember that I'm standing here. "I'd like to actually talk about my kid? Since this is an admissions event . . . shouldn't we be asking Stephen questions about the school? Isn't that what Babs instructed us to do?"

All three of them stare at me, not saying a word. They look blindsided. They look like they're mentally cringing. I realize, instantly, almost as soon as the words are out, and it's too late to take them back, how awkward I must sound. How out of touch. It is all so clear, now: this isn't an event for actually talking about our children. No one else is taking Babs's directions seriously. The tea is for schmoozing. For connecting. For being effortless and sophisticated. I now seem anything but.

I don't wait for them to answer or, worse, laugh at me. I set my drained glass on a nearby piano and turn to find Babs. She will talk to me about Easton. After all, it is her job. She is the one person here who truly matters.

I locate her by the window, partly hidden by the crowd, and grab one more champagne. I need a prop, something solid to hold on to; in spite of my conviction, I'm feeling shaky.

I walk straight toward her, my brain working overtime to decide what to lead with. A well-placed comment about Eli or a question about Easton's foreign-language curriculum?

Inches from Babs, I am deciding on the former: much better to regale her with a cute Eli story than ask a generic question she'll never remember. That's when the woman standing directly between me and Babs moves to the side, and in the opening she leaves in my POV, I see who stands there, hidden until this moment.

Lauren. Talking to Babs intently. Holding her attention. Just the two of them.

Fucking no. This can't be happening.

I down my drink in one gulp and screw up my courage.

"Oh, hi." I channel Madeline, and Ingrid, and I hope I sound like them. Confident, sociable, not an emotional dumpster fire. "I'm Sarah. Lauren's good friend Sarah. I've been dying to talk to you, Babs! Is now a good time?"

Lauren looks pained, like the air around us has turned sour. Babs, who has no reason to be anything but gracious, smiles warmly at me. "Absolutely! Lauren and I are discussing Easton's fundraising efforts."

"Of course you are!" I say, cheerful. "I bet Lauren is already pledging to the campaign! So like her! Generous to a fault! Right, Lauren?"

Lauren looks at me with a mix of something I can't categorize. Annoyance? Anger? Shock? The alcohol makes it hard to tell.

"I bet she told you all about her daughter, Trixie, too!" I beam.

"Beatrice," Lauren says solemnly. "She doesn't go by Trixie."

"Sorry, right! I always forget because it's what my son calls her," I explain. "Twi-xie! But it makes sense you wouldn't put that on her application materials. We all leave out the worst bits, don't we? Like that phase Trixie went through where she kept biting that other child at preschool! You probably won't write an essay about all the therapy you did to get her to stop doing that! Not Trixie's fault, of course; that other little boy was very annoying . . ."

I trail off, noticing that I've once again managed to completely stop the conversation cold. I don't care this time; I press on.

"Is anyone here talking about Easton, or is this all just a ruse? I don't know if it's the champagne, or what." I hold up my now-empty glass. "But I feel like everyone's in on a joke, like you're all pranking me!"

Lauren fiddles with her bag strap again, looking strained. "Beatrice never bit a child," she pleads to Babs. "I think she has the wrong person." Babs, who for the first time all evening looks uncomfortable, vaguely nods. "We aren't, um, friends. I don't really even know her."

Doesn't know me? That bitch! That couldn't be further from the truth.

"We know each other," I counter, feeling a strange calm overtake me. Calm with the certainty. Calm with the knowledge that I'm right. No matter what Lauren says, or how she tries to spin it, the truth is the truth, and Lauren can't change that. No one can. "She's a liar."

As soon as I say it, I feel something shift in the air around me. Perhaps it's the fact that Babs and Lauren seem to fade smaller and smaller, like they're standing across some kind of line in the sand, and I'm distinctly on the other side. Or perhaps it's the fact that I know I've drunk too much and gone too far. I feel tears prick in my eyes.

What have I done? And why, oh why, have I done this again?

"It said tea," I pipe up, feeling the room sway around me. I have to fix this. Somehow, I must. "Tea would have been a wiser choice. Think about it. For next time." I suddenly feel so tired.

My head is spinning. I have no idea whether I accomplished my goal, though I'm certain that, at the very least, I was memorable. That will have to do. Deep down I feel the seed of disappointment in myself growing. I know that by tomorrow, when I am sober and thinking clearly, I will have to sit with the weight of how I handled things. How badly I screwed up, once again.

Get out of here. Have to. Go. Leave.

I shuffle my feet automatically as I mumble a goodbye to our hosts, Genevieve and Lance. The last thing I remember seeing before the door shuts behind me is their family portrait, the six of them grinning from their perfect family pedestal.

Chapter 13

The next day, I wake up to piercing light in my bedroom and the worst headache I've felt in a very long time. But far worse than the pounding in my temples is the shame. I remember everything that happened up until I left the Williamses' home. I was drunk, but that doesn't mean it isn't all seared on my brain. Every excruciating detail.

I may have sabotaged Eli's chances for a spot at Easton . . .

I fear I may not recover from a dive down that rabbit hole.

I sit up in the empty bed and place my hand on Adam's unoccupied sheet, which feels cool to the touch. He's been up for a while. Something about the brightness of the light seeping through the cracks of our curtains makes me uneasy, and I wonder why. Then I grab my phone from my nightstand and notice that it's 9:30 a.m.

Fuck. I slept that late, on a Monday morning? Adam must have taken care of everything, and I never even woke from my stupor to help him. As much as I'm disappointed he wasn't there with me at the tea, as a support system and deterrent—would I have acted the way I did with him at my side?—I'm grateful now that he let me sleep in, and to his credit he will likely not bring up my hangover either. I don't deserve this treatment, but such is Adam. Loving to a fault.

By 10:00 a.m., I've popped several Tylenol, showered, thrown on jeans and a top at random from my closet, and am sitting down in my kitchen, a black coffee in one hand, my laptop in front of me. I reflexively go to the fridge to grab eggs, but my stomach clenches at the sight of them, and I quickly shut it. Even my body is punishing me.

Now, as I sip my coffee, the dirty breakfast dishes wink at me from the sink, crust still stuck to them. It is the evidence of my failure staring me in the face. I resolve to make sure to have the kitchen spotless by the time Adam returns from work. It is the least I can do.

The coffee is hot, too hot, and scalds my tongue. It awakens something in me—or is that the jolt of caffeine hitting my system? Excessively tall Ingrid looms large in my mind. Before I can stop myself, my fingers are typing "Ingrid on Time" and "Instagram" into my search browser. In moments, I've found it: her fabulously curated page, splashed with her serene daughters' faces as they pose in elegant gardens and on classic New York City streets. In every single shot, they wear long, floaty dresses—the infamous caftans. I scroll through the photos, feeling myself getting sucked in. Feeling the pull of her brand, which is ethereal and aspirational and wish fulfillment at its finest. Her younger daughter, who can't be more than three, is a showstopper, with rippling blonde curls, and the older, the one applying to Easton, has darker-blonde locks and a mischievous look to her. In many of the pictures, the dresses are matching. Mother and daughters in batik! Mother and daughters in a Pucci print! But instead of feeling vaguely *Sound of Music*–esque, the swath of fabric covering all three of them has a couture vibe to it. Custom made, not homemade. The dresses give off an unachievable air, which I know is the entire point.

I am taken in by it. By them. This is not a regular family; if you told me they were wood nymphs, living on a higher plane than the rest of us, I would believe it. As I scroll from photo to photo, unable to resist their pull, I notice that Ingrid's daughters never smile and seem wholly unimpressed with their roles. I imagine that is part of what makes people flock to this page in droves. Five hundred thousand people, to be exact. Even I know this is a lot of followers.

Ingrid is equally coy in the pictures. They are flattering, and she looks enviable in every one. I remember what she told Stephen at the tea—that the inspiration finds her, and it is simply her job to channel it—and nearly spit out my coffee. Bullshit. Each one of these shots has been photoshopped to death, hundreds snapped to land the perfect one. Nothing about this page is even remotely spontaneous.

I hate Ingrid, I conclude. Hate her for her unsmiling daughters. For the caftans. But most of all, I hate how she stole any feeble thunder I've managed to rustle up. And rendered me nearly invisible in the process.

Heat rising in my chest at the memory of how useless I felt standing next to those three, I force myself to close the browser window.

I click on Facebook, heading straight to the one page that always calms me. It's the group I joined several years ago that is the epitome of inclusive, and welcoming, and, unlike Easton, a true level playing field. It boasts thousands of members, and hardly any of us know who the others are or have met each other in real life. But we all have one thing in common, and it's the one thing that binds us. It's also the one thing I can say with certainty we wish was not so: our children all suffer from severe allergies.

I haven't logged on in a few weeks because my focus has been splintered, so I'm behind on the posts. There are hundreds I've missed. Parents asking for tips on helping their kids read food labels. Moms bemoaning how trying it is to attend birthday party after birthday party, toting a nut-free cupcake in their purse that their child can pretend to enjoy, while every other kid indulges in an elaborately decorated and themed cake.

These posts by strangers, reaching out into the void for compassion and commiseration, soothe me. They are like a benign drug, sending serotonin to my brain. My heart rate begins to slow, my anger dissipating, as I like post after post, sometimes commenting with a supportive I feel you! or an It's so hard sometimes, Momma. Sending hugs!

This is my life. Eli is severely allergic to peanuts, has been ever since he started solids, and I am a reluctant expert on the subject. I am practiced; I am routinized. I tote snacks with us on every outing to avoid the unknown. I exclusively book our family on airlines that are nut-free. I'm that mom who spoke intimately with the preschool director before Eli's first week, getting her reassurance that no nuts would be allowed in his classroom. I have prepped and prepared him since the age of one—when he first tried peanut butter and his throat closed up—that he absolutely may not accept food I haven't preapproved for him. It has always terrified me to imagine him on his own one day, making these judgment calls for himself. It scares me to death.

But here, in this group, I feel secure. It's familiar, and much as it pains me, I consider myself a pro. None of this is an expertise I particularly relish, but I long ago resigned myself to being an "allergy mom," and I accepted my fate. Loving Eli has meant doing everything in my power to keep him safe. While many of these posters have one-year-olds and are just starting their allergy journeys, I've read every book, looked into every research study. I figure if I can lend that knowledge to any of the other parents on here, then I'll have a purpose. Perhaps doing this will inject meaning into the whole thing.

"Sarah?" a voice calls out, and I startle, not having heard the front door open. I've been so lost in the feed.

"You came home?" I respond, jumping up to deal with the dirty dishes. I haven't even accomplished that, and it is the one thing I said I'd do before Adam returned.

"You're on the Facebook group again?" Adam says. Dammit. I haven't shut the tab.

I rush to explain it away, to make him see why I need this group, how it makes me feel. But he's heard it all before. "Some of these people are my friends," I say lamely.

Adam doesn't answer; he simply sets his bag down on the barstool and grabs a water glass. He looks tired.

"I'm looking out for you, honey. You have enough to think about. Other people's allergies are not your problem."

The words make my skin prickle. Adam means well. But something about the way he dismisses this group, time and again, rubs me the wrong way. He simply can't understand why I feel so connected to these other parents. I chalk it up to a mother's love, that particular brand of heartache moms feel for their kids that they say men don't experience, at least not to the same degree. I have always made Eli's allergies front and center. Taking him to his appointments. Researching clinical trials that could help him grow out of it. Adam's always thought of Eli as a regular little boy with a minor limitation, never acknowledging the lifelong burden this allergy places on our son.

"Can I make you an espresso?" Rehashing this won't be good for either of us.

"No, I'm good."

"Adam, look. About last night," I say, grabbing the sponge to aggressively scrub crusted eggs from a plate. I can't look at him. I'm too ashamed. "I drank too much, at the tea. I said some things . . . hopefully not things that will derail us," I add, feeling the desperation rising in my voice. "Lauren was there," I finally say, exhaling.

Adam stares at me. "You saw Lauren?"

I nod.

"It was horrible, Adam. She was horrible."

"I bet that was hard for you. Very hard," he concedes, rubbing his temples as he pulls out a chair and finally sits, facing me. "But—"

"But what?"

"I went all the way to the office and then turned back because there's something we need to talk about."

"Oh." I abandon the sponge and plunk down on one of our molded plastic kitchen chairs. "Are you . . . ? You seem mad." I feel small, like a child. "I'm sorry I slept in today and missed breakfast. You know I'm never hungover. That's not me—"

"I'm not mad, Sarah!" I study his face. It's true: he doesn't seem mad. Tired, yes. Like his very soul is fatigued. "I'm not mad, but I do have something to tell you, and I want you to listen and actually hear me this time."

"I always listen," I remind him, but not nastily. It's a fact.

He sits down across from me and folds his hands together. For someone with such a boyish face, he looks so stern that it makes me want to cry.

"I've given this a lot of thought, and I think we should stop the application process. The Easton application process." He emphasizes *Easton* as though I won't know what he means. It's vaguely insulting. I know. Of course I know. "It's not healthy, Sarah. It's all you talk about. You've lost all perspective . . ."

I stand up abruptly, knocking my knee on the polished steel table leg.

"You have no idea," I tell him, my eyes welling with tears. "No idea what it's like, how hard it is . . . Adam. I said things. Did things."

Fuck, my head is throbbing, and not just with the aftereffects of the champagne. This conversation . . . Adam's insistence that we stop the application process . . . it's too much. I know what I did, and pretending it didn't happen is no longer an option. I see myself downing that fourth champagne. I remember how I walked up to Babs and Lauren and started picking. I hear myself voicing that comment I made about Beatrice, insisting on calling her Trixie, and bringing up that humiliating biting incident. It was true; everything I said was true. Lauren is a liar. I wasn't wrong.

But that doesn't mean I should have said it. I said all of that, out loud, in front of the one person in the room Lauren and I both wanted to impress. I didn't just ruin things for her. I probably came close to ruining things for Eli. And Adam wants us to quit? Throw in the towel?

My heart pounds as I try to grasp onto a solution, but I'm groggy. Fucking hangover. How can I make this right? I will reach out to Lauren, much as it pains me, and apologize. But Babs, what to do about Babs? I have to make her understand.

But even Adam can't see it. And if he isn't behind me, backing me up, how can I expect Babs to be? Besides, I need him. We were a unit, a team. It is families they accept at Easton, and those families have to be 100 percent committed.

I need to think. I need time.

"Go back to work," I implore him. "We can talk tonight."

———

I'm at the door of the gallery a mere thirty minutes later, after hopping a Lyft down to the Lower East Side, to Ludlow and Grand. The Simone Clark Gallery is named after its owner, and from the outside, it is as simple and industrial as they come. A squat, concrete prism of a building that bleeds into its neighbors, all glass and steel in the front, it is what's inside—the art itself—that holds any beauty. But that's the trick of it, isn't it? The frame should be as plain as possible to let the artwork itself sing.

In this case, the artwork is not paintings or sculptures but spare photographs. Six-foot-tall, black-and-white portraits stretched over unframed canvases, as up close and personal as they come. Even through the window, I can see the pores on the faces of the subjects. They are arresting, these photos, raw and honest and bleak and unnerving, all at once. A woman smiling so wide she seems high on life. An older man, in his seventies, with deeply set crow's-feet and the expression of someone who's lived several lifetimes in one.

I know as soon as I see these that they have been taken by someone with an unusually gifted eye.

He comes to the door and unlocks it, and as soon as it opens, I step back, instantly doubting myself. Why the fuck am I here?

"I need your help," I say, and Luke studies me for a second, then grins.

"Come on in. The place isn't even open yet, so . . . hope you don't mind." I step into the space, empty but for Luke's photos on the walls. "It's just us."

Chapter 14

I'm staring at the photographs.

I can't help it—they're even more shocking without the barrier of a glass wall between me and them. I pause in front of one, a portrait of a teen. Sweat pours down her face, and her taut arms are lifted overhead in victory, as though she's scored a winning goal. The expression on her face is fierce, revealing an unexpected grit, and I feel a lurch of pride that surprises me; it's not like I know this girl or even what sport she's playing. Why do I feel so connected to her?

I wander over to the next portrait, knowing as soon as I reach it that it will be a tougher one to swallow. It's a photo of a young mom holding her newborn against her breast. Naturally, it takes me back to Eli's birth, to the hurricane of feelings that always swarms me whenever I think about childbirth or see a pregnant woman. I brace myself for the inevitable racing of my heart, which comes right on cue. Still, there's something about this portrait that almost surpasses my own traumas and lifts me out of them. It's so intimate I feel like I'm peering in on someone's most private moment. The way this woman looks down reverently at her newborn. Her bare chest, halfway covered by her baby's soft tendrils. I look away, uncomfortable.

As I move on to the next portrait, I can't help but question how they came to be. How was Luke present for these moments? It's one thing to arrange a photo session. It's quite another to be there hours after a baby's birth. Does he know these subjects intimately? I move on to the next one, the older man with the crow's-feet, and notice details, now that I am inches away from his face, that I didn't before. The rough fabric of his work shirt. The calluses on his hands, which are clasping a smaller, presumably younger hand, the hand of a child who isn't pictured. I wonder who he is and am curious to hear an account of his life, or at least what brought him to this moment, but I understand that I am not supposed to know. I'll never get those exact details. The portrait is inviting me to imagine his heartaches, his pain, not process a Wikipedia entry about the nuts and bolts of his life.

I'm completely absorbed by the time I reach the next portrait, of a woman in her thirties reclining in an Eames lounger. She's laughing, revealing perfectly straight white teeth, and she holds up a hand as if to say, "Don't photograph me, I'm not ready." The portrait would be fairly unremarkable were it not for the hospital intake band on her other wrist. It's a small detail, one I almost miss. But as soon as I notice it, the entire tenor of the photograph changes.

It's disconcerting being so taken in by these portraits, these windows into strangers' souls, and I nearly forget Luke is here, standing a few feet away. Watching me study his work. I'm startled when he speaks to me.

"We open tomorrow." His voice, though not overly loud, sounds alarming in the quiet space, echoing off the otherwise bare walls. "This is my first time showing these. So it's actually quite serendipitous that you showed up here today. I need someone to tell me honestly if they're utter crap, and if so—we have thirty minutes to tear them off the walls and load them into my truck before the boss gets here."

I recognize that he's being flip, so I smile, showing him I appreciate the joke.

"They're good," I tell him. "Really good. This might be a dumb question, but . . . are these all people you know?"

"Some are, some aren't." He doesn't offer more; I guess you aren't supposed to ask serious artists those kinds of questions. I notice he's popping the cork out of a bottle of red wine. "Hair of the dog?" He pours it into two clear plastic cups, the compostable kind you see at gatherings, and holds one out toward me.

I take it from him, though the sight of the thick, bloodred merlot makes my stomach turn. I still haven't eaten. It feels safer to fast until I feel more like myself. I hold the cup in my hand, unsure of what to do, how to turn it down. I decide to do nothing; isn't that always the easier choice?

"How did you know?" I indicate the wine. "It's eleven a.m. on a Monday."

He motions for me to sit down on the polished concrete floor, so I do, right smack in the center of the empty gallery, where I notice, now, there is zero furniture.

"Caterers will bring in chairs tomorrow," he answers, as though he's read my thoughts. "For the opening. I would have offered you sparkling water or coffee, but these cases of wine are literally all I've got." I spy several cardboard boxes resting in the corner, stacked on top of each other and labeled *Anthill Farms Winery*. "To answer your question, I knew you were wasted last night because, well, you drunk texted me. Didn't you?" His eyes seem to dance a little, and I feel a wave of panic and embarrassment wash over me.

Luke takes a sip from his own plastic cup, then sets it down before leaning back on his hand, crossing one Levi'd leg over the other. He wears a short-sleeved shirt; I notice his triceps muscle bulge as he puts weight on it. I sit a few feet from him, crisscross applesauce, as Eli calls it. If Luke looks relaxed, I am anything but. I sit up stiffly, as though I'm about to be called upon by the teacher, or playing a game of duck, duck, goose. My red wine lingers next to me, untouched.

"Guilty as charged," I breathe out. "Drunk texting. It's the gateway to a full-on felony." After I arrived home from the tea, I threw up in our bathroom, which I hadn't done since I was a kid with the stomach flu, and then slid down on the cool tile like a total cliché, my phone slipping from the pocket of my blazer onto the floor next to me. I don't recall the actual texting of Luke. In fact, I had no idea I'd even done it until he responded to me. Not right away, but this morning.

As soon as Adam left the kitchen after our chat, a ding resonated from my phone. I checked my text messages, expecting a funny GIF from friends or my mother's weekly pharmacy list, items she needed me to pick up for her.

> those teas are the reason humanity will probably die out as a species. I hope you barfed all over someone's Louboutins

My first thought was that this text had been sent to me by mistake. It seemed like a response to something, to someone. And I hadn't . . .

That's when I realized. I had. I scrolled up to find the text I'd sent him from my bathroom floor. There it was, the evidence of my debauchery.

> so on a scale of one to ten how bad is getting completely wasted at the easton tea?

The old Sarah would have never recovered from this moment. At least, not without first castigating herself for weeks, months even, and grappling deeply with her shame. But that Sarah hadn't surfaced this morning and was, in fact, nowhere to be found. I picked the phone back up and continued the text conversation, channeling all the wit and charm I could drum up. Feverishly, almost like I was in some kind of trance, I spilled all my thoughts to Luke, right then, right there. About how much Easton meant to me. About how Adam didn't get it. About how I felt like I was at a crossroads.

Luke let me pour out my soul without judgment, offering a witty, supportive comment here and there, punctuated by a few strategically placed "fuck 'em alls." I felt a kind of release I hadn't in months. I realized I needed this. I couldn't afford another misstep, another mistake, another wasted opportunity where Easton was concerned. Adam had all but told me we had to stop the application process, and I needed advice. From someone wiser. Someone who understood the landscape. Someone like . . . Luke Singer.

My options were so limited. I couldn't reach out to Jules or any of the other applicants for advice; they were my competition. As for my college friends, I was sure they were too busy to listen to my ramblings. I couldn't, and wouldn't, burden them. But Luke wasn't a competitor. And he had texted me the first time, hadn't he? And responded this morning when I was at my most vulnerable? Could he be a confidant? It was an unlikely friendship, and one sided, and perhaps I was kidding myself that he'd even care.

I was willing to take that risk.

"How'd you find me?" he asks now, swirling the wine in his cup.

"You said you were at work." I shrug. "It wasn't that hard to google you and find out about your upcoming show."

"Right." There's an awkward silence. At least, I interpret it that way. "Can I ask you something?" he continues. "It's . . . personal."

I feel my heartbeat accelerate. It's one thing to bare my soul via text, telling Luke all about how I'd gotten buzzed and practically picked a fight with Lauren in front of Babs. It's quite another to be sitting in front of this man on a bare floor in a spare gallery in broad daylight on a Monday, my husband at work, during school hours, and nowhere to be. Nowhere to go.

"I think we crossed personal last night when I drunk texted you, so sure, go ahead." I feel bold saying it.

"It's less of a question and more of a statement, but . . . I want to photograph you. May I?"

Goose bumps prick the back of my neck, and a flush grows on my cheeks. He's already fetching his camera.

"I'm not . . ." It's hardly an answer. "I don't," I try again, stumbling over my words, all pretense of boldness gone.

"You don't have to pose. You don't have to do a thing." He clicks away, crouching low in his boots, his hands working the camera and his piercing gaze on me for real now. If it weren't for the lens between us, I think I would be too mortified to continue. "Talk to me about what you said this morning, in your text," he offers. "Tell me about Easton. Why you want it so badly."

I consider his question. Why do I?

"I knew as soon as I walked into the lobby. It felt like home." I'm relaxing, and it occurs to me that this is exactly Luke's tactic. He's a pro, after all, an expert at creating a safe environment for his subjects so that they'll open up, be vulnerable with him. Does he really want to know how I feel, or is this all a strategy to get me to do the shoot? He's using me, that's clear; I'm not so naive as to think otherwise. But then again, aren't I using him too? Haven't I been, since we first met at the information session? "I guess some part of me believes Easton will make my life meaningful. Does that sound crazy? Pathetic? Sad?"

"What I think is that most people don't even know what meaning fucking is." He's still clicking away. "I think the fact that you're seeking meaning makes you a whole lot more interesting than any of the rest of those fuckers out there."

"Passion isn't going to get Eli into kindergarten." I finally stretch out my legs and stand up. I'm getting more comfortable with the camera on me. I decide he won't, he can't, show these to anyone without my permission. Right? So I can always ask him to destroy the photos. What's the harm?

Some part of me feels flattered. A warm feeling settles in my veins; this whole insane morning is starting to feel less like a failure and more like a high, like an episode out of someone else's life. I begin pacing the floorboards, and as I pace, I tell him more. About how special Eli is. About our bond. About how I almost died giving birth to him and how that changed the course of my life. About how angry I am that that happened to me. Angry at my body for not getting pregnant. Angry at the universe for punishing me with placenta accreta, after I defied it and got pregnant anyway via my fifth round of IVF.

"It follows me everywhere," I tell him, stopping to stare at the portrait of the mother and her newborn. "I'll never have this moment. When Eli was born, when he should have been nursing on my breast for the first time, I was being wheeled to the OR. They said if I hadn't been at a major New York City hospital, I would have died. There were thirty people working on me—doctors, nurses, specialists. Adam nearly went crazy with the stress. It's why he worries about me so much now."

I don't realize I'm crying until a droplet hits my arm. It happens now and again; I'll be thinking I'm perfectly fine, then notice my mascara running down my face in my reflection in a store window. I blame hormones and my traumatic labor. A therapist diagnosed me with PTSD, once. It seems to fit.

Luke lowers his camera, his face solemn. I wonder if he looks at all of his subjects the way he's looking at me now. What is that, pity? Or something else? He steps toward me, swiftly. He doesn't hesitate; he doesn't seem like the type of man who would.

For half a second, I wonder what he's going to do. And the wondering terrifies me. Then he reaches out and uses his thumb to swipe a tear that has settled on my cheek. It's the closest, physically, we've ever been, and I feel instantly aware of myself. Of Adam, of Eli . . . of how strange and unplanned and wrong this whole impulsive outing has been. My coming here, searching for Luke's gallery . . . showing up unannounced for no good reason except my own neuroses. Luke is handsome and confident and everything I'm not. And yes, I feel a certain attraction to him. But this is dangerous, like passing your fingertip through a flame. He's married to the admissions director! Audrey Singer! Am I insane? I came here to help myself, to help Eli. Not play with fire!

"I need to go," I sputter. "This was . . . you are . . . kind," I settle on. "Kind" sounds safe. Innocuous. "And those photos—"

"Between you and me. No one but us will ever know you were here."

I sigh, relieved. Adam can't know. What kind of mom does this sort of thing? What kind of good mom? None. Because they don't.

I didn't just graze the flame—I threw myself headfirst into the fire. That seems, now, incredibly rash and stupid. A complete miscalculation. A lapse of judgment. I want Adam, and home, and safety—not awkward, drunken texts and interactions with strange men on a weekday morning.

Coming here was a mistake. Luke doesn't hold the answer; I do. I know what must be done. Adam wants us to halt the Easton process, and I have to change his mind.

Chapter 15

For the next week, I was on my best behavior. Cooking us dinner every evening. Dusting, taking clothes to donate, checking off all the to-do list items I'd put off for months. Our home was spotless.

I penned a long email to Lauren, an apology letter, but in the end couldn't bring myself to send it and simply wrote her two sentences. I fucked up. I'm sorry.

She didn't write back.

After I left the gallery that morning, I spent a full twenty-four hours considering how to approach Adam about Easton. How to make him see my side of things. I could plead and cry, beg him to do this for me even if he didn't agree with it. Conversely, I could take a much more logical approach, presenting him with all the evidence of the school's superiority. But I knew that probably wouldn't work. What was truly bothering Adam about my Easton fervor had nothing to do with the school itself; it was me. He was worried that my mental health was suffering and that a competitive process like this simply wasn't worth it. Not if my sanity suffered.

There was one way to counteract that fear, and it was to show him, once and for all, that I was fine. Stable. Thriving, even. Adam hadn't witnessed my behavior at the tea, but he knew I had not been my best self. I had to override his negative feelings with positive reinforcement. He must dismiss my drunkenness as a one-off. Even though it ran counter to everything I wanted, and believed, the best course of action was to swallow my emotions. I had to be the one to compromise. I had to tell Adam that he was right.

It took every ounce of willpower I had to sit down and tell him, in my calmest and most convincing voice, that I'd thought about his concerns. That I understand them, even, and where they were coming from. That I knew he loved me and wanted to protect me from a messy and strenuous process. "If you think pulling out of the running at Easton is best, then . . . that is what we will do," I told him.

Then I refrained from speaking of it again.

Adam would come around. He would have to.

In the meantime, there was Luke. Ever since that day at the gallery, we'd been texting. A joke here, a meme there. I was determined to never step into the fire again or even light the match. We would be friends, and that was all.

But I was still curious about Audrey Singer. Of course I was! Exceedingly so. That I had managed to not google her yet felt like some kind of victory. I had come close, entering her name into the blinking white search box on my laptop on numerous occasions.

Each time, I stopped myself before going through with it. It felt wrong, somehow. Like if I crossed that line . . . I'd be somehow crossing *a* line. It felt safer not to know anything more than I'd been told, and Luke told me very little.

Of course, I knew a few details about Audrey. They were right there on the Easton website, which I'd visited countless times. She had a brief bio: U of Michigan grad. Psychology major. Two kids, Hazel and Calvin. As for a photo, there was none. Every staff member had a cartoon rendering of themselves in place of a photograph. It felt very intentional, very "Easton."

I could have so easily typed her name into Google and gotten a glimpse of her face, just a peek . . . but I resolved not to search her name further, and I intended to stick to my promise. There was no need to rush things. I'd be meeting Audrey in due time. At the upcoming tour, and after that, at the parent interview. That was another reason not to put the cart before the horse. I was still reeling from my less-than-ideal interaction with Babs at the tea and didn't want to do anything to compromise my relationship with Audrey before it even began. What if I learned too much about her and blurted out some detail that sounded stalker-ish? I couldn't rule out that possibility, given my candid tendencies. It was safer to know nothing.

I felt that even more acutely once Luke texted me the shots from our impromptu portrait session.

It was a Tuesday at 10:00 a.m., and, still on an organizing kick, I was folding Eli's summer clothes to go into storage boxes, preparing for fall. I wasn't expecting a photo to pop up unsolicited on my phone. And I was distracted enough to have not registered who the sender was, at least, not at first. All I could think, as I stared at the reddish-haired woman in the photo, was that she looked vaguely familiar.

It wasn't until I studied it a moment longer that I realized she was me.

Luke sent several more after that, one after the other, without comment. Thank God I had nowhere to be, because I was mesmerized, my folding task completely abandoned as I stared at my phone.

I was unable to reconcile that these were pictures of me. It was jarring, seeing myself from the perspective of an outsider. This wasn't like looking in a mirror, something I rarely bothered to do anymore. It was wholly different. Far more revealing, like someone pulling my skin off and showing it to me. Even my outfit seemed foreign, in spite of the fact that I chose it myself and wore it frequently: oversize James Perse T-shirt, slim jeans I'd recently bought after going down a size or two, and my face . . . that was the most startling of all. Luke had captured the full range of my emotions that day. My zeal for Easton, my anguish as I recalled almost dying in labor. And finally, the tears that poured freely down my cheeks. Luke is an artist. I got a hint of that at the gallery, when I studied his portraits. But now, it was crystal clear. These weren't lucky snapshots that happened to capture the innermost workings of my heart. They elicited these expressions from me. They revealed them. Or rather, Luke did.

I felt more vulnerable looking at them than I had in a long time. The photos brought up visceral memories of what it had felt like to stand in Luke's gallery. Of how I'd trembled when he'd approached me and wiped the tear from my cheek.

It was unnerving to admit to myself that I hadn't known then how to interpret that moment between us, and that I still didn't. Was it a friendly interaction between photographer and subject, as I'd repeatedly told myself in the days following? A commonplace occurrence, one human being offering comfort to another? It was what I'd made myself believe, ever since fleeing the gallery.

Yet these photos told me otherwise. They signaled that I had, indeed, participated in something illicit. Something I did not want my husband to know about. Adam: Eli's doting dad. Our guiding light. The best man I have ever known. Adam, who had no clue I'd been feverishly working every night on Eli's application, staying up until way too late trying out various versions of the same essay, various ways to explain how strong our son had been in the face of his allergy. How sweet he was. How kind.

Luke knew. He knew because I'd told him, in multiple text threads. He alone knew how much Easton meant to me and how my devotion to the school grew with each passing day. Which is why, when I was finally ready to submit the essays on the Easton portal, and I logged on and discovered that I'd been beaten to the punch . . .

It was late in the day, nearly dinnertime, and I sat at the desk in our bedroom that overlooks the city. I had reviewed the application essays so many times, and with such meticulous care, channeling my editorial days, that I was certain they were perfect. No typos, no possible errors. My syntax was spot-on, my fact-checking impeccable.

My heart raced as I copied and pasted all the essays into the text boxes and uploaded Eli's photo, then hit "submit," drumming my fingers on the desk while the cursor spun and spun, my whole body on edge.

Two minutes and thirty seconds later, a message popped up on my browser.

The application portal at Easton is closed at this time. We invite you to submit an application next year. Thank you.

It was the slap in the face from the universe that felt like the final death blow.

Next year? It was hard enough nabbing a kindergarten spot, and that's the easiest time to secure placement for your child.

A few moments later, I received a form email that explained what had happened. Easton had a cap on applications. With so many impressive families competing for spots, the cap helped things stay manageable and roughly meritocratic. But how had I missed this? How had I not known? In all my research, I'd never picked up on this detail. I'd gone to the tea, for God's sakes! What kind of flawed system let you get this far into the process and then rejected you without ceremony?

I texted the one person saved in my contacts who would understand. And who could blame me? It wasn't like I could commiserate with Adam; he'd have been secretly relieved, probably would have told me that everything in life happens for a reason. My mother certainly wouldn't have appreciated my desperation, and there was no one else in my life to turn to.

Luke gave me the idea to email his wife.

I was shocked when he suggested it. But he was quite clear. The system isn't set in stone, he told me. Audrey could do whatever the hell she wanted. And if she wanted to accept my application, she could.

I never would have been so presumptuous. Never would have dared reach out to her, not like that, without invitation. But once Luke said it, it felt reasonable, somehow, to email the director of admissions and ask her to make an exception. For me.

I was on my third glass of wine when I sent the first email. Getting that automated message from the Easton portal had sent me into a panic. We have plenty of wine in our beverage fridge, Adam and I, some quite expensive. But the glass I poured, and kept refilling, was not out of appreciation of varietals. It was a lifeline. I came close to popping one of my mother's Xanax, but in the end I couldn't do it. I was too anxious to medicate myself. Wine was the safer choice.

Regrettably, my email to Audrey reflected my buzzed mental state and my lack of boundaries. I was candid, too candid. But wasn't that the story of my life?

Her response, her willingness to accept my application in spite of the cap, changed everything. I dashed off version seven of my essays, triple-checking my work before she could change her mind. Before the wisp of opportunity blew away, and I was left without options, as I was not ten minutes before. I briefly wondered if Luke had put her up to this . . . or if it was true, unsolicited kindness on her part.

It didn't matter. Audrey Singer was my new favorite person.

It's why I sent her the hydrangeas, to be delivered to her office the next morning as a thank-you. It was the least I could do. I asked Luke, first, what her favorite flower was and how to make sure they arrived intact to her desk. He instructed me to address them to maintenance, to the side door, bypassing anyone at the school who might try to intercede. I followed his instructions to a T, then asked the flower shop to sign them from "Disconsolate."

———

The flowers sit proudly on her desk the next morning—which I know because I was able to sign up for a tour as soon as Audrey accepted my application into the Easton portal. With that generous act, she's given me access to the next phase of the application process, including the tour scheduler. There was one spot left, for a tour the next day, and I enthusiastically nabbed it. Someone else must have canceled. Their loss.

I text Luke as soon as I arrive at Easton, thanking him profusely for his help. Turns out, he's in the building too. We convene outside Audrey's office. She says nothing about the hydrangeas. But then again, she probably doesn't feel the need to thank me. They are the thank-you, after all. You don't thank someone for thanking you. That's not how it works.

With a pounding heart, I occupy my mind by studying the items on Audrey's desk. Of course, there are the flowers, sent by me. Otherwise, her desktop is immaculate, not an item out of place. I won't lie; I memorize every detail of it, knowing I may want to reference these tidbits later. Her keyboard and monitor: those aren't particularly noteworthy. A heart dish on her desk where she's dropped her keys. A notepad, a mug. Next to her keyboard is a canister for holding pens that looks homemade, perhaps sculpted by her son at one of those DIY pottery places. Inside it are seven white pens, three pencils, and a silver letter opener.

Even this forced attention to detail cannot quell the thoughts spinning in my mind, the questions. Has he told her about me? Has he asked her to accept my application? I have no idea. He doesn't mention me; he doesn't mention us, and I certainly can't bring up our shared history. I already offered Audrey drugs in the ladies' room. There's no way I'm going to attempt to explain to her that Luke and I hung out. That he photographed me.

He doesn't say a word to her that day. Not about any of it. At least, not in front of me.

But all that is truly irrelevant. Because I already saw Audrey, already met her in the bathroom. I have finally put a face to the name behind the email address, behind all my stalled Google searches, and now that I have, the past—all my various and sundry mistakes, the awkward interactions and visit to Luke's gallery—fade away. Suddenly, my texts with Luke, and even the photographs, seem wholly unimportant, like tiny details you flick away with your hand, the way you swat at a gnat mindlessly, never fully focusing on it.

Audrey Singer exists. She is not simply a garish cartoon rendering or a Generic Admissions Director, boss of Morgan and Babs, or even Luke's wife. She is a living, breathing woman. I can think of nothing else.

Chapter 16

Finding her address is easy. A lot easier than you might think.

Scrolling back through my text exchanges with Luke, I zero in on a few details about his wife scattered throughout the long thread. Did Luke know what he was doing when he mentioned Sculpt Pilates, a gym four blocks from their home that Audrey belongs to? He referenced it in a one-off joke about how she practically lives there. My heart begins to race as I type the name of the studio into Safari to find the phone number. Am I really doing this? I hate the idea of lying, of assuming Audrey's identity for even one moment. Admittedly, I feel an unexpected thrill as I speak her name into the phone, faking the sort of confident voice I know she would use.

I considered asking Luke directly for his address, but I couldn't bring myself to do it. There was no good reason I could concoct, no excuse that wouldn't arouse his suspicion. I ruled out telling him the truth. Much as I know this second gift is necessary, it seemed hard to relay that via text. It all adds up, in my mind: the flowers were a thank-you for accepting Eli's application. The dolls are more of an apology gift, for my odd behavior at the tour. But I doubt Luke will see it that way. It all runs counter to his suggestion that I play hard to get, and anyway, I feel embarrassed for him to know how hard I've been working to make a good impression on his wife. He won't understand or appreciate the dolls, not at all.

But I know she will love them.

In the end, I shouldn't have been so nervous. Calling and pretending to be Audrey, then asking Kate the receptionist to confirm which billing address they have on file—"Hamptons home, or New York residence?"—turns out to be a surprisingly smooth process. Kate blurts it out, not even remotely questioning the veracity of my claim to be her client. And in spite of my shaking hands and pounding chest, I get what I need.

89 East Eighty-First Street, 7E.

Immediately, I map it, zooming in on Street View, where I take in the details of the prewar co-op building. It's a fairly standard, unattractive gray brick, but it's stately enough and punctuated with a few elegant gargoyles. Luke and Audrey's is one of the condos within this larger building, which probably houses twenty apartments total. Since it isn't currently listed, I can't see 7E's interior, no matter how many times I search on Realtor.com and Zillow and Redfin, but there are two other condos in the building for sale. In the $3 million range, they are reasonably priced as far as Manhattan homes go but relatively modest within the Easton circle, where some families live in $40 million penthouses and jet off regularly on private planes. But, of course, Luke and Audrey aren't living that kind of lifestyle. He's a celebrated artist, far more well known for his talent than his wealth, and he's all the more appealing because of it.

I choose the dolls from a boutique in the West Village where I spotted them once, years ago. They reminded me, then, of some similar ones I'd had as a child, ones my mom had thrown out without realizing how much I cherished them. As I ride the subway down to Christopher Street, after the tour, I pray they'll still be there. What are the odds? I'd seen them a year or two earlier. But when I arrive and snake my way to the back of the minuscule shop, there they are in the corner, wedged between a Tiffany lamp and a box of crystals. With a warm feeling bubbling up inside me, I extricate them from their spot, certain that the universe kept them here for me, knowing they were destined for a higher purpose. I smile to myself as the lady behind the counter rings them up. No one else will think to gift Audrey nesting dolls; they are too specific a choice. Whimsical, mysterious, playful, coy, they will make her think, subconsciously, of childhood, and of Eli, and they'll give her the innate sense that we are a deeply layered and interesting family, waiting to be unboxed. I briefly think of Lauren, and how even she, with all her philanthropy and fancy charity events, will not go to these lengths on her daughter Beatrice's behalf, because she will not think of it. I find expensive white card stock in a store nearby, package it all at a local PO Plus, and deliver it to Luke and Audrey's doorman by 3:00 p.m., before school pickup.

After delivering the dolls, I drive myself mad churning over the exact language I used in my note. I hope signing it "Disconsolate" was as funny and endearing as I intended it to be.

It's not like I expect anything but a quick email from her. Even so, I keep compulsively refreshing my inbox. No response. That's when I decide to go another route. Social media, I realize, a light bulb going off as I prep dinner and throw in a load of laundry.

Locating her Instagram profile takes no time at all. Within seconds, I'm setting my own up, writing a vaguely tongue-in-cheek bio, finding a decent profile picture. I also need content for my feed, something generic that will serve as an acceptable placeholder, since I don't intend to actually use my account so much as view others' pages. One pic of Eli, one of the Brooklyn Bridge, and one of me, posing in a selfie I snapped earlier today as I walked up the Easton steps.

Is it overkill liking all of Audrey's posts? I can't help it; I've worked myself up into a bit of a frenzy. When that other woman, Olivia, comments on Audrey's most recent picture, I spot my opening. Even if Audrey hasn't thought to respond to the flowers or to my more recent card . . . one extra reminder that I exist, a jog to her memory, won't hurt anything.

I try to put it out of my head. I throw myself into organizing our closets, binge-ordering bins from the Container Store, so that I can turn Eli's room into a Pinterest-worthy oasis of order and calm. It's already my favorite room in our house, but now it will have archival boxes of all his preschool artwork. A win-win.

By the next morning, I have thought too long and hard about Audrey's silence. Is she dismissing me? Ignoring me? Or worse, avoiding me? My fingers itch to text Luke about it. But what can he even say, or do? Once again, I've been too much myself. And it has backfired.

That's how I find myself standing a block from Easton at 8:30 a.m. on a Wednesday, staring at the back of the school, eager for a chance to run into Audrey and explain myself.

But as soon as I see her walk in, conquering the back steps two at a time, dressed in a smart cardigan and high-waisted black jeans that show off her Sculpt Pilates body, I shrink away, into the trees. This is not the right time. I will ruin things again; I know it.

My fingers are dancing over my phone screen before I can stop them. A text, to Luke.

Hey I'm in the Easton hood (long story). Does Audrey have a fave nail salon around here? My hands look like I stepped out of a Maurice Sendak book. Full-on wild thing. TY!

In a matter of seconds, he responds, telling me to head to Ella's. I find the storefront quickly, wait an hour for it to open, then ask for a manicure, all the while chatting up the owner. My friend comes here a lot, I explain. Can I comp her next appointment?

As luck would have it, Ella explains while enthusiastically cutting my cuticles, Audrey is scheduled for a standing appointment this afternoon, along with her colleagues.

I settle back into the smooth pleather recliner, feeling immense relief. I have found a solution. This is something I can do for her, something tangible for all of them. I can make things up to Babs too. And after this gesture, there is simply no way Audrey won't email me a quick thank-you.

She has to.

———

Once I've sat under the nail dryer and my mani is good to go, I ask the owner of the salon to give me Audrey's cell number, fibbing that I dropped my phone in the toilet and managed to completely fuck up my contacts. For some reason, she believes me, and the white lie turns out to be a key decision.

Hope the mani-pedis were amazing! My treat! XOX.

It's a stroke of genius on my part, because now all Audrey has to do is "heart" or "thumbs up" my message. It will literally take her less than a second, and no one even half-monstrous, no matter how busy, would ignore the text of someone who has made as bold a gesture as I have.

Except that Audrey does ignore it. Because the minutes pass, and then the hours, and she still hasn't acknowledged me.

I text Luke.

Where are you?

He responds right away, saying he's at the gallery, making some minor adjustments to the way his photos are arranged.

I know I shouldn't go. I know I should put my phone away, busy myself with something else, and try not to think about Audrey Singer anymore. That is the sound thing to do, the sane thing.

I force myself to walk the thirty blocks toward the Lower East Side and Luke's gallery. It's a long-enough trek that I am determined to talk myself out of the errand before I actually reach my destination.

Spoiler: I don't. Sweaty, near hysterical, and utterly aware of what a massive failure I am, I arrive for the second time on Luke's gallery doorstep.

I have not been able to dam up the flood of reckless thoughts in my head. Audrey is ignoring, avoiding, possibly even recoiling from me. She is the key to Eli gaining a spot at Easton; that is truer than ever. She holds that power in those delicate hands, pristinely manicured by Ella. But it is more than that. It isn't just that she is, on paper, the decider of my son's future and that of so many others. Audrey is a force, and what is most baffling to me is that no one else in my position seems to even realize it. The other parents respect her, want to please and impress her, yes, because they like what she represents: a spot for their kid at Easton. They covet what Audrey can give them.

I alone adore her.

From afar, anyway. And in spite of how much she's torturing me. Or perhaps even because of it. Not just by her silence but simply by being who she is. So gorgeous, so refined, so unattainable. The two of them together, Luke and her, are like white-hot lava I continually want to touch. I am losing myself in this quest to make Audrey notice me. I know it, but I can't stop. The train has left the station, with me strapped to the front like a victim in an old western. It isn't enough anymore that I have Luke at the tip of my fingers, via my smartphone. He is utterly desirable, fuckable, even, but Audrey—she is everything.

It's hard to explain exactly why everything changed, but I can tell you when. Glimpsing Audrey's face that day in the Easton bathroom was a pivotal moment. Like stepping into Dorothy's Technicolor Oz world, with shades so brilliant I couldn't unsee them.

No, no, no, I remember thinking as I stood there, at a loss, feeling so unworthy in her presence, and, paradoxically, emboldened. Like if she noticed me, even for a split second, my life would begin again. I felt sick in that moment, close to puking, and I wanted to run away from the dizzying feeling of being in her space. And yet, simultaneously, I wanted to get as close to her as humanly possible. I couldn't believe I'd offered her drugs. It was a joke, a complete one-off. My mother had given me the Xanax for anxiety; I had no intention of ever taking it. For some unknown reason I'd tossed it in my purse that morning before the tour. I would have gone back and hid in a stall, mortified, had I not been so intoxicated by the smell of Audrey's perfume or shampoo or whatever that was egging me on with its sweet, tangy scent.

I recognized immediately that my reaction to her was overblown. That the tightening in my chest was unwarranted. That I was a married mother of a child I'd give my life for, and more, and any lust or longing I felt was some kind of trick of my overly imaginative brain.

Knowing that didn't mean I could halt it.

Audrey was perfect. Dewy skin, enviable figure, kitten-heeled boots that were the perfect height to emphasize her toned calves. I know nothing about fashion, slip on clothes as an afterthought. Audrey is thoughtful about everything she wears and does. She is luminous and stylish, and she carries herself with the slightest hint of sarcasm and disdain, as though she is judging everyone she meets. I have spent my entire life trying to please people; it's clear Audrey hasn't.

I was mesmerized.

As I followed her out of the Easton bathroom toward the lobby, I was aware of our every footfall, of every student passing us. Could they tell how infatuated I was?

I get it. That word, "infatuated." It's extreme. Absurd even. And yet, there she was. Magnetic, to the point of being impossible to ignore. So confident in every word she uttered. So effortless, swiping her flawlessly applied makeup into her bag from the bathroom counter. Plus, she had married Luke. A man who seemed so unattainable, so godlike, in a way. I wondered what it felt like to have power over a man like that. Adam had presented himself to me, at first meeting, willingly, an open book. There were no secrets to unravel with him, no cards to turn over. Ours had been a gentle love story, a cozy one; nothing epic or fireworks-esque about how we had carefully fallen in love, like two people wading in calm, shallow waters and walking effortlessly to the deep end, hand in hand.

This was anything but that.

Luke stands in the doorway to the gallery, his wide hand holding the glass door open, but instead of smiling this time, like he did when I first showed up here, his face is a mask.

"Oh. You're here." He doesn't make a move to step closer to me, and I wonder if it's because I perspired so much on my way down here. I'm a wreck, in every sense of the word. He sounds vexed, annoyed even, to see me. I have interrupted his work. Artists can be sensitive about that. Moody, volatile, even. I flush, instantly regretful. But I can see no viable alternative. Luke is my one tie to Audrey.

He still holds the door open, not exactly welcoming me in, but also not slamming it in my face. So I push past him into the gallery space, noticing that the room looks much the same as it did the last time I was here. The one difference is tables and chairs. The remnants of the opening reception. The man with the crow's-feet stares out at me from his portrait with condemnation. I avert my eyes.

As I stand on the polished concrete floor, I watch as Luke unceremoniously lets the door go. It shuts smoothly, with hardly a click. I don't wait for him to speak again. The words are escaping my mouth before I can stop them.

"I fucked up," I tell him. "Your wife hates me." I have to say it. If I don't say these words to someone, I'll combust. Luke has to be that someone. "She hasn't said that . . . she hasn't said anything. Oh, God. I'm such a fool."

He shuffles in his expensive hipster sneakers that look ridiculous on a grown man. "Look, Sarah, I'm in the middle of a bunch of stuff, and this isn't a good time."

I'm not hearing it. I won't, or can't; it doesn't matter. I have come all this way, and really, what will I do if he shuts me out the way Audrey clearly has? This is it; I am out of options.

"I sent these Russian dolls to your house. I envisioned them as completely precious and thoughtful and twee. Don't ask how I got your home address. Please. I can't relive it. It's mortifying. I was too ashamed to ask you for it directly, so . . ."

I shrug, and then I begin to cry, big fat tears pelting my cheeks. Why does this man I hardly know make me feel comfortable enough to shed my skin in front of him? Then it dawns on me. Luke must be acting distant because he already knows all this. Has Audrey told him everything?

Does he despise me too?

Perhaps they have looked at the dolls, together, and laughed. Or worse, cringed, and thrown them in the trash chute. I shrink at the thought of the two of them, together, saying things behind my back, terrible, disparaging things. I have to do something to banish these thoughts, so I make the most reckless miscalculation of my life.

I close the gap between us, storming straight up to him and putting my lips on his. The tears are still streaming; I can taste the salt, and I'm sure he can too. But as my mouth presses into his, all I can feel is his warmth and strength and the broadness of his body, solid like an oak. I'm kissing him, and I'm a total cliché. Is this what it feels like when he kisses her?

It doesn't matter that this is wrong and not the plan; it doesn't matter that I'll later be humiliated and berate myself; it doesn't matter that I'm cheating on Adam, something I've never, ever done and never, ever considered. I'm acting on pure lust, but what is most surprising is that I'm thinking only of Audrey.

We have sex right there on the gallery floor. It is cold and uninviting and uncomfortable, my knees jamming into painful spots. He aggressively bites my lips, my ear, my collarbone. There is not a single loving or tender thing about it, and I think it's how we both want it.

Afterward, we lie like starfish on our backs, side by side on the floor, staring up at the industrial ceiling. Not touching.

"You have to go."

I'm startled by his words; I haven't yet processed what just transpired. In a strange way, I've forgotten he was even here.

"This didn't happen," he says. "And it can't, ever again. I love my wife. I need you to forget you ever met me. Stop texting. Stop contacting me. Stop. Please."

I know he's right. We have done something unthinkable. I have done the unthinkable, to Adam and my son. I am officially an adulterer. Can that even be true? I have never cheated on Adam. Never kissed anyone else, never flirted with anyone else. This is so far off my script I almost can't believe it is me who did it.

Luke's words cut deep. He isn't wrong; I have been the instigator in all this—coming to his gallery, twice. Taking a drag of his cigarette that day at the information session. Giving him my fucking number. But he didn't push me away. It would have been so easy, but he played along. Didn't he?

Still, the worst part is that I haven't just hurt my own family, irrevocably. I have betrayed Audrey too.

I reach to slip my T-shirt back on. "I'm sorry." But I'm not saying sorry to him. Only to her.

———

I can't do anything but replay it over, and over, and over again in my mind. His bare back and my mouth and how we fucked everyone in our lives. How Audrey, in some strange way, was there, with us. A part of it.

Except she wasn't there. That was pure fantasy on my part. A stupid, foolish fantasy. She probably loathes me by now. And if she ever were to find out the truth . . .

It would destroy me.

I can't eat the rest of the day. I can't sleep. I sit in Eli's room long after bedtime. There is no way I can climb into bed next to Adam, pretending all is well. I am a fraud, a cheat, a liar. Not the woman he married and has been living with for a decade. He will know. He will sense it. So I pretend to fall asleep in Eli's room in the recliner.

When I see her below, on the sidewalk, bathed in lamplight, it is like an electric shock to my system.

It can't be, can it? Audrey herself? Standing outside my house, looking up at me?

I sit up with a start, every nerve in my body at attention. She is here, in the flesh. Not a fantasy in my addled mind. Not a dream, not a vision.

Breath held so tightly I might burst, I stand up and inch closer to the window, squinting to make sure my eyes aren't playing tricks. That I'm not deceiving myself.

That is Audrey. Even in the darkness, I can make out her figure, the cut of her hair. The exact shape of her profile, perky nose and adorable chin.

But why is she here? And has she seen me?

Mind racing, I cross to the door and turn on the bedroom light—a signal to her, maybe? I'm here! I'm awake!—but then flip it off again. I leave the room and shut Eli's door softly from the hallway, and nearly launch myself down the stairs, pausing in the front vestibule to calm my racing pulse. It takes three minutes for me to open the door and reach the sidewalk.

By then, I am too late. Audrey is already gone.

I waste no time hailing a cab and am on my way to her house in mere minutes.

It is simple getting up to her apartment. Rob the doorman believes every word of the story I spout, and I'm in the kitchen in no time, standing in the shadows, waiting . . . for her. Feeling my skin crawl with the intensity of what I am doing. Me, here, in her home. Their home.

Where is she?

She left my house before I did. Did she stop somewhere, at this late hour? Did she have trouble getting a Lyft? Did she walk? It seems unlikely but plausible.

When she finally does turn on the light, and spies me standing here, she recoils.

"What the fuck," she whispers, so ghostly in the half light. I feel a pounding in my chest in her presence. How is it possible that I've missed her, like you miss a lover or an ex? "I'm calling 911," she breathes.

"Don't do that."

I spin, heart fluttering, at the sound of Luke's voice. He's here. I knew that; he let me in the condo, after all. He's been biding his time, sitting in a corner armchair. We have both been waiting for his wife. Me, with fear and trepidation and wild anticipation. Him, so calm, so unruffled.

"Holy shit, Luke!" She looks pissed now. Unsure what she's walked into. To her, this must feel like some kind of ambush.

"Sorry, babe. Didn't mean to freak you out."

"Well, you fucking did," she hisses. "What is this?" She turns from her husband to me. "Why are you here?"

My throat tangles up. My tongue is dry, stuck, hardly able to form letters, much less words. This is what she does to me.

"I saw you," I breathe. "Outside my house. So I could ask you the same thing."

Audrey stares at me, suddenly frozen. I can tell she didn't know that I saw her. Not until now.

"I went to your house because you've been stalking me," Audrey finally says. "And I think it's pretty clear something's wrong with you. Luke, this woman. You have no idea."

"I can explain," I answer feebly, feeling my lip tremble. This is not how I imagined it going.

"Actually, Sarah's here because I invited her," Luke chimes in. He runs a hand through his lanky brown hair that's speckled with gray, and for a second I can't believe that I slept with this man. How did I do that? To Adam? To her?

"You . . . ?"

149

She meets her husband's eyes. He shrugs.

"Big Sur," he breathes. "Remember?"

Audrey doesn't say anything for a long beat, but finally, to Luke, she mutters, "A heads-up would have been nice."

Luke's words mean nothing to me, but it is clear what he wants. More of what happened in the gallery. Which, as far as I'm concerned, was a fluke, a mistake on my part.

I don't want him at all; that is clear to me now. My curiosity was sated when we fucked earlier, replaced by a feeling of mild surprise that I found him so attractive in the first place.

Luke is merely an obstacle now. A roadblock to the one thing, the one person, who does matter.

But the only way to have Audrey, to be with her, really be with her, is to be with them both, together . . . the three of us.

I am willing to do anything.

PART THREE
AUDREY SINGER

Chapter 17

Tea. That's absolutely the most fitting drink to serve immediately after a confrontation with your husband and his . . . whatever she is.

Sarah Price. I'm astounded by the sheer absurdity of it. By the audacity of it. And by his choice of woman. It's not that I'm shocked, exactly. There's absolutely something appealing about her. But if I'm honest with myself, no, I wouldn't have expected this.

The situation—possibly.

Her—not at all.

"Chamomile or mint?" I ask her as the teakettle begins to howl. I can't believe how calm I'm being, how blasé. But I must be, unless I want to abdicate my power, relinquish my ability to negotiate and have the upper hand. Weakness will not help me now.

Sarah's still standing there in the half light, looking like a frightened doe. I suppose she is one. Much as I find this entire episode surprising . . . mind bending, really. For her, it's likely worse.

"Let's go sit," Luke suggests, his eyes meeting mine across the kitchen island. I can interpret exactly what they say now, and I berate myself for not being able to read them earlier. All these months, wondering what was up with him. I was oblivious. Completely off my game.

Now, it's clear what he is silently asking for: Forgiveness. Permission.

At least I know now what he wants.

I steel myself. I can give all that to him.

Five minutes later, we're nestled uncomfortably on our worn-in couch, Luke and me. His muscular thigh presses into my knee as I cradle my favorite chipped mug. We are every bit the couple, the united front, even though I strongly suspect that there is much here I don't know, that I haven't been privy to.

I feel it, briefly: a flash of anger mixed with shame, and jealousy, plain and simple. Something has transpired between these two. I am not sure if I want to know what.

Sarah sinks into the leather swivel chair across from us. She's set her tea down on the coffee table, undrunk, and hugs her knees to her chest, like a child trying to make herself as tiny as possible. I make note of the fact that my anger is directed solely at Luke, at the man beside me. My husband, the partner-in-crime who cooks me five-star meals and spoons me in bed. The man who vowed, once, to love, cherish, protect, and honor me. It is hard to sit here beside him and not hate him, at least momentarily. It's hard not to feel rage. But not at her. She seems so innocent, so blameless. I can see, instantly, what it is about her that appeals to him. She's so needy. I no longer think she is the calculating stalker I once believed her to be. Yes, her actions were questionable. But within a certain context . . . this very strange and unusual context . . .

I think of her now as a pawn, a victim, a target. She no longer seems dangerous, but like someone determined to do the best for her child. Who got swept up into something much . . . more.

Who knows what active part she has even played in all this. I am desperate to find out, and at the same time, desperate to walk out of this room and escape it, and them.

I know I won't. Failure, especially in my marriage, is not an option. No matter what has happened between them, as long as Luke still loves me, I am okay. We are okay. I can stuff down the rage. I can find a way to accept, to forge ahead. Of course, I'm lying to myself, at least in part; I know that. But lie I must, and continue to lie I will.

"I'm not sure what to say." Sarah finally breaks the heavy silence. "And that's unusual for me. As you both already know." She laughs, seeming nervous. Of course she's nervous. Unless it's all an act . . .

Luke laughs along with her, and I try to join in. I'm not sure I'm convincing anyone.

"This is new to us too," Luke says, and I bristle. He talks about us, this situation, like we're discussing buying a new home or trying out wakesurfing.

"Oh good, please do acknowledge how strange and . . . unusual this situation is," I say to him, dryly, and he laughs again.

"True. This is all a bit on the unconventional side, yes."

I fight an impulse to stand up and kick him in the balls. "I don't want to know," I blurt out to Sarah, for the moment still feeling more generous toward her than him. That could change; it very well might, down the line. But for now, I don't hate her. We are in this odd ship together, and I need to make the best of it. Luke has made his choice to invite her here, and it would hurt me to try to fight it. To argue or attempt to convince him that she might be unbalanced, that it could spell trouble to bring her into our home, our lives. He would call me paranoid, and that's the last thing I want. I steel myself. "The details, I mean. Whatever you two did or said. Not now, anyway," I add.

Luke squeezes my knee, sending sparks to my groin, and I inwardly bristle. I'm actually fucking doing this.

Well, I've done harder things.

I stand up, putting distance between me and him. I have a lot of thinking to do. A lot of reconciling to get my mind straight. I must find a way to curb my resentment, but I don't have to go through all that emotional toil to determine what I will do. I know what I will do.

I spin to stand between the two of them, my mind made up. I will steer this goddamned ship or risk being plummeted overboard to wrestle with the sharks and the waves.

"I don't want to be the buzzkill here," I say, pacing between Luke, who has walked to the bar to pour something stronger than tea, and her, "but someone has to talk logistics. So let's discuss how this will work. Make some ground rules. Set expectations."

"You can take the girl out of admissions . . ." Luke smirks, stirring his Japanese whisky, his back turned to us. Us. A strange, strange trio, now. It's so unnerving and fucked up and incongruous. He and I are the team. This morning we were two. Now we are three.

And yet, if I want to save my marriage, this is to be the new normal.

"Yes, I'm organized, so sue me," I quip, careful not to sound too curt. Too biting. Part of maintaining control means reminding Sarah that I'm not the third party here. She is.

"I'm sorry, Audrey." She speaks up, timid. "I'm . . . how would this even work? Would we like . . . date?" She says it so innocently I can't help but let out a bark of a laugh.

"No," I answer quickly.

"So, it's just sex, then?" Her voice is small, uncertain.

Luke grins, turning back to face us, whisky on the rocks in hand. I bought him that whisky glass with the built-in ice wedge. It came in a set of, naturally, two. "Don't think of it so . . . concretely. Try to free your mind. You'll see. It'll be a lot easier than you think."

I want to slap him. Easy for him. He's the one who wants this. He told me so.

That's right; we've talked about this. Once before, on a grown-up getaway, when we left Hazel and Cal at home with a sitter, sneaked off for a long weekend by ourselves. Big Sur. That's what he was referencing. Our talk. "Remember?" he asked me not twenty minutes ago. Of course I remembered. How could I ever forget?

"What if we . . . wanted more?" was how he broached the topic, after our third glasses of wine at Sierra Mar, the hilltop restaurant at the impossibly romantic Post Ranch Inn, overlooking the crashing Pacific. Cal was three at the time, and the trip away from our kids was long overdue. At the time, I noted with rising resentment that he chose to bring up this topic when I was at my most relaxed. My most pampered. My most lubricated, by wine and a husband who seemed, by every count, "perfect." We'd spent the entire day in the hot tubs, wooden barrels cut into the cliffs overlooking the ocean. He'd told everyone we encountered it was our anniversary and how I'd made him the luckiest man alive.

And then . . . this.

This bomb. Detonated. There it was, my enviable life . . . the cover torn off of it to reveal a different book inside than the one I had thought I'd been reading.

It could have been worse, I told myself. He could have told me he'd cheated, or that he wanted to. He could have said he was in love with someone else, that woman he'd recently photographed or that yoga teacher Penny with the ridiculously slim frame and sleeve of tattoos. He could have left me. It had happened once before, with my ex, Samuel, so I was no stranger to being dropped like yesterday's trend, humiliated and heartbroken.

This wasn't that. This was . . . a seedling. A proposal. An arrangement. Threesome or throuple or however you wanted to phrase it. I didn't care to categorize it. I knew instantly that it was the thing Luke needed if "we" were going to last. It wasn't personal, he insisted. He loved me as much as he ever could love a person. He didn't believe in monogamy. Not entirely, anyway.

He wondered if I could open my mind. If I could do this for him.

The more I considered it, I didn't entirely hate the idea of inviting someone else into our cocoon, at least, not as much as I imagine I might have. Faced with this option—open your marriage, or watch it burn—I suppose some women might have walked, right then and there.

I wasn't one of those women.

Luke mattered too much to me. And I supposed I could come around to the idea. For the right person. The right woman.

Twenty-four hours later, as we boarded our flight back to JFK, we were talked out on the subject. It was something we agreed we weren't ready for, but we might be one day. We were simply brainstorming, the way spouses plan for retirement and vacations they want to take one day when they're empty nesters.

We didn't discuss it again. But I'd been waiting nearly two years for that shoe to drop, and here she was, in my living room, in the form of overly chatty and self-conscious Sarah Price.

She is not who I imagined as the add-on to our cozy marriage bed. In most ways, she is nothing like the woman I would have conjured in my mind. But seeing her here, now: I can't deny it. She is exactly that woman.

"We need rules," I announce, stepping into the role I know will be mine: manager. I will manage the fuck out of this situation, like I manage Babs and Morgan and the entire Easton admissions process. "First one: you can't tell a soul about this."

"Even Adam," Luke chimes in.

Adam. As in Sarah's husband. I shoot him a look. "Especially Adam!" Adam would have a motive to tell the world about this. It's my worst nightmare. "You can't tell your husband," I say, my eyes trained on her. "That is the one rule here that matters. He cannot, he must not know."

"Or we'll have to kill him," Luke deadpans.

I sigh. "He's kidding," I tell her.

She nods. "I know. I won't tell him. Why would I? He'd hate me." She chokes, and for half a second, I wonder why the fuck she is here. Why she would want to do this. Cheat on her husband and risk her happy home life. Luke and I, at least, are in this together. There is no betrayal, except what might have already transpired between them. But I am choosing to wipe our slate clean. Sarah and Adam, on the other hand . . . of course, I know nothing of their lives, behind closed doors.

"You have to understand," she says, sitting up abruptly in the swivel chair. She looks so fragile now, like she might crack in two. There's something sexy about her frame, thin as it is. Pert breasts and a slim, pale waist that peeks from beneath her sweater's edge. "I love him. He's . . . the best dad. The best husband. But . . . we aren't on the same page anymore, and . . . I need something else. Couples grow apart sometimes. It happens." She shrugs, as though that's enough of an explanation.

It is, clearly, for Luke. It will have to be for me as well.

"Can we get on with all the admin and figure out when we're going to, you know, meet again?" Luke swishes his whisky, enjoying this a little too much. But of course he is. It's all his desire, his wish, his design. I can't decide whether I want to pummel him or have sex with him right now, here on the rug. That's the thing about Luke, about all of this. I must admit, some part of me, some increasingly budding part, is excited by the prospect of what lies ahead. Of awakening the dead parts of our marriage, of our sex life.

"Hazel will be at Samuel's this weekend," I offer up, still determined to play the role of practical administrator. "If you get here at nine, once Cal's in bed . . . but what will you tell Adam?"

It's strange saying out loud the name of this man I don't know and whom I will likely do my best to never meet.

"Oh, I'll come up with something." She waves off that notion. "Dinner and drinks with girlfriends. He'll barely notice if I'm home late. He sleeps like the dead."

I take that in. It sounds reasonable. It will work.

"So we're on for Saturday, then," Luke says, as casually as if he's making a date for, well, tea.

Sarah stands up, seeming like she doesn't know what to do with herself. I walk over to the door and open it, making it clear: it's time for her to go.

"I literally don't know what I'm supposed to say right now," she offers, almost like an apology.

"That makes two of us," I answer her. Then, a thought occurs to me, and I can't keep it contained.

"One more rule," I tell her.

"Audrey," Luke groans.

"No, wait, this one's important." I steel myself, then: "Don't lie to us, okay? Not ever."

Chapter 18

I have not kept a secret like this from Chippie in a long, long time.

But I meant what I said when I gave Sarah that warning. She must not tell anyone about our arrangement. I certainly don't plan to.

I don't even want to think about what my best friend would do, how she'd react. She wouldn't judge me—absolutely not. I predict she'd be delighted. She would eat this up, at least, at first. I can imagine her glee, her millions of questions. Which is why I can't tell her.

I can't admit how out of control this situation makes me feel. And how, in some ways, that turns me on.

But after the initial shock wore off, there would be her inevitable questions. If I'm doing this for the right reasons. If I'm happy. If it's wise to let a total stranger into my life in such intimate fashion. Perhaps the questions are what I really can't face.

I wouldn't be able to answer any of her inquiries, because the truth is, I still don't know what drove Sarah's gifts and notes. And then there's my husband. He and Chippie have never exactly been simpatico, like I've always put up with Chippie's husband, Nathan, but never quite been able to see his finer qualities. Chippie's never had a bad word to say about Luke, but we always knew it was the two of us, first; BFFs before partners, till death do us part. Still, I wonder if she'd blame Luke for roping me into this. If she voiced those concerns, I'd have no way to justify my actions, because what we are planning to do defies logic. It makes no sense.

And yet, it is happening, in two days. I can hardly tamp down my nerves.

I pray I don't give myself away.

I'm browsing the marble counter at Quince where Chippie displays all her latest beauty goodies: Deep Sweep toner with papaya extract and vitamin C gel, Lotus antiaging avocado moisturizer, Hydra-Firm night cream that's $300 per ounce but promises to reverse the clock.

"But the fundraiser is in two weeks," Chippie says testily into the phone, holding up a finger for me to wait. "If I can't see a guest list by tomorrow, we're going to have to pull my support."

I tune her out. The visions in my mind are far more vivid than what's happening here in the shop. I can't get the memory of last night out of my head.

Luke and I made love, for the first time in weeks. After Sarah left, we downed two whiskys apiece, which seemed in hindsight like the right strategy. There's no world in which I could face him completely sober. I wasn't about to let Luke know how rattled I was. The last thing I would let myself do would be to rail at him, to nail him to the cross. I wouldn't accuse, or lash out. That would not help me.

Besides, my anger had begun to dissipate. It might have been the alcohol hitting my system. Or something more: the increasingly surprising feeling, bubbling up inside me, that what we were about to embark on might not be so bad.

Luke was turned on; that was plain as day. As we tumbled onto our unmade bed, I told myself it was me he wanted. His proposal wasn't about replacing me. It was about expanding our horizons.

I could almost believe it.

Here now, in the broad daylight of SoHo, I try to distract myself from the memory: my head sinking deep into the pillow, his vocal insistence that I am the sexiest woman alive . . . I scan the shop for any new tweaks to the already-chic space. The faux zebra head on the wall that Chippie commissioned from her favorite Brooklyn artist seems to wink at me knowingly as I slip onto a plush turquoise-velvet chair so gossamer soft that I'm a little nervous to sit on it.

"Hi, Audrey. Champagne? Matcha? Soothing tea? Freshly pressed Vitalize juice with kale and turmeric?"

Chippie's chic assistant, Hani, appears in front of me bearing a clipboard. I can guess she's in the middle of taking inventory, and my arrival is a nuisance, because, as Chippie's bestie, I must be attended to.

"No thanks, Hani, I'm fine," I reassure her. She nods, relieved, then scoots off in her platform clogs to take stock of the face creams.

"Get me out of here before I murder someone." Chippie floats out from behind the counter, throwing on a wrap. It's nippy outside, and we're both dressed for our weekly walk around SoHo. Me in Lululemons, Chippie in couture athletic wear. I can't identify the brand, but it's stretchy and flattering and hot pink, and her midriff, perfectly toned, can be spied in a sliver between her tank and high-waisted pants.

I steel myself. Time to put on my game face. Chippie can't know anything's different or off.

We're out the door, but not before Chippie leaves Hani with a few last instructions to go over invoices and order collagen lattes. But it takes her less than a second to grill me about Sarah as we power walk our way past the hordes on Broome Street.

"Bitch, how could you leave me hanging like this! What did you decide? Are you going to go?"

It takes me a minute to figure out what she's even referring to. Then it hits me with a zing: she's asking if I'm going to go to Sarah's home. Of course, because she doesn't know that I already went. And she definitely doesn't know what transpired after that.

"Of course I'm not going to go," I say, hoping I sound convincingly put out, slightly offended, even. "And anyway, it's old news. I haven't heard from her since that text, which means she's probably given up. Don't worry."

"Bitch has your address! And phone number! Which she got by nefarious means! And she has an inappropriate level of interest in you! I'm gonna worry."

We cross Crosby, peeling away from the throngs of furious shoppers and onto a quieter street. We used to meet up once a week during lunch to hit up a SoulCycle class, but then we realized: What was the point of exercising together if we couldn't talk? So we switched to aggressive walking.

"I promise if she reaches out to me again about anything outside the normal application process, I'll tell you." I hate lying to Chippie. But the more she keeps asking about Sarah, the more likely it is that I'll crack and reveal everything. No, I need to get her off the scent. Redirect and neutralize the whole thing.

"How's Nathan?" I ask her. It's the most neutral topic I can come up with.

"Ugh. Fine," she scoffs. "It's normal to hate your husband, right?"

"For you, yes."

"But is it? All these years, I've tolerated him, in a passive sort of way. Hate feels so . . . purposeful. But this morning when he was yelling at the espresso machine and blaming me for using up all his nutpods, I felt this wave of it. Hate. And you know what the next thing I thought was? 'Huh. That's different.'"

"That's perfectly normal." I laugh. "When Luke leaves his dirty boxers on the floor, I literally want to kill him in his sleep. Perfectly typical wifely response, I promise. You're supposed to get all passive aggressive for a week or two and turn all his socks inside out."

I'm not saying what I really want to, which is that the tolerating concerns me a lot more than any fleeting wave of hate Chippie's experiencing. Hate means you feel something for someone. Tolerating your spouse means you simply . . . don't care. But maybe the two of them really are that far gone.

When we pause for the walk signal, Chippie folds herself in two to stretch her hamstrings. "You know, when we're fucking, I think exclusively about that hot, burly chief of police from *Stranger Things*, right?"

I nearly trip over an uneven piece of sidewalk.

"Um, no, you have not filled me in on that detail previously. And seriously? Hopper?"

Chippie laughs. "I know. It surprised me too."

"But you are . . . still doing it," I confirm, feeling my cheeks flush. "That's good!"

The walking man is blinking, but Chippie stops in her tracks at the intersection, planting her Stella McCartney sneakers firmly on the concrete. "It's not good, Audrey. It's obligation. Because I married him and vowed to love him and blah, blah, blah. But I don't. As my best friend of a million years, you do know that . . . right?"

I guess I do. I hadn't thought of it in such stark terms, but when she puts it that way . . .

"So what are you gonna do about it?" I press, as several overeager tourists nearly bump into us with their massive shopping bags. I suddenly feel an intense urge to understand. I strongly suspect Luke's feelings for me have begun to waver or wane. It's why he's asked me to make this arrangement. It's why I didn't hesitate, not even for a second, to agree to it.

"Do? What would I possibly do? Jesus, Audrey, catch up. I will never divorce Nathan. He's basically the most boring person to me on the planet, but I won't. He's the girls' dad and I won't do that to them. It's too expensive and too draining and too . . . too goddamned clichéd. So I'll keep fucking him and thinking about the cop from *Stranger Things*."

I get it, I do. She'd do anything to save her marriage.

So would I.

At that moment, we both hear, in unison, the chime of our phones. Texts landing in our pockets at exactly the same time.

In a swift motion, I pull my phone out and read the message. It's from Headmaster Hurst. Chippie does the same.

Hi, Audrey. Please come see me right away about a very serious disciplinary issue involving Hazel. I'll be in my office.

Shit. I look up at Chippie, feeling the breath knocked out of me. "Hazel," I chirp.

"I got one too," Chippie says, looking dumbfounded. She shows me her phone. It's the same message, but with her daughter Winslow's name inserted instead.

Chapter 19

The outer vestibule to Hurst's office is freezing, even with my exercise hoodie on. I pull the sleeves over my hands, which are icicles, and try not to panic.

Possibilities race through my mind, but I can't, I won't let myself indulge in them. Better to wait for the details. Surely whatever is going on here won't be as bad as what I can imagine.

Too worked up to sit down, I stand, watching Chippie, who's across the room, as she speaks with intensity into her phone. She's giving Hani instructions for the next few hours. Pacing, I check my own phone; Luke hasn't responded. He should be here. So should Nathan.

The door to Hurst's office opens, and I jump, my nerves jangling.

"Come in," Hurst says, her face a mask. It's not that I expected any warmth today. This is, after all, a "serious disciplinary issue"—oh, Hazel—but the lack of emotion on my boss's face is unnerving. We aren't close, she and I, but our working relationship has been flawless. I've made sure of that. Still, right now, I'm not her employee. I'm a mother.

"Oh, good, you haven't started yet," says a voice behind me, and I spin.

I instantly feel my heartbeat start to slow at the sight of Luke. We can handle this, whatever it is, together. He rests a reassuring hand on my shoulder.

"Nathan's on a plane to Dubai," Chippie announces as she tosses her phone into her Goyard bag. "I found out from my assistant." She shrugs at me before striding into Hurst's office, Luke and I following in her wake.

"That's perfectly fine," Hurst says, waving her off and flitting behind her desk, which I can glimpse through the open door. It occurs to me that she, herself, is nervous. Fuck. If she's nervous . . . this can't be good.

When we walk through the door into Hurst's office, I am not expecting to find my daughter already sitting there. Next to her is Winslow.

I feel my heart leap to my throat at the sight of Hazel. She sits on her hands, her posture slumped, emphasizing her lankiness and youth. This isn't the preteen who begs for Starbucks and independence; this is a scared little girl. I'm hit with a flash of her as a five-year-old, toting around her Minnie Mouse purse and clinging to my leg on the subway. Hazel, my sweet Hazel, who made me a mother and changed everything for me. I feel a desperate urge to walk up and hug her, but I don't know what's appropriate. I feel frozen to the spot.

In stark contrast to Hazel, Winslow seems self-assured, confident. To me, Winslow is every bit Chippie as a girl: muscular, athletic from years of ballet lessons. Her shoulders, unlike my daughter's, are squared, her back straight as a board. She's been like a second daughter to me, ever since she and Hazel were in diapers. The playdates, the music classes . . . the girls painting their nails with glitter wash-away polish and the epic tickle matches. Neither of these girls are rebels. The time I was called to Hurst's office days ago was a complete one-off. Never in all of Hazel's life had she stepped a toe out of bounds, until then.

Which makes me wonder what is happening here. The suspense of it might kill me.

I clear my throat. "Hazel?" She turns around to look at me, and I see that her eyes have welled up.

167

Tears . . . oh, God. Those are either tears of fear and panic, for being called to the principal's office. Or tears of remorse . . . and guilt.

Please let it be the former.

I shoot my daughter a reassuring look before she turns back to face Hurst, hanging her head low. "Please, sit," Hurst instructs us, as she settles behind her desk.

Luke and I claim the chairs directly behind Hazel, and Chippie sits down next to Winslow. I don't know what to think right now, how to act, or what to say, so I say nothing. I will not speak until Hurst explains what's going on. My allegiances are split; I am both a parent here and a staff member. A mom, a friend, a wife. It's overwhelming.

"I apologize for calling you here on such short notice," Hurst begins, stacking up papers that were already neat to begin with. "But time is of the essence in matters such as this one. I'll be frank. I don't relish having to do this, but the facts speak for themselves. Both of your daughters were caught cheating on their recent history midterm."

I feel bile rising to my throat. No, no, not cheating. That cannot be.

"I'm sure I don't have to tell you what a grave matter this is, and how seriously cheating of any kind is treated at Easton. It is not tolerated." Hurst sighs, picking up a pen and tapping it. I wish she would stop. The annoying tap, tap isn't helping me get a handle on my increasingly racing heartbeat.

I feel Luke's hand reach for mine and squeeze it. I don't squeeze back—I can't. I'm doing everything I can to keep myself from coming unraveled right here in my boss's pristine office.

"I'm sorry." Luke finally speaks up, cutting into the awkward silence that has ensued. "I'm struggling here. This feels so out of character, for both girls." I wonder how he can sound so calm. Of course, Hazel isn't his daughter, his flesh and blood. He loves her, that's undeniable, but it isn't the same. All those interminable nights I nursed her. All the scrapes, the boo-boos, the monsters under the bed I shooed away. The mean-girl friends, the slumber parties she was excluded from. All the times I couldn't sleep for worry that my divorce was going to break her, that I wasn't giving her the life she deserved.

Luke can't understand any of that.

With a flash of guilt, I think of Samuel. He should be here—not instead of Luke but in addition to. I never even thought to call him.

"I'm with Luke," Chippie pipes up. "This is an incredibly damning accusation. What proof is there? Winslow?" Chippie turns to face her daughter. Even in her obvious distress, no lines have appeared on Chippie's face. Skincare as a career has a way of coming in handy, even in the most emotionally draining situations. "Is any of this true, honey? History is your best subject." I can tell Chippie's thinking this through in her mind, trying to make sense of the senseless. Why would our daughters do this?

My eyes bore into the back of Hazel's head, willing her to explain it, to prove this was all a mistake. Please, Hazel. Make this all go away.

I try to slow my breathing. I don't trust myself to speak. I've been on the other side of this, seen and heard about parents who deny the school's accusations, even when the facts stare them in the face. These are the worst-possible kind of parents, from an administrative perspective. I won't be that mom, not until I hear Hazel's side of the story and she clears this up for me. And then, if she swears she is innocent, you'd better believe I'd die going to the mat for her. Even if it costs me Easton.

"Hazel?" I force myself to feign composure. "Sweetie? Can you explain what's going on? We need to know. Was it a misunderstanding?" I have read all the parenting books. I know what to say to support my daughter without undermining Hurst. I hope.

"She did it for me." Hazel's voice comes out in a sniff of a whisper. I feel my whole body tense, and the rest of the room vanishes. All I can see is my daughter's face as she turns to look at me. Now the tears run unabated down her cheeks.

"Who did what for you?"

"Winslow!" she practically moans. "But Mom, it's not her fault. She is good at history. Insanely good. And I'm not. I can't keep all those facts in my head . . ." I want to interject that she is good, even if she isn't a natural like Winslow! But that's the thing about schools like Easton; the bar is set so abnormally high. Kids getting perfect scores on their math SATs still think they suck at it. My Hazel has never gotten anything less than a B. And still, she thinks she's not good at history. I can almost feel the physical pain of it, on her behalf.

"I texted her the answers. Not all of them. A few." Winslow shrugs. Chippie's mouth opens, but Winslow keeps talking. "Mr. Zellerman caught us. Confiscated my phone. The evidence was all there, Mom," she says witheringly to Chippie. "There's no point in pretending otherwise," she explains, "if that's what you were about to suggest. Look, I'm the daughter of lawyers. I know when it's time to plead guilty and take my inevitable punishment."

If I felt sick before, I'm beside myself now.

They cheated. They were caught. They admitted to it. We're fucked.

"We thought . . . we thought if we owned up to it right away and apologized, then . . ." But Hazel can't continue. She is a puddle of tears.

Forgetting about my job, about Chippie, about anything except the one thing that matters here—my daughter—I leap from my seat and wrap my arms around her in a vise. I don't feel tears coming because I am in shock, I tell myself.

"As my daughter has so maturely stated," Chippie says, standing up, unfolding her limber body and taking command of the situation, "they have admitted to what they've done. They have not made this process difficult, and they have apologized. That feels like quite an acceptable outcome to me, don't you agree, Headmaster?"

I tense, recognizing exactly what Chippie's doing. She's banking on Hurst wanting this to go away, and fast. Chippie is a huge donor to the school. It is not in Hurst's best interests to jeopardize her relationship with their family. But still, I can't fathom how Chippie can stand there treating this like a business transaction. Sure, she's a trained lawyer. But this is her daughter. I'm falling apart, and Chippie's picking at an unruly cuticle. Even knowing as I do that that's my friend's way of distracting herself from emotion, it's unnatural.

"I'm afraid this is bigger than an apology, Ms. Crane," Hurst says, her lips pursed. "Although I do appreciate both of your daughters' cooperation, cheating, as I said before, is not tolerated at Easton. I will be seeing both of them in front of the Honor Council at a predetermined date for a disciplinary hearing, and an outcome will be determined then. Hazel, Winslow, please return to class."

I have regained my outward composure—I must—as Hazel stands up, shakily. "Do you want to come home instead?" I ask her. I am not sure I can release her back into the wild, not after all that. I need time with her. To talk, to think this through. The room feels like a furnace. I am sweating through my clothes; I've got to get us out of here.

"I don't want to miss anything else," Hazel mumbles, staring down at her shoes. "Mom, you have to understand. I didn't want to fail."

She says it so desperately that it nearly knocks me to my knees. Luke has put a firm arm around my waist, and Chippie is leading Winslow out into the hall, where the two of them will clearly be chatting in private.

"And Winslow?" I say quietly to my daughter. "She wanted to feed you the answers?"

"She was trying to help!" Hazel moans. "She's my best friend in the entire world. She knows how much I want to go to Columbia and how impossible it is to get in from Manhattan, and how much I suck at dates and timelines . . ."

"Columbia? You're thirteen," I breathe. A baby. "College is years away." The thought of her leaving me, for college, nips at my insides. At least Columbia wouldn't take her that far away from me. But somewhere else . . . California . . . I am not ready to consider that possibility.

Hazel's face hardens. "If you honestly believe that it's too soon to be worrying about college, Mom, then you are smoking something.

Seriously. You work here. Don't you understand? Because sometimes I think you seriously don't get it." She brushes away tears and storms out into the hall, grabbing her backpack on the way.

I am stunned and shaken. I can't believe what Hazel has admitted to. She felt so much pressure she had to cheat on a test. I am gutted.

I watch Chippie hug Winslow. Neither of them is crying. They both seem calm, aloof. Winslow is the appropriate amount of remorseful. Chippie is respectfully concerned, but that's all.

Winslow starts off down the hall, her bag hanging off one slender shoulder. I know Winslow feels bad about this; at least, I think she does. But she is thirteen now. I wonder if the little girl who spent every waking minute with Hazel when they were young, the two of them putting on their own talent show at Chippie's Hamptons house, dressed in their matching unicorn pajamas—I wonder if she is still in there. I wonder who this girl really is that my daughter has spent so much of her young life with. She's your best friend's child, I remind myself.

Chippie's daughter. Practically family. People change, though. Kids change, and grow up.

I turn back to Hazel, feeling as if I'm experiencing everything in slo-mo. My child could be expelled from Easton. I remind myself that it's not a high probability; as disciplinary hearings go, most end in some kind of probation or suspension, with a community service type of consequence. Expulsions are reserved for older students who have fucked up more than once.

But still. In one fell swoop, Hazel has risked her reputation at the school, and mine. And much more important than that, I now have major work I need to do. As a parent, I must figure out why Hazel did this. All signs point to Easton being so stifling, so oppressive, that my daughter felt cheating was her only viable option, and she asked her best friend to feed her the answers. And yet, something about that feels off. Wrong.

We are out on the street, Chippie, Luke, and me, getting some fresh air, when I realize why.

Hazel would never ask Winslow to do that.

Which means it must have been Winslow's idea. Winslow has always been the bolder of the two girls. Always the one coming up with wild ideas, since they were little kids, like dyeing their hair, and pulling off elaborate April Fool's Day pranks. Hazel is the softer of the two, the sweeter; Winslow is outspoken and has her mother's edge. Chippie and I have always celebrated how well our two girls get along, reveling in the idea that they could be lifelong friends, like us.

But friendships can turn toxic. I need to protect my daughter, no matter what the personal cost.

Chippie is hugging me now and promising me it will all be all right. "They aren't going to be kicked out of school. That will not happen, okay? Audrey? Are you listening to me?"

I pull away from the hug, nodding. I hear her, but I'm numb. My sweat has turned to chills in the brisk air. "Sure."

"They won't be expelled! I will fucking commit murder if anyone even tries to suggest that. They are thirteen. They made a mistake. A bad judgment call. No one was hurt. Hurst can flunk them if she has to. That's punishment enough."

"Chippie's right," Luke chimes in. "Hazel's going to be fine. This is not a disaster. I promise."

"Come with me back to Quince." Chippie begins texting on her phone, her thumbs racing over the keyboard, taking charge like she always does. "Hani will book us spa treatments at Soho House. Cheer you right up."

She's still talking, saying something to Luke about how she and Nathan will call the Easton board and make sure this is all handled delicately, from a PR perspective. I'm not hearing it, not fully. I can't think; I am coming undone.

"Did Winslow convince Hazel to cheat?" I say to Chippie. "Because I don't see Hazel coming up with this scheme on her own."

Chippie stops talking and stares at me. "Excuse me, Audrey, but what the actual fuck are you implying?" Her voice is deadpan. She's not mad at me, I know this; but she has started paying attention.

I am not okay. She shouldn't be either.

"I'm asking if you think this was Winslow's idea." My voice is tight and calm. "She's the leader of their dynamic duo."

"So?"

"Winslow probably cooked this up. Hazel couldn't—she wouldn't . . ."

"But my daughter would."

"Well, someone came up with this plan . . . ," I answer, feeling my head start to pound. What a nightmare this is. A fucking nightmare.

"They came up with it together, remember? That's what they both said." Chippie still looks as unrattled as ever. It drives me crazy. Emote! I want to scream at her. But she never does.

"I'm not so sure that's true," I answer. Hazel hadn't said exactly how this had unfolded. Just that Winslow had wanted to help her . . .

Luke grabs me by the elbow. "Honey, let's go. I think you need a tea. Or something stronger." Luke is trying to pull me away, to extricate me from the situation before I make it worse. But the last thing I'm worried about right now is offending Chippie.

"Chippie, I love you," I say, forcing myself to calm down. She is my best friend. We go so far back it's impossible to quantify what we mean to each other. "You know I do."

"Love you, too, bitch, but . . . ?"

"You don't get it. For you this is some silly PR scandal that you can brush under the rug. For me, for us . . . I could lose my job! Which you've never understood because you walk on electrolyte water every day of your life."

"I'm upset about this, too, you know," Chippie answers. "But if you'd been listening, you would have heard me explaining that I will find a way to make this go away. For both of our girls. And take that back, Audrey, you know I'd never drink electrolyte water. It's full of hidden chemicals, and I will die on that hill."

I ignore that last comment. I'm too upset. "It can't go away. It will be on their record forever. Because they admitted it. They did this thing, Chip! We can't ever erase it. You can't snap your Cinderella fingers and rewrite history!"

"I'm not trying to."

"What am I going to do about Hazel? She's always been influenced by Winslow, and you know it. Ever since they bleached their hair in fourth grade! I bet Hazel would have stopped the whole thing, but no, Winslow is every bit your daughter, isn't she? Probably egged her on, convinced her it was a victimless crime. And promised Hazel it would all be okay. And it most definitely isn't."

The truth is, I feel like an utter failure as a mother. At the end of the day, this is not Winslow's fault, much as I want to lash out at her, and her mother.

It is mine.

"If Winslow did come up with this, she did it to help Hazel. There was absolutely nothing in it for her, and yet she took a big risk. On her best friend," Chippie says evenly. "I'd call that loyalty."

The word strikes me in my gut. Because she's right. For Winslow to do that . . . it was incredibly selfless.

It was also incredibly stupid.

"It's still a crime to help someone bury a body," I breathe at Chippie. "It was still wrong."

"And they're kids," Luke interjects, starting to look genuinely worried about me. "They'll learn, with our help. We'll get through this, babe," Luke promises, pulling me toward him.

"Together," Chippie confirms.

The mere suggestion that we're a team in this makes me want to scream. We aren't a team, because Chippie will never have to face the same consequences that Hazel and I will. And neither will Winslow. I could kick myself for letting my daughter think she was just like them. That she, too, could walk on water and live a privileged life she's merely borrowing.

I'm afraid I've made a huge mistake.

"I do need a drink," I say to Luke.

Chippie whips out her phone again. "I'll call my driver to take us to the club. You two should go for this amazing Japanese whisky that's supposed to be like an orgasm in a shot glass . . ."

The last thing I want to do is go to her fancy club and get wasted in the middle of the day. She doesn't even drink—alcohol's bad for the face—and would be sitting there plying me with booze while she's stone-cold sober. Absolutely not. I have a job to get back to. A job I need to do better than ever, now that I'm standing on shaky ground.

"What I meant is that I need a coffee because I have work to do," I snap at Chippie, fully aware I'm casting blame anywhere but at myself. "So please. Chippie. I am telling you this as my best friend. Focus on Winslow, and your own family. And I'll focus on mine."

I take Luke by the hand and start walking into the building. I don't look back at Chippie, but I wouldn't be surprised if her face were as smooth, and unaffected, as it always is.

Chapter 20

There is no handbook for how to prepare for a threesome.

I don't google it, but I doubt there's a tidy Emily Post column on the subject, and as Saturday nears, I overthink it: What I'll wear. What we'll eat and drink. The lighting, the playlist. In the end, I decide food is out and stick solely to drinks, which we'll need in abundance.

Cal's in bed, Hazel's at Samuel's for the weekend, and I nervously check my phone for texts from my ex. It's torture, coparenting with a man who provides me with the most clipped updates. Hazel here. All good. I should be with her right now. Monitoring her mental status. Supporting her. Figuring out how to have the heart-to-heart that surely needs to happen, about what she did, and why, and how I can help her make smarter decisions moving forward. But she was all too happy to leave to go to her dad's, and, legally, I can't keep her here. Samuel has custody every other weekend. It's not my place.

The truth is, I know this evening is the absolute last thing I should be focusing on. Hurst scheduled Hazel and Winslow's disciplinary hearing for next week, and I'm a wreck whenever I think about it. I've always prided myself on being good in a crisis, on my comfort with ambiguity. But this is different. It's my daughter's future, and mine. Everything I've worked and strived and sacrificed for.

I can't let it be taken from me.

As for Hazel, she's been visibly shaken since Thursday, slipping from bouts of moodiness and sullen silence into crying jags, on a minute-to-minute basis. She won't talk to me, and she all but leaped into the Uber to take her to Brooklyn to her dad's, which cut through the heart of me. I'd want to be with Samuel, too, if I were her. I'm sure his face doesn't ooze disappointment the way mine does right now. Still, it kills me to see her go, to choose him.

At night, during stretches of full-blown insomnia that I can't shake, I panic that things are unfixable. That this mistake is the first in a long line of errors Hazel will make. Errors that will categorically be my fault.

She hasn't talked to Winslow. At first, I considered the unthinkable . . . asking her to cool it off with her bestie for a bit. But as I thought about how to delicately approach that subject, Hazel did the hard work for me, telling me she ate lunch with her debate team friends, which was code, in my mind, for "Winslow and I are on a break."

I haven't heard from Chippie either. It feels strange, like I've misplaced a limb, not waking up to her sarcastic and borderline inappropriate texts. Still, I can't help but feel it's convenient, right now, that we aren't speaking. As I choose two Sancerres from our wine fridge, grab stemless glasses from the cabinet, and lower the lighting, tossing Cal's stray toys in a bin and straightening the throw pillows, I think about how hard it would be to continue to lie to her about what I'm up to.

About what I'm about to embark on.

The mere thought of it sends my pulse racing.

But there's another emotion behind that breakneck pulse, besides nervousness. It's my guilt about what's happened, about how I reacted to Chippie. I questioned her integrity. I've never handled our friendship so recklessly. Chippie is like family, and I've all but thrown her under the bus.

I peek in on Cal. He's fast asleep. Then I check the clock: 8:57 p.m. Now that it's almost time, my rib cage is expanding with every beat of my heart. I'm really doing this.

I run back to our bedroom to hastily make the bed. I probably should have changed to fresh sheets, I realize, but I'm not sure we have any because I can't recall when I last did laundry, and it's too late now. Then it dawns on me that sheets are the last thing anyone will notice . . . and it hits me, in a flash, that in choosing an outfit, I've neglected the most critical item of all: my underwear.

The thought makes my pulse pound as I tear through my dresser drawer, searching for an itchy high-cut pair of bikinis that I've never worn but that will be perfect for this. This situation. God. I slip on the panties and wiggle back into my jeans and top. At least I'm already wearing a decent bra, black and lacy, and I've recently gotten waxed. The glimpse I catch of myself in our full-length mirror as I button my jeans nearly stops me in my tracks. I'm in my late thirties. Two kids. Married, divorced, and married again. I'm fit and feel good in my skin, but I'm not the twentysomething I once was. I should be crawling into bed with tea and a Reese's Book Club pick. Instead . . .

I'm about to take a hairpin turn from the predictable path of my picture-book, married, Manhattan life.

I startle at the sound of the doorbell. It must be Sarah. Luke isn't back from the gallery, after he'd promised me in that infuriatingly endearing Luke way that he'd be here in time. If he isn't here soon, I'm going to freaking kill him.

I wrench open the door to find Sarah standing there, in the threshold, that giant purse over her shoulder, her coppery hair swarming her delicate face. I feel instant relief, which surprises me. I'd expected to feel something else . . . unfamiliarity, and unease at the sight of her, as though a stranger were standing at my door. Which, of course, she is. I hardly know anything about this woman. My five-year-old son's asleep in his room, and she could be coming here to murder us. I think of Chippie, of how she'd probably have hidden nanny cams in every available piece of furniture if she'd known what I was planning.

Another reason to keep her in the dark.

"Wine?" Sarah says, eschewing the niceties and holding out a bottle of red with slim hands that sport pale-pink polish and a thin platinum wedding band. "I thought we'd need it." There's that quality, that essence, that's so enchanting about her. Fuck! It's been the case ever since I got her first email.

I indicate the wine I've already placed on the table. "Great minds," I tell her in my most curt voice, as though we're about to engage in a business transaction. Selling a lamp, negotiating a deal. "Cal's asleep, so keep your voice down," I tell her. "Please."

"So no karaoke, then?" Sarah offers up a shy smile. She's made a joke. Cute. All I manage in return is a tight, unfriendly smile. I watch her set her bag down on a chair, then seat herself, cross-legged, on our living room rug. "This okay? I guess I'm more comfortable here on the floor than anywhere else. Job hazard. You know. All that momming, playing trucks with Eli . . . it's killer on the back, but I gravitate right toward the floor anyway. It's like I've been programmed." She stretches a bit, as if to show me what she means.

I start to laugh, genuinely. This woman is weirdly adorable. Then I stop myself. I told myself before she got here that I would go through the motions, and that is what I will do until Luke gets here. I will not give her a part of myself; I will not give up my power. This is his plan, after all. I agreed to be present; I don't owe this woman anything.

I bring the wine over, along with two of the glasses, to the low coffee table, then sit down across from her, tucking my knees under me. I serve us each a generous pour, and hand her her glass.

"Cheers." I meet her eyes and take a sip, determined not to let a scrap of emotion show on my face. She probably thinks I'm being a b-i-t-c-h. Fine. Let her.

"Okay. Cheers," she answers, averting her eyes from mine and tugging at the hem of her top. She's wearing expensive jeans that cinch at the waist and a cashmere sweater that swims on her small frame. It looks buttery soft, and I have a strange urge to reach out and touch it; I don't. We clink glasses, and as she tells me about the Uber ride over here, and how she lied about needing to listen to a Zoom call and stuffed her earbuds in so she wouldn't have to make small talk with her driver, then spent the entire ride feeling guilty about her decision, I study her every movement.

"I lie to every Uber driver. Doesn't everyone?" I gulp down my wine. "I always say I'm an accountant. No one ever has follow-up questions." I shrug, the drink already going to my head. Good! This isn't torture, but it's somewhere in that neighborhood. Being fully present here is not a welcome proposition.

"I thought it was just me," she answers, staring into her still-full glass. "But I say I'm a dentist. Okay, here goes. Audrey, I . . . I have to confess something. Like, before I implode."

My heart tightens. Is this going to be the one thing she can say to me that will break me open . . . the one thing I absolutely don't want to hear . . . that Luke really wants her? That this is all a charade because the two of them are a "them . . ." I do not want to know something about my husband that I can never unknow, that will make me question him, us, everything.

Speaking of. Luke's still not here. I check the time on my phone: 9:10 p.m.

If Luke did this on purpose . . . if this is part of some greater strategy, some calculation on his part, leaving the two of us deliberately alone . . . I gulp more wine, feeling even more off kilter than before. I don't know what either of them wants. If Sarah's still single mindedly focused on Eli getting into Easton, and that's what's driving her here, to my home. Or if she wants Luke, plain and simple . . .

I frown, then remember to wipe my face clear of any telltale feelings. Keep the upper hand, Audrey. Don't let her forget. This is my home. My living room. My rug.

My husband.

She is not here to steal Luke. And if she is, I will not let her.

"This isn't about all the gifts I sent you," Sarah continues hastily, gulping at the wineglass clutched tightly in her hand. "Ugh! I have to get this out before he gets here," she mutters. She shifts her body positioning, crossing one leg over the other, then back to how she started. It seems she's working herself up to a big reveal. I've had enough surprises and drama this week for a lifetime. I don't know if I can stomach any more. "The thing is . . . I know you probably think that Luke approached me, initially. And propositioned me, even?" I don't answer her; I am suddenly on fire, branded on my back with a hot poker. I sit as still as I can, waiting, wondering where this is going. I lied when I said I didn't want to know what transpired between these two. Naturally, I do want to know. Anyone would. "The truth is . . . ," Sarah goes on. "He didn't do any of that. It wasn't his idea. At all."

I don't move. I can't. I can't speak. Can't breathe.

"I gave Luke my phone number, after the Easton information session. Yes, he texted me after that, to be nice, it was all very friendly, two parents talking shop, but then, but then . . ." She twists her sweater hem so tightly her fingers are turning white. "I went to see him at his gallery. I let him . . . I let him photograph me."

I suck in a breath. Though I try to keep Luke's work in a box, in my head, and remind myself it's art, and it has nothing to do with me, or us . . . this feels different.

"It was all about admissions! You know how obsessed I am with Easton. How much I want to be a part of it. I had no one else to talk to," she goes on, manic. "And Luke was so knowledgeable, about Easton, and the process, and how it all worked . . . he was so generous." Of course he was. Fucking Luke. Always has to help. Can't ever say no.

"Things spiraled after that, and now I can hardly remember how it all happened. But that doesn't matter. The thing I want you to know, Audrey, is that . . ." Here, she pauses, and I see now she's trembling. "It was never him. It was never about him," she clarifies. "Well, it was, for a half second, but now, I mean, ever since the morning of the tour, when I met you for the first time . . . Audrey," she breathes, with the fervor of a fanatic. "It's only been you."

The words hit me like freezing water to my face.

"Audrey, do you really not know this already? Is it not completely and totally obvious every time I'm around you?"

My skin burns. "What? Sarah, is what obvious?"

She laughs, almost feverishly, and there's something so attractive about her in this moment. "God, you're going to make me say it out loud?" She looks up at the sky, as though she's asking the heavens for help. "Why do you think I ramble on like a freak every time I talk to you? Why do you think I sent you all those notes and followed you on Instagram like a lovesick puppy, and why the fuck do you think I'm here now? I am totally, fucking, out-of-my-mind insane—for you."

Chapter 21

I wake up, sweaty and disoriented, at 3:00 a.m., to a text from Samuel.

> Hazel fine, wants to stay a couple more days. Can take her to
> school monday

My head is pounding, and I have to extricate myself from the sheets as quietly as I can, being careful not to disturb Luke, or Sarah, both of whom are dead asleep next to me. I stumble to the bathroom to pop a Tylenol, double strength, and down sixteen ounces of water. I think I might be sick, so I lean over the toilet bowl. Nothing comes.

Luke and Sarah, both in my bed.

It's not like I don't know how I ended up here. But the rest of the night, what happened after Sarah's arrival . . .

It's a pinwheel of drunken flashes in my mind, strung together like those beads that turn iridescent when you leave them in the sun.

What transpired after Sarah's confession was a frenzied, out-of-body, kaleidoscope of the senses. Her kissing me, her lips so much softer and smaller than Luke's, and more tender; Luke returning home to find me lying on my back on that same living room rug in my jeans and bra—when had my shirt come off? I can't recall—watching the ceiling spin as Sarah ran her palm across my arms and stomach and adjacent to my breasts, both of us tipsy—no, flat-out wasted—and light headed, then all of us finding our way to the bed.

I drank because it was all too much. Hazel's cheating and my fight with Chippie and what Luke was asking of me, and Sarah—Sarah. Saying she was in love with me. She was insane; she couldn't possibly mean that. She didn't even know me. We were grown women—mothers.

At least it explained all the gifts and the stalking. She hadn't been trying to creep me out; she'd been trying to show her affection. That's almost as disturbing as her being dangerous. But then again, I wasn't sure what I preferred.

Sarah and I had downed both bottles of Sancerre by the time Luke returned, and we had already uncorked another. He seemed pleased when he found us there on the floor. The truth is, I barely registered that he was there at all. All my energy was focused on Sarah. On this elusive, and, yes, surprisingly sexy person who wasn't obsessed with my husband, as I had previously, resentfully, believed.

I was the one she wanted.

The hours after that are a whirlwind in my mind. Clothes came off. I shed all my inhibitions—the wine was crucial—and we became a tangle of bodies, of limbs and lips and hands, and skin, so much skin. And when Luke made love to me while Sarah's lips grazed my inner thighs and nipples and navel, I had to admit the sensations weren't unwelcome. Besides, something had shifted for me. I now believed her that I was the object of her affection—not Luke—and that turned me on. The hate began to dissipate, and I saw things more clearly. I didn't share her feelings of obsession, or lust, or whatever it was she felt for me. But I felt appreciated, and adored, and for the first time, not even mad about the fact that she'd invaded my home, my bed.

They'd fucked, she had told me before Luke got home. Once the wine hit my system, I had agreed to hear the whole story. Sarah explained how it had happened, how she'd visited him at the gallery in a state of panic, but, near tears, she promised me it meant nothing.

And that the truth was, she was grateful. Her interactions with Luke had brought her to me.

I was flattered and on a bit of a high as she went on about my finer points. I didn't tell her she was wrong about me; I wasn't all the things she imagined: confident, gives-no-fucks, at ease in my own skin. She'd learn, in time, if she stuck around long enough to, that I was simply good at projecting all those qualities.

I don't remember much after I orgasmed. After Luke came, I collapsed back on the pillows of our bed with our not-clean sheets, spent. I closed my eyes, feeling the weight of the wine on my eyelids, not caring what happened after that.

Now, in the wee hours of the morning, as I tiptoe into the shower and turn the tap on scalding hot, I feel more than the sick of a hangover. I feel dread. Last night, I fell into a dreamlike wormhole, where Sarah was in love with me, and I wasn't confined to being a mother, a daughter, an ex-wife . . . I was a body, submitting myself to feel every touch and shudder and prickle on my skin. But now, after the wine has worn off, and I can see things clearly, I begin to doubt. I don't know that I can trust Sarah. She says it's me she wants, and that Luke is simply a side dish to my entrée. But the truth is, I let myself believe her last night because I was drunk. And what's harder to face, but true . . . a little desperate. She could be lying to me. This could all be a ruse, a trick, and I'm falling for it, hook, line, and sinker. Worse yet, Luke could be in on it. They've slept together. He cheated. I haven't let myself fully internalize that fact up until now because it's painful and because I know, logically, that it gets me nothing. But now, I can't deny it's a possibility. Her confession could have been calculated. Luke might know everything, and they could be meeting secretly behind my back, using this threesome as a cover to be together. I can't ignore the possibility that Sarah strategically showed up first, with a rehearsed speech she'd already practiced on my husband.

I step into the shower, letting the water stream down me. It's too hot, but it's fitting. I want to emerge from this with raw, pink skin. I'm not going back to sleep, not now. I need a clear head. I'll shower and dress, go into the kitchen, and make a strong pot of coffee.

And then I will figure out how to get my daughter home.

———

Cal is up at seven. I dress him and grab a to-go bowl of cereal and his sippy cup of milk. We take the subway to Samuel's place in Brooklyn. I left Luke and Sarah a pithy note. "Took Cal to pick up Hazel. Feel free to make pancakes, but save me some. XOX." It's an absurd thing to write after a night like that.

I know I'll be waking Samuel when I arrive; the man's allergic to early mornings. I ring the bell of his house, the bottom two floors of a classic Cobble Hill brownstone that's been converted into two residences. I ring again, several times in succession, not surprised when Ruby finally comes to the door.

Samuel's new wife.

She's wearing hardly anything at all, a tiny robe, her thin, yoga-toned legs on full display. I'm used to this, to her; she is everything I'm not. Zen. Childlike. Utterly unflappable. I may present complete confidence and calm, but this woman lives and breathes it. Because she knows no better, I remind myself. Because she's never had to learn the hard way.

"Audrey!" she exclaims, looking from me, back to Cal, and then to me again. "Is everything all right? It's . . ." She checks her Apple Watch. "Eight a.m. on a Sunday."

"Everything's fine," I say, clipped. "We're here for Hazel."

Ruby squints. "Isn't she staying with us until the end of the day? It's our weekend."

I tense at her use of the word "our." It's legally Samuel's time with Hazel, but she, as stepmother, does not factor into the equation. I'm not sure her Instagram-documented wedding to Samuel under the Fiji stars, followed by an ayahuasca ceremony, was even legal.

"Can I talk to her? It's been a difficult week. You know, with . . ."

"With what?" Ruby plants a hand on her hip, looking genuinely confused. It cannot be possible that Samuel has failed to tell her about Hazel's cheating. Unless he's so unruffled by it . . . but no. That would be ludicrous. Surely they've talked about it. Surely Ruby knows . . . "Oh, I'm being so rude. Come in. I was already up making hempseed bagels. I'll give you the recipe!"

Cal follows Ruby inside, and she gives him a little pat, then searches for something in a tote bag hanging in the front hall. She fishes out a reusable bag, then hands it to my son.

"Cacao nib cookies from the yoga studio bake sale!" She beams, as though she's delivered world peace.

"Can I have it, Mommy?" Cal pleads.

"As you said, Ruby, it's eight a.m. on a Sunday, but sure, Cal, go ahead." I secretly pray he'll think her sugarless offering is disgusting, but he gobbles it up, none the wiser.

"Mom?"

I turn to the staircase, where Hazel is standing in a boxy, cropped T-shirt from Urban Outfitters that shows off her belly button ring above flannel sleep shorts. Her hair is a mess, and her face looks puffier than usual. Naturally, she's more beautiful in my eyes than ever.

"I can't believe you came here." Her clear disappointment at my arrival is a blow, but I will not let her weaken my resolve. "It's my weekend with Dad."

"And it's time for you to come home and deal with what's happened."

Ruby's eyes are flickering between me and my daughter. "So this is about . . . that."

This woman is so fucking clueless. She can't even say out loud that my daughter is in serious trouble at school. No, she wants to flit around in her yoga gear and pretend nothing's wrong. She's barely thirty and she's not a mother yet. She'll never, ever understand.

"Audrey? What are you doing here?" It's Samuel, just woken up, judging from his rumpled bedhead. He's in boxers and a T-shirt, and I cringe that I ever found him sexy. Worse, that I loved him.

"I'm here because I've let things lie for a few days, but now it's time to stop burying our heads in the sand." I know I sound completely worked up. But no one else seems remotely worried about Hazel's future. Someone has to be the adult here. It's always been me.

Samuel runs his fingers through his hair. "Hey, we've been talking about it, me and Haze. Right, honey?"

Hazel nods. "Dad's been very supportive."

I have to resist the urge to scream or punch a wall. Of course he's been supportive. He has no skin in this game. He's the dad when it's convenient. The parent who takes none of the blame. He'll "talk" to Hazel about her feelings all weekend and then go back to his real life during the week, leaving me to pick up the pieces.

"Plus, I told you, Mom, I need time. I thought you'd respect that." Hazel crosses her arms over her chest in a gesture of defiance.

"And you've had plenty of that the last few days, sweetie. But now it's time to come home and get ready for a productive week at school tomorrow." I refuse to waver. Hazel has an education and a future to think about. I haven't worked this hard for her to throw it all away.

Hazel looks like she's about to protest, but Cal's taken the initiative to run up to her and hug her legs. I feel like cheering and remind myself to give him extra cuddles later. "Mommy said we can make pancakes later. With chocolate chips!"

Hazel allows herself a small smile, directed exclusively at her brother.

"Fine, I'll come home. But after pancakes, I'm staying in my room."

I let out a breath. At least she's coming with me. We take a Lyft home, because I don't feel like dragging a sulky, pajama-clad teenager and a rowdy preschooler all the way back on the train. Plus, I need a chance to text Luke, explaining that we're on our way. Sarah needs to be out of there. Now.

We're heading over the bridge when my text is delivered to Luke's phone. I start to panic. If he doesn't get it in time . . . if his phone's on silent . . . I don't know what I'll do if I return home with my kids, and Sarah's still there, in my house.

A text response appears within a minute, and I feel myself exhale. Luke is awake, says I don't have to worry. Sarah said her goodbyes and slipped home in a taxi shortly after I left, eager to get home to her own family.

A strange emotion rushes over me as I read this. Home to her own family. I can't understand why she's risking everything she has, at home, the love of her husband and child, all because of this strange infatuation she has for me.

When we finally walk in the door of our condo, I'm relieved to find Luke in the kitchen making coffee, acting like it's the most normal Sunday in the world.

Chapter 22

We settle into a routine.

Sarah comes to our place late at night on Friday or Saturday, after Cal's asleep. During the week, we meet at our place midday. With all the kids at school, and Luke's flexible schedule, it makes the most sense for me to slip out of work for an hour or two on my lunch break, when we know that none of our children will have any reason to be around. We considered a hotel for a hot second, but it felt strange, and a little cheap, and I suppose all three of us are clinging to a notion that what we're doing is the opposite of tawdry but rather romantic in some way. Alternative . . . not trashy.

I still don't know what to think. On certain days, I wake up feeling like I'm harboring a glowing, white-hot secret, one that sets me apart from all the other Manhattan parents I know, who do anything they can to drum up excitement in their lives by hosting fancy fundraisers and renovating Hamptons homes. Luke insists what we are doing is enlightened. That we are living our lives on a higher plane, bucking societal norms and finding ways to keep the spark alive, ensuring we don't end up bored with each other and divorced. Other times, I wonder if I'm a pawn in some scheme I can't completely understand, by Sarah's design or Luke's.

Luke is happier than ever. And he isn't just interested in sex when the three of us are together. He wants me now, all the time. It's not difficult to connect those dots, and it's even easier to compare our sex life now to how it was a month or two ago, when I was worried we'd reached a plateau, and notice the glaring difference. Still, I find our arrangement nerve racking. We go from casual conversation, sipping expensive wine or whisky, with music playing low in the background, to wildly inappropriate, exploratory buffets of the senses. It seems like an unspoken rule that we never talk about our personal lives. That's happened only once, when Sarah was searching for a wine opener in a cabinet drawer and came across an old photo—one of Luke's, printed in sepia—of a woman in a cocktail dress, laughing, her head thrown back.

"My first wife," Luke tells her, without missing a beat. "Piper. She passed away. Tragically, from breast cancer."

Sarah looks shaken. "I didn't know," she whispers. "I didn't even know you'd been married before."

"It's painful to talk about her," he explains, and I squeeze his hand. The two of us hardly talk about Piper. Samuel comes up in conversation, occasionally, because of Hazel, and my ex and current husband are cordial with each other when they have to be. But Luke and Piper never had kids, and it's easier, in some ways, to pretend she never existed than to face the sorrow of her death over waffles. Luke seems to prefer not to bring her up, and I follow his lead.

One Tuesday afternoon, when I have too much work waiting for me back at my desk to let myself get buzzed, I refuse the alcohol that Luke has generously poured. It's the first time I'm here, with them, without a balm to numb my senses, and I'm wildly uncomfortable. It is Sarah who reassures me as we lie back on cool silk sheets—I've upgraded our ratty old ones—whispering in my ear that being with me is the best part of her day. And when her touch brings me to the brink, I find myself viewing our arrangement in a new light. I don't have to be the victim here, the one who had no choice in the matter; if I'm enjoying this as much as Luke is, maybe there's no harm in it. I don't allow myself to think about the future. This must be a fling, a fleeting moment in our story. Sarah cannot become a fixture. That is simply not an option.

Hazel's disciplinary hearing comes and goes, thankfully, without incident. She and Winslow are appropriately regretful and are given school community service hours, which they humbly accept. I don't meet Chippie's eyes throughout the entire proceedings, which in its own way is far more painful than the hearing itself. But I can't; I'm not ready. The chasm between us feels wider than ever. I know I must make an attempt to bridge it, eventually, but it's all still too raw.

I leave the hearing and head directly to my office, where I work straight through dismissal and dinner, till 8:00 p.m. Hazel is heading to her dad's, and Luke has reassured me he'll take care of Cal's bedtime routine.

When I finally tiptoe into the kitchen at 9:00 p.m., Sarah and Luke are waiting for me. They sit apart. A stiff drink rests on the counter. Bourbon. I assume it's for me and down it before anyone says a word.

"She's going to be okay, right?" I breathe to Luke, avoiding Sarah's watchful eyes. This isn't something I want to share with her, though I sense Luke has told her about it. I'm wary of the two of them. Suspicious. We don't talk about what happens in our "off" hours. It's all part of keeping things neatly categorized, in specific boxes, and of maintaining control. It is the only way this will ever work.

"Hazel's going to be fine," Luke repeats before wrapping his arms around me. I lean into him, smelling his Luke smell and wondering what Sarah must think of me, of this.

Minutes later, we fuck, all three of us, quickly and without fanfare. It's hasty and messy and even a little ugly, and exactly what I need to exile this day from my mind. The whole affair lasts fifteen minutes. Later, when Luke's in the shower, and I'm gathering my panties from the ground and searching for my bra and shirt, I notice Sarah sitting in the window in a robe. My robe. I don't remember loaning it to her, but then again, we eschewed boundaries long ago. She's scrolling on her phone when her hand goes to her mouth, and she straightens in the window seat, as though she's been pricked with a pin.

"Everything okay?" I ask, tentative, still never sure where I stand with her, this woman who claims to be obsessed with me.

"It's an email. From, from you."

I don't understand. I haven't emailed Sarah.

"It's from Easton Admissions," she clarifies, a tremble in her voice. "It's a form letter, signed by you, that says I won't be asked in, that Eli won't be asked in for the playdate. That Adam and I won't be getting a parent interview. It says you are very sorry but there simply are not enough spots this year to accommodate all the children and that we should apply again next year."

The way she makes this pronouncement, it's like someone's died. The light has gone from her eyes, and she drops her phone onto the cushion.

I know the form email well; it's what we send to families we've culled out of the applicant pool. In a flash, I remember that day at the nail salon, of how Morgan had dismissed the Price family and planned on cutting them from the running. I'd had no problem with it at the time; in fact, I'd been on board, especially given Sarah's emails and stalking tendencies. She was certainly not Easton material.

But now . . . I've been so wrapped up in my own life, this other side of Sarah—not Sarah the applicant, but Sarah the lover—I had forgotten all about that.

It dawns on me, suddenly, that I've been a fool not to consider this, that I've been an idiot to think we could deny Sarah a spot without her being completely devastated. Heartbroken, even. I have put Sarah's application out of my mind, so completely and categorically, letting myself forget why we met in the first place, how eager she was, bordering on obsessive, about securing her son a spot.

And yet, there's simply no way Eli can join next year's kindergarten class alongside Cal. Because of Sarah's behavior, objectively, and how unsuitable she seems for the school. But also because of this, of us. There is absolutely no way I could ever possibly let Eli and Cal be in school together. Classmates, and potential friends. Not now. The day Sarah showed up here in my kitchen, a switch was flipped, and that door closed, forever. There is no scenario in which Sarah can be a part of the Easton community or of my world. If she were, she'd remain a constant threat. How long before someone slipped, before everyone I respect and admire and work my butt off to impress found out what we had been doing . . . the mere idea of it sends sweat to my palms and heat to my cheeks. I would likely be fired for exerting my power over an applicant family . . . Hazel and Cal would be, by association, ostracized, canceled. No, Sarah must remain an outsider to our real life.

"Sarah?" Luke's standing in the doorway to the bedroom now, wrapped in a towel, his hair still shower wet. Tears pool in Sarah's eyes, and she's clearly in distress. "What's wrong?"

"Eli has been officially rejected," she responds in a shaking voice. "He's not getting a spot next year."

Luke shoots me a look, and in that instant, I know I'm fucked.

"Can't you do something?" he asks me, and I recognize that this is entirely for Sarah's benefit, but I also know, now, that what I'm dealing with here is a situation where there are exactly zero viable options. If I use my influence to get Sarah's son into Easton, then I am screwed. But if I don't . . .

Oh God. What she could tell people. What she could do. She could ruin our lives. One photo, one text is all it would take.

"I—" I flounder for the right words. I study Sarah, devouring her expression, trying to suss out what's behind her eyes, how desperate she truly is, and whether she would dare tell everyone about us, if she's that volatile. She would blow up her own family, too, but perhaps she's that unbalanced. The truth is, I don't really know her at all.

"Mommy?" I turn to find Cal standing behind me in his jammies. He must have slipped in, unnoticed by any of us.

"Cal, sweetie. Why are you up?" I feel caught.

"I had a bad dream." His lip crumples up, and I swoop him into my arms, cuddling him on our bed, trying to work out in my mind a way out of this situation. I fear there is none. The one thing Sarah wants more than anything in the world, a spot for her son at Easton, is the one thing I am uniquely positioned to give her. And if I don't . . .

"Who are you?" Cal stares at Sarah. "And why are you crying? Did you have a bad dream too?"

Cal looks at her with total honesty, the pure heart of a five-year-old kid, one who knows nothing of artifice, and it wrenches me.

Sarah lets out a sob and tries to cover it. She is studying Cal now, and I realize they haven't met before. "You—you remind me of him." Then she claps a hand over her mouth. "Sorry, I—it's this Easton development. It's over. I can't believe it's really over."

Luke has thrown on pants and now scoops up Cal into a bear hug. "Let's get you back to bed, buddy. Did you find your monster meter? The one I got you to scare away the baddies?"

"That's not real, Daddy." Cal laughs hysterically as Luke turns him upside down and carries him off.

"I—I should go." Sarah fumbles for her shoes, which are strewed on the carpet, and her jacket, folded limply over a chair.

"Wait. Cal's going back to bed. You don't have to leave so soon." I feel panic rising in my chest. I can't let her leave, not until I know how she's going to react to all this. Until I know what she might do. "Let's—talk this through. Nothing is set in stone . . ."

My wheels are turning dangerously fast. I can't promise her anything, not yet. But I can't let her go either.

"I'm sorry," she chokes as she shoves her feet into her sneakers, not even bothering to get them on properly. "I can't do this. I have to go." She is out the door, still in my robe, her jacket thrown awkwardly over it, before I can do anything to make her stay.

Ten minutes later, I'm in a Lyft crossing the city to Sarah and Adam Price's brownstone.

I have made a decision. One I can hardly stomach, but I see no other way. Eli must be accepted at Easton. But in exchange, Sarah will promise us her silence.

Chapter 23

It is what I'm planning to tell her the entire ride to her home, and it's on the tip of my tongue as I exit the Lyft, not even sure if I've properly shut the door behind me. I'm ringing her bell; there is no time for me to text her first, and I have no guarantee she'll even respond. And so I must do this here, now, in person. I have to put my finger in the dam before it, before my whole world, breaks.

Adam answers the door. With messy hair and in his pajama pants, he looks a lot less put together than I imagined him in my head, but then again, his wife has just come home after getting that news, and who knows what shape she's in.

"I'm so sorry," I tell him breathlessly. "To bother you, I mean. I know it's late, but . . . I'm Audrey. Audrey Singer. Your wife, is she . . . home?"

"She's upstairs," Adam answers, not making any move to step aside or welcome me in.

"She was upset," I try to explain, of course without explaining anything. "I was trying to help, but she wouldn't let me."

"Do you want to come in?" Adam asks, and again, I feel the weight of the world is on this man's shoulders. "She's in our son's room," he adds.

I hesitate. It's 10:00 p.m., and it sounds like Eli is awake, as Cal was. I'd had no intention of meeting Eli, but if I'm going to have to follow through and accept him at Easton, then I suppose I will meet him sooner or later. Still, it feels strange, not to simply enter the Prices' living room but to infiltrate their son's space . . . but then again, Sarah's been in my home, intimately. This is not different.

I step inside their house. It's exquisitely decorated, tastefully and traditionally, with a living room straight out of a magazine page and an open kitchen with top-of-the-line appliances and a massive kitchen island. Unlike my own scuffed and lived-in home, this one is on par with most Easton families' houses, and I feel that nagging twinge of envy I work so hard to stifle.

"Upstairs," Adam directs me, not unkindly. "First door on the right."

I nod and make my way up the curving staircase, my shoes pressing into the plush carpet runners, feeling a sense of foreboding come over me, and more than that, dread. I have let the personal bleed into my professional life. I worry I have made a grave mistake.

I press open the door that Adam indicated and find a sweetly decorated boy's room, all trucks and trains but as pretty as a Pinterest board, with Scandinavian shelving, a Flokati rug, and a whimsical lamp in the shape of an elephant that looks overly pricey for a kid's room. Sarah is sitting in a tufted, plush recliner, staring out the window. I had expected to find her crying, or worse, yelling, reacting in some terrifying way. But no. She is almost catatonic.

"Sarah?" I breathe out her name, feeling somehow unholy standing here. She turns to look at me, and her eyes appear vacant. "I was worried," I explain. "You ran out. I think we need to talk about this. Not here," I say, lowering my voice, "because I know how much we both want to keep things . . . private. But there's a solution, I know there is. Where's Eli?" I ask, scanning the room. I notice it doesn't look particularly lived in, but then again, the rest of her house is immaculate. She probably compulsively tidies, or employs someone who does.

"Eli?" says a voice behind me; I turn to find Adam standing startlingly close to me. I hadn't realized he'd come up, hadn't heard his footsteps on those plush carpet runners. I notice deep lines on his face. He's my age, I know from his application, but he suddenly appears decades older. "Why are you asking about our son?"

"I—" I don't know how to respond.

"Eli isn't here," he says quietly. "I don't know what my wife told you, but . . ."

This is making no sense, none at all . . . I feel my chest tightening. Where is Eli? Does Adam know about us? Is that why he's acting so aloof, so distant? Has Sarah told him everything, and they've sent Eli somewhere for the night, so they can hash things out? Have I stepped right into a marital hailstorm?

My heart is pounding. It's wrong that I'm here. Wrong what Sarah and I have been doing, if only because Adam didn't, or still doesn't, know. Wrong because I'm not sure I ever wanted it. Wrong because it's put me in this untenable position where I must use my influence to admit Eli to Easton.

A strong hand grips my arm, and I spin. It's Adam, who has grabbed me without my consent. Up until now he seemed entirely innocuous and, frankly, weary and sad.

I feel afraid.

"Please, go," he says with urgency. "Please don't make me ask you again."

"Sarah," I breathe out, throwing her husband's arm off me. I'm worried about her now. If Adam's a threat . . . if she's in danger here with him . . . it strikes me that I may have read her situation entirely inaccurately. Perhaps she entered this relationship with Luke and me because she was looking for an escape. Or more. Safety even. Freedom. "Are you okay?" I press. "You know I came here to help . . ."

"Eli got rejected from Easton," Sarah says, ignoring me and addressing Adam. She stands up and musters some composure. "But then, but then Audrey said we could fix things," she adds, sounding momentarily hopeful. "She said that there might be a way."

Adam stares at her, seeming so lacking in empathy in this moment that I want to slap him. No wonder she's cheating on him; he's entirely emotionless. "I thought we agreed to give up all that nonsense."

My skin prickles. That's a bit harsh, an overreaction to a school admissions process, and it gives me pause. It is not a normal reaction for him to hate Easton that much.

"We did agree to give it up," Sarah says, her voice almost begging. "But then I . . . I . . ." She sinks her head in her hands. "I wanted it so badly. I could taste it, Adam, I could feel it."

I feel the air sucked out of me. This can't merely be about admissions. Something is wrong here. Completely, fundamentally wrong. I turn to go. I can't stay here. It was a mistake to come. I want to help Sarah, but I don't know how, and I must leave, now. I'll call Luke. He will know how to help, what to do.

"Wait." Adam stops me, cementing himself between me and the door. But now he's looking not at me, but at his wife. "Sarah, for the sake of our marriage, and us, and Eli. I'm putting an end to this. Here. Now."

Ice runs up my neck. I don't know what he means, and I'm not sure I want to.

"Tell her," Adam breathes at Sarah. "Tell your friend everything. Tell her the truth, Sarah. Tell her the goddamned truth, or I swear I will do it myself."

"Tell me what? What, Sarah?" I hear the words coming from my mouth, but I hadn't intended to speak. It was involuntary.

"Tell her where Eli is," Adam says. He's still blocking the door, but he makes no move to touch me again, and I'm relieved about that. Still, I don't trust this man, and I consider grabbing my phone, readying myself to call Luke. Better yet, to run out of here and not look back. But I can't do that. There's Sarah. I have to find out what this is all about, for her sake, and for my own. Besides, I'm so dreadfully curious about what's happening here that I can't leave. I have to know.

I'm frozen to the spot as I watch Sarah walk over to Eli's bookshelf, where she lingers to study the toys and books intricately arranged there, a picture-perfect spread.

"Sarah?" I prompt. I don't want to ask, because I don't want to hear her answer . . . I'm terrified that this is something awful. But at the same time, I must ask, and I must find out.

Finally, she speaks, back turned to me, as she picks up a stuffed llama, pristine, no fur rubbed off or eyeballs missing. "What my husband won't tell you himself because he's worried I'll break into a million pieces . . ."

"That's not why. I want you to say it," Adam breathes. "Out loud."

"Say what?" My heartbeat's thrumming in my throat.

Sarah turns to face me, steeling herself for whatever it is she's about to confess. "What he won't tell you himself is that Eli isn't here. Eli hasn't been here for a year. More than a year, actually. Four hundred and two days, to be exact."

My pulse plummets to my feet. I don't understand what she's saying or what this means.

"Yes, I applied for him to go to Easton. Yes, that might sound crazy to you now, now that you know."

"Know what?" I manage to get out.

"It was delusional and insane, and I know no one will ever understand it, not fully, but I had to," she explains. "I had to."

Adam walks up to stand next to his wife, and he reaches out to grab her hand. She lets him take it.

I look from her to him, and back again, unable to speak, to move, to do anything at all.

"Eli isn't here, Audrey," she finally clarifies, "and he won't be, ever again. Eli is dead."

Dead?

Eli?

Her son?

I stare at the stuffed llama in Sarah's hands, the white fluffy fur so new, the toy of a child who never had a chance to play with it. This cannot be true. I must be misunderstanding.

"But, but the application," I sputter. I'm trying to infuse some logic here, because what I've heard defies it. I need someone to explain this to me. Because Eli can't, he can't be dead.

"I said it," she says, addressing Adam. "Out loud. Are you happy now?" I hear bitterness in her voice, but mostly I hear abject sorrow.

"Thank you," Adam breathes, pulling his wife into an embrace, and now I know, without a doubt, that my original assessment of Adam was spot-on. He isn't dangerous. He's simply a broken man.

"Eli died of a peanut allergy," Sarah explains, a far-off look in her eyes. She's not hugging Adam back, but she's not pushing him away either. She seems empty. If this is true, if what she's telling me is real, and I know, in my gut, that it is . . . there's no way she wouldn't be. "It was over a year ago. He was only four. I couldn't save him."

She stops, and it's unclear whether she has more she wants to say. Seeing her standing there, overtaken by grief—it's the most tragic thing I've ever witnessed. If I felt like an intruder before, now I feel criminal, invading their most private space, realizing that I've known a ghost of this person Luke and I invited into our home.

Their son is dead. It's unfathomable.

I don't belong here. I am an outsider, and the feeling of guilt that overtakes me as I watch her devastated husband let go of her and sit down, heavily, on Eli's toddler bed, makes me physically sick.

My thoughts career like an out-of-control truck without an available off-ramp. This is why Sarah was drawn to Luke and me. This is why she pursued a relationship with two strangers. It was her grief driving her. Her despair.

Flashes of memories pop to the surface in my mind, drawn out of the recesses of my brain and playing out like a movie trailer. Sarah always being available. Saying she and Adam had grown apart. All that time she spent, sending me gifts and notes and texts. Stalking me. Why she seemed so off, so unstable, ever since that first email signed from "Disconsolate."

And most of all: her dogged insistence that she secure Eli a spot at Easton. A school he would never, could never attend.

There was never a child to admit. And yet, she had me, and all of us, convinced.

I'm not angry. I'm sucker punched.

"I'm sorry," I blurt out, before fleeing Eli's room. They don't run after me. I walk out the front door of their house, gasping for breath.

———

My mind is a jumble as I Lyft back home. I didn't know Eli, never met him in my life, but the sickening feeling that's bubbling up in my chest is palpable. Imagining Sarah's grief, the utter devastation of losing her only child . . . I think of Cal, and Hazel, and it's all I can do not to call Luke right now and have him wake Cal up so I can FaceTime him. I'll be there in ten minutes, thirteen tops, but the wait feels almost unbearable. Once home, I will not be able to stop myself from going into his room and pulling him into my arms, smelling his sweet soapy smell, touching his soft skin, not caring one iota if I wake him up in the process.

I'm oblivious to my surroundings as we shoot through Central Park. I am fixated on Sarah, the events of the last few weeks clicking more solidly into place like missing puzzle pieces.

It explains everything. Her behavior made little sense in the moment, with this key detail missing—the death of her son. Now, I can think back on what she's done and see it in a completely new light.

It wasn't unreasonable. It was understandable. With her only child gone, there was no purpose left for Sarah as a childless mother. She must have committed to going through the admissions process because she couldn't accept that Eli was really gone. Or else she was clinging to the one role she really knew and understood how to do. The role of his mom.

My eyes water at the thought of it. A woman pursuing an empty dream in her son's memory. I feel sadness coupled with shame. Luke and I have unwittingly preyed on someone so vulnerable.

And then a worse thought occurs to me, and I have to hit the button to open my back seat window and let the cool air flood over me, lest I throw up. Did Luke . . . does Luke already know?

PART FOUR

SARAH PRICE

Chapter 24

I don't have many friends left from the Before Times. They send us holiday cards, and I'll get an occasional, infrequent email from one of my best college girlfriends, vaguely updating me on life. John got a new job! Teenagers are so insane. We're thinking of going in on a timeshare! I don't blame a single one of them for their silence, their aloofness. It's hard being the friend of someone who has lost everything.

For starters, they can't talk about their children, or, at least, they're under that impression. Isn't a mere mention of little Sasha or preteen Emma a slap in the face to a person whose only child has died? A person who can never again call herself a mother? I can read the tension in every exchange. They know they can't completely leave out the details of family life; that would insult my intelligence. But they also can't elaborate, not without feeling extreme guilt. I don't make it easy for them either. I could; I could swear I'm fine and that I want to live vicariously through their happy stories of domestic life. But there's something morbidly satisfying about letting them sit with the truth, my truth. Almost as though I want them to never forget what I live with, every single, interminable day. I don't want to make them uncomfortable. But then again, discomfort is my way of life. It would seem disingenuous to spare them of it completely.

And so, our interactions over the past year have gone from supportive and comforting to distant and pleasant. I hear a lot from my old friends about work drama, and very little else. It's not their fault, and I'm certain I'd do the same, were the situation reversed. They don't want to hurt me; they handle me with kid gloves. But the truth is, they are weary of me, and some part of them likely can't stand me anymore. No one likes the idea of never-ending grief. It goes against everything we are taught—to get back up again after a loss, to be born again from our sorrow. That's all complete and utter horseshit, of course.

Don't get me wrong; they said all the right things, initially. It's easy to comfort a friend in the immediate aftermath of a tragedy. There were the casseroles, the expensive floral arrangements that seemed to arrive at our house daily, the self-care kits and spa gift certificates and handwritten notes. The friends visiting me with grim faces to assure me that this wasn't my fault. They refrained from asserting that "everything happens for a reason," so I was at least spared that obscenity.

But what happens after the time begins to pass, and all those friends who are horrified for you have to get back to their lives? To school drop-offs and planning vacations and wiping butts and fighting with their spouses? The calls and texts became more infrequent, especially after it became evident that I wouldn't be "bouncing back" or finding a way to make meaning out of Eli's death.

Didn't they understand? His death was the meaning. I would never recover.

My online allergy friends had an even harder time. They weren't merely sickened by what had happened, like my other mom friends—they were appalled. Exponentially so. While my college friends could draw a line in the sand, between themselves and me—they were on one lucky, star-kissed shore, and I was distinctly on the other, cursed one—the forum moms' kids had serious allergies like Eli's, which meant that what had happened to me wasn't simply some freak accident, some unfortunate situation that had nothing to do with them. It wasn't a sad story they could compartmentalize, like my other friends could, because they knew, deep down, there was nothing stopping this from happening to them. I was the living embodiment of every one of their worst nightmares. They were me; they lived their lives as parents on a razor-thin edge of despair as they worried daily about their own, fragile children. And I was a constant, and terrible, reminder of everything they stood to lose.

I didn't miss any of my friends, not really. I had nothing to talk to them about. They didn't want to hear about how I couldn't sleep, could barely eat. I met their suggestions that Adam and I try for another child with contempt. I wasn't angry at them for suggesting it; it was the obvious solution, wasn't it? To have another child to hold and care for and raise? To have someone on whom to bestow all the backlog of love that was left in my heart, after Eli's death, with nowhere to go? It would bring Adam and me closer, wouldn't it? Allow us to heal?

But I couldn't be a mother again; I knew that with certainty. Adam and I went to therapy, loads of it, after Eli died. I could tell he was toying with the idea of another child. Still, I was shocked when he first suggested it, timidly, with our therapist present. It's not that the idea hadn't occurred to me, but what surprised me, truly surprised me, was that Adam seemed whole enough to actually mean it. We had gone through the exact same tragedy. We'd lived and breathed and screamed our way through it, and here he was, a year later, seeming to have come out the other side. He had been reborn, in some incomprehensible way, and I hadn't.

I reminded him, conveniently, of my placenta accreta, how after Eli's birth I'd lost so much blood I'd almost died. Neither one of us wanted me to put my life in danger again. I'd never been so happy to use that awful experience as an excuse to shut down a conversation. Wrongly, I had assumed that the gentle reminder would put an end to the discussion, but it hadn't. What about surrogacy? Adam had suggested. Adoption?

I rejected the notion and knew I'd never change my mind. But not for the reasons Adam thought, or not entirely, anyway. I told him it wouldn't be fair to Eli. That I could never, ever replace him. Adam didn't want to do that, either, he insisted. But a baby, to him, felt hopeful. I disagreed, and it wasn't something I could even stomach thinking about. The idea didn't merely upset me; it revolted me. Eli was the most special child to ever exist. I owed it to him to continue to mourn him for the rest of my life. Another baby would take me away from that mission.

But that wasn't the only reason I couldn't be a mother again. I had failed Eli. In the one job I'd been entrusted with—his safety, his life, his health—I had failed. We had tricked fate to have Eli in the first place. All that IVF and fertility after the universe had shown me, again and again, with every miscarriage, that I wasn't meant to be a mom. We'd defied the universe and done it anyway. It was classic hubris. And now we—I—was being punished.

I don't believe in destiny or religion or anything except the here and now, and yet I know this in my bones. I wasn't a good mother, because I was never supposed to be a mother at all. I paid the ultimate price for thinking I could. I never told Adam any of this; I didn't want him to feel he'd been a bad father. This was solely on me. After all, the fertility issues were because of my inhospitable womb. Not his sperm, which seemed to flow in abundance, according to the charts.

It took us five years to conceive Eli in the first place. By the time I got pregnant with him, every friend I had was on their second, even third, child. In the meantime, Adam and I had become the epitome of an infertile couple. We declined invitations to kids' birthday parties. We avoided functions centered around children. My friends were kind, too kind, planning events that had nothing to do with their kids and showering me in support and girls' weekends. I was superstitious by the time it finally happened. I think I had a right to be.

I was the happiest new mom when I wasn't riddled by paranoia and fear. That gradually eased as I got into the rhythm of taking care of Eli. Our walks, when he was an infant, around our neighborhood, the nap times where I let him sleep on my chest after nursing and never tired of watching his little sighs, his breath going in and out. After maternity leave, I went back to work. The nanny we found was delightful, and seasoned, and it felt good to walk back into my workplace to talk about books and deadlines and bestsellers. To be someone else again, besides "Mom." My son couldn't even say my name yet, and I hadn't realized how much I craved adult interaction.

That all changed a year later, when Eli was diagnosed. It wasn't immediate, my decision to quit my job and stay home with him. I debated it for months, every night losing myself in a wormhole of internet research on severe allergies. Eli's throat had closed entirely the first time he'd tasted a nut. After a harrowing ambulance ride, where he was pumped with epinephrine, and Adam and I rode white knuckled with him on the way to the ER, unclear how we'd ended up there, my world tilted sideways, and it felt like nothing would ever be quite right again. I recognized my mistake: letting myself sink blissfully into motherhood and relinquishing some of my control.

Three months later, I left my office on an impulse one November afternoon with all my things in a cardboard Amazon box, let our nanny go with a glowing recommendation, and told Adam I wasn't going back to work. Eli needed me; I was the one person, besides him, who could keep him safe. I was fortunate enough to be able to walk away from my job since it barely paid the nanny's salary, anyway. I wasn't working out of necessity, so it felt all the more urgent that I give up my career to protect my child. It wasn't a hard decision.

Eli and I spent every day together. Our outings grew more elaborate the older he got, once he could talk to me. I had known how precious he was from the day he was born, but now that thought lived in me every minute, every hour. Eli had to be protected from something bigger than both of us, and there was no one on earth, besides Adam, who understood how gravely important that role was. But Adam had to work, and so it was left to me. I became Super Allergy Mom. The forum was the first place I logged into in the mornings and the last thing I looked at, bleary eyed, before bed. I learned everything there was to learn about nut allergies and morbidly joked that some university should grant me an honorary immunology degree. I found comfort among the parents who understood me the best, on the Facebook group.

They alone knew how terrifying it is to fear food. To see danger lurking in every bite. Our children had to eat. That was the cruel twist of it all, the notion not one of us ever really wanted to confront. Unless we were one of the lucky ones, someone whose child grew out of this or could be cured by experimental treatment at Stanford, they'd be carrying around this burden for life. It was our job to protect them from nuts while making sure they didn't live a life of fear. The stress of it was maddening. I couldn't stand talking to my mom or my friends about it; unless they had an allergy kid, they couldn't possibly understand. I didn't, as they often insisted, have it "under control." I didn't need to "learn to live with it." The more I heard this from friends and acquaintances, the more I retreated into the world of the forums, letting almost everything else in my life slip away as this became my singular focus.

It was Adam who kept me grounded, who insisted we enroll Eli in preschool. He couldn't stay home forever, Adam argued. That would deprive him of all the things a child needs to thrive. Friends, stimulation, social-emotional learning. I agreed we could send him to preschool if I found one I trusted. The truth is, I'd never trust anyone else with my child, but what choice did I have? Eli couldn't stay walled within his room forever.

I don't know how I did it, how I lived with this fear always coursing through me, while simultaneously finding joy in every moment I spent with my kid, and with Adam. The three of us were happy. I could kick myself for believing we had a right to be. Why us? Hadn't I known, ever since pregnancy, and Eli's traumatic birth, that something would go wrong?

I sent him with two EpiPens that day, to the playdate. I instructed the mom—twice, once over the phone, and once in person when I dropped Eli off—not to give him a single bite to eat. Everything he needed was in his camo backpack. A lunch, a snack, a water bottle. Two EpiPens, I reminded her again. Front zippered pouch. I even showed her how to use one.

But the mom left the house for twenty minutes to pick up dinner.

The au pair made a mistake.

She couldn't find the EpiPens.

The muffins had traces of nuts, and she hadn't known because they were homemade.

Eli thought they were safe.

He was four.

It took one single, minuscule bite.

I can't think back on that day in any linear sense. I can hear the mom screaming at me into the phone, hysterical. I can picture Eli on the stretcher as they unloaded his still form from the ambulance, as I ran up onto the sidewalk, my spilled Starbucks coffee drenching my wool coat. I can recall the smells of the emergency room and see in my mind's eye the au pair sobbing and hear the click, click of the ER doctor's high heels on the tiled floor as she came to tell me that my son was dead. The multiple doses of epinephrine they administered had been too little, too late. They had not been able to save him.

You can say that everything was stacked up against him, that it was one of those terrible accidents that no one saw coming. You can say that, but it wouldn't be true. Where was my mother's intuition, after I walked down the front steps of that family's apartment building and headed to Starbucks for a coffee, feeling proud of myself for lending Eli some independence? Feeling I'd made progress, by giving him the skills he would one day need to be a successful adult?

I don't care what mistakes were made or who made them. I should never have left.

Chapter 25

I can't go back there. Not now that she knows.

She was going to find out, eventually; they both were. I knew when I began the application process that I wouldn't be able to keep up the charade, not indefinitely. There would be the child playdate, the parent interview. Eventually I would have had to produce Eli himself, and I knew this. I simply tried not to think about it. But in the brief moments when I did, I assumed I'd slip away. Withdraw Eli's application, never to be heard from again. I'd pretend we'd moved or were no longer interested. No one would have even blinked.

But that was before.

Once things escalated, and Audrey and Luke became enmeshed in the most intimate parts of me, of my day, of my world, and in fact, became the one part of my world that gave me any joy or pleasure or lifeblood . . . I had no plan at all, because there was no way out. There would be no casual slipping away. I could hide Eli's death only for so long before it all came crashing down around me, the truth revealed to them in a sickening fun house mirror.

And now, it's all I can do not to climb under the covers and hide from them for eternity.

I'm ashamed. Not because my son has died but because of how, and why, it happened. It wasn't a car accident that took Eli. A fallen bit of scaffolding or a drunk driver. It was my own failure to protect him, and that is the part of myself I deliberately bury, mortified the world will see. I am the cautionary tale, the former mother bearing her own version of a scarlet letter. Perhaps it's why I keep him so viscerally alive in my mind. I'm not delusional; I know Eli hasn't been here for more than a year. I know that going through the motions of the application process wasn't a particularly healthy thing to do. Everything I did, I did with complete awareness.

I did it because I couldn't not.

When I began Eli's application, I told myself I would indulge in the first few steps of the process, to see what it felt like, then disengage permanently. Certainly, that's what I told Adam. But once I stepped through Easton's doors, it all changed. I wasn't just hooked on the instant adrenaline rush I got from inhabiting that school. I was full-on addicted. Yes, I could imagine Eli walking those halls, being a part of a dream bigger than him or me or all of us. But also, the way I felt, lingering among those parents . . .

It was like I was still one of them.

I ached to be in their shoes with a kind of longing I didn't know was physically possible. And being in their orbit—chatting with them, sharing anecdotes, imagining there was an alternate timeline in which Eli was still alive, and rosy cheeked, and delightfully well—gave me life. Nothing else compared.

Until I met Audrey. And then I fell for her with such a force that it filled a tiny portion of the empty chamber in my abdomen, the one that blasted itself into existence after Eli died. Being with her was exhilarating, and when the three of us met at their house late at night to quite literally "fuck the pain away" . . . I discovered that I could breathe again.

Now I fear that the magic is gone. They will never look at me the same way again. Now that they know, now that the illusion has been broken, the chamber in my chest cavity exposed . . . they won't engage with me in that playful way again. Audrey certainly won't love me; Audrey will pity me.

Because she will never understand.

Who could grasp why I still walk to playgrounds pushing a stroller? Why I regularly visit Magnolia Bakery, pick out two cupcakes—vanilla for me, red velvet for him (100 percent, verified nut-free)—and devour them both on our favorite park bench? Why I continue to shop for birthday gifts for Eli?

Seeing other children hurts, acutely, especially kids who are the age that he would have been now, had he lived. That's why spotting Cal this evening was a real blow. He looked . . . not physically like Eli. Cal's much taller than I imagine Eli would be. Their hair isn't the same color at all, and no child on earth has that special twinkle that Eli had. That magic. But his five-year-old energy . . . Cal's bad dream. That little lip trembling and curling up, like Eli's used to when he was scared of the dark.

Still, that alone was not why I left their house in a rush. I've seen other five-year-olds. I don't always have to excuse myself. But tonight, it wasn't crushing sadness I felt. It was envy that knocked me sideways. The roiling, bitter feeling of jealousy, so nasty and shameful, that filled me when I saw the child in the flesh and tried to reconcile that this boy would be attending Easton, while Eli would not. This boy had his whole life ahead of him—adventures and milestones and love and heartache and laughter—and Eli would not. All because he had been born with a faulty immune system that tried to poison itself when he came into contact with *Arachis hypogaea*. It felt cosmically unfair.

Up until that point, I had tried not to think about Cal in any literal sense. He was vague and fuzzy, a mere concept, and I'd planned to keep him that way. Meeting Audrey and Luke after his bedtime meant there was little reason to think we'd cross each other's paths. But there he was, standing right in front of me in his Batman pajamas. It was too much to bear.

Now, Audrey's been gone a few hours, and it's nearly 2:00 a.m. when I log into the allergy forum, feeling myself destress the moment

I see the posts spring up. Questions about nuts at school. Questions about oral immunotherapy and getting into clinical trials. More mundane questions about recipes, like parents asking how to replicate a birthday cake their child saw on a YouTube video, minus the nuts.

I have all the info about the clinical trial at Stanford! I write in response to the first poster. DM me! Anna hasn't qualified yet but we're keeping our fingers and toes crossed that she might be a good candidate! I know how hard it is, girl—feel free to reach out!

And there it is, plain as day. More evidence that I have yet to completely face the reality of my situation.

I don't post on the Facebook forum as me anymore.

My account and profile are fake. Here, I am a perky midwestern woman named Melissa, who has two daughters (Sloane, eight; Anna, five). "Anna" has severe nut allergies.

It is as Melissa that I interact with the other parents on the allergy forum. Because no one on here wants the mom of the dead kid lurking around.

It would be too cruel. Too offensive. Obscene, even. Because what purpose do I have in going on here anymore, now that I have no allergic child? Now that I am no longer even a mother?

I received the full-court press of condolences in those early days. Notes and posts and DMs from the other members, expressing their deepest sympathies. But then it was time for me to go. To sign out of the group, permanently. To let the other parents visit the forum without a ghost haunting them . . . the ghost of who they feared, every waking moment, they could become. Me.

But I couldn't let it go, and still haven't. It is the one place I still find some comfort. The one place besides Audrey and Luke's bed.

A text from Audrey comes through on my phone, and I startle.

Can we talk?

No, I think to myself. Not now. My wheels turn, spinning so fast it's dizzying. What would happen if I simply never responded? How many times would she try to contact me? I don't want to consider that she might not make many attempts to reach me before giving up. The truth is, I ache to see her again. To feel her comfort me and hold me and allow myself to get lost in something so outside myself that it's not even my life anymore.

I don't know if I can.

"Who's the text from?"

I spin in my chair. I'm at my desk, and even though it's late and I can barely keep my eyes open, there will be little sleep for me tonight. Adam stands behind me, looking equally spent. He used to be young. Handsome. Full of sweetness and light. My failure snatched all that from him. All that's left is a shell of the Adam I once knew.

"Audrey," I tell him. No more lies. Not if I can help it. "She's a little shaken. She was shocked. Understandably."

"You're on the forum again?"

Dammit. Once again, with the browser! Adam hates when I go on here, like he hated the Easton admissions process. I quickly shut my laptop.

"I'm giving up Easton, aren't I?" I ask, defensive. "Can't I just have this? It doesn't hurt anyone!"

"It hurts you. And by association, me." His face is drawn as he sits heavily on the love seat. "We've talked about this, Sarah. You won't be able to move on if you keep doing this."

Move on. Those words that are the core difference between him and me. Him, who wants to move on. Me, who does not, and never will.

"I'm sorry," I whisper. "I'll try to stop." It's not a complete lie. I do have days where I don't let myself go on the forum. Where I don't take the stroller out or order Eli's favorite foods. Where I try to be a person who can exist in the After Times.

Adam gets up, kisses the top of my head, and leaves for our bedroom.

I open up my laptop again as another text comes through on my phone. This one from Luke.

We're worried about you.

I don't want to face him right now. Either of them. The thought of arriving at their home, alone, in the dead of night as we do, and having to confront them—two against one—and explain what I've done, and why . . . I can't do that to myself.

I am also terrified of letting them go.

They won't miss me on any fundamental level; I am sure of that. I am a plaything to Luke, entertainment for Audrey. Possibly I'm even a nuisance, since I know it wasn't her idea, this little arrangement of ours. I am aware enough to recognize that my feelings for her can't possibly be reciprocated. Has some part of me hoped that, in time, they will? Yes. But to imagine that she would miss me as much as I already miss her . . . no. It's simply not possible.

And yet, the thought of never seeing her again . . . of slipping away as I had imagined I would have to . . . leaving Easton and my dreams for Eli behind, and never being in Audrey's presence again? Smelling her Audrey smell? Watching her crack that sarcastic grin?

It's suffocating.

I can't lose Easton and the forum and Audrey in one fell swoop.

It's too dark out. There are not enough lights on outside my window, because my entire block is asleep. Before I can consider what a bad idea it is, I go to my bookmarks bar and click on the Easton website, the URL saved there months ago. As the site loads, I get a familiar rush, similar to the one that courses through me every time I log onto the allergy forum. I know the Easton dream is dead, but what if it doesn't have to be . . . not entirely? I am ready to ditch the allergy forum for good. But giving up Easton feels like a betrayal, to Eli. Like I am pacifying others: Audrey, Luke, Adam. I am not ready to let it go, so why do I have to?

I scroll through the website, noting upcoming admissions events, reading about the school's chess champions and sports team victories, the capital campaign and latest faculty hires. It is when I click on the "Events" section that I pause. An Easton fundraising gala, scheduled for next week. An auction to raise money for the school. Tickets cost $5,000 for a midlevel contribution, and that is the tier of ticket I select; I wouldn't want anyone to think that I don't belong there. Besides, the donation will go to the school, regardless of whether I can send a child there. Adam won't mind; money isn't an issue for us.

Still. What the hell am I thinking?

I can't go to this function. Audrey will be there. In all probability, Luke too.

It would be like rubbing salt in a wound, to attend this Easton fundraiser, and to have to face Audrey again. Like pressing my fingers on a recent burn, forcing myself to live in every second of the white-hot agony, the kind that sends sparks to your eyes.

And yet, a part of me wants nothing more. To be near Audrey, but in a place where I won't have to explain myself. No one talks about anything serious at parties. I would be safe. Protected by the chatter, the crowd. I know Audrey and Luke won't divulge what they know, about Eli, to anyone else there. We are each other's secret keepers, now that we have all done what we've done.

There's a floor-length silk dress in the back of my closet, tags still on, purchased for an ex-colleague's wedding I never went to; it was the week after Eli died.

My cursor hovers over the blue button that reads "Purchase ticket."

Chapter 26

As the Lyft pulls up to the home of Caroline Chippenfield Crane and her husband Nathan, I consider turning around. It's been a week since Audrey found out about Eli. Since she caught me in the lie that ruined everything. Audrey and Luke were an escape, a chance to leave my grief and loss and shame behind, to indulge in something purely sensual and of the now. That's all gone.

I thank my driver and get out, picking up my gold silk dress by the hem. It's so long that even with heels, it drags on the ground. It's November, and I'm glad I wore my heaviest wool coat. Long and black, with silver buttons.

Am I really doing this?

I haven't responded to any of Audrey's or Luke's texts. They've sent several, each. The last one, from Audrey, asked me to reach out when I felt ready. It sounded almost like a goodbye.

When I feel ready.

Am I ready now? They will be here tonight. But it's a work setting, for Audrey. Professional. She can't grill me here. I won't have to lay myself bare. It feels like the only way to face them. Alone, but surrounded by people. Alone, but not isolated.

I debated it all week. Changed my mind fifteen times, stashed the dress away, deleted the event from my calendar. Then I stayed up all night, imagining myself there. So seduced by the idea of one last Easton hurrah, a chance to see Audrey again. Now, there's no going back. I'm doing this.

I ring the bell, and a staff member clad all in black answers, welcomes me into this exquisite home. Chippie's home. I know she's called Chippie because I dove intimately into her Instagram account this week. Judging from what I've seen there, on the Gram, her home is like an extension of her. All incongruous materials, marble, steel, raw concrete mixed with plush velvet, the walls dotted with large-scale contemporary art. Furniture that is luscious and ornate while still retaining a sleek, minimalist, and intentional look. It's jaw dropping; I'm certain Chippie's hand is all over this design.

I also know from my social media research that she is Audrey's best friend. The two have been pictured together countless times: At charity balls. Fundraisers like this one. School events. In every photo, they are thick as thieves.

My heart flutters as I consider that I'm stepping into Audrey's territory. Her best friend's home. Still, I feel safer here than I would at Audrey and Luke's, where our past actions linger in every room. Where I don't know how I'd look them in the eye.

I walk inside, hand my coat to an attendant, and take the first glass of champagne offered to me. I will not get wasted like I did at the Easton tea; that is an absolute nonstarter. I must keep my wits about me tonight.

There are Easton parents, some current, some prospective, everywhere. Dressed in silks and satins, couture dresses with feathers and beads and asymmetrical sleeves. Men in sharp suits, their hair newly cut, with their arms looped around wives boasting diamond tennis bracelets and Bottega Veneta clutches. But all I can really focus on is the fact that they are all parents, and I am no longer. It is a staggeringly wide chasm that separates me from them.

But they don't know, do they? Much as Adam wishes I'd stop, that I'd never set foot in a group of parents again, for my own sake . . . I can't help it. The allure of inhabiting my former role of "mother" is too tempting. The pull is too strong.

I scan the crowd for Audrey and locate her across the room, perched next to a set of stunning gray bookcases, chatting with some parents I don't recognize. My heart flutters at the sight of her fitted navy dress, her studded leather boots, and her short, swingy hair. She hasn't seen me yet, does not know I'm here or was planning to be. It's not my intention to blindside her. I simply could not think of another way to do this. I need the excuse of the crowd, the opportunity to leave. I cannot be on their, on her and Luke's, turf.

Luke is upon me before I realize it. He pulls me into a quick hug. It's chaste, cordial. No one who saw us together would think a thing of it. But before he lets me go, he whispers, "I'm sorry."

I briefly register how truly heartfelt this sounds, coming from him, before Audrey is standing in front of me, her eyes flitting around cautiously, from me to him.

"Surprise," I say dryly. Luke cracks a smile; Audrey does not.

"Why didn't you tell us?" It doesn't feel like a confrontation. Nor does she sound angry. The question is genuine, I think.

I survey her. It's not as painful, being here, as I imagined. It's strange and uncomfortable. The reality is, nothing is painful to me now, is it? Now that I've experienced the ultimate loss?

"Why didn't I tell you about Eli?" I answer. "Or why didn't I tell you I would be here tonight?"

Audrey is about to respond, likely to say "both," when someone walks up, someone so ethereal and unreal, dressed so chicly and effortlessly, her high cheekbones cutting shadows on the walls, that I know right away who she is. Our hostess. Chippie Crane.

She swoops over in a bright-fuchsia knee-length gown, jewels dripping over her taut breasts, her hair tightly spun into an intricate topknot. She addresses Audrey humorlessly. "The girls are watching *Ferris*

Bueller's Day Off for the fiftieth time upstairs. Thought you'd want to know." She leaves without another word.

"Don't say it," Audrey snaps at Luke before he can say anything at all. "Hazel and Winslow are back on track, but that doesn't mean I'm not still angry. Okay?"

Luke nods, shooting me a look that says "What can you do?" and I'm instantly struck by the certainty that my decision to come here, to mingle in this place under the dome of Easton, was the right one. Luke is treating me normally. Not like some sad, pathetic shell of a woman. I consider that things might still be okay between the three of us. Between Audrey and me.

"Sarah?" A voice jolts me out of my thoughts. I'm not sure if I've heard correctly; between the thrumming music, the glasses of bubbly clinking all around, and the chatter of parents who're treating this evening like it's the Met Gala, it's hard to hear anything clearly.

But I have heard and wish I did not.

"Lauren." Instantly, I know that everything will absolutely not be okay.

"I had to come talk to you when I saw you walk in," she says, her voice tight. "I mean, I couldn't believe you were here, that you were still . . ."

I don't answer her, daring her to say it out loud. Daring her to do this to me. Here, now.

Lauren faces Audrey. "This is difficult, but I thought you should know. Sarah and I, we have a history—"

"She killed my child," I say.

The chatter around us doesn't stop, because no one else has heard me. But Audrey, Luke, and Lauren look stricken. Have I really done it? Really said it?

Might as well continue now. It is too late to take the words back. "Eli was at Lauren's house on a playdate with her daughter, Beatrice, when she left him unsupervised—"

"Not unsupervised," I hear Lauren mutter. "With an au pair."

"—and he ate the minuscule bite of muffin that caused his anaphylaxis."

There. I have done it. I do not feel relief in saying it, but I don't feel worthy of blame either. Lauren has all but forced my hand. Walking up here to talk to me. She could have ignored me. She could have let me be.

I am lucky the room is teeming with self-involved, oblivious parents. They are unaware of the pain that is being resurfaced. The suffering. Among them, perhaps I can hide.

Lauren's eyes well up. "You have to know. It's the worst thing that has ever happened to me . . ."

"To you?" It's such an absurd thing she's said that it almost doesn't deserve to be acknowledged.

"Truly tragic, and I will regret my mistakes that day for the rest of my life," Lauren breathes. "But that's what it was. A terrible, awful, horrifying mistake." To her credit, tears have formed in her eyes. It's not that I think they're fake or that she isn't remorseful.

It's that her remorse will never be enough.

"I didn't think this charade should go on any longer," Lauren says quietly. "I feel so terrible. I have reached out on numerous occasions, but at the end of the day, you need help, Sarah. I'm sorry." She makes a move to hug me, and red-hot-poker anger surges through me. I shove her away. Harder than I really mean to, but I can't be responsible for my actions right now. She is entirely to blame.

Lauren gasps. She isn't hurt; I hardly pushed her. But she reacts as though she's been slapped.

"See what I mean?" She finally speaks, addressing Audrey and Luke, but very pointedly, not me. "This woman is dangerous."

Luke stares at her, squeezing his glass with steady fingers. "I think it would be best if you got the fuck out of here."

Lauren looks like she's about to respond but seems to think better of it. Clutching her bag at her side, she slides off. As soon as she's gone, I feel my shoulders sag. What must Audrey and Luke think of me now?

"Oh, for fuck's sake," Audrey practically shouts, then lowers her voice, not wanting to call attention to herself, to us. "How could this have happened, Sarah? It's—it's epically unfair."

"Let's open that seventeen-year-old Hibiki whisky I've been saving, at home," says Luke abruptly. "This fundraiser is literally my worst nightmare, and not just because of that woman. It's always awful. I'll call us a Lyft."

"Would love to, honey, but there's a little thing called my job I have to attend to," Audrey reminds him. She downs the rest of her wine and sets the glass on the grand piano next to her. "Let me see how fast I can charm everyone and then slip out the back." She goes.

My head is swimming, spinning. Is it the champagne? Lauren? It's definitely, 100 percent Lauren. And Luke. What did he mean? I'll call us a Lyft. Us, as in all three of us? "I have to use the bathroom," I tell him, because I legitimately need to pee, but I also need to pull myself together.

My heart is pulsing like a metronome. Luke has invited me back to his home? If anything can ease the pain of Lauren . . . of everything that haunts me . . .

It is them. It is Audrey.

There is a line for the bathroom. Surely there are other powder rooms in this house—it's massive—but I'd get lost looking for them. Two other women stand ahead of me in line, and so I wait, accepting another glass of bubbly from a passing waiter. I hear a couple of moms behind me talking about how they're getting IV drips in the morning to counteract all this alcohol, but it's the conversation in front of me that I zero in on.

". . . anniversary of her death," says the first woman. "Which really shook me. I can't believe it. I feel like yesterday I was walking into her office, and she was cracking a joke."

"Piper Singer?" the second woman asks.

The first woman nods.

The hairs on the back of my neck stand up. Who are they talking about?

"How long has it been?" asks the second woman, who looks striking in a gown that gives the effect of having been sewn out of live butterflies.

"Seven years," says the first. "A Facebook Memory came up today. Her memorial. It really triggered me. Piper was . . ." She stops talking, abruptly, when she notices me listening in. I pretend to pick at my nonexistent nail polish. Something's nagging at me, though. I don't know what it is.

A man exits the bathroom, and the first woman makes a move to go in.

"Wait!" I cry out, sensing this is my one chance to engage her. "Why does that name sound familiar? And yes, I was eavesdropping. Sue me." I don't care what they think; I shouldn't even be here. I have nothing to lose. "Who is Piper?"

Butterfly Woman stares me down. "The previous admissions director at Easton. Before Audrey took over the job?" She regards me suspiciously, like I should know this. "Audrey worked for her, before she died. They were quite close."

"But . . . Singer?" I can't quite figure it out, why it's bothering me so much.

"That's right. Piper Singer," the first woman says exasperatedly. "She was Luke Singer's first wife."

Chapter 27

Twenty minutes and four champagnes later, I'm searching for my coat in a third or fifth or seventh bedroom. To fuck with my earlier vow that I wouldn't drink too much; that all went out the window the moment I was forced to confront Lauren. And now, this.

Audrey worked for Luke's first wife? They knew each other? They were friends?

I don't know why this development has unspooled me so much, caught me so off guard. Perhaps because I've heard no mention of it before this. It's not that I thought I really knew Luke and Audrey; our Venn diagrams have overlapped, but only marginally. I'm not fool enough to believe they've shown me every side of themselves. After all, they just learned my darkest secret, and not because I chose to reveal it to them. Adam forced my hand. Still, this revelation has shaken me.

I am glad to be alone, having left the chatter of the party behind me as I trip through the house, for some reason certain I launched my coat onto a bed. Or did I hand it to someone at the start of the night?

I open a door to a gorgeously appointed spare bedroom, but it's definitely free of coats.

I stumble down the hall and try another one.

"At least your parents don't pretend to love each other," says a voice from inside the room, and I halt, frozen to the spot. Two tween girls are lying on the floor of a media room. Sprawled on a shag rug, they're eating candy and sipping from mugs, the movie—*Ferris Bueller's Day Off*—that plays on the massive flat-screen all but forgotten.

I know instantly who these girls are. Chippie's daughter, naturally. And Hazel.

She is the one who has spoken, and I know she's talking about her mother and Luke. I can barely breathe.

"I think my stepdad's cheating on my mom," Hazel says before flopping from her stomach onto her back. "I don't know if she knows. She can be so stupid sometimes."

"Isn't it better that they pretend?" says the other girl, who is lithe, probably a dancer of some sort, with dramatic long black hair and an expressionless gaze. "I wish mine would. The crazy thing is, they actually think they're fooling us. It's so pathetic. I don't think even my little sister buys it."

I inch away from the door; I must leave before they discover me. I can't imagine what would happen if they thought I'd been listening. What would happen if anyone put two and two together.

Heart racing, I flee down the hall. Maybe my coat really isn't here. I can't remember this hallway or any of these rooms; and wouldn't someone have taken my coat, anyway? This isn't the type of party where you fling your stuff on a random bed. We aren't twenty-two and at a block party in Bed-Stuy. What was I thinking?

I wasn't, because of the alcohol, and because of what I heard those women saying. I rack my brain to recall what Audrey and Luke told me about Piper themselves. She had died, tragically, Luke said. He avoided talking about it, about her. It was too painful. Well, I'm no stranger to that.

But what does it mean that Piper and Audrey were close? How would Piper feel about Audrey having married her husband, after her death?

Still standing in the deserted hallway, I lean against a wall, clutching my phone. I open up Safari and type in her name. Piper Singer. Images pop up. The same face as the one I now remember seeing in that sepia-toned photograph that I came across in Luke and Audrey's cabinet. She is beautiful, this woman, with striking features, toned arms, and an effervescence about her that seeps through the pictures . . .

There is an obituary, and I click on it. It's full of all the usual details that inhabit a life. Born in Philadelphia. Survived by two sisters, her mother, and husband, Luke. Cause of death: heart attack.

I stop reading. Heart attack? But hadn't Audrey and Luke said she'd died of cancer?

I shake off the thought. I'm probably misremembering. Why would they lie about that?

"I found you," says a voice, and prickles go up my spine. I drop the phone. It's a voice that sends me reeling every time I hear it.

I spin to face Audrey, feeling caught. Is it weird that I googled Luke's ex-wife? Probably. "I don't want to talk," I blurt out. If she's here to rehash that whole Lauren incident, and I hope she isn't, it's the last thing I want to do.

"Then let's not." Audrey shrugs, closing the distance between us to kiss me insanely lightly on the lips. I feel my breath hitch on contact. Warmth spreads to every part of me, groin included, as her body presses to mine, the wall pinning me from behind. Oh God, I have missed her, and this. She pulls away from me, seeming to enjoy the fact that we're, for all intents and purposes, in public. At least we would be if anyone chose to walk down this hall right now. I wish she hadn't stopped. I want more. "A week ago, if you had ever returned my texts . . . I was going to tell you that we had to call things off," Audrey says, her voice breathy.

"Because of Eli?"

"Because of Eli," she repeats. I can't help but think that her daughter is off this hallway, a few rooms down. Does she know this? Would she take that chance?

"Has it occurred to you that might be the reason I didn't return your texts? Because I knew what you'd say?"

"The thought crossed my mind," Audrey responds, her mouth twitching in a half smile. But then it fades. "I felt like we'd taken advantage of you. Like you were vulnerable and couldn't have possibly been in your right mind when you . . . when you agreed to this."

Her words hang in the air, bloated, like an overstuffed balloon. I must set her straight.

"You're wrong," I tell her. "I'm not vulnerable. When Eli died, another skin grew over my existing one. It's armor, now. Nothing can hurt me."

She seems to consider this. "If you never wanted to see us again, me or Luke, we'd understand. But somehow, I don't think that's what you really want at all. Is it?"

I shake my head. It's the last thing I want.

Audrey sighs. "Ten more minutes, and I'll have shown my face. I'll leave Babs in charge of the auction, and we can go."

I nod, and she heads out to schmooze and make the school more money. My head spins like a top. I'm confused, and drunk, and the world is tilting slightly on its axis.

That conversation I overheard still lingers in my mind, but it feels distant, now. Cloudy. Like an almost-forgotten dream.

And Audrey . . . can I dare to believe it? She kissed me. She and Luke both want to continue what we've started. It was foolish to come here tonight; I know that. But maybe it will have been worth it.

———

Twenty minutes later, I'm riding in the back of an Uber, Luke in front, Audrey next to me. We don't touch, but I long to. Her kiss lingers on my lips, and it's enough to drive me to distraction. My pulse pounds; my heart ricochets in my chest like a machine gun.

She still wants me.

I still want this.

And yet . . . something isn't sitting right with me. I wish I could ask her about it, about Piper. There's probably a perfectly logical explanation for why she never brought it up. I kept my dead son from them, didn't I? So who am I to talk? I shake off the feeling. Nothing matters, not now. Eli is gone. I have nothing but this.

We arrive at their condo, and Luke relieves the babysitter. Cal is fast asleep, Hazel still at the Cranes' home, spending the night with Chippie's daughter.

We are alone.

In minutes, our clothes are shed. Body parts find each other and fit together like puzzle pieces. It has been an entire week since we've been together, but we remember what to do. Luke barely registers for me as I shiver at the sight of Audrey's naked body. Lips, hands, skin, breasts: she is exquisite, worthy of sculptors. I come, and it's the release I've needed to let go of everything that's transpired. Audrey is perfect. I am, briefly, happy. I have let my secret go. They know, now, and there is nothing left of myself to hide. It feels like a relief, them knowing. They won't bring it up anymore, unless I want them to. I feel sure of that now.

I drift off, the wine finally knocking me out, and I feel my eyes closing, lids heavy. When I wake, Luke is gone. Audrey alone lies beside me. The room is dark, but my head is clearer. I reach my hand out to lazily touch the silken skin of her arm, and she stirs, opening her eyes. She looks over at me, and for the first time, I feel she is really seeing me, without the filter she seems to apply to every person, every situation in her life.

Especially this one.

I hate to break the spell, but now the wine has worn off and the glittery high of the party has evaporated. All that is left is the reality of this, and us. Eli is dead. Easton is over, for me. I know now, with certainty, that I have attended my very last Easton event. I mourn for what could have been, but I shut the door on it. I must.

My heart rate kicks up. It's now or never. "I heard something strange," I tell Audrey, circling my fingernails gingerly on the skin of her forearm. "At the event. These two women, they were saying . . . you were friends with Piper? Luke's first wife? You worked for her, at Easton?"

Audrey's filter goes back up. She sits up, retracting her arm from my touch.

"Yes," she answers. "Piper hired me. It was shortly after Hazel started kindergarten at Easton. I needed a job, and she needed an assistant director. We became close, as colleagues often do. When she died, it was . . ." She trails off, considering her next words. "The whole community was reeling. She was beloved by the school."

I try to imagine this Piper woman who was tragically taken before her time, in her early thirties. What was she like? What were she and Luke like, as a couple?

"And then," I stammer. "And then . . . you and Luke . . . ?"

"He was grieving. Inconsolable. I understood. I had loved Piper too. Not in the same way. She was my friend, my best friend besides Chippie." Audrey pulls the sheet tighter around her. "She and I were a team, a damn good one. And that's what brought us together, Luke and me. Our shared grief. Our shared love for Piper. It wasn't planned. I never saw it coming. But it happens sometimes, you know. We waited until we were sure before we told people about us. We knew it would come as a shock. But in the end, everyone understood. They were happy for Luke." She shrugs. "Everyone likes a happy ending."

I consider this. It's true; there's no reason Luke should never find love again, simply because his first wife died. And Audrey . . . I can see it. Divorced, raising a child . . . their chemistry is undeniable. Perhaps it was meant to be.

I check my phone. It's 2:00 a.m.

"It's weird, not worrying about having to get home," I tell Audrey. "I could stay here all day tomorrow, and it wouldn't matter. No one would miss me."

"Not even . . . Adam?" Audrey stares at me, and I do see pity in her eyes, but I tell myself it isn't there.

"I think he wishes the old Sarah would walk through the door," I try to explain. "But this Sarah? This version of me? He hardly knows this Sarah. I don't see how he could possibly love me when he doesn't know me."

It's the best way I can think to express this.

"I'm gonna make some tea," I tell Audrey. "Want some?"

She shakes her head, lying back down and pulling the covers up. "Too drunk," she says, before shutting her eyes again. I extricate myself from the sheets, throw on a T-shirt and shorts strewed by the bed. They must be Audrey's. As I dress, slipping into her clothes, I consider that it's nice being able to talk about my situation, finally, without having to pretend I'm something I'm not. Does Audrey see the real me now? I wonder as I pad out of the room. I want her to.

I head into the kitchen. I will microwave a cup; I don't want to put on the kettle and have it whistle all over the house, waking Cal.

As I'm grabbing a mug from the upper cabinet, I notice a light is on, very dim, down the hall. In Luke and Audrey's office. Is he up, working? I pad over, toward the light.

The door is ajar. I can see enough through the crack to notice that Luke is looking at his laptop, his back to the door as he sits facing the window, at the desk.

A video plays with no sound. A sex video of two women. I start to turn around and flee. I definitely do not want to watch Luke watching porn . . . but before I turn, something catches my eye.

I know one of the women in the video.

Chapter 28

I do not want to be watching this.

I absolutely, 100 percent do not want to see what I'm seeing. And yet, I can't take my eyes off the video. I am locked in a kind of trance, my gaze fixed on the women on Luke's screen.

One of them is Audrey. At first, I wasn't entirely convinced it was her, not until she turned and I saw her profile. Then I knew it, with certainty. It's the woman I've spent these last few weeks pining over, lusting after. The woman I'm irrationally and unstoppably infatuated with. The woman who lies naked and asleep in the next room, who has made me feel alive for the first time since Eli died.

In the video, she wears black lace panties and nothing else. The other woman, clad in a bra and underwear, is lying back on the pillows, mostly obscured by Audrey's bare back.

This isn't porn, I realize now. It's a homemade video. I swallow against the blockage in my throat, feeling my nerves pulse in every appendage. There is no scenario in which I ever would have sought this out. Where I would purposefully have chosen to spy over Luke's shoulder as he views a sex tape of his wife. With another woman.

Still, what is wrong with me? I can't look away.

Go, I tell myself. Turn around, walk down the hall, and leave. It feels like a betrayal of Audrey's privacy to stand here for even one more second. But I continue to watch, mesmerized, as the Audrey in the video kisses the woman's thighs, stomach, and breasts, and I have to admit to myself that I'm not upset that this video exists . . . I'm jealous. I know that's crazy; so Audrey was with another woman at some previous point in time. Who knows when this was filmed? My guess is that it wasn't all that long ago; Audrey doesn't look significantly younger than she does now, so I doubt this is ancient history. But no matter when it was recorded, it's entirely not my place to care. I'm married. All three of us are. It's not my business who Audrey was with before me; we don't have anything close to a mutually exclusive relationship.

Of course, I do care. A lot. I want to look away because logically, I know I'm an intruder, a voyeur witnessing something I have no right to see. But I can't.

I try to unravel the tangle of thoughts taking root in my mind. Audrey and this woman . . . who is she? Was Audrey cheating on Luke when she made this? Does he know this woman? And did he know about this when it happened, or has he just found out? Or maybe this tryst between Audrey and this woman was not a betrayal of Luke at all but part of an arrangement they had. The three of us have an unconventional arrangement; maybe Audrey and this woman were not a surprise to Luke but something he signed off on. The wondering makes my head spin. I wipe my sweaty palms on my shorts.

Audrey's silk shorts. I'm suddenly aware of how intimate it is that I'm wearing her clothing. Her flimsy pajama bottoms. I shiver, filled with longing for her, suddenly perspiring and freezing, all at once. I should go—I know I should go. But before I can leave, I notice Audrey, the Audrey in the video, sitting up and dangling her legs over the edge of the bed. Then she stands and walks out of frame, and I get an unobstructed view of the other woman's face.

This woman . . . I squint at the screen. She's far enough away, and shot in dark lighting, that it's not exactly easy to make out details. Do I know her? But I can't possibly. Manhattan is small, but not that small.

Unless . . . could it be someone famous. Is that why I feel she's strangely familiar?

I gasp as it hits me. This woman isn't famous. And I was right: I don't know her.

But I do know who she is.

It's the woman from my earlier Google search. From the sepia photograph.

It's Piper. Luke's first wife.

My heart thumps wildly. I search for the wall; I need support. I'm light headed, bordering on dizzy. This isn't happening, is it?

We were close, Audrey had said.

Is this what she meant by close? Were Audrey and Piper . . . a couple? I never imagined when she said she loved Piper that she meant it in any way other than platonically. But here it is, evidence that they were, at the very least, sexually involved.

I feel instant dread. This is his late wife. With his current wife. My mind reels as I try to make sense of it. What must he be thinking as he watches this? Why does he have it? Why has he held on to it all this time?

I have walked into something far more complex and private than I ever imagined. Something dark and unknowable, steeped in grief and pain and loss, as well as lust and secrets and possibly shame. I pivot and stare down the dark hallway, reminding myself that Luke hasn't seen me yet. I still have a chance to quietly leave the scene. To return to their warm bed, and Audrey, and sleep this off. He'd never know I saw this, would be none the wiser.

But you have seen it, Sarah.

So what? It's not a crime to have sex or to record a sex tape. Not if you're two consenting adults and it's for your own private use. But I'm suddenly aware of how strange and fundamentally not right this is. Me standing here, in the dead of night, watching Luke watch this. If Luke were to turn around . . . I'd be the one catching him, wouldn't I? Not the other way around? And yet, that thought doesn't comfort me. This is his home. His wife. His life. I'm a guest here, a tenuous one at that.

Go. Go, go!

But I can't, not yet. Because Audrey's returned, in the video, and I'm too desperately curious to leave now, not until I've seen what it is she's holding in her hands. I'm mesmerized as she leans over Piper, who stretches up her arms. I see it now clearly, what she's holding; it's a length of rope. With it, she proceeds to tie Piper's wrists to the bedposts. I'd be the last to judge anyone's sexual fantasies; heck, I used to wish Adam had any fantasies! But I'm quite, quite sure I was never supposed to see this. Audrey would not willingly show me this video. I am certain. And that brings on an overwhelming feeling in my gut. Of guilt.

I have to get out of here. I can't unsee what I've seen, can't unknow what I know; it's too late for that. The image of Piper tied to the bed is going to be forever imprinted on my brain; there's no going back.

I make a move to turn around and head back down the hall, shifting my bare feet. But as I do, the floor creaks.

Fuck!

Luke turns, swiveling in the desk chair.

He's heard me. And now, it's clear, in spite of the dark: he's seen me too.

He slams the laptop shut, then turns back, locking his eyes on mine.

Then he smiles.

"You're up," he says, leaning back in his chair and slinging his bare feet up on the desk. Lounging, like he has nothing to be concerned about. Does he know I saw it? Can I pretend I just walked up, and it will all be fine?

"Got up to make tea, then saw your light on," I admit, shuffling my stance. "I couldn't sleep. Ever since Eli, I can't, really, ever. Insomnia. It's a whole thing."

Luke focuses his eyes on me, his smile slipping.

"I can't imagine," he says softly.

"No," I tell him. "And you wouldn't want to. So don't."

It occurs to me now, as I stand here in the darkened hallway, making idle chitchat about my dead son with this married man I've been sleeping with, that I don't know him at all. Who is Luke, really?

I open my mouth to say something. To confess all to him: I saw the video. It's on the tip of my lips, poised to tumble out.

"We weren't expecting you to come back," Luke says. "We thought for sure we were over."

Something about his tone sends goose bumps up and down my arms. It's cold in the hallway. It's November, after all. I'm wearing next to nothing, a thin tee and Audrey's scanty shorts.

"Did you want us to be over?" I finally work up the nerve to ask.

"No," Luke says. "I didn't. I don't. But you can't keep doing this, you know."

"Doing what?"

"Showing up like you did, at events. With people we know."

This is about tonight. About the fundraiser, which was at Audrey's best friend's home. It was risky to show up there, unannounced. I was focused on myself, on how I'd feel seeing them again. I hadn't considered how they'd feel. I was playing with fire when I showed up there, infiltrating their precious inner circle . . . wasn't I?

"Audrey worries about what people think," Luke says, carefully choosing his words. "Understandably so. Her job depends on it. I can't help but remember something she said, on our first night together."

I don't answer. A lot of things were said. Which one is he referring to?

"'Don't lie to us,'" Luke reminds me. "Ever."

Fuck.

It was one rule out of a few, and I'd broken it before the pact was even cemented.

Now I'm breaking it again. I saw the video, I want to tell him. Why were you watching it? What does it mean?

"I—I'm going home," I say, my cheeks burning with shame. I can't bring myself to tell the truth, no matter how much I know I should. "I have to get up early."

Another lie. A glaring one; Luke knows I have nowhere to be. No job, no child, barely a marriage.

"You sure? It's late."

I nod, feeling his gaze on me as I begin to back down the hall, my body as tense as a stretched rubber band. In the safety of the living room, away from his watchful eyes, I scoop up my bag, coat, and gold silk dress, which is lying on the living room floor in a puddle. I don't remember when I took that off; I was probably wasted.

Heart pounding, I inch toward the front door. Audrey is asleep; I won't wake her, not now. I rip off the T-shirt and shorts and slip on the dress and my long wool coat; I don't want to leave any of my possessions in this house, abandoned. I have a primal urge to erase all evidence that I was here.

No one's done anything wrong, I remind myself. This is all confusing and upsetting and jarring, but nothing appalling or disgraceful has happened here. Nothing illegal or particularly shocking, and certainly nothing criminal. I saw Luke watch a video. That's all.

But if that's true, then why do I feel like I've been punched in the gut?

You know why, Sarah.

It's not the existence of the video that disturbs me. It's Luke's reaction. On the surface, he was friendly enough, wasn't he? Our conversation was even pleasant. But things took a turn. He reminded me that our entire relationship is predicated on a lie. He knows it, Audrey knows it, and I know it. From the very beginning, I've kept a part of myself so hidden and cordoned off. How does one ever recover from that? Do they trust me? Will they ever?

And can I trust them?

I have never considered Luke my friend. We've been using each other. Drawn together in our own individual and fucked-up ways, we entered into an arrangement that I'm sure could be categorized as emotionally risky, from every vantage point.

I didn't care, initially. I did, and still do, have nothing left to lose.

I turn my phone back on to hail a Lyft, noting one text from Adam hours ago, asking me to check in. My driver arrives, and I climb into the back seat of a black BMW. But as I race across the park, through the abandoned New York City streets, to my home, it dawns on me that this feels different, now. I wasn't able to characterize it in the moment; I was too overwhelmed by the video, too guilt ridden to see it. But now I do see it, clearly.

Luke's words tonight sounded suspiciously like a warning. Don't lie to us. Ever.

For the first time since I met Luke and Audrey, I must admit. I'm afraid.

PART FIVE

Chapter 29
AUDREY SINGER

This isn't my first rodeo, is what I'm thinking as I drag my hungover limbs out of bed. It's 6:30 a.m., and Cal is calling to me from his room to get him dressed. Headache or not, I must confront my weekend, post-Easton gala. Post . . . whatever you want to call what happened last night. Most of it's a blur of current and potential Easton parents vying for my attention. Lavish outfits and champagne poured freely from $800 bottles. Now the bed is cold and empty. Sarah was here . . . I remember that. She has likely gone home, and Luke is probably up working. He's never hungover, or if he has been, he hides it well.

Luke is, in fact, nowhere to be found. I'm cooking eggs when Hazel walks in the front door from her sleepover at Winslow's.

"It's seven a.m.," I say, glancing at the microwave clock. "I didn't know you could go outside at this time on a Saturday without melting."

My daughter throws me a glare.

"How was it?" I ask, handing her a plate of scrambled eggs as she plops down at the kitchen island next to Cal, who's gobbling Cheerios. I don't let on that I'm hoping for some tidbit on Chippie, since it's been more days than we've ever gone without speaking. All my doing, but still. I miss her.

Hazel stares down at the plate. "I'm plant based now, Mom. Or have you forgotten everything I summarized for you about the Netflix documentaries I binged while I was locked in my room?"

I grounded Hazel after the cheating episode. What I did not count on was her becoming vegan in the process.

"Chippie's mom remembered," Hazel says, eyeing the eggs with disgust. "She made us acai bowls."

Now it's my turn to glare. "She made them?"

Hazel pouts. "Fine, asked her chef to make them, same thing. And we ordered tofu burritos for dinner. Her idea. Anyway, I'm not hungry." Hazel pushes the plate away, and I wonder whether Chippie's taken a special interest in Hazel's new diet merely to send me some kind of passive-aggressive message: that she is paying better attention to my daughter than I am.

"Can I have your eggs?" Cal's leaning over his sister's plate, eyeing them.

"Sure," she says, ruffling his hair. "But you know they're dead baby chickens, right?"

"Hazel," I warn her, but Cal just laughs, thinking she's joking, and scoops up a bite from her fork.

My phone dings from beside me on the counter. I reach for it. Sarah.

We need to talk.

I text furiously back.

Now's not a good time can it wait until Monday?

Sarah responds, almost immediately.

No. It can't.

I scan through the recesses of my brain to try and remember what happened last night. Sarah showed up, unannounced, at Chippie's brownstone. That gold dress, which, I had to admit, was flattering on her increasingly thinner frame. That awful bitch Lauren; God, how did that woman have the balls to stand there and act like Eli's death was triggering, for her? It disgusted me, and I make a mental note to strike Lauren's daughter, Beatrice, from the Easton applicant pool. Harsh, I know; it isn't the five-year-old's fault her mother doesn't know when to let sleeping dogs lie. I'd wanted to slap Lauren myself, had felt a physical pang in my chest as she stood there, taking the moral high ground. And after, when I found Sarah upstairs, seeming so lost, I was surprised to find myself kissing her, wanting to be close to her. Feeling I could help ease her pain, somehow. I don't love this woman, am not sure how much I'd even miss her were she gone. Still, she's become, in a few short weeks, like that new pair of socks you've tried on and have decided to order in bulk. Comfortable. Reliable. Even with all her issues: her grief, the way she chatters uncontrollably and seems to have no sense of self-awareness . . . she is easy to be around. On top of that, she makes Luke happy. An alarm goes off in my head: What about you, Audrey? What makes you happy? But I ignore it. Like I said, this isn't my first rodeo.

But Piper and I, and Luke. We were happy once too.

That's when the memory crashes onto me like a crashing surf wave. Like hard drugs to a willing vein. We were lying in bed, Sarah and me. It was the middle of last night. Sarah circled her fingernail on the skin of my arm; it felt good.

She asked about Piper.

She asked about Piper!

There is smoke coming from the pan; I've forgotten to switch off the burner. I turn the knob, racking my brain, grasping to remember if I explained it all effectively away. If I satisfied Sarah's curiosity enough for her to let the whole thing go.

Sarah can never know. Luke and I agreed on this point, years ago, after her death. Our past was sealed shut, locked in a box, our business, no one else's. Piper had died, and we were wrecked. That's all anyone ever needed to know about the situation.

If Sarah starts asking questions . . .

I turn on PBS Kids for Cal and step into the shower, turning up the heat on the dial. Hotter. Hotter still. I need to wake myself up, to bring clarity to my brain. Hazel can watch cartoons with Cal while I get my head on straight.

If Sarah starts prying. Pushing buttons not meant to be pushed . . . then she might realize. She might catch on to the fact that she isn't the first.

I was the first.

I scrub every inch of my body with a loofah, working to erase the memories. Memories of how I began working for Piper when Hazel was in kindergarten. I'd snagged a partial scholarship for her—divorced single mom, with a dad who was struggling to get his architecture business off the ground. The funds didn't even cover a quarter of Easton's tuition, not to mention extras, like acceptable clothes. The truth is that I wasn't sure I'd be able to keep her there, not on the salary I was making in my HR job. When the assistant admissions position became available, reporting directly to Piper, I jumped on it. It paid even less than I was making but came with a shining benefit: 80 percent of my child's tuition, covered. Guaranteed until she graduated from high school.

I was all in.

Piper and I hit it off immediately, from my first interview, and I lay in bed every night after she hired me thanking the universe for gifting me this golden opportunity. As long as I kept my job, then Hazel would be set, and she would be able to stay. I would do this job for twelve more years and love every minute of it, and I'd never give anyone cause to doubt me, or, God forbid, fire me. This job, with its average pay and little autonomy, meant everything to me. The job and I were meant to be. No one cared about Easton more than I did. No one needed this like I did. I resolved to make Piper love me so much that she'd never let me go.

I didn't mean it in the literal sense.

But we were a good team from the outset. Piper reminded me of Chippie. Not nearly as privileged but in a neighboring stratosphere; she seemed to inhabit the world of Easton with an ease that I admired and envied. She was staff, but she belonged. Our working relationship started off entirely professionally. We were cordial and well suited to teamwork. I was type A; she was an Enneagram 3. We were a well-oiled duo within three months of working together, and even Babs, who was one notch above me, one notch below Piper on the Easton admissions hierarchy, seemed to approve of me. In part because I kept the reality of my life under the radar, the fact that I was bitterly single after Samuel had unceremoniously dumped me. The fact that I rented a small junior one-bedroom in Brooklyn and subwayed in every morning, a forty-five-minute commute, with Hazel, who learned to read on the A train. I became adept at hiding who I was, with pristine secondhand clothes from Poshmark and subtle tricks to ensure I looked and behaved every inch the part of an Easton mom.

It was a minor miracle I'd gotten Hazel into Easton in the first place. I think my essay is what did it; Piper told me later that she'd been moved by my ode to Easton, my recollection of what it had been like as a scholarship student there, myself, decades prior. It was an easy assignment. The words had flowed out of me in one sitting: How the school had become a foundational part of my very self. How I had befriended current donor and legacy Caroline "Chippie" Crane at the lunch table, or, rather, how she had befriended me: the girl with the scuffed shoes and an alcoholic mother, the girl who had nothing Chippie had and coveted it all. When Chippie graced me with her friendship, I instantly flourished. Girls wanted to be friends with me. Everyone wanted to date me. Chippie seemed to like that I came from nothing, and though we never discussed it, I had a suspicion that she initially intended to use it against me. To manipulate the vulnerable girl that I was. She never ended up doing that. Good thing, because, at the time, I would have withstood any abuse to stand in her shadow, reaping the benefits of being best friends with a Crane.

Hazel must have that future, I wrote in the essay. Easton was in my blood, and it would be in my daughter's too. Looking back, I can acknowledge how similar I sounded to Sarah, in those first, pleading emails she sent me. It's why I responded to her. It's why they landed. Minus the dead son, she is the old me. The one who longed to be a part of Easton so badly that I would have done anything. Anything.

In those early days of working together, Piper rarely spoke about her husband. I knew she was married, no kids. She wasn't sure she wanted them. When I met Luke that evening at the Press Lounge, when he was photographing the event as a favor to his wife, I had no idea who he was. Who he belonged to.

Our meeting was one of those aha moments, when you realize that your life up until that point has been bland and joyless: a duller version of what it could be. Samuel had extinguished my spark. Luke offered to reignite it.

But when Piper walked over, later that night, and draped her arm around his waist, and I put two and two together—this man is my boss's husband—I realized I'd been too quick to think I could have a happy ending. I had no business hoping for that. Samuel had reminded me that marriages don't work out. He had left as swiftly as my father had left my mother and me. Hazel and I were destined to be alone, just like the woman I reluctantly call "Mom."

When Piper led me by the hand that evening, out onto the brisk Manhattan street, and kissed me—Would I come over next weekend, to their place? No strings. No pressure. No expectations—I was stunned. Stunned that she asked; stunned that I said yes. I'd never done anything like that before, had never even considered it. I'd had a string of terrible boyfriends in college and had made out with a girl once, but that was the extent of it. I'd met Samuel, and we all know how that ended up. My whole life up until that point had been about being good, and good enough. Good enough to belong at Easton. Good enough to be worthy of my father's love and Samuel's. Good enough to fit in. My skin sizzled as her warm fingers grazed my arm, and I knew in that moment that I would say yes to anything those two suggested.

And so, it began: my first rodeo. Not that night, but the next Saturday. Piper admitted to me weeks later, when the three of us were drifting to sleep, naked and splayed out on the plush carpet of their apartment, empty wine bottles littering the floor after a night of indulgence, that she and Luke had been looking for me for a while. She said no other "applicant"—we both had a good laugh at her lingo—had fit their criteria. The person had to be exceedingly discreet. Exceedingly attractive. And most importantly, she and Luke had to agree. That was the hard part, she confessed. Several acquaintances were considered, many discussions were had between them, but none ever got the dual sign-off . . . until me. According to Piper, Luke had been intrigued by me from the moment I walked into his viewfinder. He had photographs of me to prove it.

And so began our arrangement. It was breezy, and uncomplicated, the who, what, when, where, and how of it easily determined. The place was the same: the condo Luke and I live in now. I showed up at their house when I could, when Hazel was at her dad's, or when I had a sitter. We didn't have to be careful, not like we are now; there was no Cal to wander into the room, and Hazel was young enough not to ask where Mommy had been once I returned to our apartment. It was effortless, like falling in love, and off a cliff, all at once.

I assumed that at a certain point in time, the arrangement would sour, or peter out, or they would get sick of me, or me them. But they didn't. And I didn't. In fact, I felt so alive in those rendezvous that I had a hard time imagining ever letting them go. They made me feel like I belonged to something, pitiful as it sounds now. I began to rely on them, like family, not just for sex but to talk about life and my own struggles; in a way, they became my home.

Separate from how I felt about the three of us was how I felt about Luke. I loved him: that was clear. I wasn't sure how I would ever manage if they decided to toss me out like Samuel had. I needed Luke. I had a sneaking suspicion that he and I were meant to be, that if he had never met Piper five years prior, he and I would be married, with the condo, contemplating children.

Of course, I didn't tell him that till much later, after Piper was gone. And I certainly never told her. Perhaps she suspected it; now I'll never know.

I step out of the shower, grab a towel to cover my dripping body. I must talk to Luke. He alone can put me at ease. Even if Sarah suspects there is more to the story of Piper and me than she knows, and I remind myself that she knows nothing, except that we worked together . . . that is very little. Luke will know how to nip it in the bud, before she ruins us. He always knows what to do.

"I'm going back to Winslow's," Hazel calls out, and I spin, my body barely covered by my towel, to find her standing across from me with an overnight bag. "They understand me there."

I stare at her, uncomprehending.

"They what?"

"I told you I was vegan, and you willfully ignored that fact. I told you Easton is too stressful, and you grounded me. How is that going to help anything? I need a friend, Mom. Not . . . not this." Hazel grips her bag, her knuckles showing through her skin. "God! You pretend to be so enlightened, but the truth is, all you think about is how things affect you. Your perfect life. Your perfect job. Chippie said I can stay as long as I want. I just needed more clothes."

Before I can even open my mouth to stop her, she's out the door.

I sink onto my disheveled comforter, still not dressed, not sure when I will be able to lift my limbs to walk to my closet. I am losing Hazel. And Chippie is winning. I know I'm Hazel's mother and that Chippie can never take her away from me. Chippie is simply holding Hazel up where I have failed her.

I stand, letting my towel drop to the floor. Hazel needs a therapist; I have the number of one scrawled on a birthday party invitation stashed in a kitchen drawer. It's clear I don't know what to do, how to reach her. I need help. I will call the therapist on Monday, beg for her soonest appointment.

But first, Chippie.

I pick up my discarded phone and begin typing a message.

Thanks for having Hazel, can you please let me know how she is? I know I've messed up. She needs help, and so do I

But before I can finish typing, my phone dings, and I abandon the text I'm writing to check my other messages. I have nine new texts since I've been in the shower. None of them from Luke. Where is he?

I'm still wet and shivering as I read the texts, each one causing more goose bumps to emerge on my skin in quick succession. Each one from Sarah. Each one more desperate than the last.

Call me.

Where are you?

I know you're busy but it's important.

Please whatever you're doing can wait.

I know I'm not a part of your life and I know I haven't been truthful about things but this is different. You have to believe me when I say something is wrong.

I'm coming to you.

Audrey. Please, we have to talk.

We have to talk.

We have to talk.

Chapter 30
SARAH PRICE

Robert the doorman lets me into Audrey and Luke's building, no questions asked. He recognizes me from all the nights I've shown up, late, for our meetings, and he has no reason to think they haven't invited me here this time too. He buzzes me through.

I knock softly on their door two times, pulse pounding in my throat, and it opens. I was not expecting Cal.

He peers out at me, quizzically. "Are you here to see my mommy?"

I nod, heart hammering. What have I done? I am certain all visitors get announced by Robert first. This will come as a shock to her and Luke, just like my appearance at Chippie's brownstone startled them last night. Hadn't Luke specifically asked me not to do that again? But Audrey's ignored all my texts. What if I had asked Robert to buzz and she had refused to let me up? Refused to see me?

I can't think of another way.

Cal lets me in, and I feel vaguely guilty. I have now taken advantage of a five-year-old child in order to weasel my way into the Singers' home.

I remind myself I'm not doing this for me. I am thinking about one person now.

Cal leads me inside, asking if I want a snack or to see his trucks. I'm distracted, but bantering with him is easy. I'm smiling a lot and complimenting his rocket ship pajamas. It's second nature, talking to a child of this age. I haven't done it in over a year. Still, judging from how effortlessly I interact with him, it must be like riding a bike, I think with an agonizing pang. I haven't forgotten how to mother; I have simply lost the chance to practice.

"Is your mom here?" I ask him.

He nods. "I can go get her!"

He runs off, and I survey the living room. It's exactly as I left it last night in a mad rush, in the middle of the night, after . . .

I try to push the image of Luke out of my head. The way he sounded. The way he looked at me . . .

Audrey is upon me. Clad in a towel, straight from the shower. I feel a surge of something electric in my nerve endings but shake that off. I am not here for that; I'm here because I'm worried. About her. I don't matter; this is about what I saw last night. How I felt when I left. Like something was very, very wrong.

"Cal let me in," I tell her.

I see her shiver, visibly, and feel the need to reach out to her. To explain. I haven't used Cal, haven't sneaked up here to frighten her. I've come because I've been awake since I left here at 2:00 a.m., trying desperately to think of someone else to turn to. But there is no one else.

"Is Luke home?" I whisper.

"I thought he was with you," she answers, her voice tight.

"He isn't," I tell her, shaking my head.

"Cal, honey, do you want to watch another *Peppa Pig*?" As she squats down to her son's level, I'm hit with an unexpected wave of emotion watching her with him in this way, still in her towel, unvarnished, her truest self: This is motherhood, I think. This is Audrey as a mother.

She is Cal's whole world. Just like I was Eli's, and he mine. If there is any scenario in which Luke might be hiding something from her, any chance he is a threat of some kind . . .

Cal trots off to the TV, and Audrey straightens up, her eyes narrowed.

"Can I get dressed, first? Or is this so urgent I have to stand here in my towel?" She perches a defensive hand on her hip. "Come on. You can talk to me while I throw on some clothes."

I trail her into the bedroom, noting that the bed is still unmade. I was lying there last night, I remind myself. Not six hours ago. On those sheets. Tangled in Luke and Audrey. And yet, everything feels different now.

While she flings off her towel and I pretend I can't see her naked form as she slips on panties and rifles through her drawer for a slouchy sweater, I tell her why I'm here.

"I couldn't say this in a text," I explain. "What if he saw it?"

Audrey stops midwiggle from sliding her hips into a pair of jeans and stares at me. "Who? What if who saw what?"

"Luke. Thank goodness he's not here. Audrey, last night. It was two a.m., or two thirty, I don't remember. I was making tea. The light was on in Luke's office, and . . . and I walked over to see what he was doing up. I know it wasn't my business . . ."

"Just tell me what he was doing up."

"He was watching a video." I turn to make sure the door has completely shut behind us. I don't want to risk Cal overhearing. "It was of you and another woman." I don't say the word "sex"; it's clear what I mean. "And yes, I looked. I know it's fucked up. I know I shouldn't have. I'm human, okay?" I have no good explanation for why I didn't leave. I will have to hope she understands. "At first, I didn't know who the other woman was, but then, it hit me. That photograph I'd seen in the cabinet. The video was of you . . . and Piper."

Audrey pulls her sweater down. I feel relieved; talking to her half-naked was distracting. Now she stands in front of me, seeming to barely breathe as she takes in what I've just said.

"There isn't a video." She says it resolutely, as though by saying it, she can will it to be true.

"I saw it," I insist. "Do you honestly think I'd make this up? Luke was watching it. I don't know why. Why he had it? Why he wanted to look at it? It was the anniversary of her death," I say, remembering that tidbit of information I'd learned from the Easton mom as I'd waited in line for the bathroom. That feels like it was years ago, when it had been a mere ten hours prior. How can that be? "I suppose he wanted to see her again?" I venture, though it sounds strange coming out of my mouth. Why would Luke want to remember his deceased wife by watching that video, of all things?

Audrey is standing very still, not speaking; it's so unlike her that it sends chills up my arms and legs.

I'm afraid to ask, but I must. "Did you know Luke had a video like that saved? Where, how did he get it? Had he seen it before, before last night?"

"Of course he'd seen it," she finally answers. "He's the one who filmed it."

Chapter 31
AUDREY SINGER

Fuck. She has seen it.

The video that Luke swore he erased. That we erased, together.

It was supposed to have been expunged from the cloud, from Dropbox, from wherever the fuck else it was stored, where he had stored it. After Piper died, we needed a clean slate. It was not safe to have any connection between the three of us recorded. Not because we had done anything wrong but because the court of public opinion doesn't care about right and wrong. It never has.

Why does Luke still have it? It's all I can think as Sarah prattles on, explaining how she shouldn't have stood there watching and knows it was a weak thing to do, and she hopes I can forgive her.

I don't care about forgiving her. What I need to do, now, is damage control.

I could kill my husband. He alone is responsible for this, after all. Keeping that video. Watching it while Sarah was in the house. No doubt, he did have a hankering to see it on the anniversary of Piper's death. Men are like that. Sentimental in the most bizarre ways. I could strangle the fucker.

I do a quick calculation in my head. How to best ensure that Sarah walks out of here and does not keep digging into business that is decidedly not hers.

"You are not special," I tell her, feeling the words sting on my lips because I know they sound cruel; I mean them to be.

Her eyes glaze over. "I didn't think I was," she says quietly. "But thanks for the acute reminder."

I walk to the door, peek out. Cal is parked in front of *Peppa Pig*. Hazel is gone. Fuck! And my text to Chippie hasn't been sent! But at least I can put out this fire, first, and troubleshoot my troubled daughter later.

I shut the door again, making sure it clicks. Then I turn to face her. She looks dazzling in the morning light, the way it reflects off her copper hair. This is the last time she's going to be here. Things are going to have to come to an abrupt end. She cannot be in our lives anymore. She's too much of a liability. She has seen too much. We are over. I feel a pang of sadness wash over me, but it's superseded by practicality. Think of Cal. Think of Hazel, I scold myself.

"You aren't special because we've been here before, Luke and I. When he was married to Piper . . . they invited me in," I say, feeling my voice hitch. "I was you, in another lifetime. I was the third wheel to their twosome. And the three of us, we were a thing . . . for a while. Until she died, and then . . . and then everything I told you last night was true. Luke and I realized we still needed each other. We came together in our grief. God, did you really not suspect?" I'm not giving her any chance to answer me, I'm so caught up in what I'm saying. So desperate to get this off my chest. I don't love Sarah, but some part of me wants her to understand the role I've played in all this. "Did you think I'd never done this before? How many women would just say 'Okay, sure, babe. I will disrupt our marriage by letting this rando into our bed'? Of course we'd done it before."

"I guess I never thought about it," Sarah admits. "I guess I thought . . ."

"You were special," I remind her yet again. "But the truth is that Luke doesn't believe in monogamy. Never has. Piper wasn't a fan either. Her other relationships, her monogamous ones, hadn't worked out. She felt a traditional marriage set her up for failure, and she didn't want that pressure again. Luke felt the same way. Opening things up like this gave them both what they wanted. Less pressure to be everything to each other. When he and I got married, I knew more than anyone how Luke saw things. I represented it. In the flesh. I was the literal embodiment of everything he believed, and didn't believe! I wasn't an idiot. I knew the time would come when he would want more. When he would seek it—you—out. I married him knowing that. I married him okay with that; I had to be, if I wanted him." I shrug, hoping that laying this all out for Sarah will make her see. See me, see him, see all of it. She can't possibly judge me, not after cheating on her own spouse. Luke and I, we have been nothing but honest with each other, and with her.

"I thought that video had been erased," I explain. "But I guess Luke kept a copy somewhere. It doesn't matter now, does it? All that matters is that you saw it."

Sarah looks like she's trying to work all this out. Like I'm speaking a language she has no knowledge of, and she's trying and failing to translate. Catch up!

"I need one thing from you," I tell her. Please, God, make this work. It has to work. "I need you to promise you will leave and never tell a soul about this. About Luke, and Piper, and me. I could be fired. I would be. I'm certain of it. I know it wasn't a crime. That doesn't mean any of my colleagues or a single person at Easton would understand. Piper died the night that video was filmed," I say, fighting tears that I wish would stop; they won't help me, not now. "It was a tragic fucking nightmare, and they would misinterpret it. Easton people are polished. They are perfect. They would never understand us, if they knew. They would never even try to understand the choices we made. The choices you made. Would they?"

Sarah shakes her head, no, and I know I've got her. I'm saying this in a way she can't argue with. This is essential.

"You and I, we are the same. The other parents, they would cancel us. And I don't give a fuck about us! But my kids. Hazel, Cal. They are my everything. I know you understand that . . ."

"Of course I fucking understand that," Sarah whispers.

I feel it, a pang of gut-wrenching guilt. I am using motherhood—my own, and her lack thereof—to persuade her. I feel terrible about it, but this is not about me. This is about my son and daughter. They come first, full stop.

"Here is what is going to happen." I lay it out for her. Patiently. Clearly, so there can be no misunderstanding between us. "Luke and I will never breathe a word to anyone about Eli, about how you applied to Easton when he . . . when he . . ."

"Was dead," she supplies.

I wince, but I must continue. "We will never tell anyone about that. We will part ways and put all this behind us. But you have to promise me you won't tell anyone about this. Not ever."

Sarah's eyes are wet. "Of course I won't tell anyone," she answers. "I came here because I was worried about you. Do I have to say it? You know why. I'll go," she chokes, then slips out the door and is walking down the hall before I can stop her.

———

I don't know if I've done enough. She seemed to get it. But Sarah is unhinged, I remind myself. It's not her fault; her son is dead, and she has lost herself, entirely. That's also the problem. She has nothing left to lose, and it shows. She swore she wouldn't breathe a word, but the truth is, I don't trust her.

I must act. I have to.

I do the only thing I can think of. I furiously text the mom of Cal's preschool bestie. Can Cal hop over for a playdate? Sorry so last minute. This admissions season is killing me! So behind! Ugh!

In moments, she says yes, and after I've left Cal safely at her house, I hail a Lyft to Sarah's. This might not work. And if she's home, I'm fucked.

I text Luke that Cal's at a playdate and Hazel has gone to Chippie's house. Call me. Important.

Still, I get no answer from my husband. That fucking gallery. I bet he's been there since 5:00 a.m., poring over images, his perfect images.

I ring the Prices' bell.

Adam answers. Once again, he's dressed in business casual but slightly rumpled, giving the impression that he hasn't properly taken care of himself in ages. I suppose he hasn't.

"Can I come in?" I ask, feeling mild déjà vu. The last time I stood on this doorstep, I asked the same thing.

He doesn't respond but opens the door wider for me to enter.

"Is your wife home?" From what I can see of the house, it's pristine, just as it was last time. Not a book out of place, not a dirty dish in sight.

"No," Adam says. "And I don't know where she is, so don't bother asking."

"Good, then I'll be brief. Your wife has a problem."

"You think?" he asks, raising an eyebrow at me. Again, he seems weary, not angry. Exhausted, not belligerent.

"It's worse than you can possibly know," I tell him. "She stalked me. Like, full-on *Single White Female*–level stalking. Buying me gifts. Following me to my nail salon. Sending me texts, sussing out where I live." I take in a breath, feeling guilty about what I'm doing but praying it works. "She had me believing Eli was alive." I hope I don't pain him too much in the process of unburdening myself. "She crashed the

Easton gala last night! Had it out with that Lauren woman, the woman from preschool who . . . who . . ."

"I know who Lauren is," Adam says.

"Sarah's been sleeping with my husband. I'm sorry to have to be the one to tell you, but surely you've noticed she doesn't come home at night. It's because they are together sometimes. I've made my peace with it, but this isn't about me. Sarah's lost it, Adam. Really and truly. I'm worried about her. About her safety. And, to be honest, yours and mine. Please—get her some help. Therapy. Medication. Something. She's saying crazy things about me. Things about me and my husband's first wife. It's all because she's jealous, because Luke told her he didn't want to leave me for her. It doesn't matter, though. I just want to make sure she's okay. I don't blame her, really. Luke is hard to resist. Most women can't. I know I couldn't."

I pause, hoping my version of this story is landing. I need him to buy it. It's still the truth, though taken slightly out of context.

Adam doesn't respond, and for a fleeting moment, I wonder what he is going to do. I wouldn't be surprised if he screamed at me. Slammed the door in my face. Or completely broke down.

He does none of those things. He looks fatigued. Like nothing I say can hurt him.

"I need you to go now," he finally says, opening the door and making it clear I am no longer welcome. And so, I do. I've said what I needed to. I hope it's enough.

Once I'm outside, on the sidewalk, I double over, feeling like I can't breathe. If Sarah talks . . . if her digging around causes anyone to start asking questions . . . she must be shut down. She must not be believed. Because if she is . . .

My entire life as I know it could implode.

One thing is absolutely certain. She cannot, she must not know what happened on the night that Piper died.

Chapter 32

SARAH PRICE

She wants me gone. That much is clear.

I don't stop to talk to Robert on my way out or look where I'm going and am almost flattened by a yellow cab as I cross the street, tears streaming, mind reeling.

I'm not special. But then, I've always known that, haven't I? It's why the events of my life have played out the way they have. It's why I'm so self-aware. Too much so. It's why everything I've done has ended in disaster and heartbreak. Why I failed Eli. It's not new. And yet, I must admit that hearing those words coming from Audrey stings, and it still does, in a particularly rapier-like way. Perhaps because I had made myself believe that she had seen, and liked, the real me.

But how could she? I almost never even showed her that side of myself. I delayed that unveiling until the inevitable moment when she discovered that the woman she'd been in a relationship with was a bombed-out shell of herself. When she learned that my son was dead, that I was nothing but a beach swept over by a tsunami, empty of visitors, littered with jagged glass and debris.

Is that it, then? Am I being tossed to Fifth Avenue, never to see or hear from Audrey and Luke Singer again?

That thought is unbearable.

In the short time I've known them, they've given my pathetic life meaning. Perhaps it's a fucked-up meaning, one that has significance only to me. What does that matter? I needed them. I needed her; I still do. I couldn't admit it to her face moments ago, that I care about her. Dare I say it? Even love her. I have a feeling she suspects it, regardless.

She has tried to buy my silence with a promise. They'll keep my secrets; I'll keep theirs.

What Audrey doesn't understand, the calculation she has made inaccurately, is that their silence is worthless. What do I care if people know Eli is gone? Can't she see that I'm already a pariah? That it isn't their approval I'm looking for, at all, but my own? It hurts that she thinks I'd tell anyone about us. About them, and Piper.

Can't she see I only care about one thing now, because it's the one thing left—protecting her? Audrey is a bright light in my otherwise dim, hazy world. I know I'm infatuated, obsessed, whatever you want to call it. I've had feelings for other women in my life, but not like this. Not with this intensity. This level of devotion. The idea that I'll never be with her again is not one I can accept.

I cross the street, this time making sure to wait for the walking man; it won't do anyone any good if I'm flattened by a bus. A blue SUV anxious to turn bears down on me, honking. I ignore it; I have the right of way. Still, the noise is oppressive, and it causes my palms to sweat. I hold my hands up to my ears to shut out the sound. But I'm shutting something else out too. A thought that invaded my brain the moment Audrey tried to shut me up.

It's the real reason I ran out of her condo, eyes streaming with tears.

All I want is to keep her safe.

But is that what she wants for me?

Or is there an uglier truth staring me in the face, just like that SUV? And how long can I keep ignoring the voice in my head that's telling me: Don't trust her?

My phone dings with a text. I whip it from my pocket as shoppers and commuters quickstep around me. They bustle to get to places that matter to them. I have no such places. Not anymore.

I look down at my screen, praying it's her. Is she asking me to come back? Does she wish I hadn't left?

It's not Audrey. It's a text from Luke.

Sarah. You there?

I tense. How to respond to him?

Yes I'm here.

I need to see u. There's a reason I saved that video. I couldn't talk about it last night . . . Look this is hard to admit. I've been protecting her all this time, but the fact is—I can't let this go on any longer.

Chills ripple up and down my spine. Let what go on? What is he talking about? This doesn't sound like the cool, casual Luke I'm used to. Or is this the Luke from last night, the one who issued that warning?

I told her I erased it. But that video is the only evidence I have of what happened that night. That awful, awful night. I love her, and so I did everything I could, but the guilt it's eating me up. I'm worried about u. Meet me at Easton in an hour, around 10, at the atrium on the roof. We need to talk in private. Please. I've been wanting to tell you for so long. Just didn't know how.

I don't dare breathe as my fingers type out the words.

Tell me what?

. . .

I watch the three little dots appear, blinking in place. I'm trembling as I wait, because I know whatever Luke has to tell me . . . I am almost certain that it will change everything.

I'm sorry to tell you this, but I can't hold it in any longer. Someone else has to know. U have to know, before—

My hands are shaking so violently I almost drop the phone.

Before what?

. . .

Audrey killed my wife.

———

I'm not an idiot; I know I should approach this situation with caution. Luke claims Audrey killed Piper. It's ludicrous, of course. After I receive that text, I stare at it, hands shaking, breath held, for a good five minutes, telling myself it's a lie. That it's insane. Categorically impossible. Which it is.

Unless it isn't.

And if it isn't . . . anyone in my shoes would connect the dots and fear for their own safety. It's why Luke claims to be warning me, isn't it? Because if Audrey killed Piper, if that's even remotely plausible, then there's only one reason she did it.

To keep Luke for herself.

Here I am, the third wheel to their idyllic marriage. If I believe there's even the slightest chance he's telling me the truth, I should be worried. More than that: I should be downright terrified.

But anyone else in my shoes wouldn't know Audrey the way I do. They wouldn't see her the way I do.

I simply can't believe she would do something like that.

Unless, of course, I'm missing something. Something foundational, something fundamental.

Would Audrey resort to murder if she were desperate enough?

I hurry toward Easton on foot. I have an hour before I'm supposed to meet Luke. It's 9:00 a.m., and he suggested 10:00. The crisp air feels good as I clip down the street, heading north from Audrey and Luke's building.

I see it all so clearly now, in a way I hadn't been able to before. Audrey was a footnote in another lifetime, a lifetime where Piper was alive. It's so strange, peeling back that layer of their history and seeing it now, without a filter: Audrey, who has always seemed so in control, so confident, was not always in charge, was she? At one point, she had more in common with me than I ever imagined.

I can't help but wonder, in a never-ending loop: What transpired behind closed doors, before, after, and during the filming of that video? Who controlled the strings? Was it Piper? Luke? Or had Audrey turned the tables somehow? Had they forced her into a position where she simply had to? If I could get my hands on that video . . . but I know, deep down, it would be a futile exercise to even try. Surely Luke has it stored under lock and key, password protected. No, my best bet is to stick to the plan. Meet him at Easton and hear him out. Find out why he'd write something so twisted and provocative. So salacious.

But what if . . . ?

I can't stop the thought from forming.

What if what he says is actually true? Could Audrey have done something like that? Something so vicious and psychopathic? I shake the thought off as I tackle a busy crosswalk, dodging an aggressive mom with a stroller and business folks rushing by me in heels and expensive suits. It's Saturday morning, but they all look like they have somewhere important to be. For a moment, I'm wistful; that used to be me.

I never responded directly to Luke's text, that text. I agreed to meet, refraining from further comment, and focused on the logistics. How would we get into the building? Would we be alone at the school? Luke assured me that we would; according to him, the school calendar had no events planned for today. Easton would be empty.

Naturally, I'm wary as I approach the school's intersection. I check my phone, hoping for a text from Adam. He was asleep, of course, when I got home at 3:00 a.m., and I left this morning before he got up. I've told him via text where I'm going, even dropping him a pin, and I've dashed out a quick message explaining that I'm worried about Audrey and will text him if I need him.

There's been no response.

No texts from him after the one he sent last night, at 10:00 p.m., before going to bed. I know he's seen my most recent messages. It's the first thing he does, without fail, every morning: switch his phone off "Do not disturb" and take stock of the world, responding to friends and colleagues, his college WhatsApp group, while he drinks his coffee.

Which can only mean one thing. He is actively choosing to ignore my texts, and me. The thought of his silence sends a weight from my heart to my stomach. Adam always responds to me; even in our worst days, our nightmare days, he never wavered. Does this mean he is finally through with me? Have I pushed him, at last, too far?

And another, far more urgent fear creeps in: I was counting on him being a text away. Because as much as I try, I can't shake the memory of the look Luke gave me last night. It's burned onto my brain.

I reach the school building and take in a short breath at the sight of it. It's as majestic as always, standing guard on the corner with a curious mix of rigor and whimsy that pulls at my heartstrings. How can

Easton feel like coming home, when I know my son will never cross the threshold?

I pass through the unlocked gate and walk around to one of the side doors as Luke instructed me. I pull the iron handle; it's heavy, but it opens. Luke must have unlocked it, which means he's upstairs, waiting. For a moment, I see his face, from last night, looming large in my mind: the face of a man who caught me watching something forbidden. I shake off a creeping feeling of dread and remind myself that the Luke from the gallery—the Luke I slept with there, when we were as alone as two people can be in New York City—was gentle. And generous. Aloof? Yes. But also, kind. He had good reason to be short with me when I saw that video. Maybe I've misjudged the way he spoke to me. Maybe it was a warning, but of another nature. If he really thinks Audrey did this . . .

But no. She can't have. That kind of accusation, it's . . . preposterous! He must know this. He must know that in sending that text, he would throw me completely off balance.

Is that what he intended? Was that accusation merely a strategy of some sort, to get me to drop everything and come here? And what if . . . ? Is it possible it wasn't just Audrey who wanted Luke to herself, but the two of them were conspiring together, harboring some kind of twisted agenda? Are they both complicit in Piper's death? And was it simply that, a death—or, hard as it is to stomach, an actual murder? But then again, my imagination is probably running wild, and I should take Luke's text at face value because he is just trying to help me. If that's the case, then can I trust he has reason to accuse his own wife of something so egregious? And if I do trust him, what does that mean for Audrey . . . and for me?

These thoughts swarm my brain like vicious wasps as I tackle the steps two by two up to the rooftop atrium. I reach the final flight, and in moments I'm up to the top, where I grab the handle of the door to the roof, my heart galloping in my throat.

I hesitate on the landing. Once I open the door fully, there will be no going back. I will hear Luke's side of things. He may very well show me something I am not expecting to see—the rest of that video, or something even more damning—and if he does, there is a chance that everything I believe will fall to pieces, crumbling into dust, like an ancient city wall at my feet.

I should turn around. I should not be doing this. It's the familiar, persistent refrain of these last several months. Don't do it, turn back, stop this before you hurt Adam. Stop this before you hurt Audrey. Or yourself.

But the words are fruitless, because I have already made up my mind. I will see this through. For Audrey. For me. It's imperative that I know the truth.

I'm on the roof now, making my way through a perfectly mani-cured atrium of benches, pathways, and verdant plants. Easton employs two full-time landscapers; it's easy to see why. Even with winter at our heels, this garden is lush and bursting with delicate blooms. I wind my way to the center of the atrium, aware of the city laid out before me, just beyond the edge: other Upper East Side rooftops, boasting community gardens and lounge furniture, a few rooftop pools. I don't dare make my way to the edge to glance over it; I don't need the height to throw me off balance. I'm nervous enough.

Where is he?

I stop short in front of an archway covered in vines. Luke isn't here. But someone else is.

Chapter 33

AUDREY SINGER

Piper Singer died of a heart attack.

I know why Luke told Sarah it was cancer; no one asks questions about cancer. It's identifiably tragic. A heart attack at thirty-four begs a lot of questions. Questions he didn't want to have to answer, because answering them would mean having to explain. What Piper was doing when it happened. Who found her. Where she was. Why we were all there. Together.

The answers have haunted me ever since that night. Not because I assign blame. I know what happened was a freak occurrence. Piper had an undiagnosed heart condition. No one could have known about it.

Still, I've asked myself this question over and over, ever since that night seven years ago: If I hadn't passed out at 11:00 p.m. If I hadn't been so drunk, asleep on the living room sofa, when Piper went into cardiac arrest. If Luke hadn't been in the shower . . . if he'd come back into the room five minutes sooner . . .

I try to shut down this line of thinking, and every time, I fail. The thought comes my way, anyway, racing at me headfirst with the force of a Mack truck.

Would Piper still be alive?

I glance down at my phone, at the text thread between Luke and me, his last message confirming that he'd be here. At 10:00 a.m. See you soon.

So where is he? And why is Sarah here now, on the roof? It makes no sense that she has come. I told her we were over, made it clear we could no longer continue. That we must part ways and keep each other's secrets.

A shiver of fear courses through me. Sarah stalked me once. She could do it again. How could I have been so naive as to believe she would simply . . . go?

"How . . ." She looks past me, then turns and scans the roof deck. "Where is he? Where's Luke?"

I stare at her, not comprehending. "Luke was meeting me here. How the fuck did you know that? Are you hacking into my texts? Have you been watching me somehow?"

"Watching you? How?" Sarah strides past me now, still looking around. It must all be an act, because she fucking followed me here. She must have.

"Stop lying," I implore her. My head is pounding, and all I can think is that I'm never drinking that much again. Luke should be here. We were supposed to meet here, in private, to figure this out, together. And now I have to manage Sarah all on my own.

"I'm not lying! I swear to you." She turns to face me, and even now, she looks like the Sarah I've gotten to know these last few months. Sad, frayed at the edges. Not threatening. Not dangerous. Yet something is niggling at the corners of my mind, telling me this isn't right. Nothing is right. It may never be again.

"Luke texted me to meet him here." She whips out her phone. "He said he needed to talk to me. Alone."

She's about to walk up to show me her phone screen, but I wave her off. I don't need to see that text. I'm several steps ahead of her. I know why Luke must have set this up. He wants me to fix this, somehow. To make sure Sarah never bothers us again. Problem is, I don't know how.

I pace, turning away from her, my wheels turning. I've already asked her to keep our secret. Begged her. Think, Audrey. Think. I spin, facing her. I must consider this from her perspective. I must consider what she wants. If Luke and I are simply a fling to Sarah, a distraction from her infinite grief, it makes no sense that she can't just let us be . . . unless.

"You don't love me," I tell her. She takes in a breath that's more like a gasp, then inches back from me. I've got her now. I've pinpointed the reason she won't let me, this, go. "You don't even know me, Sarah! Look, I'm flattered. And I have to admit, as I've gotten to know you more, we've really had quite the ball together, but . . ."

"Oh, a ball. I see. But you're done with me now?"

"It's not that!" I'm so frustrated I could scream. "I never meant for this to be more than a one-off! Don't you get that? I love my husband. We're happy together. You were an itch he had to scratch. That's all."

"And you were that same itch," Sarah says, her voice even. Commanding. It seems like she's gaining confidence with every passing moment. Weak, self-doubting Sarah has left the building. "You told me yourself. Luke and Piper were happy. And then . . . and then what, Audrey? What happened to her?"

"She died," I snap, trying to remain calm. I must be careful not to piss her off; that is critical. But it's hard to control the hot spring of emotion bubbling inside me. "Suddenly, of a heart attack."

"Luke claims otherwise."

The world goes sideways. No. He would never.

"You're mistaken," I tell her. "Piper died after some mildly aggressive sex, some kinky sex, but it was nothing, nothing that would have killed a perfectly healthy woman. She had a heart defect she wasn't aware of. None of us knew, until after she died. It was an accident."

"An accident you two must have covered up somehow," Sarah considers. "Or you wouldn't be so secretive about it now."

"I told you that too. Yes, we hid what we were doing. We couldn't tell anyone. We had our reputations to consider."

"Reputations that are more important than a woman's life?" Sarah's looking at me now with something akin to disgust, and even though I don't want to admit it, it stings. "Reputations that are more important than the truth?"

"You're twisting my words," I hiss at her. I turn my back to her and begin to walk. Toward the edge of the roof, where all of Manhattan glows underneath us in the misty morning light. "What does it matter if we told the police we'd been together that night, all three of us? It wouldn't have changed anything! She died. Her heart gave out."

"But you lied. To the police."

I stare out at the city, my city, the one that has both eaten me alive and fulfilled my wildest dreams. "That isn't what I said."

"But it's what you meant. Isn't it?"

I won't respond to that. I can't. Where the fuck is Luke?

I am at my wits' end now. If Luke is MIA, if he's left me to do the dirty work, then I have no choice. I must end this thing between us for good. It's the only way.

Chapter 34

SARAH PRICE

I can't bring myself to utter the words out loud: Luke says you killed her.

If it's true, what then? She will deny it.

And if it's not? Would she even believe me? I could show her the text, but she'll either claim I doctored it or refuse to talk to me about it at all. Because the truth is she is still defending what she did with Luke. I am convinced they have lied about what really happened to Piper.

"What happened to her, Audrey?" I am moving toward her now, closing the gap between us. She must not avoid my questions. She must not brush me aside, wave me off; not now. "How did Piper die? And if you say one more time it was nothing—"

"It was—"

"I'm calling bullshit on that." I feel myself steadying, and I'm not used to it; where is this boldness coming from? But I know, deep down: it's because I have nothing left to lose. The Sarah who exists post-Eli can do whatever she wants. Say whatever she wants. I have lived the worst-possible outcome. Nothing can truly hurt me anymore. "Something happened that you aren't telling me, and it's either because you're protecting Luke or he's protecting you. For God's sake, Audrey!

Who cares about your perfect life? It means nothing, don't you see that? Because when it's all taken away, in the blink of an eye . . ."

"That's your story," Audrey answers me, finally spinning to face me. "Not mine."

"No, your children are alive," I remind her. "It's ironic, isn't it? How much I should resent you for that? Despise you for that? I don't, for the record. But I know things you don't. Have seen things you'll hopefully never see: Your life falling apart. Everything you care about, whisked away. You still have your life, Audrey. You still have your kids, your marriage. Do you think your reputation even matters to those vultures you call friends? Do you think they'd even miss you if you were gone?"

A hand clasps my arm. She's spinning me toward her, her fingers digging into my flesh, her eyes on fire. We are centimeters from the wall, all that's between us and a four-story fall. I whip my face away from hers and catch a glimpse behind me of the street below. I've never liked heights.

"You know nothing about my life," Audrey breathes, her fingernails prodding into my forearm so hard I'm certain she'll leave a mark. "I bet you grew up with a Tiffany rattle in your bassinet. A silver spoon in your mouth. Nannies and Hamptons homes and a trust fund at your fingertips. I didn't."

I yank my arm away from her grasp, shaking her hand off me.

"You know nothing about my childhood. Because you've never bothered to ask. But even if what you said were true, money doesn't solve everything." I'm pinned between her and the concrete wall. Her eyes look unfocused now, and even as I remind myself this is the Audrey I fell for, I haven't ever seen her like this. I don't like it. I don't like being afraid of her.

"Oh, God, that old pathetic cliché! Of course money solves problems. When you've had to scrape your way to every single success you've ever had in your life. When your mother's an alcoholic and your dad abandoned both of you when you were four, never to pay child support again. When you've worked harder than everyone else. Sacrificed more than everyone else. But I wouldn't expect you to understand."

I feel the constriction in my throat, the wall pressing into my back. I'm frozen to the spot, unable to move, not because I really think she will strike me—or worse, push me. Would she push me? Don't look behind you, Sarah. The height, suddenly, feels dizzying.

"I do know you," I say. "We aren't that different, you and I. We're mothers who'd do anything for our children." But even as I'm saying it, I don't know how much I believe it. Not anymore.

Audrey loves Cal and Hazel; I fully believe that. She and I probably would have had a lot in common, once. Before Eli died. The woman I used to be, that doting mother, lived in Audrey's world. I see it all now, so clearly. That's the woman who could have fit in at Easton, who would have relished being a part of the PTA and the moms' groups and toting snacks to soccer games. But now . . . now I am not like them. Not like her. I can't be, not ever again.

"I was looking for something that day I met you. Easton. A lost dream. Something alive and hopeful and aspirational. You embodied that for me." I'm shaking. It's raining hard, now. The rain feels welcome, like it's washing away my sins. "But I'm done trying to prove myself to you. Done trying to immerse myself in you. Done expecting you to save me, when we both know you can't." It's pouring sheets, and we're soaked to the bone. Impulsively, I take one teeny step toward her, closing the gap between us, and grab her drenched face in my hands. I kiss her on the lips, hard, knowing this might be the last time I ever do this, knowing it should be. They are as soft and inviting as ever, even slick with freezing rain. Our teeth clang, and it's awkward and uncoordinated, but she's kissing me back. The Sarah of one hour ago, ten hours ago, would have interpreted this hopefully. But This Sarah knows; it was always an illusion. I can't linger. I must not. I wrench myself away from her.

I turn in the direction of the stairs. It's all so crystal clear. Audrey and I are over; we have to be. The love I feel for her I know now is an obsession. Seen from this angle, it looks twisted, and, in hindsight, woefully misguided. I may never know if it was love at all. That's not important now.

I'm running to the exit. I can't look back or I'll cave. Audrey needs me, doesn't she? But she doesn't want me. She never has. I must move on. I must let her go.

I shove open the door to the stairwell, run through it, and hear it slam behind me.

Inside, out of the rain, I pant from the exertion, from the desire coursing through my body. It physically hurts to have walked away from her, but I know it will hurt more to keep doing this to myself. Not when she doesn't want me.

Is this how Adam feels?

I shake my coat out and pull my phone from my pocket, thinking one thing now: I must talk to my husband. What have I done to him, all these months? How could I have betrayed him like this, left him hanging, and wondering, and alone in our bed, every night, with hardly so much as a note to let him know that I was okay, and not off dead in a ditch somewhere—and for what? A woman who doesn't love me? Who never has? I know what I have done. I have been so focused on obliteration, on refusing to face the life that looms ahead of me, of us, without our son.

Have I obliterated my marriage in the process?

I type out a text to him with wet fingers and stumble down the stairs. Three flights to go, and I will storm out of this place, directly into the torrential rain, and go tell him myself. I hope it's not too late.

The soles of my sneakers are slick from the rain, and I trip, or slip, on a concrete step. As I do, my phone flies from my hands, shattering onto the landing far below me, the crash reverberating throughout the stairwell.

I probably am too late. All the "I'm sorrys" in the world won't matter, not after what I've done. And I don't just mean the cheating. It's the taking him for granted that has likely hurt him the most. Who in Adam's shoes would even hear me out, now, after the way I've treated him? After all I've done?

I race down to retrieve my phone, tears marring my vision as a specific memory of Adam floods my mind. It was weeks after Eli's death. My days were filled entirely with nothing. Eli's funeral was over, the arrangements made, the last flowers had drooped and shriveled and the final food delivery was carefully stored in the freezer or thrown away.

Adam insisted we go for a walk. I resisted, at first, but eventually capitulated. It's not as though I had any good argument as to why I couldn't leave the house, and fighting with him didn't seem worth the trouble.

We covered the city that day, walking numbly around the reservoir. Through the park. By Rockefeller Center and past Bloomingdale's and a hundred other spots that populated the New York City I knew and loved when Eli was alive. Adam said nothing to me that whole time. And when we were finally spent, and we felt, somehow, like we'd wiped our souls clean, having traversed most of our city without him, we huddled inside a diner and collapsed in a booth. Adam ordered eggs for himself and coffee for me. It was bad, tasted like soap, but then again, so did everything I ingested in the first year after Eli's death.

When we finally spoke, it was I who said the first words. "Leave me," I told him, point blank.

He didn't look surprised. Was he expecting me to say something like that? He did know me, better than anyone else.

I explained that I was a shell. A bitter, hard one, like the exoskeleton of some prehistoric turtle. I was hiding in that shell, and I would never emerge. I wouldn't be hurt if he left, now. I wouldn't blame him, and it would probably be better that way, if he saved himself.

Of course, he told me no. He wouldn't leave. There were two important reasons to stay together. The first, that we were the only two people in the world who knew how special Eli was, and that reason alone was enough to remain a couple. We were Eli's parents. We had to stay connected, or else we'd risk losing the one thing we had left of him—our shared memories. Memories no one else could ever appreciate, not like we did. Second, he still loved me.

He placed his hands over my own on that dingy table and told me that I'd have to physically dispose of him if I wanted him gone.

Remembering Adam's words now, I feel my breath hitch, my torso heaving as I round the last corner of the stairwell, fighting for air. My confrontation with Audrey triggered a downpour inside me, like the deluge happening outside. I locate my phone on the floor and pick it up. Fuck! The screen's cracked, and it's not turning on! I step down and land hard on my ankle on the bottom step, feeling it twist into an unnatural right angle. Sharp pains shoot up and down my leg, and I can practically feel the break. Dammit! I let out an involuntary cry as I stand back up on it—oh Jesus, it hurts—and limp forward as the throbbing overtakes me. I grit my teeth against the pain and push on the door to the interior of the school, my useless phone stuffed in my pocket. I'm in an interior corridor now, and I need to find my way to an exit, but I'm disoriented.

I'm frozen in front of a long line of classroom doors, unsure which way to head, when someone yanks at my injured ankle—fuck, that hurts—and I go straight down, the back of my head smacking the polished wood floor. I cry out in pain and utter terror as a hand grabs my hair, hard, pulling me up.

PART SIX
SARAH PRICE

Chapter 35

All I can think as I'm dragged down the hallway of the school is that I should never have come.

I swing my arms to get purchase on the floor, but I'm helpless, despite trying to grab at the wooden slats; my fingernails scrape futilely against them. My butt, back, and heels bang on hard ground, then run roughly across carpet, the fibers from the rug burning my legs even through my jeans, the pain in my head unceasing from the firm grip on it.

In my mind, looming like a nightmarish, sinister monster, is Luke's text: Audrey killed my wife.

Anyone with any sense would have been terrified by that, by any interpretation of what it could mean, and would have taken more precaution. But I believed in her, didn't I? I loved her. Never thought her capable . . . but have I so categorically misjudged her? Is she actually capable of violence . . . or worse, murder? Is Audrey, against all my gut instincts, a killer?

I clench my teeth against the pain and pray for one thing: to be released from this temporary hell. Even if that means something far, far worse is next, for me, it would still be preferable to being hog-tied like a calf in a rodeo. My ankle hammers relentlessly, and my head feels like it's on fire. Is my hair going to be torn out at the root? Does it even matter, now?

At last, I feel the pain in my scalp dissipating as the hand lets go of my hair; I'm deposited in a heap on a cold marble floor. With the blinding pain gone from my head, I can see well enough to make out where I am now: the Easton lobby. I get my bearings, sit up, my limbs feeling like they've been pummeled. I don't let myself focus on the physical agony. I can't, if I am to survive.

It is then that I see her, splayed out on the ground a few feet from me.

Every atom of my being stands at attention, awakening with fear and dread, as I move gingerly to my feet and find myself face to face with my attacker.

Luke.

God fucking dammit. It is him.

He's standing a foot from Audrey's body, surveying her, like a person might contemplate a piece of particularly boundary-pushing installation art in a gallery. Or a black-and-white photograph, I think with a gasp. In this moment, I finally have the confirmation I need: something is desperately wrong with him. Fundamentally so.

With a start, I feel my feet moving toward her—I must help her! I must!—but I force myself to replant them firmly on the ground. Going to Audrey's aid could mean instant death for me. I have no choice but to play this game carefully.

I focus on Luke, standing there in the soft morning light that filters through the stained glass windows. What a gorgeous place this is. A place I revere, where I dreamed Eli would spend his formative years. Where now, unless I am wrong, or I put up one hell of a fight, I may spend my final moments alive.

"Is she dead?" I manage to choke out.

"No," he answers. "Not yet."

With horror, I try to guess what he means. Not yet? Is he saying we are going to wait here until she dies?

Luke doesn't keep me wondering for long. Arms crossed over his chest, he paces the length of the marble floor. His words are calculated and icily flat, distinctly lacking in emotion. "You, dear Sarah, are going to finish her off."

Finish her off? "What the fuck?" I spit. "Why would I do that?"

He stops pacing and studies me for a moment with the gray eyes I once found so captivating, so alluring.

He smiles at me.

A smile that makes every nerve ending in my spine tingle with fear, and the realization that he is enjoying this.

"You will do it because she doesn't love you." That smile is still plastered on his face. Never in my life have I felt so sickened by someone's pleasure. "You will do it because you're pathetic, a loser, the worst kind of person imaginable—someone no one gives a shit about."

I gasp, audibly. That isn't true—he's fucking with you—he's a maniac, a sadist.

Luke surveys Audrey's prone form again, then, with his gloved hand, tosses a knife onto the ground in between us.

"You thought I didn't know?" Luke goes on. "How much you've pined for her? Fantasized and longed and probably got off thinking about her? Of course I knew! And now you've told her how you felt, and she didn't reciprocate, did she? Because she never cared about you. Everything she did was for me—for us—because she was so scared shitless she'd lose me. You could have been anyone. You were anyone, to her. A body, a no one. A literal placeholder. How does that make you feel?"

Don't take the bait.

"You want me to kill your wife." The words sound hollow and insufficient. I must make sense of this, this madness. And I must buy myself some time. "Why?"

Luke laughs. "Audrey is posing—has posed—a quandary in my life. One that didn't have a solution . . . until you came along. It was kismet, I see that now, our meeting. I'd like to take full credit for it—for spotting you. But even I must admit, I believe luck had something to do with it."

I don't answer, I simply stand there, trembling, longing to do something to help Audrey. Knowing I can't, not without risking my own life. Getting myself instantly killed won't help either of us.

"How fortunate was I that you walked into my life at precisely the right time. It was in this lobby, wasn't it? Where you first noticed me?" Luke muses. He's loving this, revisiting our very twisted meet-cute; that thought sends shivers up my spine. "I knew from the moment I noticed you that you would solve all my problems. You were so broken. So innocent. So trusting. So . . . utterly worthless."

I tense at those words—they make me hate him, and myself, with a white-hot passion. Still, that hate can't drown out my fear. We are alone; Audrey is incapacitated. My heart beats in my chest with a ferocity that I am sure he must hear. Someone come, please, I beg the universe.

"And after I kill her?" I breathe.

Luke looks up out of the windows, the light hitting his face in such a way that he seems carved from stone. "You will kill yourself. Oh . . . does that come as a shock?" He turns his head to meet my eyes again. "But surely you saw that coming. What I need, Sarah, is a murder-suicide that can all be traced back to your psychotic stalking of my wife. I have to thank my own intuition, in choosing you, that you would play it so perfectly, though even I couldn't have predicted you'd go so far as to send those gifts . . . the notes . . . the texts . . ."

I feel a vise squeezing my chest. This cannot play out. It's absurd, insane! He won't get away with it. Will he?

"You have a son," I breathe. I don't say aloud the words that tug at my insides. You will be taking away your child's mother. Forever.

"Cal and I will weather this. He's too young to even understand. I'll find him a new mom, a better mom. You can't really argue Audrey was so skilled at that particular job. Hazel can live with her deadbeat dad, and Cal and I will move on and pick up the pieces. People do it every day."

I'm nauseated, choking. What a sick, twisted fucker.

I feel my brain fogging over; I can't think straight, but I must. I must. "Your plan will never work. You attacked Audrey," I stammer, still searching for something that can stop this train wreck before we all become casualties.

"Wrong again. I would never have struck my wife. She fell down the stairs after you showed up here to confront her. You told her you wanted to be with her, forever, and she rejected you, Sarah. That's when you chased her down the stairs, and she fell. And now . . . you are going to finish what you started."

"Why?" I ask, feeling the rising despair in every one of my words. "Why do this? Why resort to this?"

But I don't really want to know. Because if he tells me, if he confesses—I'm doomed.

"Our marriage was over." He shrugs.

"So get a divorce!" I hiss.

Luke laughs, bitterly. "I can't divorce Audrey. She is the one person in the world who knows what really happened on the night my ex-wife died."

I stare at him, fixated on his face. "You . . . you murdered Piper?"

"No. While I'd love to take credit for her untimely death, all I did was facilitate a natural ending to her life."

I'm struggling to breathe.

"None of us knew she had a heart defect," Luke goes on. "It was undiagnosed. How could we have? She was the one who wanted to be tied up, who was into the BDSM, the role-play. It was harmless: kink light. I enjoyed it, I won't deny that, but we were careful. I am nothing if not careful. Besides, it never went too far. Piper was simply unlucky; the incident triggered a lack of oxygen, a specific heart event . . . we'll never know all the details, will we? Not without an autopsy, and no one in her family requested one. Why would they? There was no foul play. When Piper went into cardiac arrest, and Audrey was asleep in the living room . . . I seized a golden opportunity. It was even more inspired than I realized, at the time." He smiles, stands a bit taller.

"You—" I almost can't say the words. They are too horrific. "You finished her off?"

"I didn't have to. She died there in our room, of natural causes. All I did was refrain from calling an ambulance. It was her time, after all. When Audrey woke up and came back in the room, she tried to revive her, but it was futile. Piper had already lacked a pulse for a good twenty minutes. I told Audrey how things would have to be. She would leave. She absolutely would not call the police or tell them that she had been there. We would remove all evidence of our encounter that evening, resetting the condo to exactly how it was before our night began, and leave Piper in our bed, untouched. I would go to my gallery, where I would say I had been all night, if asked. No one ever did ask. When I returned home late that night around four a.m., after a long stint in the darkroom, and discovered my wife dead, no one questioned it. She had been unlucky, her death was tragic; it all fit neatly into a box. There was no need for anyone to suspect a thing."

"But there could be," I say, feeling my throat closing as I put the pieces of this depraved jigsaw puzzle together. "If Audrey decided to talk. If you threw her to the curb, and divorced her, and she decided to get her revenge. It's why you kept the video," I say, the realization suddenly coming to me. "The real reason you held on to it. You wanted to be able to use it as evidence, to make a case against her, if you had to. But this . . . this is much easier. If Audrey were to remain alive, you would always live with the nagging worry that she would reveal what you did."

Luke nods. "Bravo. You aren't as dumb as you look." He laughs, and I shrink into myself. I finally have my answer, but this small victory feels like anything but. Luke was ready to get rid of Piper, and the universe did it for him. And Audrey . . .

She went along with Luke's scheme. Didn't call 911 herself. Was it because she truly believed nothing could be done for Piper? Heart attacks don't give you time to ponder what to do. Piper probably was beyond saving. Audrey must have weighed her options and decided that telling the whole world the truth about their arrangement, and that she was there when this transpired, wasn't worth it. It would ruin her reputation, and Hazel's young life, and what would it do for Piper? Nothing; she was already gone. And if Audrey truly believed Luke had been in the shower the whole time, unaware his wife was dying . . . and I had to think that she did . . . then she chose to protect him over outing the truth, because she loved him. Because she coveted a certain life she'd been chasing ever since she'd attended Easton. Had she secretly been pining for Piper's job as well as her husband?

I glance over at her motionless form. Regardless of what she knew or didn't know, what she wanted or didn't want, she is alive, now, barely. And so am I.

"I'm waiting," Luke prods me. "Pick up the knife. I recommend the neck. It will be quickest."

I walk over to the knife and gingerly handle it, aware that in doing so, I'm putting my fingerprints all over it. Then I step back from him, feeling every hair raised on the back of my neck.

"Adam will come looking for me." I am despairing now, aware of how little time I have left to extricate myself from this horror show. "He will never rest until he finds me, and no matter what you do to me . . . he will tell everyone the truth. That I'm not capable of this. That I would never hurt Audrey. Or myself."

I am holding the knife up, defensively, not moving, not breathing.

"I'm sure that would be absolutely true," Luke answers me, his face drawn in an expression of faux compassion. "If Adam were still alive."

What? Adam . . . no. *No!*

He's lying.

He must be. He has to be.

Adam, dear, sweet Adam. No. Fuck, no.

"I don't believe you," I growl. It's another one of Luke's tricks, his setups. He wants me to feel desperate, so desperate I'd do anything. Kill Audrey. Myself. No, I won't do it.

"Believe me or don't, it's the truth." Luke shrugs. "You're all alone. You'll find out soon enough—oh nooo, but you won't. You aren't leaving here alive."

"You didn't—you wouldn't kill Adam! You don't even know him. You'd have no reason to!"

"Except for all the reasons you just so eloquently laid out," Luke reminds me. My stomach flips; the room starts to spin. He is right—fuck—he is right . . . was Adam a loose thread he had to take care of before coming here? Before forcing Audrey and me to play his sicko *Squid Game*?

Oh no oh no oh no . . .

"Adam called me this morning—you must have already left the house." Luke circles Audrey, like a predator rounding in on its kill. "He was so frantic—sobbing, if I'm being truthful. What a baby. 'Boo hoo hoo, leave my poor wife alone, she's fragile, vulnerable. She's been through enough.' Big sob story; I'm sure you can imagine."

I can't imagine; Adam would never capitulate to a fucked-up human like Luke. If he did call him—did he? Did he still care enough to?—then it was probably to make it known he wouldn't stand for it. For this . . . oh fuck. If he threatened Luke . . . if he made it clear he'd make life difficult for him . . .

It's my fault if Adam is dead.

"You'll be caught," I gasp. "It'll be obvious you did this—"

"It will be obvious you did it." Luke grins. "Your hubby died at your home. Your fingerprints are everywhere. You told him you were leaving him, for Audrey. When he tried to stop you, you slit his throat. One of those crimes of passion you always read about. Of course, once you got here . . . Audrey didn't want you either. Boo fucking hoo is right."

"You twisted, fucking psychopath!"

I lunge at Luke with the knife.

I lunge, and I miss.

Fuck, I miss! He dodges my swipe; I slash futilely at the air instead. He knocks the knife from my hand; it clangs noisily to the floor as he kicks at my injured ankle, throwing me off balance from the excruciating pain and knocking me to the ground. I scrabble to get up, unsure if my leg can withstand the pressure to hold on. But hold on I will, because this sicko isn't going to kill me, or Audrey. And if he's already killed Adam . . . no. Thinking of Adam won't save me, not now. I must focus. No distractions. I will not die. Not today.

Luke shoves me backward toward the wall; he's too strong—he can so easily overpower me—and now his hands, which once explored every inch of my body, are around my throat.

"You can't do it yet!" I gasp. "If you kill me now, there goes your murder-suicide!"

His hands tighten around my throat, crushing my windpipe.

"Don't flatter yourself into thinking I ever really needed your cooperation," Luke breathes. "I'll take care of both of you, and then I'll tell the police I was terrified for my wife—terrified of you, because you are an unbalanced and deranged stalker who has been hounding her for months now. I realized what was happening and came here to warn Audrey, but I was too late. You had already shown up, ready to declare your devotion to her. When Audrey rejected you, you pursued her down those stairs, killing her before taking your own life."

I can't say it because my windpipe's being crushed, but if he strangles me, my death will never be viewed as a suicide, and he will be caught. I'd feel smug in this revelation except that it won't save me. Empty victory. The same thought seems to have occurred to Luke, because he suddenly loosens his grip. I gulp in air—God, I've never tasted air this sweet!—and try to push him away, but he's wrenched my arms behind my back and is holding the knife to my throat.

"Suicide," he reiterates. "You killed Adam, then Audrey, and then, with nothing left to live for, you slit your throat with the same knife."

With his left arm, he holds me in a death grip, then reaches his right hand to the front of my body to trace my artery with the blade, as though I'm the one doing this to myself. With dread, I realize he's too calculating, too smart not to cover his tracks. He has strategized from the very beginning. From the day he first met me. I feel a surge of anger that makes my temples pulse at the thought of him plotting to use me like this. At the way he must have viewed me: A pawn. A victim. A prop. Nothing more.

I won't let this fucker do that to me again.

Desperate now, more desperate than I've felt since those blindingly painful days after Eli first died, I bite Luke's right hand, the one gripping the knife, as hard as I possibly can. I've never bitten anyone before; the taste of metallic blood startles me. He yelps but doesn't let go. "You fucking bitch," he swears, grasping me tighter. I see the knife glinting near my face and shut my eyes tight. If this is the end, I won't watch it . . . I won't give Luke the satisfaction.

Eli. Think of Eli. If I'm dying, I want my last moments to be filled with memories of him. Lazy days in Central Park, hot chocolates in our hands and hot-air balloons in the sky. Monster trucks and *Goodnight Moon* and cuddles, cuddles, thousands of them. His trusting eyes. My wilding cozy in his sleep sack, asking for one more song. Mommy comes back. Always comes back . . .

I hear an earth-shattering crack; my eyes fly open. He has released me. Stunned, my heart slamming into my chest with the force of a pile driver, I spin around to see a transformed Audrey, weakened, but not defeated, standing behind Luke, who has collapsed to the ground. In her trembling hands, a Tiffany table lamp.

"Run!" she screams, dropping the lamp, which clatters and crashes to the ground, splitting apart. I spy the knife on the ground a foot from Luke's body and grab it as I scramble after Audrey. She knows this school like the back of her hand, and I do not, outsider that I am, so I follow her to the closest door. She tries it, but it's locked. Dammit. "This way," she growls, and I'm on her heels as we head in the opposite direction, this time finding the exit mercifully open. We scramble down a first-floor corridor and approach a door. Fuck. Footsteps behind us. Luke's. Heart raging, I don't dare look behind me. If he's on our tail, we can't stop, can't lose a second. Can't hesitate, or we're done.

We are inside now—we're inside Audrey's office!—and she is pushing on the door with all her body weight to slam it shut. I am gunning toward the landline phone on her desk when I hear her scream. Fear prickles up my spine; I turn back to see the door flying open, toward her, knocking her back onto the floor. It's Luke—of course it's Luke. He picks her up by a foot and launches her across the room with such force that she flies into her desk. Her head glances the edge, and blood begins to stream from it.

"Audrey!" I scream. She reaches her hand to her head, touches the viscous crimson liquid that's pouring forth. I make a move to go to her, but it's a miscalculation; I should have tried to run. Luke grabs me and holds me back. I swing the knife at him, but he knocks it from my hand to the rug. Help. Please, somebody. Help. I twist and fight, clawing and attempting to knee him in the groin, elbow him in the face, but it's no use; he's too fucking strong.

"You let Piper die," Audrey sobs. "You fucking let her die! I didn't want to believe it. I thought it might be true, but I fought it, I banished the whole idea from my mind because it was too monstrous to be true. This was her office. Her job. You were her goddamned husband. I should have told the police everything. I should have fucking done something . . . instead, I ran to you . . . I trusted you. I married you! I let this happen. I let it happen . . ."

I feel Luke tightening his grip on me, his arm around my neck squeezing so tight I can't get air in, and I see Audrey look up from her bloody hands. The world seems to spin as I focus on all that dark red. I push fruitlessly against Luke's restraining hold.

I'm not coming for you, Eli. Not yet. I'm not ready.

I will not die—not now. Not here. Not if I can help it. Out of the corner of my eye, I see Audrey slide her hand to the knife. She nods at me. I do not react; as it is, I can barely breathe.

And Luke . . . Luke is laughing.

"You loved every minute of our life together, Audrey Wilson," he barks. "Piper's body was barely cold before you climbed in bed with me. But I'm the monster?"

"Let me go!" I scream, biting down hard on his arm again. I taste blood. He yelps but clings tighter.

"Let go of her, you motherfucking psycho!"

Audrey lunges at him with the knife, and his eyes turn to steel, all remnants of his laughter dissipating as he lets go of me and reaches to overpower her. He's grabbing her by the wrist, blocking her from making contact, when I feel behind me for the letter opener from Audrey's meticulously tidy desk, never taking my eyes off Luke and Audrey as my fingers close around it. Thank God Audrey's a neat freak and it's where it's supposed to be. Without thinking, without hesitating, I tighten my grip around the opener, lift my arm up, and stab Luke in the neck. Hard as I possibly fucking can.

He goes down. He goes down! Clattering to the floor, clutching his neck and the silver stick jutting out of it. Luke makes a gargling noise, eyes wide in terror as he fumbles at the letter opener, trying futilely to pull it out. Fighting for air.

Audrey strides up with a heavy marble bookend from her shelf and rams it over his head, ensuring he is dead.

Luke is still, his body rigid. His eyes roll back in his head.

He is gone. We are safe.

Audrey stands there, still as a statue, the bookend still in her hands. She's probably in shock. I know I am.

I sink to my knees on the threadbare rug. Perhaps the adrenaline is wearing off because I feel intense pain radiating from my ankle and fatigue like I have experienced exactly once before in my life: when I stood in the hospital, hearing a doctor inform me that my son was gone. That one bite of a muffin had ended his life.

I am fading, now. So very tired. From my knees, I start to fall forward, unable to support my body weight, my own head. I collapse on the ground as I vaguely register Audrey speaking into the phone to a 911 dispatcher before I sink into unconsciousness.

————

From the laptop of Adam Price:

This is difficult to write, for several reasons:

(a) I'm a terrible writer.

b) I don't plan to actually give it to you, so it's probably pointless.

c) the whole exercise is mortifying.

But my therapist—who used to be our therapist, before you decided she could no longer help us (you were right; there is a limit to how much a human who hasn't experienced tragedy can help those who have, no matter how well-intentioned). Anyway, my/our/your former therapist said it might be healing for me—for "us"—so I will give this journaling thing my best effort.

I would do anything to see the light go back on in your eyes.

And so, that is what I have done. Anything. Everything. I have waited. I have hoped. I have supported your dreams—even the most unreasonable, and absurd, like applying to kindergarten on behalf of our dead son—until I could physically no longer stand it. I have gone to bed alone these last few months, falling asleep watching mindless drivel and reruns, while I wondered where you were, and who you were with.

I have forgiven you carte blanche, without even knowing what I was forgiving. And now I ask, I plead with you, really. Will you do the same for me? Because you are the one person who can give me what I want.

I want us back, in whatever meager form that might take. I know it will not be the old "us." It will not even remotely resemble the shiny couple who read their vows in front of family and friends on a warm spring day, and meant them. Who never could have imagined being tested in this specific and agonizing way. No, that "us" is long dead. But perhaps this "us" can emerge as some lesser version, some shadow of us. Some bootleg, pirated, taped-together-at-the-seams version. That, I would happily accept. That might be enough.

(Never giving this to you. For the record).

EPILOGUE

SARAH PRICE

Six months later

I lock the front door of our home for the very last time, then test the handle.

Satisfied it's securely shut, I turn and head down the front steps. My ankle aches, even all these months later, an old wound that may never heal, not entirely. Some never do. I pass the **SOLD!** sign in front of our once-happy home. I am doing this. I am finally moving on.

I'm not, of course. Not really.

Luke killed Adam. I was determined not to believe it, not to let it be true. As I sat there in Audrey's office, shaking from the shock, I stared at Luke's body, and all that blood, convincing myself that he had made it all up. An invention by his sick, destructive mind, it had all been a cruel trick, and the police would rush to my house to find Adam sitting there, calmly drinking his coffee.

I was wrong. Oh God, I was wrong.

What they found at my home was a bloodbath. Adam was lying on our waxed kitchen floors in a pool of red. His throat was slit, as Luke had boasted. His phone lay on the counter, smashed and useless, and our Nest cams unplugged. The Wüsthof chef's knife from our knife block, a wedding gift, lay on the floor beside him, my fingerprints all over it from the last time I'd chopped carrots. Luke was right. It did look bad for me.

But he had not counted on Adam recording the whole exchange, from the moment Luke had walked in the door, via the nanny cam I still kept hidden in a bookcase facing the kitchen. Even before Eli's allergies emerged, when I was still working at Random House, I was never able to stray far from him without the reassurance that I could check up on him. I'd installed those cameras throughout the house. Our nanny had no problem with them and approved of me popping a look at the cameras from my desk. She knew I simply needed to see my boy. To know that he was happy and being treated kindly; that he was well and safe.

After Eli's death, I never uninstalled them.

The nanny cam is what saved me. Adam saved me. He must have made sure it was plugged in and streaming before letting Luke in the house. I was briefly questioned by the police but quickly released once I told them how to access the camera footage. There it all was: Luke's twisted, violent act from start to finish. I have never watched it.

I want to remember the Adam I knew, the Before Adam, the Adam who never gave up on me. Who, unbeknownst to me, put up a valiant fight and never stopped fighting for me till the cruel and bitter end.

Adam and Eli are never far from me; they accompany me everywhere I go. Every outing, every mundane chore. It took me months before I could fall asleep in my house again. For a long time, I stayed with Chippie, who graciously put me up in one of her many extra bedrooms and cared for me like a sister, a daughter. Eventually, I picked myself up, came home to face the brownstone. I would not live here anymore; I couldn't. I needed to get ready to list it. To say goodbye. My husband and son were with me when I sifted meticulously through each of their items and decided which sparked joy, which were precious to me, and which no longer held meaning. Naturally, I deemed them all precious, at first. But I pushed myself to let Eli's toothbrush go, and Adam's sweaters and wool socks.

I kept the furniture, our books and decor. They are in storage now, until I decide on a permanent home. I'm not ready to root myself anywhere, not yet. I tell myself I will travel. I tell myself I will be the millionth person to try to write a memoir about my life, about what it was like to be a mother to my boy, and then to lose him, and that I'll probably be the millionth person to fail. But all of it seems a little more hopeful now, in spite of the daily pain that knocks me to my knees every morning when I wake up and remember: they are both gone. And I had a hand in it all.

It has been half a year since Adam's death—since Luke murdered him—and at times it feels like an eternity. Other times, it's like a mere moment has passed. I have once again been forced to confront my never-ending guilt, as I must acknowledge that it was my fault Adam died. My failure. My mistakes. My two most precious humans are gone because I couldn't keep them safe.

I don't take the stroller out to Central Park as much anymore. I might eventually sell it, too, like I've sold so many other things.

I make my way to my neighborhood café, Toastery, and push the door open. I move swiftly to the table where Chippie and Audrey are already perched, splitting a scone, both of them sipping lattes. They wave as I approach and smile warmly. It's hard to think back to the people we were, Before. We aren't the same, and how could we be? The Audrey of Now is like a bird who has been trodden on, and nearly died—only to be revived in its last hours. She has emerged from her trauma with feathers that shine in the light and talons that are sharper than ever.

Chippie, with her penchant for true crime, had apparently been suspicious of Luke from day one.

"I haven't trusted that guy since the day you first got together with him," she told Audrey when she arrived at the school in the aftermath of Luke's attack and wrapped her best friend in a death grip of a hug. "I have a file this thick on all the fucked-up shit Luke Singer has done. The cheating—oh, yes, the cheating. All these years, the cheating. The psychological torture of you and Piper. The emotional manipulation of all three of you. I am delighted that he's gone."

Turns out, she'd been tracking our whereabouts using Find My Friends on her phone, looking out for Audrey like her own personal Boo Radley. Surveilling her even when Audrey refused to speak to her.

"Sit," Audrey says. I take the open spot across from her. It's spring; I slide off my light jacket and drape it over the back of my chair. "But also, eat."

I accept a piece of the scone Audrey offers me. Before biting into it, I hesitate. Will I ever stop assessing the possibility of a baked good containing nuts? I'm quick to remember Eli is gone, and I don't suffer from his allergy. The scone is safe.

Chippie pushes a latte toward me. "No foam, nonfat. And I asked them to add half a drop of stevia but no fucking more." She smiles at me, her influencer smile that shows extremely white, Invisaligned teeth. In her lime-green jumpsuit and platform clogs, her oversize purple Telfar bag on the floor at her feet, she looks vaguely like she stepped out of Eli's favorite show, *Yo Gabba Gabba!* The outfit makes me smile. I'll never again think of Chippie as a privileged dabbler. She alone saw Luke's true colors from the start.

There is no need for pleasantries. The three of us chat every day, at least by text. Audrey and I touch base every morning, and we often fall asleep in our own, separate homes with our phones on, each of us staying silent while the other drifts off. This practice staves off the nightmares. We understand each other, now, but we are not that kind of "us" and never will be. It's not in the cards, and perhaps it never should have been.

We have been through a lot, the two of us.

The shock. Our injuries, significant enough to require treatment, and rest. And, of course, the hardest part of all: Audrey breaking the news of Luke's crimes to her children. In the end, the unvarnished truth sufficed, for Hazel, anyway. Cal is still too young to understand. He misses Daddy, and one day, he will have to learn the truth, but not now. Hazel and Audrey started therapy that very next day, and in spite of the trauma of what Luke did to her mother . . . Hazel seems better than ever. It's a cliché to say that tragedy brought them closer, but it did. Even Samuel has stepped up to the plate. Ruby hasn't stopped delivering hemp cookies for Cal, at least twice a week.

Audrey dreaded what would happen once the news got out that her husband had turned out to be a maniac psycho murderer. But what she didn't count on was how beloved she was, and still is, now more than ever.

"So, I invited Chippie to join us for coffee this morning because she's very intimidating, and I am going to ask you a question now that I don't want you to say no to," Audrey announces.

I sigh. What's this going to be about?

"Easton admissions have spiked in recent months. In spite of . . . well, everything. And I can't keep up with all the applicants. I need another assistant."

Is she joking? I open my mouth to answer.

"Before you shoot me down, think about it. You love Easton. You're the school's original fangirl. Those essays you wrote . . . your bordering on religious fanaticism for the school . . . how can you not see how perfect you'd be for this job?"

I don't speak. What to even say?

"She offered me the position, but I could never work for this bitch," Chippie deadpans. I can't help but laugh. "You two, however, seem to make a really good . . . team."

I sip from my cup, feeling my cheeks burn from the attention of these two. I couldn't possibly take that job. It would be absurd.

"Think about it, okay?" Audrey flags down the waiter before turning back to face me with a smile that still slays me. "Nobody belongs at Easton more than you."

Acknowledgments

The idea for this novel took root in my brain after a coffee date with a friend, where we briefly discussed preschool (yes, preschool!) admissions. It's strange how a seemingly ordinary hour of conversation can lead to something much bigger—in this case, a story that refused to leave me alone, that forced me to wrangle it into something beyond a wild fever dream. It would still be a half-formed dream if it weren't for the many people who guided, supported, and advised me throughout the writing process. First, to my editor, Danielle Marshall: I could not have imagined a more insightful and enthusiastic champion of this project. You recognized what I was trying to do from day one, and I am endlessly grateful for your expertise and vision. Thank you, thank you. (I'll use fewer em dashes next time. I promise.)

To my fearless agent, Victoria Sanders: how many ways, times, and in how many forms can I express my thanks?! (I'll keep trying.) You are a wizard, and I am so lucky we met. To the entire team at VSA: Bernadette Baker-Baughman, you are a lifeline! Christine Kelder, thank you for everything you do. Huge thanks also to Sylvie Rabineau at WME, for your tireless support and passion for this book.

Benee Knauer! This book would not exist without you, nor would it be any good! Thank you for your steadfast belief in me and this story. You are stuck with me now.

Thank you to the entire Amazon Publishing team. Your hard work to bring books to life is so critical, and I am grateful to everyone from marketing and publicity to copyediting and cover design. Speaking of, thank you to Eileen Carey for the stunning-with-a-touch-of-creepy cover and to Kyra Wojdyla and Jen Bentham, Stephanie Chou and Bill Siever—I am indebted to you for your meticulous attention to detail.

Matt Sadeghian, Leigh Brecheen, and Stephen Breimer: thank you for being 100 hundred percent in my corner.

To the Chippies in my life—Winnie, Alexa, Victoria, Bill, Nidhi, Amy, Cathleen, Stephany, Sonia, and all of the many, many friends who continue to navigate my various voice-to-texts and answer my frenzied questions: you're the best. Jessica: thank you for teaching me how to write (my name) . . . and so much more. Nicholas, Amy, Jacob, Ray, and Sonya: thank you for the unconditional love. Sofia Bresciani and Laura King: I'd be lost without you, but you already know this.

Thank you to Carolyn Schweitz and the entire Gold Leaf Literary team for working your magic! Thanks also to the most prolific CPs, Winnie Kemp and Billy Hanson. Writing Retreat 2024 must happen, or else. To my parents: thanks for the rides to all those rehearsals. I would still love a ride, even now.

Last but not ever least, thank you to my family—Ethan, Leo, Quincy, and Naomi—you make it possible for me to escape into unknown worlds and return to the safest (and most fun!) reality. I will still attempt to write you a middle-grade book, but it won't be as good as *Gregor*. Leo, you're cool. Quincy, don't ever stop making art. Naomi: let's do "knock-over."

Ethan: two words for you. Door, and monkey. Thank you for being you, and for still combing through every aisle of the grocery store even when I try to convince you not to. I love you, always.

About the Author

Photo © 2021 Kathleen Sheffer

Rebecca Hanover is the *New York Times* bestselling author of the young adult series the Similars. After graduating from Stanford University with a BA in English and drama, Rebecca joined the writing team of the CBS daytime drama *Guiding Light*, where she earned an Emmy Award. She now writes novels full time from her home in San Francisco, where she enjoys matcha lattes and a complete lack of seasons. *The Last Applicant* is her adult debut. When she isn't writing, she can be found in a yoga class or reading anything Dav Pilkey with her husband and three kiddos.